Wild Is the River

WILD
IS THE
RIVER

BY

LOUIS BROMFIELD

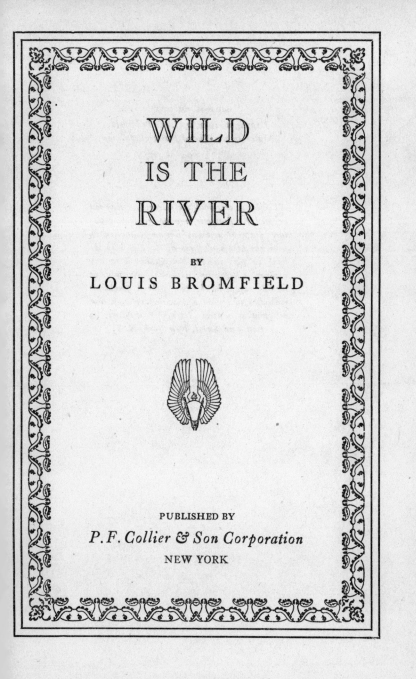

PUBLISHED BY

P. F. Collier & Son Corporation

NEW YORK

Wild Is the River

ONCE he turned the corner out of Dauphine Street, the noise of the rioting faded until at last there was only dark silence broken faintly by a distant pistol shot or the scream of a brawling harlot. The Street through which he walked, close against the house walls in the shadow, was like a passage through a city of the dead, with every shutter and door tightly barred and here and there a thin glowing sliver of light where some resentful, respectable Créole still remaining in the ravished city, sat watching and listening, plotting perhaps against the invaders. The echo of his footsteps ricocheted back and forth from one wall to another—click, clack, click, clack. He was a tall big man and the steel on the heels of his army boots made a sharp clear sound like a pistol shot each time they struck the stone pavement.

He walked unsteadily for he had had too much champagne at La Lionne's establishment before the fight began and now the "hants" were after him again, those "hants" which only surrounded and attacked him when the malaria, picked up in the swamps of Virginia, returned or he became tired and bored and a little drunk. He had started the fight at La Lionne's out of boredom and once it gained the proportions of a riot he had slipped away out of the back door into Royal Street. And now the "hants" pursued him, coming out of old churches and town halls and still white houses all over New England to torment him—"hants" from which he would never escape because they were in his blood.

The moon, rising hot above the bayous beyond the city came suddenly above the roofs of the houses and painted the empty silent street in black and silver. The heels still went click-clack, click-clack on the stone *banquettes*. A cat slithered quickly from one side of the street to the other, black in the clear metallic light. Then suddenly even the distant isolated screams and shots were no longer heard and he was in the remote section of the quarter, near to home.

"Home!" He did not speak the word but the sound of it echoed in his brain. Home was a long way off. Boston would be full of slushy early April snow now, the whale-oil lights shining yellow on the Common and the Public Gardens, the snow in Beacon Hill Streets brown with the droppings of the fat horses which drew the carriages of Mr. Adams and Mr. Saltonstall and Mr. Lowell. That was a remote and distant picture. It was nearly two years now since he had seen it. It was a long way off, farther even than the hundreds of miles which separated the cold, middle-class, half-English City from this street where he walked in the moonlight.

Here the houses crowded close to the muddy pavements, the windows shuttered and barred beneath the high galleries of grill-work overhead. That distant, clean air cooled by the melting snow was a long way from this warm mugginess, scented with the smell of wistaria and thick fertile odor of Delta mud.

Tipsily he thought, "I must pull myself together." Something had happened since he marched away from the Common as a volunteer. He hadn't thought about it until tonight when in the quarrel which started the riot La Lionne had slapped him and said, in her broken English, "Why can't you drink champagne like a gentleman? You're the kind of Yankee who shouldn't drink at all."

He hadn't had time at the moment to think what she meant; he had been too eager to vanish as the quarrel spread out of the mirrored ballroom into the hallway and at last into the street outside. After he had knocked down two men—the strangers who had insulted him—he went out by the back door into the alley. He liked a fight but it wouldn't do for an officer who held the profitable post of Collector of Revenue of the Port of New Orleans to be shot or arrested in the most expensive brothel of the town. There had been other scandals, but even a favorite of a General in Command of a conquered and ruined city could be involved in a scandal too many. There wasn't much law in New Orleans, but there was such a thing as becoming ridiculous.

He raised his hand and touched his cheek gently. It was bruised all right. Tomorrow it would be swollen and dark blue. The stranger had got in one good blow before he fell, his head striking one of La Lionne's gilt chairs. As he touched his cheek, the memory of the fight returned to him briefly and at the same time his heart

[2]

beat more quickly and he was sorry he had run away instead of staying to the end. The blood rushed through his veins and the muscles of his arms and across his abdomen tightened. His whole body tingled. It was a quick sudden sensation, almost like the thing he experienced in the arms of La Lionne. He liked fighting, as a ram or a young bull liked fighting. He even liked the slight pain of the bruise as he touched it with his hand.

But the sensation passed quickly and he was aware in a hazy fashion that he had reached the blind alley where he must turn in to reach the side door of the big house. For a moment he felt again a shadow of the indignation which had seized him when Old Seraphine told him that she could not give him a key to the main entrance of the big house. She had said there was no key because the old Baroness de Lèche had taken all the keys when she fled to the plantation at St. Claire—all but those to the side entrance on the *impasse*. That, he was sure was a lie, but from the look in her broad mulatto face, he knew that nothing would make Seraphine yield. A Yankee entering by the big door was something she could not tolerate.

The *impasse* was in the shadow and while the balconies above were bathed in moonlight, the cobblestones were in blackness. Stumbling, he felt his way along the wall until he reached a small door. Here he halted and leaned against the building, pushed back the long skirts of his regimental tunic and drew a great key from his pocket. It slipped smoothly into the key-hole and turned in the well-oiled lock. War or no war, occupation or no occupation, victory or defeat, the great de Lèche house was kept in order.

As he pushed open the door and stepped out of the darkness into the open gallery inside, the whiteness of the moonlight blinded him for a moment. There was a thick scent of jasmine and wistaria in the warm air—that peculiar voluptuous smell which troubled him when he wakened in the night, even when he had come only a little while before from La Lionne. Then the moon blindness passed and he saw the familiar details of the big garden and court-yard with the galleries running round the four sides, the clumps of bamboos, the fragile palms and the big jars and pots with camellias and mimosa and dwarf acacias. At the same time he heard

[3]

the cool sound of the little fountain and beyond it the faint tinkling music of a piano.

For a moment he stopped in the shadow of the gallery, listening. Then, thrusting the key back into his pocket, he said, half-aloud, "Damn that music!" And at the same time across a patch of moonlight he saw the figure of Old Seraphine coming toward him. She was very fat and she walked rather like a duck. He heard her soft voice, "You all right, Major?"

He answered her, "I'm all right, Seraphine, thanks."

He walked perfectly steadily he knew. His voice was all right. But it did not matter. Seraphine would know he had been drinking. She knew everything. These French Quarter negresses were different from the ones in Virginia and the Carolinas . . . maybe because they were an odd mixture of jungle and voodoo and French and Spanish civilization. They were shrewder and more witch-like.

His head was a little clearer now. He heard her saying, "That young Captain Wicks is here. Ah let him go up to your room!"

"Damn it!" he thought, but to the old black woman, he said, "That's all right, Seraphine. Good night." He slipped a gold piece into her black hand. "I've forgotten about that for a long time." Then he slipped past her toward the stairs. "Damn it!" he thought again, "Why did David turn up tonight?" Why had David waited all this time until after midnight to see him?

In the sitting room on the second floor of the house overlooking the garden Lieutenant David Wicks had been waiting for more than an hour. For a long time he sat studying the room in order to pass the time, and so, although he had been there many times before, it was the first time he had ever really seen it. For he was young, not yet twenty-one, and had not yet learned how much one can discover from houses of their owners, of their history, indeed of whole civilizations. And because there was so little that was sensuous in his training and background he would probably never, until he died, notice such things as beauty of line or of stuffs or of colors. He had come to notice this room now only out of boredom, in order to pass the time. And he did not feel it, for all its beauty, a sympathetic room, partly because everything in it was so different

[4]

from the rooms and houses he had known all his life, and partly because its beauty made him feel disturbed and uneasy. The lovely line of the armchairs was too delicate and frivolous, the brightness of the light walnut and pear wood seemed giddy after the solid bourgeois heaviness of the mahogany and rosewood he had always known. And the great round carpet with its voluptuous design of faded swans and roses had no air of solidity and worth. He was sensitive—he had written poems at Harvard as a freshman—but it was a sensibility without sensuousness, and so he distrusted this feminine graceful room as he might distrust a woman who wore scent or too much lace, with her bodice cut too low. Not even Tom's sword thrown carelessly across one of the delicate carved chairs, the belt falling to the faded rose and gray carpet, failed to give the room a touch of safe masculinity. It seemed only to make it worse— as if somehow the sword were mating with the chair before his very eyes.

And then presently someone began to play a piano and sing in a room on the opposite side of the garden. Although music did not stir him very profoundly he knew about it because Aunt Tam was a blue-stocking and had tried to pound music into the heads of Agnes and himself. Aunt Tam had been to Paris where her uncle had been Ambassador and she knew the French and Italian operas. And so as he listened, it dawned upon him after a while that the unseen woman on the opposite side of the garden was singing an aria of Mozart from an opera called "Il Re Pastore." When Aunt Tam was younger and he was a small boy, Aunt Tam had tried to sing it, badly, but well enough for it to have become fixed in his unmusical memory through countless banal repetitions in the drawing-room on Pinckney Street. It was the difficult cadenza which fixed the thing in his memory . . . the cadenza with which Aunt Tam had struggled and met defeat. Now, sung by the voice of this unseen woman, it was liquid and glittering as quicksilver.

The memories roused by the cadenza made him feel homesick and roused again the dormant gnawing desire to escape from this disturbing, unreal city. Back in Boston he would be safe once more. In Boston there were so few temptations. Everything moved in its own groove. Everything was planned, arranged in advance. The air was either bitterly cold or feverishly hot. In New England there was no warm scent of jasmine and acacias but only the clean smell of maples and pines. In Boston his mind never seemed to run away with him into realms which could frighten him. In Boston his very body was different. Down here it had become something alien to his mind and spirit. It had become a kind of enemy with which he was always wrestling like Jacob with the Angel. In Boston there was no liquid, silver sound like the voice on the opposite side of the garden singing the aria from "Il Re Pastore," a sound which conjured up improper thoughts and visions. He hated this place. People at home would think him lucky to be living safely on the fat of the land with the army of occupation, but he knew he would rather be fighting in the front line in Virginia or Tennessee. There, with all the mud and vermin, he would feel cleaner than here in this strange foreign city.

He wished that Tom would return so that he could deliver his message and return to the hotel. He was glad that he didn't have to live in this house with all its luxury and voluptuous femininity. A bed, a washstand, a bureau in the hotel were better. The life there was raucous and noisy but at least it held no temptations for him. The painted noisy women who frequented the hotel bar never tempted him. They only offended his sense of the fastidious. His room was just a room, plain, ugly, a hotel room—but safe. Not like this room in which he sat.

At last to pass the time and keep his mind from wandering into treacherous paths, he took the worn pack of cards from among the mess of papers on Tom's desk and sat himself down by the light of two candles in silver holders to play bezique, playing like a man with two natures, against himself. He played with a curious cold detachment in which there was no heart. It was thus Tom Bedloe found him when he came in from the gallery.

Tom stood for a moment in the doorway, balancing himself a little, his strong legs spread apart, because he was a little tipsy and because the sight of his fiancée's brother, even though he had been prepared for it, filled him with displeasure. He didn't feel like talking to David now; the boy seemed strangely out of place in this room with its elegant French furniture and the faint scent of wistaria in the hot air. There was something about the boy, something about the pale face, the blond hair worn long in the military

[6]

fashion of the moment, which seemed at once anemic and feminine and reproachful. It wasn't that David said anything or even, in his sly way, looked disapproving; it was merely that his presence and the extraordinary likeness to his twin sister was disturbing. He had that pale beauty which in a girl was lovely but in a young man was, to Tom, at once annoying and faintly evil. He did not like David; he could not think why he had asked for David as his aide except that his sister Agnes had wanted it and the last time Tom saw Agnes he had been in a mood to agree to whatever she desired. It had got him nothing, not even so much as a kiss with a little warmth in it, from that mouth which was so like David's pretty mouth. No, the sight of David annoyed him, as if it were a reproach —especially now when he had come straight from a brawl in the establishment of La Lionne. What he really hated, he thought at sight of David, was the boy's fastidiousness and purity. And those were the very things which roused his passions even at the memory of David's sister, Agnes.

All these things went through his brain hazily as he stood in the doorway, as well as another thought which had become more clear of late—that although he was himself a New Englander, he was, with his wild appetites and his recklessness, a black sheep and an outcast. He was a swarthy pirate born unaccountably into a world of respectable merchants.

David, standing there across the room from him, *was* New England. David and his sister Agnes *were* New England. They were Boston. He himself was New Bedford. No, he wasn't even that. He was just a black sheep. He thought, "To hell with it!" And then turning himself from surliness to charm, he said, "Hello, David. What can I do for you?"

The two men were only a few years apart in age but Tom's tone was patronizing and that of a man immensely older.

David said, "It's some clearance papers from the custom's office. The *Orion's* new captain wants to sail in the morning and can't until you sign the papers."

Tom unbuttoned his coat and sat on the chair behind a table covered with papers. "Has he paid his fees?"

"Yes," said David, "I have it here."

"In cash?"

[7]

"Yes—in cash." He took from the inside pocket of his coat two federal bank notes. Tom looked at them and thrust them not into a drawer of the table but into his own pocket. "Give me the papers," he said.

He signed them quickly, aware that David's blue eyes were on him. He looked up quickly, half-hoping to catch a look of suspicion and accusation in the boy's eyes, but in the candle-light the pale blue eyes were perfectly expressionless. "There," he said, handing over the papers. "Was there anything else?" He saw that David was looking at the raw bruised spot on his cheek bone where that damned cheap carpetbagger had got in one blow before the fight really began.

David, blushing unaccountably, turned quickly away and said, "I had a letter from Agnes."

"Good," said Tom. "Is everyone well?"

"Yes. She gave me a message for you."

"What?"

"She said she hadn't heard from you for nearly two months. She said she understood how busy you must be. She didn't mind for herself but that Aunt Tam and the others were always looking at her and pitying her."

"To hell with them," said Tom. "They think a Tom Bedloe isn't good enough for an Agnes Wicks—and all of them getting rich out of selling burlap blankets to the Union Army for wool and shoes with paper soles. To hell with them!"

In the soft light David flushed. Although he was aware that his father, his whole family had been insulted, he said nothing. In the silence the dim sound of the square piano and the woman's voice singing on the opposite side of the big garden filled the room, taking possession of them both. David awkwardly said, "Have you seen her yet?"

"No."

"She has a pretty voice. She's a widow, I hear."

"A widow?"

"Yes. Her husband died last year. That's why she's here from Paris—to look after the estate."

"She must have courage to come to New Orleans in the midst of a war. Where did you hear all of this?"

[8]

"Madame Delaplaine told me. She runs the hotel."

"Do you like it better than being quartered in a house?"

"Yes. In a way it's quieter. You don't feel hostility all about you. I get more work done." The pale sensitive face seemed to grow narrower.

"And write more poetry?" Tom smiled suddenly, a dark, almost fatherly smile which changed the whole expression of the unhappy handsome face. He was sorry suddenly for having been rude to the boy. And for a moment there came into his gray eyes a look of affection born of the boy's sudden swift resemblance to his twin sister.

"Yes," said David shyly.

"I'm glad. The war will be over some day. Then you can go back to Harvard and write poetry about snowstorms and spring and be happy. As for myself I think I'll stay in the Army and go out West . . . as far from New England as I can go." He stood up and came around the desk to where the boy was standing. Putting his arm about David's shoulders, he said, "That's all for tonight, Davy. Go along home and get some sleep, and don't worry about anything. I'll write to Agnes tonight . . . I promise . . . so Aunt Tam and the other old cats won't be able to pity her."

"Thanks," said David. "You know how they are."

"I certainly do—a nest of old cats—that whole lot of your relatives." He let his arm fall from the boy's shoulder and said, "Whenever you want to go out and see the high life, let me know. I'll show you everything. It's something you oughtn't to miss, Dave . . . New Orleans in war time occupied by an army. It's a wide open town. You never saw the like. You ought to find yourself some fun."

The boy looked away from him and said, "All right, Tom. If I ever feel like that. Good night." Shyly he held out his hand. The older man took it. Then the boy went away, out of the door and along the moonlit gallery above the garden, wrapped in an aura of loneliness.

When he had gone, Tom stood for a moment thoughtfully, watching the doorway through which the boy had disappeared. The hot mist of the bayous was fading and in the doorway the

[9]

sky showed a deep blue sprinkled with stars. The boy irritated him now less than he puzzled him. What did he want—David? What was before him? What did anyone want? What did he himself want . . . power, wealth, admiration? He didn't know unless it was that he wanted everything—everything you could wrest from this God-damned unhappy world. What was the use of worrying about it? What the hell? For a second he was suddenly envious of David, of David's tranquillity and peace of mind. Then the old uncontrollable vitality took possession of him again and suddenly he kicked over one of the frail chairs and began taking off his clothes, throwing them carelessly on the sofa until he was naked save for a pair of under-drawers. He had a powerful body, young and strong and hard for all the wildness of the life he led. His curly black hair he wore cropped short against the fashion of the army.

Stripped of his clothes he felt freer. The heat of the night no longer seemed to stifle him. He could breathe now. His limbs felt free and his head seemed more clear. He thought, "This is a hell-hole! If it's like this in April what must it be like in mid-summer?"

Then for a moment the heat, the heavy dampness, seemed to blend in an odd fashion with the sound of the music coming from the far wing of the great house. He stood listening, his round curly stubborn head cocked a little on one side. It was pleasant music, gay with a gaiety he had never encountered in other music. Vaguely he remembered the song, as one of many sung by La Lionne when she performed for him alone in her own apartment above the bar and gambling rooms. It was a song from an operetta which she said was the rage of Paris—something called "La Grande Duchesse." But it sounded different now. The woman singing it sang with a pure, clear voice, executing the trills and roulades simply and elegantly. It sounded quite different from the way La Lionne sang it in her husky champagne music-hall voice. The singing he heard now was, he became dimly aware, art.

But the sound only annoyed him, stirring the blood in his veins, upsetting him. He wished she would stop singing and go back to France whence she came, this damned widow who was too proud even to let herself be seen by a damned Yankee.

Then he remembered his promise to write Agnes and after pouring a glass of brandy, seated himself at the table to write. He had not thought of Agnes for days but the sight of David had stirred again the knowledge that she was desirable and the kind of woman one wanted for a wife. La Lionne might be fun, and the tantalizing, unseen woman on the far side of the garden might be romantic, but Agnes was the sort of woman one married.

For a long time he hesitated, tipsily considering how to begin, and then remembered that there was only one fashion, the fashion he had always used since the moment of their engagement when for a day or two he had believed that life would be impossible without possession of her blonde loveliness. He did not feel that way now but the fact remained that he was still her fiancé. When the war was over he could decide one way or another. It was impossible in any case to think of marrying during the war. And he did not trust himself. Although he did not feel her indispensable to his happiness at the moment, he knew that at sight of her the old passion might stir again with violent life. He would write now and the thing would be done. In any case restlessness and the heat would not let him sleep. The fight and the bruise had in some strange way roused his desire.

So, after a gulp of brandy, he wrote firmly:

My darling:

I am a dog for not having written before now, but in the confusion of the occupation and in the disorders following the arrival of your uncle, the general, I have been working day and night.

Here he paused a moment, thinking, and then with decision wrote, *The General has come to count on me more and more and lately he has turned over to me the collection of all port revenues. This has added a vast amount of work.*

Again he paused, trying to think what to say. A pen in his hand was as clumsy a weapon as a club. He could never make it say what he meant it to say, even when he was afire with passion and sincerity, and now, when he sat down to write a letter which must sound loving when there was not much love in his heart, he found it doubly difficult.

He poured himself a drink of brandy and listened for a time to the sound of the voice from the opposite side of the garden. Damn it! How could he write to Agnes with that sound in his ears.

But after a time he took another drink, looked at the paper and read the last lines—*"This has added a vast amount of work. . . ."* Then he grinned and thought, "and a lot of money in my pocket." But you could not write that. You couldn't quite put it on paper, even if Agnes' relations were getting rich out of graft and fraudulent army contracts in Boston. They were mealy-mouthed hypocrites. They had not the courage to loot frankly and openly like General Wicks and his staff.

So he wrote, *David is very well and so am I. David is, I think, getting used to the roughness of army life. New Orleans right now is a good test. It is the most lawless, wildest damned city in the Union. But I rather like it.*

It was going better now. He was beginning to let himself go, perhaps because he liked New Orleans just as it was. He liked living in it. He liked talking about it.

He wrote, *I don't know when I'll have leave—not for a long time, I should think, with all the troubles we're having in reorganizing the city and stamping out lawlessness. You would think New Orleans wasn't a part of the United States, if you judged by the pride and stiff-neckedness of the inhabitants. Why, some of them can't even speak English. We have a job on our hands, Agnes. There's even a secret organization bent on assassinating union officers and officials. It's not as safe as some people would have you believe.*

Well, that's all the news I can think of. I hope you are well and not too worried about me. I thrive on this kind of life. Give my friendly regards to the members of the family. I am always your devoted fiancé. Thomas.

For a moment he sat back in the chair regarding the letter thoughtfully. Letter writing was always a great effort, and writing now in the damp heat with his brain numbed by La Lionne's champagne was doubly exhausting. After a moment he took up the pen again and very carefully he wrote, *P.S. I miss you very much.* X X X X.

His instinct about women had dictated the last line. Taking up the wax which Madame de Lèche had left in his room as if he were a guest and not an unwanted rough soldier billeted upon her against her will, he sealed the letter. Then he discovered that he was smiling, over what he did not quite know, unless it was with satisfaction that life was so good, so exciting, so filled with sensual delight and that the letter was after all a pretty smart letter.

He was aware then that the music on the opposite side of the garden had ceased, and for a long time he sat quite still, listening, even straining his ears, in the hope that it would begin again. While he sat there he forgot Agnes altogether and thought only of Madame de Lèche, wondering what she was like, and why her pride prevented her even from showing herself, why she had come back from Paris in the midst of war. Old black Seraphine had told him boldly in her mumbo-jumbo English that her mistress dared not show herself in the streets so long as there were carpetbaggers and free slaves and damned Yankees about. That must be because she was beautiful. An old or an ugly woman would be safe enough, even on the disorderly streets of New Orleans.

What would she be like—a woman who had lived half her life in Paris? He knew what La Lionne was like but you couldn't judge from La Lionne. She was eternal, a woman of her own special class and profession. La Lionne was not a lady. La Lionne was not even a beauty; it was other qualities which made her a success. But this woman who would not see him . . . who lived always hidden away like a harem woman on the other side of the garden . . .

The music and singing did not begin again, and presently with the champagne and brandy in his veins he began again to grow restless. He knew then that he was not going to sleep, that it would be another of those nights when tormented by heat and mosquitoes, he would turn and toss and groan, thinking of La Lionne and the delights of her establishment, and of all the other women he had known and the wine he had drunk and the roistering he had done. For a wild moment he thought, "Damn her and her pride! I'll break in and see her! I'll kick open the door!" But he knew that he wasn't drunk enough for that.

Then the thought occurred to him that although he had never seen her, she had probably seen him many times, watching through the closed shutters as he came in and out. And the thought brought a little tingle of pleasure down his spine. Even now she might be watching him as he sat there, half naked, in the heat—the shutters open to welcome the faint stirring of the tepid scented air.

Then suddenly the lights went out in the rooms on the opposite side of the garden and save for the light in his own room the old house was dark. A parrot chortled wickedly in the gallery across the garden. "An evil bird," he thought, remembering the cascades of Créole French with which it mocked him each time he entered or left the house by daylight. And he knew then there was no peace in his soul nor any sleep in his body that night. The woman across the moonlit garden was in his blood, and there was, he knew, only one way of getting her out of it. He would have to return to La Lionne and have more champagne and patch up their quarrel.

And so, loathing himself and his restlessness, he put on all his clothes again, this time taking up the belt and sword from the chair and buckling it about his narrow waist. Then quickly he put out the lights leaving only the flame of the whale oil lamp on the carved *escritoire*.

In the gallery he stopped for a moment listening to the tinkle of water in the little fountain in the center. He wanted more champagne badly. In the heat he was sweating and his head ached. The part of the house opposite still remained silent and dark. For a moment he thought, "What if I crossed over now and broke into her rooms?" There was nothing to stop him. As an aide of the General he was safe. Weren't they all here to pilfer the Rebels of New Orleans? Gold and women . . . everything. It was their right. Hadn't the general issued an order telling his men to treat loyal Secessionist women like women of the street? But again he knew that he was not drunk enough. No, there was only one thing—to go back to La Lionne. Then his thoughts were checked by the faint sound of a bell tinkling in the part of the house across the garden.

He listened but the bell did not tinkle again and uncertainly he descended the creaking wooden stairway from the upper gallery. Past the pots of camellias he made his way in the shadow as far as the side entrance into the *cul-de-sac*. At almost the same moment, he discovered the waddling figure of Seraphine coming toward him. The old negress made a sudden inarticulate sound of surprise, a pig-like grunt with the old shade of contempt in it.

She said, in her queer English, "Ah thought you was in bed, Captain. Ah seen your light go out."

"I couldn't sleep."

[14]

The old woman hesitated while he searched his pockets for the key to the gate. Then she said, "You'd better go back to your bed, Captain. It ain't a night to be roamin' about. Ef'en you go out you might get into trouble."

"I can take care of myself, Seraphine."

Then she did a surprising thing. She stepped in front of him and put her own key in the lock, saying, "It ain't safe for you to open that gate jest now."

The gate swung back and as he thanked Seraphine and stepped forward to go out, he discovered that the gateway was not empty. Through it stepped a man. He must have seen Tom's figure silhouetted against the moonlight of the garden for he stopped short, and then recovering himself, he stepped quickly, with no sign of greeting, through the doorway and into the shadow of the gallery behind Seraphine. He was gone quickly, like a ghost, leaving behind only the impression of a waxen face beneath a broad-brimmed black hat, a slight limp and an empty sleeve.

The apparition startled Tom and left him for a moment as if paralyzed, looking down the gallery where the figure melted away into the blackness. It was the voice of Seraphine which roused him. She simply said, "Bien?" softly, as if she had included him in the secret of herself and Madame de Lèche, as if she also said, "Well, are you going to hold your tongue?" He felt a moment of tipsy embarrassment and then said, "Good night, Seraphine," and went through the gate leaving her to close it behind him.

In the street he hurried, why, he did not know exactly, except that he wanted to be with La Lionne, quickly, to drink her champagne and forget the senseless, idiotic torment roused by the shadowy idea of a woman he had never seen. But there were other things too which hastened the tread of his feet, an odd feeling of jealousy and a desire to escape the torment, but most of all, fear— a fear compounded suddenly of many elements.

The *impasse* was narrow and dark as a vault and when he reached the street and turned toward the Place d'Armes the way was scarcely wider and no lighter save for the intersections where a patch of moonlight splattered between the narrow shuttered houses. This city of which he had just written to Agnes with such enthusiasm, had become suddenly a dark, hostile and menacing place. Behind these closed shutters there were people, old men and women, people in middle life, even children and slaves freed now, but finding no joy in their imposed freedom, who hated him. Worse than that, they had a contempt for him. He had known it all along; he had felt it day after day, each time as he passed one of them in the streets; but his animal vitality had helped him to ignore the insolence and pride of their glances which said, "You are no better than a burglar—looting the city like a common ruffian. You are a common Yankee—an uncivilized brute!"

Those glances, those airs, had not mattered before. Secure in his own health and arrogance, he had not thought of them. And now suddenly in the silence of the dark streets where his own footsteps echoed back and forth from wall to wall, the eyes returned to haunt him, the eyes of women and men and children and black women, their heads enveloped in brilliant colored *tignons*. They were there in the darkness, eyes without faces, glaring at him as if they were illuminated by an unearthly phosphorescence, and in the forefront were the eyes of a shadowy woman he had never even seen.

All because, a little drunk with champagne, he had listened to the singing of a woman he had never seen, met an old black woman in the shadows and saw a waxen-faced phantom slip through the gateway into the house of Madame de Lèche. Who was he . . . that phantom? A lover, no doubt, of that woman he had never seen.

Not even the presence of the Army and the carpetbaggers from the North could change the cold hostility of this city. The dreadful heat was hostile, and the heavy scent of flowers that came from the balconies and over garden walls, and the oaks with their trailing garlands of gray funereal moss. There was in it none of that spare, clean, sterility of Connecticut and New England, none of that steely quality which in the end had bred the anemia of David and the crystal purity of Agnes. As he hurried through the dark, stifling street he was thirsty suddenly for that spare purity. He wanted passionately to see again the white restraint of the New Bedford Meeting House and see snow on the Boston Common. All this heat and voluptuousness and fertility became a sudden nightmare, a conspiracy to corrupt and strangle him.

He thought, "I must have been drinking too much lately. I'm

[16]

beginning to imagine and see things." For the contemptuous eyes were there again staring at him through the darkness—eyes which were eloquent, saying, "You are a damned crude Yankee, a shop-keeper, a ruffian, a thief."

And then with a sudden leap of the heart he saw, as he turned a corner, a glow of light from the part of the city bordering Canal Street and heard what he thought was the sound of ribald singing, but almost at once he discovered that the music he heard was that of the frogs in the ditches and marshes in the low-lying land along the river. "Frogs," he thought, "singing in the cemeteries where the dead are buried above ground lest the corpses become water-logged."

A hundred yards more and the street was no longer black. The eyes were gone, their phosphorescence dimmed by the lights of the gambling rooms and saloons and brothels. The sound of his own footsteps no longer pursued him. He thought, "A hundred steps more and I will have champagne. That will pull me together."

A hundred steps more and he turned in at a wide door into a big room lined with mirrors and gilding. At the far end stood a bar backed by mirrors which reflected hundreds and hundreds of bottles of every color and shape, bottles which glowed like jewels— the emerald of *crème de menthe*, the topaz of *chartreuse*, the clean diamond clarity of gin. Around the walls were gilt tables and chairs where sat a wild and strange assortment of men and women. Some of the men were in uniform, others in flashy clothes. Some had removed their coats and sat in shirt sleeves opposite women dressed in ball gowns, most of them mulattos and octoroon girls who made three brilliant blondes and a girl with auburn hair seem to have no color in them. On the floor two couples waltzed to the music of Offenbach, listlessly, badly, for the two men were too drunk to preserve either rhythm or balance. The music came from a band of colored musicians seated in a gallery above the bar. The room smelled of stale tobacco, smoke, sweat and spilled wine, but over the scene hung two great chandeliers of crystal, brilliant, sparkling, the pendants revolving slowly as the weight of the dancers stirred faintly the frame of the old building, anchored in the mud upon which the whole city was built. It was an expensive and elegant place, the establishment of La Lionne. Only men with pockets bulging with money could afford it. In the whole room there was not one citizen of New Orleans. There were only Union soldiers and carpetbaggers.

For a moment Tom stopped in the doorway surveying the room. The men with whom he had had the fight were not there. Only the shattered mirror opposite the bar remained as evidence of the riot which had happened there three hours earlier. He was sorry the men had gone; the sight of the lights and women and champagne stirred his blood again. He would have liked to have finished the fight. For a moment he would have preferred a fight to La Lionne herself.

Then a girl called Clélie came up and spoke to him, leaving a man in a wildly checked suit who, completely drunk, sat snoring, his head on the table buried in his arms. She slipped one soft arm about Tom's waist and said, "Bon soir, M'sieur Tom. Buy me a dreenk?" He only freed himself and asked, "Where is La Lionne?"

"She has gone to bed," the girl answered. "Buy me a dreenk! La Lionne is veree tired."

"I came to see La Lionne."

Then he crossed the room, ignoring the tipsy greeting of three or four of the men and all of the girls. The men greeted him because he was important. He was the General's aide and favorite. The girls greeted him because they knew that he was becoming richer every day. It was nice to have a rich client, but nicer still to have one who was young and stalwart and handsome and accepted by anyone as experienced as La Lionne. In each head was the same thought, "Perhaps one day he will grow tired of La Lionne, and then he might turn to me!" His entrance into the ball-room was like the entrance of a stallion into a herd of mares.

In the boudoir of her flat above the ball-room, La Lionne sat before an enormous gilt framed mirror shaking the gold powder out of her hair. It was a trick she had learned long ago. Hortense Schneider used it and Cora Pearl and Miss Howard, the darling of the French Emperor. She shook out the dust on an old copy of the Picayune spread on the dressing table in front of her. Of course it wasn't real gold dust. Maybe Hortense Schneider and Cora Pearl used real gold dust as people said, but not La Lionne. Nevertheless, the stuff was expensive and there wasn't any common sense in throwing it away when it could be used over and over again.

They had called her La Lionne long ago in Paris when she was no more than sixteen. It was Duc de Morny who had given her the name at her "coming out" party. She didn't remember any longer who brought the Duc—twenty years was a long time especially if you had led a life as varied and exciting as that of La Lionne. The bastard brother of the Emperor, twirling his mustache, had looked at her and said, *"Mais c'est une jeune Lionne—une belle, très belle, jeune lionne,"* and the name had stuck.

It suited her, with her broad slavic cheek-bones, her tawny hair and her sinuous body. Now with her corsets off the body was little heavier than it had been then. There were a few fine lines about the corners of the nose and eyes, but otherwise she did not look much older. Looking at her reflection in the mirror she thought, "I look harder . . . *plus dûre* . . . but after all tonight I am tired." The thought depressed her. Throwing the tawny hair back over her bare shoulders she began removing the rouge.

She could, she thought, have gone the way of Cora and Hortense and had the same sort of career. She could have had her carriage and her horses to drive up the Champs Elysées and out to Auteuil. She could have had her own palace and jewels, but that was not what she wanted. Perhaps even at sixteen she had always been too independent, living like a man, choosing her lovers instead of being chosen by them. Never had she known the disgust and boredom of having a lover who was old and fat. No, she had always chosen. That was why now, at thirty-seven, she had a lover ten years younger than herself, a handsome, accomplished lover who was devoted and so far as she knew, faithful . . . faithful she thought proudly—because there was no younger woman so attractive or amusing or accomplished.

And she was as rich as Hortense or Cora with all their jewels and horses and chateaux because she had been a clever business woman. *Quelle femme d'affaires!* She had earned her own money; it had not come to her from lovers as gifts. All the houses she owned along the Boulevard Poissonière she had bought with money she had made and saved out of the establishments in Lyons, Paris and Marseilles, and never had she made so much money as in New Orleans. Just before the war with cotton booming, the money had rolled in. Then for two years, times had been bad and she would have gone back to Paris save for the money she had invested in an establishment which she could not sell. And now again with the coming of the Yankees, times were good again, better than they had ever been because the Yankees, looting the city, had pockets stuffed with money. As clients she preferred the *New Orléanais*. They weren't so crude and they made the girls far happier than those men who took off their coats and spat on the polished floor and made love like rabbits. But business was business. They brought in money, rolls and rolls of it.

Another year or two and she would go back to Paris for good. She'd buy the house in the Square Chaussée d'Antin ... the most elegant and celebrated house in the world, the gayest and gaudiest in the style of Louis Quinze. And then she'd buy a house in the country in Périgord and live there most of the time and rest and rest and rest and become respectable and respected and go to early Mass on Sunday, walking across the Square under the neatly trimmed linden trees, up the little flight of steps into the chapel where the curé would be waiting to say, "Bon Jour, Madame Duchêsne." That was her mother's name. Her father's name was Poldinski, so her mother had told her. But you couldn't call yourself Madame Poldinski and live quietly in a small town in Périgord. "Madame Duchêsne" sounded respectable and very French.

Leaning back in the plush and gilt chair she forgot about the rouge and sat staring in front of her, but she did not see the reflection of a reddish-blonde handsome woman; she saw the green and gray village and heard the sound of the bells ringing for Sunday Mass. And there was La Lionne only she was Madame Duchêsne now, sober, sedate, dressed in black, giving money to good works and resting, resting, resting.

And then through the music of the phantom church bells came the sound of other music, the music from the ball-room belowstairs, the can-can music out of Orphée en Enfer. Slowly it crept upon her consciousness drawing her back, away from the image of the quiet little village into another world of Paris—of mirrors and gilt and gas light and plush—the silly, tragic, theatrical world of Napoleon

III and Morny. That was the world of Hortense. "Orphée" was her great success—"Orphée" and "La Belle Hélène." And suddenly she was filled with nostalgia and loneliness. Tonight, just now, she would have liked to be in Paris and be gone forever from this strange, hot city with its perfumes and evil smells, its cholera and yellow fever and magnolias and azaleas.

The music had changed suddenly. The melody of Offenbach was finished and in its place was the sound of a banjo and black big 'Ector's voice singing, "With a banjo on my knee." That sound brought La Lionne back to the image of herself in the mirror. The paleness of the face frightened her. She thought, "It's this *sacré* heat!" And at the same time the picture of the plague of four years ago returned to her—the heat and the croaking of the great frogs, the flaming barrels of pitch lining the streets at the edge of the *banquettes*, lighting up the charnel wagons that carried off the dead; the silence in the streets, the terror in each house where one by one the inmates dropped, turned livid and died in convulsions and filth. The image of the green, evil memories blotted out even her own image in the mirror.

"As soon as I can find a buyer," she thought, "I'll leave this accursed town and go back to Paris."

She was afraid and tired and alone.

From belowstairs came again the wild gay music of the can-can and for a second the sound distracted her, changing the image in the mirror to the drunken gaiety which she knew so well since the Yankees and carpetbaggers had come to town. She saw it all—the yellow plush and gilt and mirrors, the girls tired by now and bored by the drunken roughness of the clients, kicking and swishing their skirts contemptuously. Her thoughts fastened suddenly upon Clélie. Clélie was a wonderful dancer and a beautiful girl. When she herself went back to Paris she would take Clélie with her. The girl would have a great career there where her delicate *café au lait* beauty would not go unappreciated as it did here in the Café Imperial.

She sighed, wishing for the old days, when only gentlemen visited the establishment and she took pleasure in sitting at her own table until the dawn came up across Lake Pontchartrain and turned the vast muddy Mississippi the color of rose.

Then her reverie was broken by a double knock at the door and, startled, she called out, "Who's there?"

A voice answered "Tom"—a voice of peculiar timbre, deep but clear and arrogant, a voice which by its mere sound relighted the fires of her stupendous animal spirits. The quarrel and the fight earlier in the evening had wearied her, and when she had seen him leave after knocking down two drunken carpetbaggers in succession, she had felt for one brief second that she was dying. Her heart had stopped beating and she had gone suddenly faint in the fear that he had gone out of the door never to return. She fancied the picture of herself as a woman of character who lived like a man, but lately she had been troubled by the doubt that she was no different from any other woman, that time and fate had caught up with her. She was no better than any other woman of her age with a *maquereau* years younger than herself. It did not matter that he was an officer in the American Army. He had all the makings of a *maquereau*—vain, spoiled, egotistical, selfish and beautiful, with a kind of animal beauty which always made her feel faint like any common *grue* at the sight of her pimp.

And so the shrewd, handsome, hard-headed, tired woman- -no longer young, frightened of so many things, of the plague, of New Orleans, of the Devil, of poverty, of death, came alive again and the image in the great gilt framed mirror suddenly took on color and was young. Her heart cried out, "Entrez, mon bien aimé. Prenez moi! Prenez mon corps! Prenez mon coeur! Prenez tout! C'est à toi!" But her head and her pride prevented her. Her head said, "He is a Yankee—a barbarian. He does not even understand French." She heard herself saying in a curious cold voice that was strange to her, "What is it you want?"

The voice from beyond the door said, "I want you. Let me in, Félice." And then the sound of the knob turning and of a muscular shoulder thrown against it. The door was locked as it always was, for belowstairs there were often men, rough and drunken, who preferred La Lionne to any of her girls and sometimes tried to force themselves upon her.

Then heart and desire slew reason and she said, "Wait! In a moment."

And with her heart beating, she quickly rouged her lips and

cheeks and gathered her hair, tawny now and free from golden dust, fastening it with one heavy golden comb. The newspaper containing the dust she whisked away into a drawer of the dressing table. Then she went to the door and unlocking it, turned the handle.

He came in quickly and putting his arms about her, buried his face in her white shoulder. He held her thus for a long time, and when at last he freed her, he said, "Tell Ernestine to bring champagne."

"You've had enough!" She did not like him drunk. He became quarrelsome and difficult. With her Frenchwoman's instinct and taste she disliked mixing drink and love-making.

He only said, "Damn it! I feel gay!" He pulled the bell rope himself and faraway in the house a bell jangled. The noisy music of the can-can had stopped belowstairs. Its sudden absence made the hot night suddenly still—so still that you could again hear the croaking of the frogs in the marshes along the river.

He unbuckled his belt and threw it and his sword across a chair. Then he unbuttoned his tunic and threw it over one of the gilt chairs. The shirt he wore was of white lawn—a shirt, she thought suddenly for no reason at all, that was part of the loot of the ravaged city. They said the Yankees had stolen not only all the money they could lay their hands on but silver spoons and forks, and even women's clothes, as well. They called the General himself "Silver Spoon." For a second she felt a flash of contempt but that passed quickly in her passion for her lover. It was thus she liked him, for the shirt revealed the beauty of his body, that body more perfect than any she had ever seen, which obsessed her and humbled her pride and made her like any common woman, a mere female like any other. And because the thought humiliated her pride, she stifled it and gave herself over to her passion.

She noticed the bruise on his cheek and took up a bottle of one of her own scented creams to dress it, but he would have none of it. The disagreement over the champagne had irritated him.

Even when the champagne came, borne in by Ernestine—a big, very black negress, so powerful that she sometimes threw out drunks and noisy men, single-handed—his mood did not improve. She tried to behave as if there was nothing troubling him. She asked where he had gone after the fight—why he had returned, a thing he had never done before once he had gone away.

"I couldn't sleep. The damned heat and the mosquitoes."

And all the while she talked, saying trivial, idiotic things like any of the girls belowstairs, she kept thinking, now that she had put away her pride, how much she loved him—the high color, the broad shoulders, the flat narrow waist, the stubborn nose, the sulky sensual mouth, the arrogant clear blue eyes, the cropped curly dark head. "He is like a bad little boy," she thought. A charming bad spoiled little boy in whom there was something splendid and noble which one day might emerge, a nobility touched by the splendor of an animal. Then she heard him speaking, saying something which had lain, she knew shrewdly out of her long experience, all the time behind the sulkiness.

He was saying, "What is Madame de Lèche like?"

She shrugged her shoulders and drew the peignoir closer about her as if she were withdrawing from him a little. "Which Madame de Lèche?" she asked, although she knew quite well. "There are two. The old Baroness and the daughter-in-law . . . the one they call the young Baroness."

"The widow," he said abruptly. "The young Baroness."

"I have never seen her."

"You must have heard of her."

"I have heard it said she was beautiful." And almost at once she was sorry she had spoken thus. "But very possibly it is because she dazzles the provincial Créole families. She is Parisian."

"Oh, Parisian!" he said, but from the timbre of his voice she could not tell what he meant. The music had begun again downstairs, a waltz now.

"Of course," she said, "I should hardly meet her. We don't move precisely in the same worlds. Have you not seen her?"

"She hasn't shown so much as the tip of her slipper."

"They are a proud family."

"Damn their pride . . . come here. Sit on my knee."

She came over, obedient as a child, yet feeling ridiculous in her pride. She was jealous and angry, jealous absurdly in a blinding flash, of a woman neither of them had ever seen.

[24]

He felt her body stiffen and said, "What's the matter? Don't you love me any more?"

"Of course I do."

She kissed him and called him "cher" and behaved as she had always done, but there was a difference. Desire—the desire for which she had always felt contempt—fought with her pride, for she knew that while he sat there with his arms about her, he was thinking not of her at all but of that other woman he had not seen . . . that Baroness de Lèche. "The young Baroness" they called her. Out of her long experience with men, she divined that he had come back tonight not out of love for herself but because he could not sleep. She knew his kind of man, although she had never met a man so arrogant, so passionately willed, so challenged by obstacles. He was not in love with the Baroness de Lèche. How could he be when he had never seen her? He was in love with the idea of her—that she was contemptuous of him and would not see him, that he considered himself irresistible. He had come back to her with Madame de Lèche on his mind. He was using her as a makeshift mistress.

She wanted to say, "Go away! Never come back here again! I never want to see you!" But at the same time the touch of his hand, even the sight of the head covered with curling black hair that was so wiry and seemed alive with vitality, rendered her will quite powerless. She could only say, weakly, like any silly woman, "Don't think of her. It will do you no good. The de Lèche family are all proud as devils. She wouldn't spit on a Yankee." She wanted to say, "How could you think that a woman from the Paris of the Empire would bother with a ruffian from Boston. How could all that is Parisian and Catholic and civilization itself mix with the son of New England shop-keepers?" But she held her tongue, for she knew that although he himself blackguarded Boston and everyone in it, he'd never permit others to deride it.

But somehow he must have divined what she was thinking, for he said, as if talking to himself, "To hell with her pride. To hell with contempt! Let's not speak of her. Let's forget her!" Then he seized her and kissed her with that wild fury which lay at the very roots of her shameful subjection. It was, she knew, with her ancient instinct, the fury of a baffled, divided, unhappy man who sought

[25]

to lose himself in love-making as he sought to lose himself in drinking. Even while he kissed her, she thought, "Some day he will destroy himself unless he finds peace." And she found a sort of perverted macabre delight in yielding to him, in trying to help him to forget whatever it was that tormented him.

They drank another bottle of champagne, and La Lionne, the business woman, the proud and independent femme du monde, became a weak and silly creature like any cheap sentimental girl in the arcades of the Palais Royal. But for this she would at that moment have exchanged all her jewels, all the houses on the Boulevard Poissonnière, even the chance of that long, long rest in the little town in Périgord as Madame Duchêsne. Once she threw back her head and in an odd strangled whisper called upon God to save her.

Belowstairs there was another fight. Ernestine the great black woman, with voodoo curses, threw a drunken carpetbagger into the middle of Royal Street. The band stopped playing at last and Clélie and the other girls found their way, with aching feet, up the high stairway to their beds. And at length he lay, peaceful and asleep while she sat watching, thinking that he looked like a small boy, a naughty small boy whom everyone was always certain to spoil.

Outside the sky turned rosy above the bayous and the frogs ceased their croaking and presently she heard the bells of St. Louis' squat spire ringing for early Mass. Rising she dressed quickly and throwing a shawl of black lace over her head, went down the stairs and through the ball-room smelling of stale wine and cigar smoke, past the overturned chairs and the shattered mirror and out into the empty silent streets.

She was going to Mass to pray for her soul, to be delivered from the spell the devil had cast upon her, to pray for her freedom and to escape from the slavery of her body. In the doorway of the old church she came face to face with a woman younger than herself, a woman of curious beauty whose violet eyes and black hair shone through the lace of the shawl which she wore over her face. The woman returned her glance quickly and then cast down her eyes, but in that second there was an odd flash of understanding between them. La Lionne thought even that the younger woman smiled as if to reassure her, a smile even of friendship,

[26]

almost of sisterhood. La Lionne waited to allow her to pass in the door first and then with a feeling of sickness, thought, "That must be her. That must be the young Baroness." And before she entered the church she profaned the portal by murmuring a prayer, "Oh, God, Oh, Mary, grant that he never sees her!" For she *knew*. She was afraid of what she had seen because out of her long experience she knew what it was.

In the house in Pinckney Street, Aunt Tam and Agnes were ready to leave. The chill spring sun of April in Boston came through the big white framed windows casting little lozenges of violet colored light on the heavy mahogany, the thick, durable carpets and the chaste white rail of the tall curving stairway. Minnie and Bridget, the cook and chambermaid, were there, Minnie twisting and untwisting her apron and Bridget crying silently and commending little Agnes and Aunt Tam to the care of all the saints she could think of. Sure, Miss Agnes and Aunt Tam would have need of their attendance, going off like this among niggers and foreigners and rebels.

And in the foreground stood Ethan Wicks, solid, phlegmatic, bearded, reassuring, a tower of strength in the presence of so many hysterical females. Living always in a house filled with women, he was perpetually forced into the role of "keeping a steady keel." And so he had an air of studied calm and outward indifference which sometimes was far from the true state of his inward feelings. There were even times when, forced to act as a counterweight to screams and tears and sobs, he found himself making decisions against his own inclinations and judgments simply in order to create an impression of calm and order and common sense. He was aware now, as Agnes and Tam were ready to leave, that he had allowed them to go simply because all the others in the family, nearly all females, had wailed and called the whole idea of the trip nonsensical and dangerous. In his heart he was troubled but he knew now that it was too late to change his mind and forbid them to leave. In the first place it would have given the women an opportunity to patronize him and say that, of course, they had been right all along; and it would have given the impression of weakness, a thing which he had learned long ago could never be risked by a man who governed the finances and ruled the major decisions of eleven women relations. His daughter Agnes and his spinster sister-in-law Tam would have to sail on this quixotic voyage. Even if they were captured by Confederate privateers or were ravished by the strange wild people of Cuba, or were shipwrecked in the Mexican Gulf—even if they themselves wanted to turn back, he would still have to stick by his decision.

Once, long ago, when David was born, he had hoped that a son, another man in the family, would take some of the burden from his shoulders; but years ago he had given up that hope, for David wasn't much better than the women. He was a poet. Imagine a solid Boston merchant like Ethan Wicks having a poet for a son!

For the Wicks weren't artistic or intellectual like the Adamses and the Lowells. They had always been a solid Whig shop-keeping family, in which a poet was no less than a calamity.

Looking at Aunt Tam, a good many people thought she would have the common sense and level head of a man. Aunt Tam looked like a horse, and had ideas about the enfranchisement of women and was a friend of Margaret Fuller and Bronson Alcott, but inside, her brother knew, she was the most sentimental and hysterical of the lot. Whether her exterior and her advanced opinions had thwarted her in the role of doting wife and mother or whether her spinsterhood had given rise to her advanced opinions, he could never quite make up his mind.

He had his hat in his hand and a woolen shawl over his shoulders, for despite the deceptive brightness of the chill sun, dirty snow still lay unmelted in the shadows of the Pinckney Street houses.

Terry, the coachman, drove them to the station down the long slope of Beacon Street. On the doorsteps and the sidewalks neighbors recognized Terry and went inside the house to talk in hushed voices about the madness of Ethan Wicks allowing his daughter and sister to go away in war time to a captured Confederate city. It wasn't, they said, as if you could count on Aunt Tam in a pinch; she was giddier than little Agnes herself.

It was a small town, Boston, more like a village than a city, where everybody knew the affairs of everyone else. Two or three women, wiser or perhaps more fleshly than any woman in Boston was supposed to be, shook their heads and expressed doubt that it was either Agnes' affection for her twin brother or the invitation of her Uncle General Wicks which drew her and Aunt Tam to New Orleans. More likely, they thought and said, it was the attraction of that dark and seductive figure of Tom Bedloe, a ne'er-do-well, an adventurer, a rogue if there ever was one, but a man who stirred shaming thoughts in the bosoms of many a respectable woman. He had but to enter a drawing-room to disturb the whole atmosphere, to heighten the color of a normal woman and brighten her eyes. But marry him. . . . No. They couldn't understand Ethan Wicks allowing his pure young daughter to be engaged to marry such a rake. They would sooner see their own daughters in the grave.

And so as the fat horses of Ethan Wicks drew them down Beacon Street toward the station, the curtains of front windows in house after house were whisked aside while middle-aged wives, old maids and even young spinsters watched the carriage carrying poor little Agnes Wicks toward a horrible but seductive doom.

And in the cabriolet little Agnes sat beside Aunt Tam, holding muff and reticule in her lap, facing her father, watching his broad, sombre dull face. In her heart she was a little frightened, not so much by the adventure which lay before her, as by the knowledge that for the first time in her life she was leaving the protection of the heavy man opposite her, the man who had made every decision for her since she was born, who sheltered her and provided the solid comfortable house in Pinckney Street and the old house surrounded by orchards at Dedham. Between these two establishments her whole life had passed, secure and solid and uneventful save for the death of a kitten or the tempestuous visits of Tom Bedloe.

Watching her father, her thoughts kept straying in an unmaidenly fashion to Thomas, for although when she was alone in her bed at night she thought of him as Tom and even "dear" Tom she had never in her life called him anything but Mr. Bedloe or Major Bedloe and once or twice Thomas.

The women behind the curtains on Beacon Street had been quite right; it was not Uncle James Wicks who drew her to New Orleans or even her brother David; it was Tom Bedloe. It had been Tom Bedloe from the very beginning, from the moment he had stepped through the doorway of Eliza Trent's drawing-room and she had noticed the curly head, the blue eyes, the high color and the wide tormented sensual mouth. Something had happened to her in that moment and it had gone on happening ever since, without relief, without change, relentlessly. And presently it had changed her whole character. From a simple, naïve child, she had turned secretive and even crafty. She had plotted, more by instinct than by reason, to meet him accidentally, to lead her father into the trap of asking him to supper on Sunday evenings. For the first time in her dull, quiet life, she had experienced excitement.

Brought up protected and sheltered by her father and Aunt Tam, she knew nothing whatever of life. She had not even the faintest suspicion of what it was in her that made her plot and connive to see Tom Bedloe. She merely knew that she had to do it. She supposed that she was in love, although the violence of her feeling was far more intense than any emotions she had found described in the few decorous novels she had read. Her own feeling was like a delightful illness which caused fever and even delirium and dreams of the wildest and most exciting nature.

She knew, by intimations and whispers and by her own woman's instinct, that Thomas was "wicked," but that made it all the more exciting. She was not even quite sure of just what wickedness he was guilty. But she liked the idea because it was exciting, and always in the back of her small Boston mind there was a thought, "Perhaps I can change him. Perhaps I can tame his wildness and make him a good and virtuous husband." Knowing nothing whatever of life, this seemed to her in the long watches of the night a comparatively simple thing to do.

When she did not hear from him for weeks at a time, she grew troubled and quiet and even ill. If he were killed, she told herself, she would never marry anyone but give her own life to good works. She would wear black for the rest of her life—becoming black of course—with a little veil falling from the back of her bonnet. But it was not the prospect of his death which troubled her so much as the idea he might have found some other girl he liked better than herself and that he had forgotten her. So she wrote to him, three times each week, letters which outwardly were dove-like and innocent and simple, but in reality were masterpieces of craft, reminding him by instinct of the things which had led him into asking for her hand . . . such things as her innocence, her freshness and her youth. How or why she did this, she had no idea, but once Aunt Tam, who included reincarnation in her all-encompassing passion for new and faddish doctrines, had said, "Agnes, my dear, you are what is called a very old soul. You know so much more than you could possibly have learned in your present brief span upon this earth." It was her solid father who had replied, saying, "I don't know about all that rubbish, Tam, but there are times when it seems to me Agnes is very near to being a minx."

And so when her Aunt, the General's wife, had written suggesting that she and Aunt Tam might like to visit New Orleans now that David and Tom were both there, Agnes had been very quiet at the supper table, like a mouse, behaving as if the idea were too preposterous even to discuss. It was Aunt Tam who had received the suggestion with enthusiasm. Aunt Tam who had lived in Paris and was a friend of advanced creatures like Margaret Fuller and Louisa May Alcott and Harriet Beecher Stowe and had travelled a great deal, even making a trip through Sicily on a donkey. Aunt Tam thought it a wonderful idea, with no perils at all. She treated it as if the trip were no more than going from Boston to Dedham. She did not even allow Agnes' father to interpose an objection. And when at last Aunt Tam paused for breath, and he asked Agnes what she thought of the idea, she said, meek as a lamb, "it would be nice if we could visit Aunt Louisa and we could make a comfortable home for David. He wasn't made for a soldier's life and he's very homesick" with not one word of Tom, although all the time his dark, delightful and troubling image was there in the back of her heart and mind. Her heart beat like a trip hammer and her brain raced with ideas of drawing him back to her.

So for three weeks they had toyed with the idea, Aunt Tam full of enthusiasm, Agnes always quiet as a lamb, docile and submissive, until presently the idea no longer seemed preposterous, even to her father, but as simple and usual as the annual migration to the place at Dedham. Then quite suddenly without his knowing exactly how it happened, he found that Agnes was treating the thing as already settled. She was getting ready her wardrobe and had the trunks down from the big attic, and when Ethan Wicks expressed surprise, Agnes cried a little and said that of course she thought it was all settled, and Aunt Tam attacked him, saying that he couldn't change his mind now and disappoint them both, and as the two women began to maneuver the decision into the proportions of a scene, Ethan Wicks gave in and pretended before all the women folks in the family that it had always been his idea, and that a change would do both of them good and that New Orleans now must be a very interesting place. Under the guardianship of General Wicks they would both be as safe as they were in Pinckney Street.

It was Agnes' idea that their arrival should be a surprise to poor homesick David, and of course to Tom as well, because otherwise Tom might give it away to David.

And so now here they were in the cabriolet driving to take the train to New York to embark, two lone women, upon what could be an exciting adventure, and Agnes, sitting meek as a mouse, was praying that her father might not change his mind at the last minute and was saying to herself, "I *will* have him. No one else shall have him, even if I have to go to New Orleans and get yellow fever to keep him."

The cabriolet stopped suddenly and her father opened the door and they walked into the station and there was the train and in fifteen minutes she was leaning out of the window as it moved off, waving her lawn handkerchief bordered with lace out of the window to her father, with just the right number of tears in her eyes to make the departure moving.

In New Orleans Uncle James Wicks ruled like a Persian Satrap. Ethan Wicks knew his brother well enough, for they were only three years apart in age and had played together in the old orchard at Dedham and gone swimming in the icy waters of Maine beaches where Jim had bullied every boy smaller than himself and assumed a God-like attitude of unimpeachable rightness upon every subject under the sun. When Jim returned from West Point to visit at Dedham, his arrogance and self-assurance was so vast that their father had been moved to remark, "Jim is as absolute as God, only God is sometimes wrong."

The General who now ruled the conquered city of New Orleans

was the same insufferable male, older and more hardened, whom Ethan had known as a boy—a man, stumpy and vulgar in build with the chest of a pouter pigeon, who ruled like a Hun chieftain over the civilized Louisiana city. Beside him on the Satrap's throne sat his wife, Louisa, a woman who made virtue a profession, converted thrift into avarice, and regarded comfortable living as sinful and wicked. For the two of them the whole of the United States, both north and south, was a shiftless and corrupt community save only that corner known as New England and even New England was a sullied place in comparison to Aunt Louisa's native state of Maine.

In the splendor of the most beautiful house in New Orleans the pair ruled over the stricken, once rich city, like a New England justice of peace and a school-marm. And Uncle Jim was also a martinet and a militarist, whose little army world he would have made a model for the whole of civilization. They were peasants in a palace—frost-bitten, penurious New Englanders in the midst of a Latin City set down in a splendorous, half-tropical climate. Ethan Wicks, though a dull man, was no fool. He did not like his brother James and he was even less fond of James' wife, Louisa, but of one thing he was certain—that so long as James and Louisa ruled New Orleans with an iron fist as if it were a New England village, his daughter, little Agnes, was safe.

For all their iron-handed virtue, James and Louisa had at least two weaknesses. One was money, and to get money, almost anything short of murder was justifiable under the New England belief in "smartness." A man might be a pillar of sexual righteousness in his community, he might claim God as his brother, but this did not prevent him from being "smart." Being "smart" was not only excusable; it was a virtue. Men like Bronson Alcott, who could not feed and shelter his own family, were fools but men like Ethan Wicks who sold shoddy blankets and paper soled shoes to the Union Government for its soldiers were "smart" and admired. And General James Wicks was "smart." He and his wife Louisa lived as frugally as peasants; they had no desire for wealth because of the beauty or graciousness of life it could bring them; they wanted it to hide in socks or beneath mattresses or to bury near the privy at the end of the garden. And for a "smart" man, New Orleans, rich and prostrate and helpless, her wharves filled with sugar and war-time cotton, her banks filled with money, her great houses with silver and rich furniture, was a chance for plunder seldom tossed at the feet of a "smart" New Englander. After one good look at the situation, Uncle James sent for two or three business men friends from the North and the sanctimonious gang went to work. And at the same time they set to work to rescue the souls of the New Orleans rebels from their whoring and wine drinking, their duelling and their frivolity.

The other weakness the General and Aunt Louisa had was Tom Bedloe. From the moment they had seen him in Ethan Wicks' house at Dedham, he had captured their imaginations. In an odd way he had had upon them somewhat the same effect he had had upon little Agnes. He was like themselves, a New Englander, but he was a black sheep. He had a kind of wild beauty and a warmth and a vigor which neither of them and very few other New Englanders had ever known. His mere presence brought something into their lives which had not been there before. That he was wicked, Aunt Louisa knew as well as did little Agnes, and she knew what his "wickedness" was, that he could not resist women, but in some strange way she did not mind his "wickedness" so long as she was not brought face to face with it. What she did not openly recognize did not trouble her, and there were times when, in secret, she found it pleasant and titillating to speculate upon the rascal Tom's amorous life.

And so General Wicks had made him a Major and his *aide*, partly because he found Tom's amoral point of view convenient. When the General did something "smart" there was neither suspicion nor accusation in Tom Bedloe's eyes. There was perhaps, a humorous twinkle, but no more than that, and a humorous twinkle you could ignore, pretending not to have noticed it. So much did Uncle James and Aunt Louisa like Tom that they relinquished to him one of the plums in the plunder of New Orleans. General Wicks made his *aide* the Collector of Port Revenue, with a hint that here was a great chance for "smart" business. So Tom, with a twinkle in his clear blue eyes, took over the post, provided as favorite of the Tetrarch and Tetrarchess with a rich and beautiful promise. In three months he had already done very well for himself.

It was late afternoon when he wakened in the red and gold bedroom in the establishment of La Lionne. Belowstairs, the bar and the ball room were already crowded and the music had begun. For a moment, on wakening, he did not know where he was nor how he had come there. His head ached and he felt sulky. When Ernestine answered his angry ring, he asked the great negress where La Lionne was and received the answer that she was belowstairs acting as hostess. Then Ernestine brought him a gin drink with which to start the day.

"What day is it?" he asked her.

"Sunday," said the big black woman, "but it's nearly over." He reflected upon the difference between Sunday in New Orleans and Sunday in Boston, where there was no gaiety and few people even appeared in the streets.

Instead of going away Ernestine stood watching him, her great ebony arms bared to the elbow, on her hips. Her figure was feminine with enormous buttocks and great breasts but her strength was masculine. As he drank he closed his eyes to ease his aching head and when at last he opened them Ernestine was still there, at the foot of the bed, a kind of magnificent ebony Nemesis in her brilliant *tignon*. She was as vigorous and barbaric as the room was decadent and over-elegant.

Looking over the rim of the tall glass, Tom thought, "Maybe she's going to throw me out." The passionately interested stare of the woman annoyed him. He emptied the glass and then said, "Do you want anything, Ernestine?"

She took her hands off her hips and leaned on the high foot-board of the ebony and mother-of-pearl bed. She was a free negress from Natchez with an adventurous nature, who had been to Atlanta and Charleston and even as far north as Nashville. La Lionne treated her as a confidante. In a small way she ruled the Café Imperial, the lieutenant in command after La Lionne.

"What do you Yankees want here in New Orleans?" she asked.

It was a question he found suddenly difficult to answer. Dully he searched his brain for a reason but none came or at least only a weak one. "It's war time," he said. "We captured the city. We've got to hold it."

"It ain't any place for you," she said. "If you Yankees stay long enough you'll be done up proper—women and drink and the climate. You Yankees ain't tough enough for New Orleans."

That was an odd thing to say to a New Englander—that a New Englander wasn't tough enough for a soft, decadent city like New Orleans. But this morning his aching head gave him a faint intimation of what she meant. Before he could think of an answer, she said, "And there's things goin' on."

"What sort of things, Ernestine?"

"Plots and things." She rolled her eyes. "I like you, Major Tom. I wouldn't like to see you get hurt or mebbe killed. Why don't you git out of here while the gittin' is good?"

Weakly he answered, "I've got a job."

"And there's Madame. She likes you a mighty lot. She had a mind to go away to Atlanta when the Yankees came, but after she laid her pretty eyes on you, Major Tom, she give up the idea." For a second she was silent and then she said, "It ain't good for a young fella to be mixed up with a woman like Madame. No, sir, it ain't good. It ain't healthy." Then quickly she added, "Only doan you ever tell her ah said so."

"I won't," said Tom.

Ernestine stood up straight thrusting out her great bosom with an air of finality. "Ah like you, Major Tom. Ef'n you was to take my advice you'd head yourself right away from this town afore the sickness gets you or mebbe a bullet in the back."

"Thanks, Ernestine."

"You doan want a cup of black coffee or nuthin' more, do you?"

"Nothing more," said Tom.

Then she went out leaving him to consider what she had said. Her speech had been like the croaking of the frogs along the levee and that smell of warm, wet, sickeningly fertile mud which sometimes drifted over the city when the hot wind blew from the gulf, filling him with a curious nervous indefinable sense of depression and doom. Plots and things. Assassination, voodoo gatherings, the quiet extinction of Louisianians who had been friendly or even moderately polite to General James Wicks and his pilfering Army. With a sickening feeling at the pit of his stomach he remembered the hangings of rebels who had raised General Wicks' ill humor . . . strong, healthy young men one minute, loving life and women perhaps as much as he himself loved them—the next minute simply jerking, dying, fighting bodies at the end of a rope.

Maybe Ernestine was right. Maybe he ought to go away. Dully he fell to regarding the room.

It was lush, over-elegant, with heavy curtains of red brocade hanging voluptuously from beneath heavy gold baldaquins, with chairs and a *chaise longue* of mother-of-pearl and ebony brought all the way from Paris. Now as he drank, he regarded the room in all its details with disgust.

He thought, "A trollop's bedroom, if ever there was one!" And again he felt a sudden longing for the chill austerity of his own childhood bedroom in New Bedford.

In the mood of satiation he did not even think now of the young widow in the old house where he was quartered. She belonged to another part of him, the Tom Bedloe who was like a young bull forever looking for new adventures. And that Tom Bedloe had disappeared now or was at least dormant, lost in remorse and a cloud of good intentions.

With a bad taste in his mouth, an aching head and the sickening odor of La Lionne's scent in his nostrils, he dressed, putting on the soiled ruffled shirt which once had adorned some duelling New Orleans dandy. There was a streak of the dandy in himself, he knew—the kind of dandiness that came of vitality and health, which drove the cockerel in the morning to seek the top of the dung heap to shake his brilliant feathers and greet the sun. He dressed quickly, filled with a desire to escape the hot, vulgar room and the heavy scent of La Lionne. He did not want to see her.

Outside the sun was setting and the faint croaking of the frogs had begun, and as he buckled his sword, thunder broke the suffocating stillness of the room with a sudden roar. It was a kind of thunder he had never heard before, dull and muffled by the misty heat. He thought, "I will go home and change and go to the General's for supper." They always had a welcome for him, even on short notice. He knew he was the favorite of General Wicks and "Aunt" Louisa and unscrupulously he played on the knowledge.

"Aunt" Louisa was always trying to save him from the gutter. He suspected that if he had been ill-favored and pimply instead of good-looking, her zeal would not be half so great. Now, feeling hot and soiled, he welcomed the thought of a spare New England Sunday evening supper. He had had enough of *bisque d'écrevisse* and blood-heating gumbos. He would change and dine early and respectably at the General's and then go home and write a letter to Agnes—not a labored indifferent dull letter like the one he had written last night but a tender loving letter worthy of her purity and goodness, worthy of that childlike sweetness which made him love her when he thought of her. Agnes could save him. It seemed that he himself had not the strength. He was sick of scent and champagne and sultry love-making.

The first great warm drops of rain had begun to fall as he came out of the back door of the Café Imperial. They splattered about his feet on the *banquettes* where his weight on the badly laid flagging forced through the crevasses the mud upon which the whole city was built. The sickening faint smell of a hundred and fifty years of offal and death swallowed up and dissolved in mud, drifted through the falling rain and mixed with the faint warm scent of the wistaria on the grilled balconies. As he walked, he hurried partly to escape the oncoming storm and partly out of impatience to have a bath and wash away the scent of La Lionne which was as unbearable to him as the smell of the mud. The thunder pursued him, muffling the rising chorus of frogs as the warm rain fell faster and faster. But before he had gone a dozen blocks, the shower became a downpour.

It was like no rain he had ever seen. The water fell in thick warm sheets. In it there was nothing cool and refreshing. A faint, muggy mist arose from the crude flagging of the *banquettes*. Water from the roofs overflowed the shallow gutters and poured down on his head and shoulders. One expected rain to be cool and refreshing but here in these narrow streets it was like a downpour in hell, serving only to increase discomfort and misery. The dirty water flowed in the gutters and rose half way to the tops of his army boots. He did not attempt to seek shelter for in his tired dulled mind was the thought that somehow all this water would serve to cleanse him.

At the *impasse* which led to the courtyard door of the de Lèche house the whale-oil light was extinguished and in the darkness he stumbled through the rain over the cobblestones, fumbling for a long time when he arrived at the door to fit the great key into the lock. Inside the gallery it was dry save for the mist that drifted in from the garden as the downpour beat upon the flowers and plants. As he climbed the stairway he discovered that there was a light in his sitting-room and he thought, "It must be David come back again," and he felt a sudden tinge of annoyance.

But as he entered the open doorway he saw that it was not David at all but a woman. Standing she was, with her back toward him, a slim straight, elegant back rising from the folds of a great crinoline skirt of yellow banded with ribbon. The light from the candles beyond gave her a dim but radiant aura of light. The noise of the rain drowned the sound of his footsteps and without turning she continued what she was doing. Beside her stood a fresh bouquet of flowers, camellias and some kind of lily mixed together, but it was not the flowers which occupied her hands but the pile of papers which lay on his desk. He divined then suddenly that this was the young Baroness and that she was searching for something among his personal belongings.

He started to speak and then, his mind suddenly awake and alert, he was silent and turning, he went back into the gallery where unbuckling his sword, he allowed it to drop to the floor. The clatter rose above the sound of the rain and when he again appeared in the doorway she had turned toward him away from the papers and was busy arranging the bouquet of lilies and camellias. She did not turn toward the door although he was certain that she knew he was standing there. It was an excellent performance she gave, apparently absorbed in the arranging of the flowers as if she were completely alone. For a second he stood there watching her, all his weariness and boredom gone, his heart pounding again beneath the soaked blue broadcloth of his tunic.

The yellow dress suited her with her white skin and black hair. She was, he thought, all his passion for women driving him on, perhaps in her middle twenties, and dressed as if for a party in a gown cut low to show the throat and breast, a throat that was ivory and lustrous now in the light of the candle. He could not see the

[39]

color of her eyes for as she looked down at the flowers they were hidden by the long dark lashes, but the curve of her lips caught his attention, full and voluptuous and rouged in the Parisian fashion. Her mouth was large and the nose delicately cut but a little too arched at the bridge. He had, he thought, seen more beautiful women but the very perfection of their beauty had made them seem cold. There was a glow about this woman, a physical glow that was like the aura of light cast about her by the candle. And there was a style about the clothing and the way she held herself which gave promise of pride and spirit.

Then, his mouth curling a bit at the corners, he said, "Good evening."

Again she gave an excellent performance, even to the start of surprise, as if he had frightened her. She looked up at him and he saw that her eyes were dark though not brown or black. The yellow dress suited them too. She said, "Good evening. I hope you'll forgive me. I brought you some flowers."

He had expected her to speak with an accent, or perhaps that she would speak no English at all. The English was perfect. It was the way English people spoke English.

"It's very kind of you," he said. "A man living alone has no time to think of such things. I'm Thomas Bedloe."

"Yes," she said, "I've seen you. I've watched you go out in the morning. I'm Madame de Lèche—the one they call the young Baroness."

In spite of the dignity and the fine show of manners, he was aware by the faint glint in her eyes, that inside she was laughing at the comedy they had just played.

"Won't you sit down and have a glass of port?" he asked.

But she refused, "Thank you very much, but my grandmother would be very angry if she knew I was here alone in your rooms. She is the one they call the old Baroness."

"You would be quite safe."

She smiled, a slow, curious insinuating smile, full of mockery. It was at the same time a bold and wicked smile full of knowledge and experience. "Unfortunately, it is not safety which matters in my world so much as appearances. You see, you have never called. Officially I still do not know you."

"If I called would it help put things right?"

"Perhaps."

He was aware as they spoke that she was studying him, that she was noting everything about him—his head, the way he held the sword, the shoulders, the cut of his tunic. It was the kind of look he expected from women like La Lionne, an appraising almost bawdy look, and yet it was different, perhaps because of her dignity and pride. He was thankful she could not see the pilfered shirt with its frills all soiled and crumpled from the debauchery of the night before.

"I thought none of you would receive a Yankee."

"We have been waiting for you to call. It's very dull, being shut up always in this house—never being able to go on the street without being insulted by Yankees."

He knew she was lying and that she had asked him to call only because he had trapped her pilfering his papers and a little because she found him an attractive man. There was a boldness and self-possession about her that fascinated him. She conceded nothing. She stood her ground with brazen assurance.

"I apologize and hope you will believe that all Yankees are not alike." He heard his own voice and it had a curious, artificial sound like the very words he spoke, as if somehow he had been forced into the role of actor.

"It may be," she answered, smiling a little.

"When may I call?"

"Tonight if you like. After we have dined."

"When do you dine?"

"We should be dining now. There is the bell." As she spoke dimly through the rain came the familiar sound of the silver bell which Old Seraphine rang to summon the family from the more distant parts of the big house. "I shall have to go. And you shouldn't be standing there in those soaking clothes with the sickness about."

"There is no fever in New Orleans," he said. "General Wicks has cleaned up the town and quarantined all incoming ships."

She smiled again, "Your General Wicks may believe he is God but there are things he cannot control. The fever is here. The nuns have three cases now in St. Louis. It has come in from th⁻ land side, from up the river."

She turned then and coming round the corner of the desk she passed him. "If you'll forgive me, I'll go before Grandmother discovers where I have been."

"You speak excellent English," he said. "I was afraid when I saw you that I shouldn't be able to speak to you."

"My mother was Irish and I was brought up by an English governess. It was my first language."

She went out into the gallery and for a moment he stood watching her as she went along the long passage to the far side of the house. As the shadows and the falling rain blurred and hid her figure, he felt a sudden pang that was like a faint sickness. It surprised him, for out of all his experience, he had never before known quite that sensation.

When she had gone he went to the desk and picking up the papers there, he went through them carefully trying to discover what it was she had been seeking. There were many things she might have discovered, evidence of dishonesty and intrigue and cheating, but he doubted that a woman's mind, much less the mind of so seductive and feminine a woman, could have discovered just where the secrets lay in all the disorderly heap of invoices and sailing papers and quarantine orders. There was nothing, not even the faintest hint of what it was that drew her into his room. Perhaps it was only a woman's curiosity, to pry into his life, discover and read his private correspondence.

Then as he undressed and bathed, he wondered whether she had been in his room before tonight, going through his belongings, discovering bits and pieces which she put together like a picture puzzle to make the whole that was himself and his disorderly life. And he remembered that two or three times when he had come in at odd hours, the silver bell had rung as he came into the door of the lower gallery, as if someone had been on guard to warn of his return. It might have been the old negress, Seraphine. At the sound of the bell, Madame de Lèche could have disappeared into the far portion of the big house before he reached the upper gallery.

The idea of going to the General's house for dinner was quite gone from his mind now, along with all the weariness and the good intentions. Now that he had seen the young Baroness at last he was in no mood for a New England dinner.

Intuition and experience told him that this woman was unlike any he had ever encountered. In that first glance he had been aware of a kind of challenge to combat, as if it were a man who stood there opposite him.

When he had dressed he walked impatiently up and down the gallery outside watching the windows through the flooding rain for the moment when the candles were lighted in the long salon abovestairs. And as he walked his thoughts went this way and that to many things. He thought of himself, quietly, almost humorously, as if he were quite outside this energetic, violent body which was always upsetting all his plans, all his good intentions and driving him into trouble and danger and folly and dishonesty. It was his body's restlessness and hunger for excitement which had driven him to run off on a whaler as a boy. It had driven him into the Army. Its recklessness and bravery, its animal delight in violence and danger, had brought him success and even in a small way, fame. It was his body, his good looks and high spirits which had made him the favorite of General Wicks and his smug, plump wife. They loved him because he was beautiful, not because he was good or trustworthy or honorable. They loved him not even because he was a humorous scamp, a perfectly frank and unashamed scoundrel, but simply because his physical presence titillated their sense of life —a ray of brilliant light in the dull monotony of their own narrow existence. He did not love either of them in return. He only felt contempt for them.

Then he thought of Big Ernestine's warning to get out of this strange heathen city that was such a strange mixture of mud and gallantry, of perfumes and stenches, of flowers and disease. It might be stronger than himself; it might, as Big Ernestine said, be his ruin. Suddenly he remembered the figure of the man with the empty sleeve and the white face beneath the broad black hat who had passed him in the shadow of the doorway, and it occurred to him that perhaps he was one of those of whom Big Ernestine had spoken—the ones who might put a bullet into your back, the ones who had already left a score of bullying negroes and cheap crooked carpetbaggers dead, with a cross cut on their brows, in dark alleys

[43]

and narrow silent streets. And he thought, too, of the young Baroness' remark that the sickness had returned, the dread yellow fever which carried off hundreds to a filthy disgusting death. He dreaded death as a young animal might dread it, if an animal could have foreknowledge of death, because there was so much in life that was sensual and exciting. But he dreaded death itself, which he had faced a hundred times, far less than the prospect of a sickness which reduced man to the level of a brute turning him into a vomiting, defecating, helpless animal who turned black and began to decay before he was dead. The fever was a horrible disease and the thought of it creeping into the city out of the swamps and bayous or sneaking up the wide muddy river on some filthy foreign boat, brought a shiver of horror and a sudden desire to run away, to flee to the north into a world that was clean and cold like the first snow of December in New England. In the damp heat, he shivered suddenly, thinking, "Perhaps it would be better if I went back and married Agnes and became a good citizen." And then looking across the drowned garden he saw that the candles in the long salon were lighted. They had finished dinner and she would be waiting for him.

There was a very old woman in one corner of the room, thin and immensely wrinkled and wearing a black lace shawl over her head and a great number of diamonds that glittered in the soft lights of the candles which burned in sconces dripping with crystal. The young Baroness sat at the square ebony piano placed close by the tall shuttered windows and beyond her he saw the man who had passed him in the shadow of the doorway. The man was dressed all in black with a stock furbished with a cascade of white lace, no whiter than the intense, delicately chiseled face above it. Like the very old woman he had glittering black eyes. The room had a curious decayed quality of rose and pale blue, silver and crystal— a curiously feminine room with an enormous mantelpiece of pale pink marble below a heavily carved and gilded mirror. Old Seraphine was there in a frock of white and cherry colored stripes with *tignon* of poison green and candy pink.

As he stepped into the doorway he saw it all clearly as a picture, perhaps because it was all so foreign, perhaps because it was the first time he had been received by a New Orleans family. The General and Mrs. Wicks had appropriated a famous and beautiful house, but the General put his horses into the slaves' quarters and Aunt Louisa had immediately destroyed the whole character of the place by arranging the house to suit her spare Maine taste. There was a glow about this room which warmed everything in him that was sensual.

At sight of him, the young Baroness rose from the piano and crossed the room and the young man with the white romantic face stood up.

"You were very punctual," she said.

"I watched the lights." But he knew that she was mocking him and that she was aware all the time of his impatience.

"This is Grandmère," she said, presenting him to the old woman. "It's unfortunate but she speaks only Spanish and French and a little Italian."

The old woman leaned forward a little in her chair, holding out her hand to be kissed with a gesture so imperious that to his own astonishment he found himself kissing it. The old woman said nothing but only gave him a sudden brilliant glance from the intense black eyes, a glance of appraisal which was almost a physical manifestation as if she had touched him.

The pale young man held out his hand and the young Baroness said, "This is my cousin, Baron de Lèche."

The cousin's eyes were the eyes of the old woman, black and brilliant, but without the life and the burned-out passion behind them. They were cold eyes, the eyes of a fanatic with something of madness in them.

He said, politely but coldly, "I hope you are comfortable in our house."

"Very comfortable, thank you. A man could not well be more comfortable—even with fresh flowers in his room put there by your charming cousin."

The man glanced quickly at the young Baroness, a cold opaque glance, yet full of questioning. The color came into her face and Tom thought, "I scored there."

He had a curious sensation of being upon quicksand, feeling his way inch by inch lest suddenly he disappear into a quagmire of hostile mystery. He was aware of the resentment in the old woman and the young man, a resentment which came from the injured pride of the conquered. And he knew too that behind the two pairs of black eyes there lay a savage contempt for himself as a Yankee, a barbarian, an uncivilized yokel. It was a feeling so strong that he experienced a sensation of acute awkwardness and discomfort, as if the sleeves of his jacket were too short and his boots soiled with mud and his waistcoat covered with spots. Without thinking he glanced quickly at his image in the huge mirror and what he saw reassured him. He was more a male than the waxen-faced Baron with the empty sleeve. Suddenly he suspected that that was why the man had given him a glance of such profound hatred. The young Baroness had that quality of arousing rivalry between men, not because of her beauty which was peculiar and in the judgment of some people, dubious, but by something, some arrogant female quality which lay just beneath the surface. He knew that his revelation about the flowers had displeased her, but only for a moment. Then, with the wickedness which sometimes looked out of the blue eyes, he divined that she enjoyed the feeling of jealousy it had roused in her cousin.

The cousin said, "The Baroness is unconventional—sometimes to the point of folly. I suppose it is her Irish blood. My family resented my cousin's marriage."

The young Baroness laughed, "Yes, there was not enough money. I had no *dot*. My husband was in love with me. But I've learned about money. I've become very clever about it . . . more clever even than the Lèche family."

Suddenly the old woman in the corner said, "*Qu'est ce qu'elle dit?*"

The Baron translated quickly and the old lady said, "*Honteux! Sans gêne!*" and rattled a small diamond studded contraption she carried. It was made of black enamel and onyx with a dozen small boxes studded with diamonds attached to a gold chain. The sound was like the rattling of bones.

A tiny dog of a breed Tom Bedloe had never seen before came into the room and went directly to the old Baroness, leaping into her lap and making the collection of articles she wore at her waist clatter again like old bones. Then, all in one moment it turned, raised its nose in the air and sniffing, detected the stranger in the room. Searching with its rheumy eyes it found Tom Bedloe and leaping down again, ran screaming and yapping at him. It was the young Baroness who came to his rescue. Placing herself between the dog and her visitor, she kicked it with a sudden swift viciousness. The tip of her tiny slipper struck the animal in its belly and it set up an hysterical screaming.

The old woman, who until now, had been sitting rather like a waxwork in Mr. Barnum's Exhibition, suddenly was galvanized into a fury of life. Screaming a flood of French and Spanish at her grand-daughter-in-law, she rose and picked up the horrible little animal and gathering it to her thin old breast, changed her tone abruptly and covered it with a torrent of endearments.

The Baron said, "You should be ashamed of yourself!" And the young Baroness said in French, "I apologize, grandmère. It was only that he was annoying our guest. I did not mean to kick so hard."

Bedloe could not understand what she was saying, but he was aware that the look in her dark eyes belied the tone of her voice, which was silky and conciliatory. The eyes were filled with sudden hate—the same concentrated hatred which had gone into the kick at the offensive, yapping dog.

To Bedloe she said, "You must forgive our bad manners among ourselves. It is a passionate family. I am quite gentle by nature but I have become savage in self-defense."

He found himself in an odd situation, as if he were not in the room at all, save when the young woman addressed him. It was not only that the three of them appeared to hate each other and were shameless in their hatred but that he could understand only half of what they were saying. Whenever he spoke, some simple phrase, stiff and polite, it had a hard artificial sound. It took a great deal to make him feel uncomfortable but he was miserable now, wishing he had not come at all. For a moment the strange girl no longer seemed attractive to him. He thought, "What am I doing here? Why did I come? They all hate me, perhaps the girl more than the other two?"

But almost at once he knew again why he had come. The girl, he saw now, was not as beautiful as he had thought her; she was in fact, not beautiful at all. It was not that which attracted him now but something inside her, some fire. He was aware again of the sense of challenge. He was aware too, that the eyes of the cousin followed every move, every gesture and he thought suddenly, "He is in love with her, in spite of the hatred between them." It was all subtle and uncomfortable, complicated and sinister, like nothing he had ever before experienced. He heard himself saying, nervously, "You sing beautifully, Madame. I've listened to you night after night."

The Baron answered before she could speak, "I'm sure the Baroness was aware of that."

Quite calmly she answered, "I was aware of it, Amedé. Twice, through the shutters I saw him standing in the gallery listening. I do sing well and I have a good voice too. I am pleased and flattered when anyone finds my singing pleasing."

The old woman again asked, *"Qu'est ce qu'elle dit?"* and when the Baron had translated, she repeated again, *"Honteux! Sans gêne!"*

Bedloe said, "Perhaps you will sing for me now?"

"With pleasure." She rose and went to the piano and at the same time the old woman, picking up the dog under one arm and the rattling collection of diamond studded objects in the other, rose and said gravely, "Bon soir, Monsieur" to Bedloe and went out of the room. He rose at her imperious departure and stood looking after her. She seemed not to walk at all but float, as if she had at some time in her life trained for the ballet.

"Grandmère," said the young Baroness smiling, "cannot support my singing. I think she hates music."

As the old woman went from the room she left the door open behind her. He could see her black figure moving down a long corridor lighted by candles, glittering yet soft-colored like the room in which he stood. As if to claim his attention from the handsome old woman, the girl struck up a stirring roulade of notes against the sound of the hot rain. As he turned she began to sing the aria from "Il Re Pastore" which David Wicks had heard as he waited on the other side of the garden for Bedloe.

Tom knew little about music, only that which pleased him sensually, and he was pleased now, not only by the sight of the young Baroness at the piano but by the lovely architecture of the aria she sang so effortlessly yet with such grace and art. She sang in

[48]

Italian so that he understood no word of what she was singing, yet it produced upon him an extraordinary effect. In a little while all the uneasiness, the sense of discord, even of hatred, in the room seemed to vanish. The faint weariness returned to him and the sound of the music was as if the girl stood beside him stroking his aching head softly. It was incredible that the girl in the yellow dress singing so tranquilly could be the same who a little while earlier had kicked so savagely the old woman's horrible little dog.

When she had finished the last delicate cadenza, limpid and soothing as the note of a silver bell, he opened his eyes and saw first of all the young man with the white face and empty sleeve. He was watching her. He had forgotten the hated visitor.

Then she sang again and again, "Voi che sapete" from *Figaro* and an aria from Gluck's *Orféo*. Outside the rain ceased and a sudden gust of wind rising from the distant gulf blew out three candles in the sconces, leaving the figure of the girl herself in the shadow. An extraordinary sleepiness came over Bedloe, in which, sitting with his eyes closed he saw her quite plainly, the gentle curve of her throat and the blue black of her hair and the dark blue-violet eyes and the mouth that was enticing but somehow ugly because there was evil in it. Yet its very ugliness was fascinating. The image was fixed there in his mind forever. Dimly, out of his experience, he thought, "I shall always remember her thus."

Then the music came to an end and he opened his eyes and she stood up, very straight with that curious air of pride. At the same moment the door opened and Old Seraphine came in followed by a very old negro in rough country clothes with a face like an ape and a poll covered with white wool. He seemed excited and pushed past Seraphine.

He made a curious kind of shuffling curtsy and then began to talk wildly in the *patois* of his parish. Once or twice the young Baroness answered him and once the cousin spoke. Then suddenly she said something to him very sharply and Seraphine, taking him by the arm, led him forcibly away. He turned once and began again to speak rapidly but the Baroness silenced him with a cry, "Tais-toi, Théophile. Je te parlerai demain."

Then smiling she turned to Bedloe and said, "He is frightened because the fever has broken out at Bel Manoir. That's one of our plantations. It's quite near . . . frighteningly near, on the other side of the river."

The extraordinary sleepiness born partly of physical exhaustion and partly by the hypnotic effect of the music refused to leave Bedloe. Mechanically he said, "I'm sorry. I'll tell the General. He'll stop them coming into the City from that side."

The cousin answered, "That will do no good. It spreads like magic. It flies through the air. It is worse in wet times like this."

Then abruptly Bedloe said, "Goodnight," still in the power of a curious dazed feeling as if he were sleep walking. As he crossed through the gallery above the drenched garden, he heard the bell at the door opening into the *impasse* tinkling faintly and as he turned the corner he saw, in the fitful light of a moon half obscured by flying clouds the figures of two men moving along the lower gallery.

He fell asleep almost at once and slept, dreamlessly unaware of the damp heat until the burning sun was high above the steaming city. When he wakened he lay for a long time trying to remember what had happened the night before. It returned to him in fragments, with a feeling of unreality, as if the whole uncomfortable experience had been no more than a dream.

The *San Cristobal* bound from Havana for New Orleans reached the mouth of the Mississippi nearly three weeks after sailing from Havana. She was a dirty ship, Spanish owned, out of Valencia laden with tobacco, hemp, tin pots, olives and leather for New Orleans to trade for cotton which she would carry to Liverpool, now that the warehouses of the great city had fallen into Yankee hands and the money for the cotton would no longer go to the Confederate Treasury but into the pockets of the men who occupied New Orleans.

For ten days she had battled hurricane head winds round the end of Florida and for five days with her pumps working day and night, salt water had swept her decks, covering hatches and pouring into holds, wetting her cargo so that from below deck there rose an overpowering stench of rotting hides and soaked tobacco and rancid olive oil. For five days the Captain had prayed thrice daily to preserve the *San Cristobal* from destruction and to rescue her crew from the imminent prospect of hell. He was a lean, sallow man and a profoundly religious rascal who had in his day commanded slave ships, participated in a murder or two, and been involved in privateering expeditions which bordered closely upon piracy. He was a man who found little in life or in the human race to astonish him, but on this voyage he had encountered something new and astonishing in his whole experience, and that was the presence on board his ship in one of the two dirty cabins which sometimes carried passengers, of two ladies from Boston, one very young and virginal and pretty and the other an amazing female the like of which he had never encountered even among the dragon duennas of his own country.

They had come alongside his ship as she lay in the shadow of Morro Castle, coming alongside in a leaky harbor boat rowed by a gigantic and very black negro in ragged shirt and trousers, who spoke a strange mixture of Spanish, French and English. In this curious babel of tongues he made known to the Captain what it was they wanted. The young girl and the horse-faced woman were, he said, American ladies from the port of Boston. They had come as far as Cristobal de la Habana as passengers on an American Army transport bound for New Orleans. The ship had been driven off her course by a hurricane and, leaking badly, had put in at Havana. It would be at least a month before she could sail and the American ladies were in haste to arrive at their port of destination. Would the Captain of the *San Cristobal* take them as passengers? They were important people, related to the General in Command of New Orleans.

From the rail of his dirty ship the Captain had watched the two women while the giant negro shouted up his message from the leaky boat, debating whether or not he wanted two women to complicate a voyage with an unruly cutthroat crew. The girl was certainly young and very pretty, and blonde, which made her more dangerous but also more desirable. The horse-faced woman who accompanied her certainly had a formidable appearance; but in his Spanish heart the Captain knew that in Spain duennas had been known to have been outwitted before now. In fact Spanish legend and literature (of which it must be said, the Captain knew next to nothing) was full of stories in which lovers got round ugly old women.

The news that the two ladies were related to important personages alarmed him, but the alarm was nullified almost immediately by the shouted information that they were also ladies of wealth and would pay well for the privilege of passage in the dirty old *San Cristobal*. So the Captain, being an avaricious as well as a lecherous fellow, invited them aboard and showed them a large and rather elaborate cabin ornamented with black carved oak, which had been built long ago to carry the owner of the ship when he travelled from Valencia to the West Indies on business.

It was a rather gloomy room with a single small window high above the built-in beds and it smelled of rancid olive oil and pitch. The Captain watched the two women while they inspected it, wondering that two women of wealth and distinguished position should have any desire to travel on such a boat as the *San Cristobal*. The only Anglo-Saxon women he knew were the women of the ports and certainly they were hard and capable of taking care of their own interests. But these, obviously, were not ladies of the port. Some very urgent reason, he concluded, must have driven them even to consider such a boat.

At last, grumbling, he named a price which was three times the ordinary passage from Havana to New Orleans, and after a minute's consultation, was informed by the big negro that the ladies accepted. Then, for a moment, the idea of kidnapping or robbery swept like the shadow of a cloud over the hard brain of the Captain.

They informed him that their names were Miss Agnes Wicks and Miss Abigail Jones and when the Captain could make nothing of this in the jargon of the big negro, they wrote down the names for him on a bit of paper the horse-faced woman took out of her reticule. Then the big negro informed the Captain that the ladies would like to come aboard after dark the night before sailing.

After paying him fifty American dollars they withdrew, leaving the Captain to bite the gold pieces and ruminate whether he had been wise to accept them as passengers. Whatever happened, their presence on the boat for ten days or a fortnight could only mean trouble. The girl was too pretty and too young. And it was odd that they wished to come aboard at night.

When the leaky boat drew up to the stone quai, Aunt Tam gave the big negro a coin and after saying, "Tomorrow night, César, at nine o'clock," they left him and entered a *calèche* drawn by a team of bony flea-bitten mules and drove off by a round-about way to the Grand Hotel de Salamanca.

It was a small and very dirty hotel built round a shabby patio furnished with plush and tired palms, overrun by cockroaches and made musical at night by hordes of flying insects, but it was the *Grand Hotel de luxe* of Havana. They could, it was true, have stayed aboard the troopship *Allegheny* which lay anchored in the bay. It would have been cleaner and the food would have been plain, clean, army food instead of course after course of tomatoes and veal cooked in oil, but aboard the *Allegheny* Aunt Tam would have been denied the freedom without which she found life insufferable.

The Commander of the *Allegheny* was an acquaintance of General Wicks, a sturdy man of the sea who believed that woman's whole duty was to remain at home, care for the children and await her sea-faring husband's return to breed, and so he showed no great approval for Aunt Tam's emancipated ideas. At first he had forbidden her to live ashore, but when the routine of the whole boat was upset by her constant demands to be set ashore or be called for day after day, the Commander, worn down, conceded that perhaps, if he were ever to accomplish the re-conditioning of his vessel, it would be better for her and her niece to move ashore, not however without strings attached to them. He had no liking and a great deal of mistrust for all Latin people and so the idea of two Boston ladies living unprotected in a corrupt city like Havana was intolerable to him. To Aunt Tam's great disgust he posted sentinels in shifts outside the door of the cockroach-infested room occupied by herself and her niece. Thus it was impossible for either of them to move without the knowledge of the solicitous, female-protecting Commander.

But Aunt Tam was not to be defeated in her rôle of pioneer tourist. Accompanied by Agnes she set forth each morning to absorb the color and picturesqueness of this squalid foreign city. Although at times Agnes felt misgivings, neither stenches nor filth nor disease, nor muggy heat nor parasites dampened the ardor of Aunt Tam. These things became translated in her eager transcendentalism into color and picturesqueness and beauty. Mr. Emerson or Mr. Alcott would not have noticed them, and Margaret Fuller would have found them, even the cockroaches, filled with sociological interest. Besides the enthusiasm and vitality of Aunt Tam were boundless. Her trip on a donkey through bandit-infested Sicily had made her an object of interest in Beacon Hill drawing-rooms for many years. How much longer would these tales of adventure in a barbarous country like Cuba make her interesting before they lost their lustre. She had no intellect like Margaret Fuller or Mr. Emerson but she was a rabid and excellent reporter and a passionate tourist.

And with it all she was a friendly person to whom people were simply people without regard to race, creed or color. A palace had no greater interest for her than a thatched hut with a fire burning in the middle of the earthen floor. Each muddled conversation with their occupants and several lines of "interesting" notes were entered in a notebook labeled "My Journal" which she carried with her in her reticule, even to bed in case inspiration overtook her in the small hours of the night. Nor was a difference in tongues any hindrance. She was remarkably gifted as a pantomimist, so gifted that on occasions she and Agnes found themselves surrounded by crowds of natives who watched her with the same interest and fascination they experienced at a performance of a travelling puppet show. And her quick, superficial mind had a way of picking up key-words in any tongue with remarkable rapidity. These she strung together like beads on a string, without the faintest concern or need for grammar and syntax. French was the only tongue for which she had any pretensions and that she spoke badly with a flat English-Boston accent which transformed it from a beautiful and elegant tongue into something which sounded rather like the clatter of wagon wheels on the cobblestones of Beacon Street.

So, dragging Agnes with her, she penetrated with her simplicity and innocence, the hovels of poor *mestizos* and the grilled aristocratic patios of Spanish Créole families. Because she was a strong

Abolitionist she took special interest in the negro quarter. Here she found freed men and escaped slaves, and talking to them she filled a whole notebook with jottings to relate to Mr. Alcott and Mr. Garrison and Harriet Beecher Stowe, when she was once more in Boston. Here it was that she came upon César, the great negro who rowed them out to the *San Cristobal*.

She found him in the market talking to a pretty quadroon seated among piles of melons and radishes, garlic and brilliant red hot peppers. She opened conversation with the quadroon by asking the price of the peppers and buying a whole string which she stuffed, wrapped in a plantain leaf, in her voracious reticule. Then in her curious Spanish she managed to chat for a time with the quadroon girl who now and then emitted shouts of laughter at Aunt Tam's queer turn of phrase—shouts which were drowned in the louder laughter of the great black negro.

In her friendliness Aunt Tam was likely to tell personal details of her life to any stranger, and so now she managed to convey to the quadroon girl the fact that she and her niece were on their way to New Orleans. In this information, the big negro showed a great interest.

"La Louisiane," he said in a homesick voice and a queer jargon that surpassed even Aunt Tam's extraordinary speech. "Mon dit nègres free all time now in Louisiane."

Aunt Tam, in English, explained that every negro was free now that General Wicks, whom she was going to visit, was in command of New Orleans. Then quite simply the big negro said, "*César va avec,*" and left his quadroon girl and accompanied Aunt Tam and Agnes back to the Grand Hotel de Salamanca.

In the morning when they made an early sortie from the hotel he was waiting outside, his white teeth exposed in a grin, his black skin showing through the rents in his torn yellow shirt. From then on he accompanied them each day wherever they went. There was no being rid of him and in a way he was a convenience, for with him at their side carrying all the articles purchased by Aunt Tam as souvenirs, they were no longer annoyed by pert and bawdy remarks concerning the blonde prettiness of Agnes. After the second day, Aunt Tam took to giving him a coin or two in the evenings when he left them to the mercy of the cockroaches at the grilled doorway of the hotel. He went off to spend it all in a brawling night with the quadroon girl. He was satisfied. He had never been so rich before. And so without any plan of any kind he became a kind of body servant to Aunt Tam and her niece.

But Agnes was growing impatient. For the first few days she had found the exploration of Havana in the wake of Aunt Tam amusing and novel, but after a time the food, the lumpy bed, the welts which she discovered on her fair skin each morning, began to outweigh the glamor and excitement of foreign travel. And in the bottom of her heart, like a little worm gnawing, was always her impatience to get to New Orleans to find Tom Bedloe and rescue him, to save him for herself. It was remarkable how the thought of him disturbed her, haunting her nights, popping suddenly into her little brain at the sight of some Créole dandy whose swagger or darkness brought the image of him suddenly to mind. She felt haunted and driven, but the haunting was a delirious sensation, partly pleasure, partly agony and apprehension, and as the obsession grew, Havana and the Grand Hotel de Salamanca and the insects and smells and food became more and more unendurable.

But for her impatience Aunt Tam would perhaps have stayed on and on in Havana, extending the range of her tours accompanied by the great black César further and further into jungly country districts haunted by bandits and other lawless characters. It was only the protests of Agnes and the growing paleness of her cheeks which led the indefatigable virgin at last to approach the Commander of the *Allegheny* upon the subject of their consequent departure. They went to noonday dinner on the transport *Allegheny*, rowed out by César who had a friend who owned the rickety, leaking boat, and learned that the ship would be forced to remain for at least another three weeks, since sufficient supplies of oakum, tar, etc., needed for the repairs seemed very nearly unattainable in the slip-shod corrupt Spanish port.

This news Agnes, holding her peace, received with a pang thinking, "I shall die. I shall contract a fever and die if I am forced to remain three weeks more in this filthy port." Even Aunt Tam found the delay excessive, and rather as a feeler, put forward the idea of taking passage on some civilian ship.

The suggestion only brought an explosion from her friend, the

Commander, "Impossible, Madame!" he said, "There are no civilized packet boats sailing from here to New Orleans . . . no packet boats upon which a decent woman could trust herself. The idea is out of the question."

The reply made Agnes' heart sink. This might go on and on forever, until Tom forgot her very existence in the company of the belles of New Orleans. Her knowledge of New Orleans life was slight, only what she had picked up during an education spent at a fashiónable and expensive but superficial school in Boston, and her conception of New Orleans was of a languorous city, flower-laden and scented, entirely populated by exquisite and seductive young women of Créole origin and immoral French educations. And so the prospect of three more weeks delay, not to count the possible fortnight for the voyage itself, filled her with despair. She began to cry and Aunt Tam said, "There! There! My dear! We must be philosophical! It will turn out for the best! There is still so much to be seen in Cuba."

But in her heart Aunt Tam was not philosophical at all. She was crafty. She had dealt with strong men like the Commander before. Her father had been a "strong" man and her brother Ethan Wicks was one. "Strong" men were only to be overcome by deceit and craft as long as women, deprived of political rights, were treated as half-wits.

So Aunt Tam smiled at the Commander of the *Allegheny*, sighed and was outwardly philosophical, but in her heart she had a plan. That night when she returned to the Grand Hotel de Salamanca she held a jargon conversation with César and in the morning he returned with the news that a ship called the *San Cristobal* would be sailing for New Orleans in two days time. That afternoon they visited the ship and arranged passage with the dubious Spanish Captain.

But escape was not easy for there was always the sentry outside their door who would inform the Commander if he saw them leaving with their baggage. But now Aunt Tam had begun to relish the plot and to enjoy all the sensations of a conspirator making an escape, and Agnes, at the prospect of flight from the dirty hotel, had color in her cheeks once more and a light in her blue eyes. So between them they arranged with the mustachioed and swarthy proprietress to have the baggage lowered during the day into the courtyard at the back of the hotel, and at eleven o'clock the night before the ship sailed the two women themselves climbed down a ladder to the courtyard where César and a mangy *calèche* awaited them. In the hot darkness the big negro rowed them out to the *San Cristobal* and when they climbed up the ladder over the side he cast adrift the leaky old boat with a kick of the foot and followed them.

On the deck when Aunt Tam sought to give him a gold piece and dismiss him, he only grinned and shook his head saying, "César go la Louisiane avec."

At the Grand Hotel de Salamanca a new sentry came on duty at eight o'clock in the morning outside the door of the room occupied by Miss Abigail Jones and her niece. For eight hours he remained there without seeing any trace of the two ladies, and when he was relieved in the late afternoon he reported that the ladies must have gone out early in the morning as he had not seen them during the whole day. It was only at nine in the evening that the second sentry became alarmed and pushed open the door to find the note left by Aunt Tam. By the time it had been delivered to the Commander of the *Allegheny*, the *San Cristobal* was well on its way toward New Orleans, and nothing was left for the Commander to do but to curse in sulphurous language all women with advanced ideas who would not trust their lives to strong men.

On the morning after sailing Aunt Tam, trying to open the door of her cabin, found the door blocked and for one brief exciting moment, she believed that they were to be imprisoned and held for ransom. Then with another shove she managed to push the door open an inch or two and discovered that the obstacle obstructing it was only the massive figure of César. He had slept the night on a hempen mat, a murderous looking knife in his belt.

Standing up, he grinned at her and said, "César sleep here. Mauvais hombres all around."

For a moment she thought, "What a story to tell them in Boston." And for another moment she wished that her brother and the Commander could see her. After a frightful breakfast of some bread and coffee and eggs cooked in oil which she and Agnes ate in their cabin, she set to work on her journal, writing page after page in headlong overcolored prose which sometimes gave scant consideration for grammar. She failed to notice that Agnes had gone out to take the air on the deck, until the door was suddenly flung open and Agnes came in, her cheeks bright red, her blue eyes flashing, less frightened than angry.

"It's intolerable, Aunt Tam. I can't walk on the deck."

She told her story breathlessly. Twice she had made the circuit of the main deck and each time when she passed any of the crew they made rude noises and obscene gestures.

"What sort of gestures?" asked Aunt Tam, with an innocent almost scientific interest.

"I don't know what they meant and I couldn't possibly show you, but I know they were meant to be insulting."

"You must be quite sure," said Aunt Tam, "before I speak to the Captain."

At this Agnes' face grew even more red. "The Captain?" she said, "Much help he'll be! After it happened, I stayed at his end of the ship in front of his cabin. He came out to walk with me, and he *pinched* me!" Here she burst into tears, crying out, "Oh, Aunt Tam, I wish we had never left Boston. I wish we hadn't run away from Havana. How do we know they're going to New Orleans at all? They're probably taking us to a pirate island to murder us!"

She was frightened now, perhaps for the first time in all her brief and sheltered life, not nearly so much by the thought of being carried off and murdered as by the gestures made by the men on the deck which she did not even understand. There was a terrifying, shocking, mysterious ugliness about their leering faces and the look in their eyes, something which in an odd way was related to the whispered, shadowy ugliness that came into the faces of some people when they whispered of Tom's "wickedness." She was tired and depressed and hungry and a little seasick and for a long time she lay with her head in Aunt Tam's lap, sobbing while the older woman tried to comfort her.

When she had recovered a little, Aunt Tam said again, "What did they do? Show me so that I can complain properly to the Captain."

Then Agnes, sitting up, made quite innocently, and shyly, an obscene gesture as old as time itself.

"I'm sure I don't know what that means," said Aunt Tam, "but it does look reprehensible. I'll speak to the Captain at once. You had best lock the cabin door while I am away."

Then she left Agnes and went out on the deck. The ship had begun to roll a little and the eggs cooked in oil, which she had eaten more as an experience than a pleasure, were not resting well. But her mind was scarcely less troubled than her stomach. It was the puzzling gesture which disturbed her, principally because she did not understand it. If she had known its meaning, she would doubtless have dismissed it at once under the head of experience, but in her innocence it became mysterious and sinister and even corrupting. For herself it did not matter but for Agnes it was different. For the first time it occurred to her vaguely that perhaps the whole trip had been the sheerest folly.

It would have been bad enough even if the transport had gone directly to New Orleans. She thought, "Perhaps running away like this on a strange ship and a Spanish ship at that, *was* unwise!" She would ask the Captain to put them down at the next port, only there was no port on the way.

As she walked unsteadily up and down, she was aware that the crew, at their tasks, were watching her and she tried ignoring them, but this was impossible for every few paces she could not help seeing one or two murderous faces out of the corner of her eye. They were, she admitted, decidedly worse appearing than any men she had ever encountered before—unshaven, ragged, filthy and depraved, not at all like the nice sailor boys on the *Allegheny*. Even during her donkey trip through Sicily she had never seen anything like them. They went about their tasks, holy-stoning the decks made greasy by the long dissipated stay at Cristobal de la Habana, repairing ragged sails and splicing ropes in the rigging, but each time she passed near them, they looked up and grinned, showing yellow teeth with great gaps between them.

She had no illusions about her appearance. She had, indeed, long ago become reconciled to her plainness—so she did not believe they grinned at her for reasons of seduction. She kept repeating to herself what she would say to the Captain, trying at the same time to control her stomach by that inner force of will which she had discussed with Mr. Emerson on several occasions.

Then suddenly she heard loud bawdy laughter and forgetting her intention to ignore the tormentors of Agnes she turned and saw that a fat bearded man, obviously the clown of the crew, was making the dreadful gesture at herself.

Flouncing and bridling with fury and indignation, she went quickly to the cabin of the yellow-faced Captain, thinking at the same time that she must go quickly and get the interview over with before she became actively sick.

In her haste she did not trouble to knock but pushed open the door to find the startled Captain bending over a greasy chart. Pressed by the emergency she began to talk at once, partly in English and partly in bad French, neither of which the Captain understood. In her voice and manner was all the fury of outraged womanhood aggravated by the uncertainty of her stomach.

The evil Captain, understanding not a word, divined from her manner and out of his own shopworn conscience the reason for her indignation. He merely stared at her, his face quite blank and stupid, and Aunt Tam, aware suddenly that her speech was conveying nothing to him, fell instinctively into her principal resource when confronted by a foreign tongue. She resorted to pantomime, ogling him to his astonishment, rolling her eyes and repeating, "Comme ça! Comme ça!" but the crisis came when, carried away by her own pantomimic eloquence, Aunt Tam, the friend of Margaret Fuller and Mr. Emerson, made the gesture!

For a second the blank expression on the evil face of the Captain changed to one of astonishment and even alarm, and then before it had time to wrinkle with laughter, the astonishing woman was gone out of the door, to be sick.

In an odd fashion the strange interview was more effective than if the Captain had understood every word that Aunt Tam shouted at him. When he had finished laughing, he told his mate what the plain, middle-aged dragon from Boston had done, and the mate told the boatswain who passed it on to the crew, so that by evening the story was known, even to the scrofulous cabin boy. And when the two women came out of their cabin in the evening to take the air, the men they encountered on the deck grinned, but there was no bawdy laughter and the awful gesture was not repeated. In some strange way, Aunt Tam, perhaps by the very grotesqueness of her simplicity and innocence, had managed to shame them.

The next day nothing at all happened save that the *San Cristobal* began to pitch and roll in a choppy sea. Whether the two ladies could have continued the rest of the voyage without annoyance no one could say, for on the third day the wild fury of the hurricane coming out of the Gulf of Mexico burst upon the ship, ripping half her sails to shreds, carrying away spars and half the fore-mast. Hour after hour, for six days the ship was carried now east, now west, now north, now south at the mercy of God; and God was merciful for neither the crew nor the superstitious Captain, both paralyzed by terror, did much beyond praying and working the pumps to save the ship.

In their cabin, Aunt Tam and little Agnes stayed for six days living upon chocolate and the biscuit and water which black César managed somehow to bring them in the moments when he was not helping to work the pumps. At first both women were terrified and then after a few hours, the misery and discomfort of the pitching ship dulled the edge of their fears. They did not, like the Catholic crew, spend their hours wailing and calling upon God and the Virgin Mary. Instead both Agnes and Aunt Tam fell to considering God and the hereafter seriously for the first time in their lives. Until now, God and the after life had been no more to the older woman than subjects for rather superficial, intellectual discussion in Boston and Concord drawing rooms; and Agnes had never considered either subject at all, merely accepting the conventional Episcopalian concepts stamped upon her by an evasive father.

In the darkness, for it was nearly as dark by day as by night, the two women lay lashed into their beds, alone yet united for the first time in an odd fashion, considering the past and speculating upon the future in case they escaped. Once or twice when the fury of the hurricane seemed to abate a little, Aunt Tam attempted to rise and set down her reflections in her journal, but after a scrawled illegible line or two, she abandoned the idea and simply lay still, her eyes closed, retching and clinging to her bed. And after a time both of them fell into a condition of dullness and coma in which night and day no longer existed, and even the chocolate and the stale water no longer had any interest. Twice Agnes passed into unconsciousness and out again, lost mercifully for a time in the delusion that she was at home safe in the drawing room of the Pinckney Street house with melting snow under the windows. Then came a time when she forgot even Tom and the reason for having come on the voyage, she began to pray only that she might once again see Boston and her father. All the boldness, all the assurance born of her very innocence, was gone.

Then one morning the hurricane was gone as quickly as it had come and the San Cristobal, rocking gently on the swell which followed, limped over a sunlit sea of brilliant blue, worked by a crew shaken, enfeebled and full of repentance. The repentance would have worn away as repentance does, but for the fact that the second day after the hurricane died away, two bodies sewn in torn sail cloth with rusty iron at their feet, were slipped over the side into the Gulf. Aunt Tam and Agnes came on deck at the very moment the Captain and three members of the crew stood by the rail, caps in hand, until the plank on which the first body lay was tilted and it slid into the water. When the Captain saw them, an expression of alarm, almost of horror came into his dismal face and turning, he walked quickly away from them toward the fo'castle.

It was a curious look, so sinister that it alarmed even Aunt Tam. All that day and the next they had no sight of the Captain but whenever one of the crew passed near them he did a curious thing. Each man held up his hand, forefinger and little finger extended, and spat toward them seven times between the fingers, his face at the same time contorted by a look of fear and hatred.

It was black César who brought the explanation. He came in after dark to their cabin, his face grey in the candle light. Closing the door behind him, the whites of his eyes showing, he said, "Mauvaises nouvelles, the black sickness is in the bateau. Two men dead yesterday. Three more today."

The expression "black sickness" puzzled Aunt Tam. When she questioned César he crossed himself and went into an excited and unintelligible jargon accompanied by a horrible pantomime in which his powerful back arched and his head jerked until the whites of his eyeballs showed. It was only after a long time that

Aunt Tam was able to make out what he was trying to tell them. It was that five of the crew had already died of cholera.

But that was not all. The crew, it seemed, believed that the two women were witches—*sorcières*—and that it was their presence which had brought the hurricane and the cholera. Their virtue was safe enough now, César told them; there was not a man on board the ship who would touch them, save to throw them overboard into the blue waters of the Gulf. Below deck there had been plotting and only the sudden revolting death of two more of the men had diverted them from ridding themselves of the two ladies from Boston. Now it would not longer be safe for them to leave their cabin.

"César stay dédans," explained the big negro, touching his knife. "Arrive Mississippi soon."

For a moment Aunt Tam recoiled, thinking that she preferred death to the violation of her modesty created by the presence of the great negro inside their cabin. She thought, "This is impossible. It cannot be happening in the middle of the nineteenth century."

In the end it was the thought of Agnes which made her yield. Agnes was in her care; it was herself, Aunt Tam, she admitted with a sense of guilt, who had tricked Ethan into letting them come on the trip, she herself who had conceived the idea of running away from the Grand Hotel de Salamanca upon a voyage which, with the fear of death upon her, she saw now was madness. Somehow, by some means, she must bring Agnes safe to land. After that nothing would matter. Nothing would ever matter again. Never again would she go about looking for excitement to make herself interesting.

And so she yielded and César slept *inside* the bolted door with his knife beside him. Agnes cried again and, at last, mercifully fell asleep, but Aunt Tam remained awake, starting up each time she heard footsteps outside the door. Once, several men came outside the door and stood there for a long time, now whispering among themselves, now silent, listening. They tried the door and finding it bolted, mercifully they went away again.

During the day she slept a little and tried to cheer Agnes who was white and weak from seasickness and lack of food. The second night she stayed awake all the night and about four in the morning, the freshness went out of the air and a damp muggy heat seemed to pour in through the open window. The clean smell of salt air went away and in its place there was a damp smell of rotting vegetation and mud. The boat no longer rocked at all and when daylight came and she looked out of the window, they were no longer in the open blue sea. The water was mud-colored and as far as the eye could see there was nothing but yellow water and a flat expanse of mangrove swamp, a prairie of deep emerald green surrounded by dirty water.

Shaking César awake, she called to Agnes, saying, "There's land outside. We're safe!"

When they went outside on the deck there was not a man in sight. The ragged half-furled sail drooped in the hot damp air and the red and yellow flag hung like a damp rag. As far as they could see there was no other ship nor on the land any sign of habitation or of life of any sort. The big negro went to the forecastle and shouted but there was no answer and going inside he found it empty. His voice echoed back from the empty stinking hold. There too there was no living thing save the rats.

At last the three of them went to the cabin of the Captain and pushing open the door, they found him there, his head resting on the dirty chest. A bottle stood beside him and the air reeked of stale cheap brandy.

Shaking him awake, César held him upright, and there occurred between them a mad conversation complicated by the drunkenness of the Captain and the jargon of the big negro. At last when César had extracted what information he could—enough to discover the full desperation of their situation, he let go of the Captain's shoulder and the man fell back again to the table, his unshaven face against the dirty chart, drunk with boredom and evil and brandy. Then César explained.

The crew had all left the ship. There was no way of working it farther. Even if the cholera-infected ship could be worked, it would not be allowed to pass the twin forts, Jackson and St. Philip. That was the orders from New Orleans from General Wicks himself.

"But General Wicks is my brother. We are going to him," Aunt Tam said in her bad French, and then understood at once the stupidity of her remark. There was no way of seeing General Wicks, no way of sending him word. Besides she wanted only to leave the stinking, horrible ship, now. Once free of it, she felt that everything would be all right.

Agnes did not cry. She sat down suddenly because of weakness and the heat, and when Aunt Tam said, "Don't be frightened, my dear. We'll find a way out." Agnes said bluntly, "I'm not frightened. I wasn't ever really frightened. I was sick."

Again it was César who had the solution. He knew this country. It was *his* river. He knew every inch of it once he was out of the tangled delta. If the American ladies would trust him, he would bring them safely to his master's plantation and from there they could have a fine carriage to drive in style into the city. It would not be an easy trip and it might be a long one, but if they would trust him, everything would be all right.

Aunt Tam considered the idea, but Agnes, suddenly practical, interrupted. "I don't see what else there is to do," she said. "Otherwise we might be here till doomsday."

She was feeling a little better now that the boat was still, and for the first time she felt irritation at Aunt Tam, not because she had suggested the flight on the *San Cristobal*—she herself was equally to blame for that—but because Aunt Tam's reaction, her mind itself, seemed so hopelessly romantic and divorced from all reality. "Anyway," she added, "I've no desire to die of cholera."

So César managed to get a big dory over the side and with ropes managed to lower their telescopes, valises and two heavy tin trunks filled with finery for New Orleans into the dory. With these stored in the stern he helped the two ladies to a place that was safe if not too comfortable, and casting off, he swung the smaller boat away from the stinking *San Cristobal* and close into the shore out of the sluggish current. The foul stench of the ship faded away and presently in its place there was only the strong fertile smell of the mud and the mangroves.

César began to sing as he rowed, a curious, deep-throated river song in the language of his parish. Aunt Tam said to Agnes, "Sit on the bottom of the boat, my dear. Put your head in my lap and try to sleep." Then she raised her parasol, holding it so that it shielded her and the fair head of the girl. She thought, "Well, we're out of that!" But almost at once she was forced to rouse Agnes for

[66]

the dory had begun to leak and the muddy water was wetting the skirts of the tired girl.

Sleepily Agnes sat beside Aunt Tam and almost at once fell asleep again with her head on the older woman's shoulder. Sitting very straight, Aunt Tam held the parasol above them while César, still singing, pulled the heavy oars, his black skin drenched in sweat. A great sand crane rose heavily out of the mangrove swamp and an alligator slipped with a splash into the muddy water. A curious ecstasy rose in Aunt Tam. She was thinking again of Margaret Fuller and Mr. Alcott and what a story she would have to tell them. It was very good to be alive. God had been very good to her, giving her a life so full and rich with adventure.

For nearly a week La Lionne neither saw Tom Bedloe nor had any message from him, but she knew what he was doing and what had happened to him, for there were many ways for news and gossip to travel in a city like New Orleans, a city compounded strangely of negroes and French and Spanish and all the riff-raff of a great port. The news came to her from Big Ernestine.

Day after day the big negress had watched her mistress grow more distracted and more irritable, neglecting her business, being rude to customers and sharp with the girls. She had even slapped Clélie her favorite, because the girl had complained of being tired, and she had gone early to bed again and again when the big gilt and mirrored ball-room was still filled with customers. Each night the class of customers grew worse—weasel-faced Yankees and raw-boned up-river men and *mauvais Kaintucks* who in the old days would never dared to have come beyond the confines of Tchou Pitoulas Street. There were fresh quarrels and brawls each night. Twice the carpetbaggers had dared to bring in negroes, one a very black man, the other a mulatto free man with an evil reputation called Faro Sam.

All this big Ernestine watched with distress and misgiving. A Bourbon at heart, she saw the whole world in which she had always lived, prosperously and enjoyably, falling into ruin before the Yankee invasion. The Café Imperial was becoming like the crib joints and the low cafés along the levee. What use were the mirrors and chandeliers and yellow plush in a world where there were no gentlemen? What good were the excellent Burgundy and Bordeaux wines and the champagnes and brandies for men who would as soon have swilled beer from a trough? She grew weary of subduing obstreperous and drunken patrons and lost all her zest in a good fight. And she began to consider what was to become of her, where she was to go when the whole thing came to an end. She might go north to Ohio or New England where, she heard, the negroes were treated like kings, or she might go to Paris with Madame or she might buy herself a cabin out of her savings on some remote bayou and live there like a queen among the other less fortunate negroes.

But the immediate present troubled her. One night there was certain to be a real riot and a murder among the carpetbaggers and white trash and then the Governor of the city would close the place and Madame would have nothing in return for all the money spent on the crystal and mirrors and plush that gave the place its tone. The thing to do was for Madame to sell out and go away to Paris, perhaps even to New York where there still were gentlemen—gentlemen who still had money and could appreciate the quality of an establishment such as the Café Imperial.

But what worried Big Ernestine most of all was the rapid degeneration of Madame's character. It had begun, she knew, from the moment Major Tom came in on that first night after the big riots and the hanging of young Mumford, to sit sulkily alone in a far corner of the room. Madame had gone forward to greet him as she would have gone to greet any new client, but in a little while there was a difference Big Ernestine had never noticed before in the hard veneer of her professional manner. On the second night and the third he returned, and after that he was always there sitting in the corner of the room at La Lionne's table and finally in her own sitting room above stairs. He was, Big Ernestine knew, not quite a gentleman, at least not a New Orleans gentleman, but that did not matter; with her woman's understanding she knew that the Yankee Major had other qualities which made it quite unnecessary to be a gentleman. Principally among them was the quality of excitement; he had only to come into a room to cause things to happen.

It was the quality of excitement, Ernestine knew, which had

undone her mistress. From the moment he appeared, a curious change came over La Lionne. She no longer paid the same meticulous attention to the affairs and conduct of the place. It was as if somehow she had entered another world, a kind of dream world over and above the gaudy establishment which had always been her pride. Most extraordinary of all, there were nights when she forgot completely to go over the books and receipts.

And then at last when he stayed away, she became altogether distraught, like a dazed half-mad person, like a *grue* whose *maquereau* had deserted her. She lost all dignity and throwing herself on the great mother-of-pearl and teakwood bed, she would lie weeping for hours at a time. She had violent migraines and once for twenty-four hours she stayed locked in her room refusing to eat or drink or come down to the ball room to keep the place in order.

So at last, Ernestine decided that something must be done. If it went on like this, the business would go to pieces and the establishment sink to the level of any waterfront café. Tactfully, she suggested that Madame communicate with Major Tom, asking him to return, but this idea La Lionne rejected with fierce and angry pride. Should La Lionne who had dominated every man she had ever known, suddenly throw herself at a man's feet imploring him to return? No, she screamed, that was impossible.

After two days, Ernestine again approached her with a new idea, an idea to which La Lionne agreed at once. It contained a grain of hope, and at the prospect of that hope, she brightened and sat up in her great bed. There were difficulties, quite large difficulties, but Ernestine thought she could get round them. To carry out the plan, they would have to have hair and nail parings of both La Lionne and Major Tom. The first part was, of course, simple enough and Ernestine thought she could cope with the second part. She was a friend of Old Seraphine, the de Lèche servant. They came from the same parish. Seraphine might steal the hair and nail parings out of friendship or she might have to be bribed. And they would have to have the services of Mama Tolanne, the withered old mulatto witch, who lived in her own house by the levee and was honored and feared by half the town. That too would cost money. Mama Tolanne could make a potion that would bring him back to her.

"Money!" La Lionne cried out, throwing herself about in her anguish, "What is money to me? *Rien!* What good is money when one is wretched and has no wish to live?"

In all the talk, while Big Ernestine sat by the side of the bed holding the white hand of La Lionne, she kept back two things, first her knowledge that it was the young Baroness who had kept Major Tom from coming to his mistress and second the story that the young Baroness was herself a witch and that she had practiced voodoo in Martinique when she had gone there as the bride of the Baron Louis. There were even mutterings among the de Lèche slaves that she had had something to do with his decline and death by consumption.

When she had finished describing her plan La Lionne cried out, "Go! Go at once to Seraphine!"

But the big negress said, "There is one more thing, Madame. Ef'n I was you ah'd sell the concern. Things is going from bad to worse. Even Clélie is beginning to carry on like a she-devil! And the customers is gettin' worse and worse. And now there's fever comin' in from across the river."

La Lionne, without turning, made an answer which came, muffled from the depths of the pillows. "Find me a buyer. I'll sell it quick enough. Who's to buy it?"

"Ah'll find you somebody, Madame. Ef'n I was you ah'd get back to Paris. There ain't no future in New Orleans with Yankees all over it like flies on a yeller dog."

It was already ten o'clock in the evening when Ernestine left by the same back door out of which Tom Bedloe had made his devastating escape. She left the place with misgivings, aware that her mistress would refuse to come downstairs even if a riot broke loose which destroyed every mirror in the place. Before her lay two courses, one to go to the house of the Baroness de Lèche and the other to go direct to Mama Tolanne's house. Seraphine might be at either place. If she was at Mama Tolanne's she, Ernestine, could kill two birds with one stone; so after a moment's reflection she set off in the direction of the river.

As she walked through street after street, now turning this way, now that, the lights, the air of life and gaiety diminished and for a time she went through a quarter beyond the Pont Alba Buildings where every house was shuttered and only an occasional yellowish light threw a long dim shadow beyond her on the narrow *banquettes*.

It was a long walk and the air was hot and Big Ernestine was in no haste. She had all night to accomplish what she had set out to do; if trouble broke out at the establishment, the military would have to take care of it. She was getting restless again and filled with ideas of roaming. She might go to Paris or Mobile or Natchez or even Atlanta, although she didn't care much for Atlanta or Atlanta society, either white or colored. According to Ernestine's Louisiana standards there wasn't a gentleman or lady in Atlanta. For Ernestine was a snob; at La Lionne's establishment she had been on intimate terms with most of the fine gentlemen of New Orleans and the surrounding parishes.

As she walked she came presently out of the darkness of the proud Créole houses and into the half-light of another world. Here there were fewer lights than in the heart of the rich city and they were less brilliant, yet it was a world teeming with life. Black men and women and children sat on doorsteps of slatternly wooden houses, unpainted and falling into decay, or walked the muddy roadway built upon old trash and garbage. Twice she passed rows of brick houses with shuttered doors where girls black and brown and yellow stood in the doorways, their half-nude bodies silhouetted against the faint glow of the night light behind them. They screamed with laughter and made obscene jokes with the men who passed by to inspect them. Some of the shuttered doors were closed with a faint glow or only blackness showing between the *Louvres*. Most of the men were colored men but among them appeared occasional white men, foreign sailors, swarthy and dirty, with gold rings in their ears from the ships which had swarmed to New Orleans to carry away cotton and sugar now that the blockade was lifted. There were tall, gangling, coarse-jawed men in rough clothes, the *mauvais Kaintucks* from up the river. The croaking of the frogs in the swamps along the river hung in the air, a wild accompaniment to the occasional music of a guitar or a banjo, music as bright and as gay in all the filth and desolation as the brilliant *tignons* and skirts of the negro women.

Through the crowd, Big Ernestine made her way, aloof and proud, like a great ship advancing through swarms of dirty bumboats. Everyone in the quarter knew her by sight, the famous Big Ernestine from the Café Imperial. Most of them at some time or other had had a glance at the magnificence of the place beneath the shuttered, high swinging door which opened on the street. As she passed, men on the street or girls from the shuttered doorways called out sallies, some of them funny, all of them obscene. And Ernestine answered them back in kind, bettering them each time in her retort as a burst of loud laughter rose from the crowd on the street.

At last she came to the edge of the quarter where the clustered, swarming houses came to an end. Beyond, half in the black shadow of the high moonlit levee, straggled a half-dozen houses no better than the other miserable shacks save for one which stood apart, a small house built like a doll's house, a copy in miniature of a great plantation house. Along the front was a high shallow portico not more than two feet wide with slender columns no more than three or four inches in diameter. From the portico descended a double stairway. Across the front fell the black shadow of three cypresses. The house was extraordinarily tall and narrow and set above the soggy mud upon piles like stilts. It had been painted white once but only flakes of the paint remained, enough to cast a kind of phosphorescent reflection in the pool of black water where the river had seeped through the levee.

The pavement ended a little way beyond the last house of the Quarter and from there on Big Ernestine had to pick her way through the mud and reeds, avoiding puddles of stagnant water that stood in the narrow path. In a little while she had reached the house and climbed the rickety narrow stairway and was standing before the door of Mama Tolanne's house. From somewhere inside came the sound of weird singing, punctuated by the rhythm of a muffled drum.

She knocked once and then again and again but still there was no answer. The croaking of the frogs seemed to grow louder with mockery. The curious moaning sound punctuated by the nervous rhythm of the drum continued. Slowly, when there was no answer, cold fear began to steal over Big Ernestine. She began to remember the weird stories of Haiti and Martinique in which the dead were summoned from the grave to serve old women like Mama Tolanne.

Then abruptly the door was opened by a tall, thin yellow negro who, recognizing her, stood aside to admit her and then quickly closed the door and bolted it.

Inside the whole house consisted of a single large room with a great fireplace at one end in which a fire had nearly burned itself out. Near the fire stood two women and beside it squatted a thin, very black negro with a long neck like a bird, beating a tom-tom. His eyes were opened but the eyeballs were rolled back until only the whites were visible; at each third augmented stroke, he jerked his head until the bones of his neck cracked. On the floor lay a naked octoroon girl, her body rigid in a trance. Over her bent the wrinkled ancient black figure of Mama Tolanne herself. She was muttering and groaning and now and then with a gesture of lightning quickness she would throw a pinch of some powder on the coals which, flaming up, cast a flashing irridescent light over the faces of those in the room and revealed the sheep's skulls and stuffed alligators that hung on the walls. The room smelled of urine and burnt flesh.

For a long time Big Ernestine stood silently watching the rigid figure of the naked girl on the floor; then slowly, furtively, she raised her eyes and regarded the figures of the two women. One she saw at once was Old Seraphine; the other woman wore a long black cloak with a hood which was pulled forward over her face. After a moment, Ernestine realized with a start that the woman was not a negress; even in the shadow of her hood, the face was very pale. She was young, too, and slender. Then she saw that it was the young Baroness de Lèche.

She knew at once that she would have to put off the interview with Seraphine, since obviously she had come with the young Baroness and could not leave her long enough to go into the complicated and secret details of Ernestine's mission. She would have to wait until the ceremony was finished and then talk to Mama Tolanne herself.

It was over in a little while. The old witch threw a final pinch of powder into the fire and gave a hair-raising scream. At the same

[73]

moment the drummer stopped his monotonous beating and sat upright, rolling back the pupils of his eyes and staring about him as if he had suddenly come from another world. The naked girl on the floor, stirred, moaned and sat up, looking about her with the same expression of astonishment. Ernestine observed that she was a very beautiful octoroon, not more than thirteen or fourteen years old. Then Mama Tolanne straightened herself with a sudden wheezing sigh that seemed to come from the tip of her naked, claw-like toes. She wore a curious headdress of feathers and periwinkle shells above a coal black Senegalese face immensely wrinkled, with the skin hanging in folds. The skinny yellow negro threw some shavings on the fire and as the flames leapt up, illuminating the room, Old Seraphine gave Big Ernestine a curious look which said, "I cannot speak to you now."

Then without a word, Seraphine gave the yellow negro a gold piece, the young Baroness drew the hood of the cape across her face and the two women went out the door. When the yellow negro had closed and bolted it Mama Tolanne did a curious thing; she turned toward the door and raising one hand, the left forefinger and little finger erect she spat through it seven times as the men on the *San Cristobal* had done when Aunt Tam or Agnes appeared on deck. Then she addressed the yellow negro who brought a bottle of rum and two cups and inviting Big Ernestine with a kind of weary elegance to seat herself in one of the dilapidated chairs, she herself got into the crude bed at one side of the room, propped herself up with a couple of enormous and greasy cushions and settled down for a gossip. The octoroon girl made no move to put on any clothing but stood, naked and unconcerned near the fire drinking rum from a rusty tin cup with the air of a wild and beautiful animal.

The old woman, between sips of rum, commented on the great heat, and the fever that was stealing in on the city, asked after Big Ernestine's health and then craftily inquired after the health of La Lionne.

Big Ernestine at first evaded the question. They spoke in a *patois* of their own, a kind of French, sprinkled with English and Spanish words and corrupted on the part of Mama Tolanne by hazy distant memories of Senegal. Propped up in the bed, her black eyes glittered in the dim light. At last, after many false starts, Big Ernestine came to the point.

La Lionne was badly off, she confided, shaking her head and going into the symptoms.

"L'amour?" guessed Mama Tolanne.

"L'amour," echoed Ernestine, "for a Yankee."

Mama Tolanne put her head on one side and cackled, "For the same young Yankee that the young Baroness is after. I know!"

This was somewhat of a revelation to Ernestine. Again she sparred for time, but presently decided that the best thing to do was to come to the point.

"Was that why she come here tonight?" asked Ernestine bluntly.

Yes, that was why, the old sorceress admitted. The young Baroness wanted to fasten the Yankee "Tom" to herself.

This again threw Ernestine into doubts. If Mama Tolanne was putting spells on Major Tom on behalf of the young Baroness, she could not at the same time put spells on him to bring him back to La Lionne. But after more gossip and talk of the weather during which Big Ernestine considered this point, she said, "I guess maybe I'd better be going. I came for the same thing."

Mama Tolanne chuckled wickedly into her rum. "Don't tell me you're after Major Tom too?"

No, explained Ernestine, it was for La Lionne. "I suppose," she said, "you couldn't work a spell both ways." Mama Tolanne didn't answer her directly. Again she chuckled wickedly and observed, "That Yankee must have somethin' wonderful for two women to be after him like that . . . two women like La Lionne and the young Baroness."

"He's excitin'," remarked Ernestine. Then, after a pause, she asked bluntly, "What for, Mama Tolanne, did you spit after her?"

"You ain't got any right to ask such questions, Ernestine," the old woman said.

" 'Cause you're afraid of her," taunted Big Ernestine.

"Ah ain't afraid of no white woman. No white witch is powerful like a black witch."

"Mebbe you doan like her?"

"Ah doan like her. It ain't healthy for no white woman to go meddlin' around with black people's voodoo."

Ernestine let the subject drop again. They had another tin cup of rum. Ernestine did not drink much and never while on duty at the Café Imperial, but now she wanted to get something out of Mama Tolanne. So she had another cup. Presently she said, "Mebbe gold could undo a voodoo."

"Mebbe it could," said Mama Tolanne.

"Mebbe a couple of bottles of Madame's best rum could help." Mama Tolanne chuckled again, "It sure could."

So after that Ernestine went to work on her. She told Mama Tolanne the whole story, and Mama Tolanne talked too, much more than was ethical for a professional witch doctor. The rum warmed both their hearts and they settled down to gossip. Mama Tolanne called out to the naked octoroon girl, "Euphémie, you'd better git your clothes on and git yourself home before that yellow boy gets you into trouble. Ah doan want your ma after me!" The girl picked up a kind of bright yellow shift made of calico and slipped it over her head. The yellow negro said something and the girl slapped him. Then they both went out together, followed by the black negro who had been beating the drum; and Mama Tolanne was free to talk.

Mama Tolanne said that the young Baroness had her mind set on Major Tom. She was out to get him, and she had to be secret about it because if New Orleans people found out about her running after a Yankee, it would be the end of her, what with her own cousin wanting her too. She was a bad woman, Mama Tolanne said, and all she thought about was gold. Seraphine hinted that she had possession of all the de Lèche property—the big house, the plantation Bel Manoir and all the gold in the Planter's Bank. That was why the old Baroness and the husband's cousin had to stick by her, even though they hated her. Only now the Yankee General had possession of everything—all the cotton and all the gold in the Planter's Bank, and even the young Baroness couldn't touch any of it.

Ernestine, a little dizzy from so much rum, listened to everything the old woman said. She saw that Mama Tolanne was talking too much under the influence of the same rum. There might not be another chance like this.

Then the old sorceress said an odd thing, "Ah ain't seen this young Major Tom but ah'm feelin' sorry for him."

"What for you feel sorry for him?" asked Ernestine. "Ain't he got all the women a runnin' after him?"

"Ah doan know nothin' worse for a man than havin' a lot of women runnin' after him. It ain't healthy havin' two women like La Lionne and the young Baroness runnin' after you. It ain't healthy for no young man. Ah wouldn't want to be in his boots." She shook her head and cackled and the feathers and periwinkle shells in her wooly hair waved and rattled.

Then, as the warmth of the rum stole over them and they began to sweat, the two of them fell to talking about their own adventures and the men they had known. Mama Tolanne could even remember a black boy back in Africa before she was transported. And at last when they were quite tipsy, Ernestine veered back again, a little unsteadily, to the point . . . the business of fixing up a spell to bring Major Tom back to La Lionne.

Mama Tolanne finally agreed that for fifty gold Yankee dollars and two bottles of rum, she could undo the spell she had barely finished casting on the sought-after lover, and transfer its effect to favor Ernestine's mistress. Then they had a night-cap of rum and Big Ernestine set out unsteadily along the planks laid in the mud back through Congo Square toward the Café Imperial. It was nearly dawn when she reached the back door of the establishment. The lights were out in the ball room and when she listened outside the door of La Lionne's room she heard only the sound of her mistress' regular breathing.

On the long way back she had come to a decision. She would tell Madame nothing of the gossip she had heard from Mama Tolanne. She was afraid of what La Lionne might do. A woman like that in love with a man ten years younger might do anything.

At the General's a party was under way, not a very gay party for there was a scarcity of women and the two women who constituted the entire female element were neither young nor very attractive. One was the General's lady, Aunt Louisa, and the other the wife of the Quartermaster General, a crow-faced woman from Indiana. Between them there was no love lost for the General's lady looked upon the Quartermaster General's wife as a savage out of a log cabin and the Quartermaster General's wife, Mrs. Theophilis Gilpin, by name, looked upon the General's wife as a Yankee harridan. Mrs. Gilpin would not have been at the party but for the fact that she was the only other Yankee woman in New Orleans, and she had been called in when every New Orleans woman invited, even those who had showed a semblance of friendliness toward the Union troops, refused. Even those who sought favor for the sake of their property, and there were a few, dared not to appear at General Wicks' since his order that New Orleans women who did not salute the Union flag and fawn over Yankee soldiers were to be treated as common prostitutes.

It was in fact a grisly party, without wine, with nothing stronger than a weak lemonade punch concocted by the hand of the General's wife. The guests were nearly all fellow officers of the general, inferior in rank, who, no matter how much they hated him, could not refuse his invitations. There were all sorts and types, some regular Army men feeling contempt for the few volunteer officers; these in turn feeling hatred for the West Point men. The only men not in uniform were two ill-favored cousins of the General, who had been summoned to New Orleans to take part in the general looting, and the poor Mayor of the City who had come in the hope that this act of diplomacy might help his fellow citizens to save their cotton, furniture and silverware from the plundering horde.

The Mayor was a thin, delicate little man, dark and sensitive and proud, and the whole evening was for him filled with humiliation and agony, not only because his pride was again and again trampled under foot but because in his heart he felt only contempt for most of the men in the two big drawing-rooms. He remembered them, these same rooms, as they had been when the house was occupied by the MacTavish family—rooms which had a glow about them of crystal and flowers and color, when they echoed to laughter and music, and there was champagne and planter's punch at such a party, and pretty women instead of these two Northern dragons who moved about among the officers with arrogance and vulgarity because they were the only two females on a desert island. Somehow the bleak touch of Aunt Louisa's hand had altered the rooms more even than the barbarians now encumbering them. How it was done, the Mayor could not divine, and in his weariness he did not even try. He only thought from time to time what strange creatures these New Englanders were, so bleak and tactless, all sharp corners, with no ease or elegance. How could they ever have been citizens of the same country?

Twice during the torture of the interminable evening, the gentle Mayor had moments which were mildly pleasurable, once when David Wicks approached him with politeness and asked questions about the history of the old city. The boy was agreeable to look at with his longish blond hair, clear complexion and blue eyes. He had good manners and a sensitive intelligence, something of which the Mayor had found no trace in his contact with the other military men. They had talked for a little while in a corner until the wife of the Quartermaster General had rudely snatched the boy away.

The other moment had come when Tom Bedloe talked to him. This time it was not the sensitive intelligence which touched him but a sort of animal warmth and friendliness and a curious kind of understanding. He seemed different from the others, a kind of buccaneer, who had no interest in the petty prides and triumphs. He was cheery and there was no condescension in him, and in an odd way you felt his contempt for the others in the room, not for their barbarity but for their meanness, because there was something ordinary and limited about them, something cautious and commonplace which denied living or sought always to draw profit out of pleasure.

The Mayor found himself smiling, unaware that part of the cordiality in the young man arose from a perverse pleasure in showing the others that he respected the Mayor and preferred his company to theirs. But whatever the reason for the warmth, the few minutes spent in the young man's company, relieved a little the dull misery and humiliation of the evening.

In their conversation, the young man said presently that he was quartered in the house of the de Lèche family and quite bluntly that he found them a strange family.

For a moment the little Mayor seemed frightened. Then he said, "Yes, they are a strange family. They have spent a good deal of time in Paris. I used to know the old Baroness when she still went about . . . a very strange character. Once she took twelve slaves with her to Paris simply for a ball." He smiled gently in reminiscence of the story. "The night of the ball she placed them, six on each side of the great stairs, each holding a lighted torch. They were the finest young negroes from the plantation and they were quite naked. It created a sensation. When the protests of her guests came to her she only said, in her deep voice, 'Mais ils ne sont que des bêtes. Pourquoi habiller un taureau?' 'But they are only animals. Nonsense to put clothes on a bull!' " The little Mayor chuckled a little, "Yes, the old Baroness was a card!" Then he sighed a little. "And very beautiful once . . . like the Empress." Then quite suddenly he asked, "Have you seen the young Baroness?"

"Yes."

"I hear she too is beautiful."

Bedloe said quite simply, "I have seen more beautiful women but never one quite like her."

"They say she is mixed Irish and French blood. It is not a good cross. No up-river cattle breeder would ever make such a cross except to produce a curiosity."

"She is a remarkable woman."

"Her husband was her cousin," said the Mayor. "They had to have a dispensation for the marriage. After that no one in New Orleans would receive them."

Then the General's wife broke up the conversation and took Tom Bedloe away with her to have a gumbo. It was an outlandish dish, she said, much too highly seasoned, but the negress whom she had for cook could not learn to do simple cooking, no matter how hard the General's wife tried to train her.

It was while they stood by the buffet that a soldier appeared in the hall outside saying he had a message. The General's wife, standing opposite the arched doorway, saw him, a thin white-faced man, with a look of terror in his eyes and a dark splotch of blood on his tunic. Although he had asked only for the General, she divined disaster and with short, quick firm steps she left Tom Bedloe standing alone and walked into the hall. What was the General's business was hers. After all, her friends at home said hers was the better head of the two. In a crisis, the General could not make a proper decision. More often than not it was Aunt Louisa who in fact stood at the head of the Army of Occupation. At this moment she smelled a crisis.

Tom Bedloe watched her, thinking what a horrible woman she was, fat, solid and hard, but using her femininity unscrupulously to faint or scream hysterically when her will was crossed. He had no pity for the General. In his way he was no better. He could not hear what the white-faced soldier was telling them, but he saw the General's lady suddenly grow scarlet with anger and begin to berate both the General and the helpless soldier. Her plump red face seemed to swell and her body to quiver with rage. Lazily, still grinning, he walked toward the little group.

As he came nearer, he heard the General's wife saying, "It is an outrage! Every able-bodied man in the city ought to be hung." She turned suddenly to the General. "If you had any backbone that's what you'd do . . . whip all of them as if they were niggers and then hang them!"

He heard no more for he suddenly thought of the Mayor, and turning away walked to where the gentle little man was trying to show amusement at a dirty story being told by a red-faced blubbery Colonel.

Quietly Bedloe said, "You had better come with me. There is trouble."

"But I couldn't without saying good night to my hostess."

Tom laughed, "Leave that to me. I can manage her." Then his face grew serious and he said, "Believe me, sir, I am telling you the truth. Come with me. I'll be responsible. Come, I'll show you the way." The thought of having the little man humiliated any further was unendurable to him. Some trouble, some violence had occurred and the Mayor would be held responsible. Gently he took the little man by the arm and led him away.

"I know the house," said the Mayor. "I've known it since I was a little boy. You see, the MacTavishes were my friends."

"I'll go with you," said Tom, and like a hen mothering a chick he led the Mayor down the long wide stairway beneath the great chandelier of crystal and out into the magnolia-scented darkness. As they passed out the doors, there came to them the whickering of horses quartered in the lower floor of the house.

The house was on the garden side of the city and unlike the old quarter, the gardens here lay about the outside of the house instead of being on the interior surrounded by the house itself. From beyond the cast iron fences came the scent of crêpe myrtle, magnolia and the first tuberoses, thick, sickening in the hot dampness of the night.

As they walked, the Mayor said, "It is a most unfortunate position, being the Mayor of a conquered city. The enemy does not like you for opposing him and your own people hate you because they think you do not do all you can to help them. You have been very kind to me tonight."

Tom laughed in the thick darkness. "I couldn't see you being bullied by the General's wife."

In a little while they came nearer to the dim glow of Canal Street which divided the old city from the new. As they approached, Tom said, "I'll leave you here, sir. I understand. It would not be well for you to be seen walking in the streets in a friendly way with a Union officer."

The little Mayor started to protest politely but Tom Bedloe knew that in his heart his companion was relieved. In the darkness the Mayor bade him good night and again thanked him. Then he went off bravely, very straight and slender, as Tom, smiling, stood looking after him. It would be bad enough for the little man to be seen with a Union Officer, how much worse for him to be seen with a Union Officer who was also the Collector of the Port, and robbing all his fellow citizens.

As he walked away toward Canal Street, he was troubled by the innocence and gentleness of the little man who day after day, night after night, strove to keep peace in his city, protect his people and preserve his dignity as well as theirs. The man made him ashamed of his roguery. He sighed and kicked a piece of stone broken from the banquette. Well, when he was through with this job, he'd clear out and marry Agnes Wicks and go into the West and lead a different, decent life.

Then he crossed Canal Street, picking his way through the mud that oozed up through the ancient cobblestones, and as he reached the other side he noticed suddenly that without thinking, he had crossed at Royal Street and was quite near to La Lionne's establishment, so near that he could hear the music of the negro band playing in the room with the mirrors and yellow plush. For the shadow of a second he was tempted to turn in and see what was going on, but immediately he knew that if he went inside he would see La Lionne, and although he had heard no word from her since the night he crept out of the back door into the flooding rain, his instinct told him that he would encounter scenes, hysteria, screams. Perhaps even he would be forced to remain, something he had no desire to do.

And so he passed the door and continued on his way along Royal Street toward the quarter dominated by the de Lèche house whither without thinking he had been bound since the moment he took the arm of the little Mayor and led him down the stairs. He was returning "home" early, in the hope of seeing the young Baroness before she retired to bed.

Since that first bewildering evening in the drawing room on the other side of the drenched courtyard, he had seen her twice. Once in the early morning when, unable to sleep because of the heat, he had dressed early to go to the port office. As he came out of the room she was playing with a tortoise-shell cat in the garden beyond the singing fountain. She, too, could not sleep for the heat and she had come into the garden clad only in a nightdress with a *peignoir* thrown over it. It was a nightdress the like of which he had never seen before; even La Lionne had nothing like it. It was of some shimmery thin material, gauze-like, gathered just beneath the breasts and ornamented with scarlet ribbons. Now and then as she played with the cat, the pale green *peignoir* fell open.

For a second as he watched, he felt that he should turn away, but the temptation was too great and he hid himself, smiling, behind the wistaria that climbed up the iron grill work.

For a long time he watched her, thinking again how it was that a woman who was not beautiful should still be so fascinating. It was perhaps her body which now he saw, without shame, for the first time unhidden by great crinolines. Whenever she moved it was with the same supple grace of the cat. He remembered now that even in the first evening when he had come upon her clad in the yellow ball dress, she had possessed the same grace of movement. Even the clumsy dress had not hampered her.

[83]

She threw a ball for the cat and each time the cat captured the ball and grew bored with it she followed him along the path and threw it again. Hidden in the gallery, Tom was aware that it was impossible to move down the stairs and out of the door without her knowing that he had been watching her. There was no other course but to go back into his own room, and it seemed to him a silly thing to abandon so pleasurable a spectacle. It did not matter so long as she remained in ignorance of his spying.

At last, wearied of the game, she threw herself down on a kind of outdoor sofa in the lower gallery, where she lay back, the *peignoir* open, one hand trailing over the side to stroke the arched back of the cat. It was a lovely picture, like the aphrodisiac drawings which some member of the Lèche family had left hanging in his bedroom, drawings signed by Fragonard.

Then suddenly the silver bell rang, and he heard the voice of Old Seraphine calling, "Baroness, yo coffee is fresh and hot." At the sound of the old negress' voice she rose lazily, gathered the *peignoir* about her, and went into the house, the gold mules she wore on her feet clattering across the stones of the gallery. As she entered the wide doorway she looked back over her shoulder toward the garden and laughed, and for the first time it occurred to him that she had known he was there all the time behind the wistaria-covered pilaster, and he felt the blood rising into his face. In some obscure way, she had made a fool of him.

Then he had seen her again for a moment one evening when, just before he was going out for the night to gamble at a house in Chartres Street, she came again to his door. This time she did not come inside but only stood on the threshold, saying, "I came to see if you were comfortable."

He grinned, "Perfectly, thank you." And he looked at her boldly with his eyes smiling, as if to tell her that he had watched her in the garden and that he knew she had been aware of it. The look in her own eyes was a perfect answer.

She said, "I had hoped you would come calling again."

He could not say that he had not come because he had found the first evening bewildering and unpleasant. He only said, "I have been very busy. Now the port has opened again there is a terrible amount of work." And then he felt a little silly, knowing

that they were both standing there making idiotic formal speeches
which had nothing to do with what was in their minds and hearts.
He thought, "She is a bold one," and said, "I would like to call
again another night if I may have the permission."

"Certainly, my friend. This time I will try at least to keep Grandmère out of the way. She is sour because she is no longer young.
You must forgive her. She was a great beauty once. It is misery
for beauties when they fade."

Suddenly he said, "Won't you come in and sit down? I have
nothing to offer you but some port."

She smiled again, "No, thank you. Tonight is not the proper
time. Old Seraphine will be ringing me to dinner. If there is anything you need, you must call on us."

Then she had gone away, leaving him bewildered again and
feeling like an awkward yokel. She was a lady and yet she behaved
like a trollop, or perhaps it was only that ladies behaved like that
in Paris. He had never met any woman like her, with grand airs,
and yet inviting and bold all at the same time.

What she had done was to fix her image in his mind so that the
memory of La Lionne scarcely existed any longer for him. A dozen
times during the day, he would find himself, sometimes during his
work, sometimes in the middle of a conversation, sometimes over
a drink, suddenly lost in a kind of fog from which only her image
emerged, now in the yellow ball gown, now in the night dress, now
in the black gown with a fichu she wore as she stood in the doorway. He no longer remembered Agnes at all save when David's
pale face and blue eyes brought her to mind for an instant.

And so tonight, instead of going on from café to café, from
gambling house to gambling house, he was returning home to bed
early, on the chance that he might have a glimpse of her or, better
still, that by some miracle he would find her alone or in such circumstances that he could break down somehow that half-mocking
air of grandeur which separated them as man and woman. He did
not even know her Christian name; he had never even heard it.
He only knew her as the Baroness de Lèche or the young
Baroness. "Tomorrow," he thought, as he walked through the dark
streets, "I must ask Seraphine."

The moon came up later now and as he turned into the dark

impasse which led to the courtyard entrance, he had to feel his way along the wall until he reached the door. The great key slipped into the lock at the first try and grinning in the darkness, he thought, "That is a good omen. It means the way is easy."

The garden inside was in darkness save for a patch of light which came from the open French door of the drawing room on the upper gallery. Again he smiled for this, too, was a good omen. Perhaps she was there, alone.

Quietly he climbed the stairway and walked along the gallery to the open doorway. He had stepped into the light before the people in the drawing room heard him. He had even stood there for a second or two before they became aware of his presence. There were three men in the room, the dark cousin and two strangers, both young. One of them was seated in a chair and beside him stood Old Seraphine holding a basin beneath his arm which had been bared to the elbow. The young Baroness bent over him, bathing the arm from which came a thin trickle of blood. The water in the basin held by Old Seraphine was red with blood.

It was the young Baroness who noticed him first, although she stood with her back to him. As if she *felt* his presence she turned and said, quite calmly, "Good evening. Won't you come in?"

The others turned quickly. Old Seraphine screamed and very nearly dropped the basin.

Quite calmly the young Baroness said, "We have had an accident . . . if you can call a duel an accident. My friend here has been wounded in the arm." Then very grandly, she introduced the two strangers, "My neighbor, Monsieur MacTavish and my friend Monsieur Delaplaine."

Tom Bedloe bowed and said, "I should be glad to be of help if there is anything I can do."

The two strangers and the cousin only stared at him in a hostile fashion without speaking and the young Baroness moved a little nearer. She said in a low voice, "If you want to be of help you will go away. Duels are forbidden by law. My friends would prefer it."

So there was nothing for him but to go away. When he had bowed and gone, the doors were closed quickly behind him shutting out all the light save for what filtered through the openings in the shutters.

He scarcely slept at all that night and twice he rose and partly dressed to go to the Café Imperial and find La Lionne, but each time he went back to bed deflated because the image of La Lionne no longer brought any feeling of excitement.

In the morning when, over his coffee in a café in Chartres Street, he read the *Delta*, the only paper permitted to be published by the General, he found a bit of news which made all the disconnected incidents of the night before suddenly fit together like the pieces of a picture puzzle.

He read, *"A dastardly murder was committed last night near the corner of Bourbon and Toulouse Streets opposite the opera house when Mr. Lucius M. Willock, a northern merchant in New Orleans to buy cotton, was shot to death by two unknown assailants believed to be members of a traitorous gang known as The Defenders. With him was Colonel Marcus B. Danton, of the staff of the General in Command of New Orleans who received a bullet in the right shoulder. The cowardly assailants made their escape into the darkness, leaving the dead and wounded gentlemen lying on the banquettes. One of the assassins is believed to have been shot in the arm by the orderly accompanying Colonel Danton who bravely drew his carbine and fired. . . ."*

The rest of the article was a denunciation of New Orleans and her citizens, filled with threats of hangings and shootings, all bearing evidence of the vituperative violence of the General's wife.

Tom Bedloe put down his paper and grinned. The death of Lucius M. Willock could only be regarded as a benefit not only to the city of New Orleans but to the human race. He knew him as a tall, lean, weasel-faced thief who had come to the prostrate city to batten upon its misery, buying up even furniture and women's clothes, coddling "bad niggers," wriggling his way into politics for the greater plundering that was to come once the freed negroes ran the State. And even the wound of Colonel Marcus B. Danton—the pompous bastard—did not alarm him. It might take some of the starch out of his shirtfront.

Now he understood the scene in the hallway at the General's party and the curious tableau in the old de Lèche house. For a little time he sat pondering the story and then suddenly there came, in a flash of inspiration, an idea of how it might be turned to his own advantage. He had found a way, perhaps, to break down that puzzling wall which separated him from the young Baroness.

Calling for a pen and a piece of paper, he wrote, "I saw nothing last night. I understand nothing. Do not be alarmed." He did not sign it but he addressed it to the Baroness Louis de Lèche and calling a boy, gave him a coin to deliver it. Then he walked out into the broiling sun to go to his office. After all, the omens of last night might be good after all.

On that first day of their strange journey up from the Gulf through the Delta country black César rowed all day through the heat against the sluggish current of the great river, keeping always inshore near the fringe of mangroves which thrust their bare gnarled knees into the shifting treacherous mud. Here the current was less strong but the heat was more stifling for the low-lying vegetation cut off the faint breeze that stirred the thick green leaves. The heavy dory made the going difficult and now and then the keel caught in the mud of a hidden bar and there was nothing to do but let the current of the river turn the boat and carry it back into deep water. Every hour or two, the big black man would fasten the boat to the overhanging vegetation and rest, his great shoulders heaving with the effort, the sweat pouring down his broad ebony face.

Opposite him Aunt Tam sat very straight holding the parasol over the sleeping Agnes to save her milk white skin from the ravages of the sun. The girl slept with the dead sleep of the very young, only stirring faintly once or twice when the boat eased, with a faint jolt off a mud bar. The older woman was tired, but she was wiry and tough and the excitement of the adventure kept her awake; and there was the life in and about the mangrove swamp which they skirted—the alligators, the great turtles, the glittering clouds of aigrettes, the crows, the gulls, the water snakes—a teeming life that seemed to inhabit and infest all the vegetation which covered the fertile alluvial mud. In a way she was thankful for the abandonment of the *San Cristobal*; aboard a big ship they would have been forced to keep to the middle of the river where the current ran swift and strong, far from the shore. They would have seen nothing of this fascinating life at close hand.

And as she sat opposite the great black man she kept thinking about him, wondering at his devotion, speculating upon what went on inside his heart and mind. He was like a great friendly dog, simple and good-natured. Sometimes, after he had rested for a time, he would sing until the heat and the exertion forced him to stop and give all his strength to the simple business of pulling the heavy dory upstream. Occasionally they exchanged a few words, Aunt Tam speaking her tram-car French and César his jargon of three languages. Even on that first morning a new relationship between them began to come into being—a kind of friendship founded upon a sudden sense of recognition between two utterly simple and kindly people. Sometimes they did not speak at all but when their eyes met as César leaned back on the oars, the plain horse face of Aunt Tam would soften into a smile and César, responding, would show his perfect double row of shining white teeth. What they were saying to each other—the gaunt spinster from Boston and the great negro—was quite simple. They were saying, "What a wonderful and beautiful world this is, so filled with things which make you feel happy inside . . . things like the glistening beauty of the white aigrettes, and the lovely suspended timeless grace of a great sand crane rising in flight, and the comic ugliness of the alligators and the deep rich green of the mango leaves and the fertile smell of the life sustaining mud carried down from the great plains and wooded hills of far off Iowa and Illinois and Ohio and Kentucky and Tennessee."

Aunt Tam had really never had time in all her life to think about what people were like inside or about the wonders of being *inside* of nature and creation itself. Always she had been too busy with ideas ever to touch and penetrate the beautiful simplicity of reality. Always in the world in which she lived, she had, breathlessly, been struggling to keep up with the brilliant minds of Mr. Emerson and Margaret Fuller, trying to create and hold a place for herself in a world far removed from realities which concerned itself with the exterior of *things* and the interior of abstractions. And in the end she had fallen into a breathless confusion in which her catalogues of exterior things kept in her journal was the only order.

The first signs of what was happening to her she neither recognized nor understood. She only knew that since the moment she had followed Agnes down the ladder from the window of the Grand Hotel de Salamanca, a vague but powerful new element had come into her existence. From the moment she left the deceived and tiresome Commander of the *Allegheny* behind her in the harbor of San Cristobal de la Habana, she had felt her soul and spirit growing. The sense of beauty she had experienced even in the midst of the hardship and terror of the hurricane; there had been in the pounding sea and the howling wind and the darkness a kind of magnificence in which she herself had participated in some strange fashion. And so in her heart she had never really been frightened because she was all the while on the *inside*, a part of the whole spectacle. If she died, she was a part of it, and she would go on and on just the same, because in some puzzling fashion she had left behind her all the *exteriorness* of the life in Boston, all the endless talk and writing, all her own brother's dreadful material sense of property and possessions. In her heart she was still puzzled, but the new excitement prevailed. It was as if she could feel herself growing.

Sometimes César would grin and in his jargon say, "Look at old man turtle a-carryin' house right on his own back, steppin' down into the water, pullin' in his head and toes if old man alligator gits after'n him. Dey ain't no alligator wants to chew up Mr. Turtle's shell and digest it," or "De aigrette is de bird of Hebben. When de gates of Hebben opens up Monsieur and Madame Aigrette is goin' to be de first birds a-flyin' in." And he called the great cranes "Granpa Crane!" affectionately, as if the wise birds were in some way related to him. And Aunt Tam would smile back at him and try to remember all he said and told her so that she could write it down in her journal when they stopped for the night.

It was funny! It seemed to her that she had always felt the same affection for animals and birds that black César showed, only she had never showed it or been allowed to show it. In her world they had always been more interested in the color of the feathers of a bird, or its Latin name or the history of its migration or the number of eggs it laid; they had never any feeling of the bird itself. And the discovery made her feel warm and happy inside. It even made her feel differently about the girl who lay asleep beside her, her blonde head on her shoulder. It was as if until now her niece had been an *object*, something detached and apart from her, a very conventional object of which she had been very fond. But this was different, this new feeling. It seemed to illuminate Agnes and black César and all the world about her, even the ugly alligators and turtles.

About noon she saw a ship slipping down the river. It lay well out in the middle of the river, its sails hanging limp, being carried down by the current. When she told César of her discovery, he stopped rowing, turned quickly to regard the ship and then deftly drew the dory in close to the mangroves, so close beneath the branches that it was very nearly hidden.

When she asked why he had done this, he explained that these were war times and that one could not tell who was an enemy and who a friend. And while he was in Cuba he had heard that the river and the inlets and bayous were infested with every sort of scoundrel—deserters, escaped war prisoners, men who had broken jail during the siege; and there were always the native bad characters, the Sabines who were part Negro and part Indian, escaped slaves, and desperadoes of all sorts. You couldn't know in these times who was aboard a ship like that or what they were up to.

When he saw her expression turn to alarm as she listened, he grinned and added, "Doan you worry, Miss Tam. You just stick by César. This is ma country, this river country. César knows every bayou and *raccourci*. Ah'll git you safe into New Orleans."

In half an hour, the schooner drifted so far downstream that it was lost in the mist of heat over the water and César, taking up the oars, set the dory upstream once more. About three o'clock in the afternoon, Aunt Tam sighted another boat, this time a steam vessel with a plume of black smoke which drifted before it, and again César executed the maneuver of hiding under the mangroves. As the boat steamed past them Aunt Tam thought from its flatness and the great height of its paddle-wheels it must be a gun-boat, although she could not make out whether it flew the

Union or the Confederate flag. It was a long way off across the muddy immensity of the river and the flag hung limp.

If it had been a Union gun-boat they would have been safe but she could not know for sure and in any case she was beginning to doubt whether she wanted to be rescued just yet.

About sunset a faint breeze came up the river from the Gulf and presently César drew the dory close into the branches and standing up on the highest part of the boat he studied both banks of the river for a long time. Then he loosened the boat again and turning it, set out across the river.

The current carried them slowly downstream but César, it seemed, had calculated on this and as he reached the other shore he allowed the boat to drift close to the mangroves until it had slipped down river for about a hundred yards. Then with a couple of powerful strokes of the oars he thrust the bow through an opening scarcely wide enough for the boat to slip through and they were suddenly in a hidden lagoon where the still water was clearer than the water of the Mississippi and reflected the reeds and the mangroves like an oval mirror.

As they entered the lagoon César grinned at Aunt Tam as if to let her know how clever he had been. Then he said, "We camp here all night—a little further on big island."

The boat headed for a narrow opening at the far end of the lagoon and as they passed through this they came into a new world.

There were no longer any mangroves but only grotesque gnarled trees that stood up to their knees in black water. They rose to a great height and shut out the fading twilight less by the thickness of their green-black foliage than by the long garlands of moss that hung like great strands of graying hair from their topmost branches. As the boat slid into this dim, still, enchanted world, the aigrettes perched in the treetops set up a great screeching and, flying high into the air, caught the rays of the dying sun on their white plumage and bent them downward into the gray wet forest and the still water so that the whole place seemed suddenly illuminated.

It was at this moment that Agnes stirred and waking, opened her eyes. For a little time she lay half-dazed by sleep, her head still on the shoulder of Aunt Tam. Then slowly the wild alarming cries of the birds and the white of their reflected images in the dark water roused her and she thought, still befogged with sleep, "I have died and this is the world of the dead." Even when she saw the black face and grinning white teeth of César before her and felt the touch of Aunt Tam's hand, the illusion still remained. Perhaps they too had drowned in the hurricane.

Then Aunt Tam asked, "Are you all right, my dear?" And with an effort she answered, "I'm all right. Where are we?"

Then Aunt Tam explained and César put in a word or two.

The girl was hungry, hungrier than she had ever been before in all her secure and well-ordered life. Hazily she thought, "It must be awful for people who really don't have enough to eat." She did not feel like talking. She only wanted to stretch herself like a waking kitten and watch the tall black cypresses and the dark water slipping past. The aigrettes had circled about and were now sitting again in the tops of the trees.

Then the dory came again into a small round lagoon with a kind of island on the far side. Here there was solid earth and out of it growing great low-branched live oaks so thick that beneath them there was no vegetation but only dried brown leaves.

César, grinning, said, "We stay here tonight."

Once the chest César had brought was put ashore on the island, he vanished tactfully into the reeds that grew at the far end, leaving the two Boston ladies to attend to their toilettes and make themselves as comfortable as possible. Aunt Tam retired to a thicket on one side of the open grove and Agnes to another similarly placed, and after a little time each emerged.

In the peculiar circumstances in which they found themselves, so unlike anything they had imagined even in the wildest flights of Aunt Tam's fanciful mind, there seemed remarkably little to talk about. One or the other might have said, "How extraordinary that only six weeks ago we should have been sitting safely beside the comfortable fire in Pinckney Street," but that seemed a remark so obvious that neither of them made it.

They did remark to each other upon the unearthly beauty of the spot and upon the cloud of white aigrettes which, apparently overcome by curiosity, had now abandoned the tall cypresses for the upper limbs of the spreading wild oaks just above their heads. The birds kept uttering wild cries and shifting their positions so that the tops of the trees were in a perpetual state of agitation.

Then Aunt Tam seated herself on the chest and opening her reticule took out a pair of scissors and lifting her skirt began cutting the threads which fastened the fashionable crinoline frame into her voluminous skirt.

"It is of no use," she observed. "It's only a fad in any case and a great nuisance getting in and out of the boat."

As she ripped her way to the higher reaches of the skirt, she said, "Now, my dear, you'll have to help. I can't reach any higher and I can't reach the back."

So Agnes lifted the skirt and after a moment's snipping, the crinoline frame fell about Aunt Tam's ankles and she stepped free of it with a shake of her skirt, saying, "There! That's better They're all nonsense anyway!"

Then in turn she freed Agnes from her contraption, and standing off to regard her, she said, "You're much prettier without it, dear Now we can climb about as we like."

At the same moment Aunt Tam noticed the reeds moving as i some animal were advancing toward them, and after a moment a whole section of the reeds appeared to detach itself and come in their direction. It was César returning. He carried on his broad back a whole bundle of reeds to make a thatched shelter for the night.

Deftly he went to work, grinning. In a few minutes he had erected a frame and covered it with reeds, making a dry rather pleasant dog house. Then he went away again and returned in a little while with more reeds for their beds. Agnes went down to the edge of the bayou to wash her hands and face, but Aunt Tam watched and after a little while she was seized with an overwhelming desire to participate in the pioneer work. So César set her to gathering wood for the fires that were to keep off the millions of mosquitoes which had already begun to buzz in clouds in the blue twilight.

César, it appeared, had thought of everything. Once the shelter was made and the fires started, he opened the chest and brought out hard biscuits and salt and pepper, an iron kettle and som salt pork. Then he disappeared again. Aunt Tam and Agnes seated themselves on piles of reeds inside a ring of small fires and listened to the night sounds that had begun at dusk to arise from out of the great swamp—the splash of alligators, the hoarse croaking of great bull frogs, the occasional cry of a bird. It was a lost and lovely world and they both felt extraordinarily peaceful and happy. Aunt Tam was very tired and all the excitement was beginning to wear off a little.

Presently she said to Agnes, "What are you thinking about?"

"I'm thinking about Tom and David and Papa and what they'll think when they discover we're lost."

"It's nothing to worry about. We'll be in New Orleans before the news could reach your father and Tom and David don't even know we're coming."

"But Uncle James and Aunt Louisa will, and they'll tell the others."

There was a silence with the night sounds breaking the stillness. Then Aunt Tam asked abruptly, "Are you really in love with Tom Bedloe, my dear?"

For a moment Agnes was silent, bewildered by the suddenness of a question which very likely Aunt Tam would never have had the boldness to ask back in the house in Pinckney Street. The girl tried to examine herself, but getting back no answer, she said, "I don't know, Aunt Tam. I don't know what love really is."

"I'm sure I couldn't tell you," said Aunt Tam, "but I thought you might know."

Again after a little silence, Agnes said, "I only know that I want to see him more than anything in the world, and that when he's near me I feel different . . . all excited and happy and a little crazy so that I'm ashamed of myself afterward. I feel as if I'd do anything in the world to keep him and be near him."

"Well," said Aunt Tam, "that sounds like what love is supposed to be. I only asked because I wanted you to be sure. He makes me feel excited too, especially when he jokes with me, but I wouldn't call it love."

They got no further with their discussion, for out of the shadows, beyond the drifting wall of smoke, César appeared looming up

[95]

like some giant out of the swamp. He carried the iron kettle and it was filled with oysters.

First he filled the pot with water from the bayou and put it over the fire and then squatting on his haunches, he shucked the oysters and cut the salt pork into small cubes. Then with his great knife he chopped the herbs he had gathered into fine pieces and emptied the lot into the pot. After it had boiled for a time he added salt and pepper and a few onions he had brought out of the chest and then at the last the sailors' biscuit which he broke into fine pieces and poured into the stew. The smell that came from the boiling pot was stronger now even than the odor of the smoke from the fires or the damp peaty smell of the swamp itself. It was quite dark before César, with the air of a great chef, produced two great iron spoons from the chest and said, grinning, "Mangez! Good mangez!"

But Aunt Tam said, "What about you, César?"

"César mangez after."

She attempted to argue but it all came to nothing. The great negro would eat what was left.

Then as Aunt Tam and Agnes ate, sitting on bundles of reeds, the moon came up behind the tall cypresses hung with Spanish moss on the far side of the lagoon and overhead the aigrettes, stirred into wakefulness as if by a false dawn, chortled and shook their glistening white feathers, and Aunt Tam forgetting, despite her hunger, to eat, sat for a long time enchanted by the beauty of the night and the sounds of the bayou, thinking again how fortunate she was to be alive in so lovely a world.

And even Agnes, nearly desperate with the hunger of a healthy young woman, was aware of the strange soft loveliness that had the qualities in it of mystery and eternity. Toward the end of the excellent and savory meal, she sat, staying for a time with the great iron spoon poised, looking out of the lagoon, dreaming, barely conscious of reality.

The strange adventure started in far off Havana was beginning to have an effect upon her as well as Aunt Tam. In this moment she was happy, in a way she had never before been happy, with a kind of ecstasy which blotted out everything that she had left behind her, all the neat little life, the protection of her sober father, the imbecilities of her private school, the thin arid quality of Boston itself which was like October air in stony New England. In the stillness as the moon rose steadily above the black cypresses, it seemed to her that she could feel her soul expanding. The soft air faintly stirred by a breeze from the Gulf caressed her cheeks.

Quietly, without disturbing her, as if she understood the turmoil which had begun inside the heart of the girl, Aunt Tam pushed the iron pot toward César. Quickly he finished what was left in the pot and then leaning back against the chest he began to sing in a deep voice which took on a new beauty in the voluptuousness of the setting. He sang in his own *patois*.

> *Malle couri dan deser*
> *Malle marche dan savane*
> *Malle marche su piquan doré*
> *Malle oui ca yu de moin*

The voice rang high and clear in the stillness of the night. Although Aunt Tam understood very little of the *patois* French she knew enough to divine that what César was singing was a song of homesickness, for the plantation and the country from which he had run away. There was verse after verse each time bringing a refrain.

> *Sange moin dans l'abilateur ce la la?*
> *Mo gagnain soutchien la Louisane*
> *Malle oir ca ya de moin!*

On her pallet of reeds Agnes understood nothing of the song. She had slipped down now into a lying position, her head resting on the crook of one elbow, looking out across the water. The dreaminess still enveloped her, and through it she was dimly aware of César's music, as if it came from a great distance. Now and then a thought took form, lazy, voluptuous thoughts, strange to her. She wondered what it was like to be a man, what Tom was really like inside himself, behind the good looks and the easy, half-cynical manner. And presently she found herself thinking of the gesture made by the sailors as she passed them on the deck of the *San Cristobal*, and what it meant. They were strange thoughts in the mind of a young virgin from Pinckney Street.

Then the singing ceased suddenly as César rose to put more wood and damp leaves on the smudge fires. As he bent over the dim flames he said, "Tomorrow we eat better. Demain we come into César's pays. . . . César's country."

They slept well, even Agnes who had slept all the day. Outside the thatched shelter, César lay on a pile of reeds under the open sky.

In the morning they set out again on their journey but they did not return to the great muddy river. César took them further and further into the vast swamp. When Aunt Tam asked when they would arrive in New Orleans he explained that they were not going to New Orleans at all. New Orleans was a *mauvais* town now, filled with Yankee soldiers and bandits from up North. He had heard about it from sailors in Havana. It was not a safe place to take the ladies. He would take them first to his own country, to the plantation that was his home. Then if it was safe he would conduct them to New Orleans.

When Agnes heard the news, she began to cry. Aunt Tam tried to comfort her but experienced very little success, perhaps because she herself did not mind if they never reached New Orleans. Sitting there holding the parasol over Agnes, she was happy. She would have so many things to write in her journal when they camped again for the night.

César, now rowing, now poling the boat, took them through forests of cypresses and great meadowlands of reeds, following the serpentine course of the bayou, now and then taking to a *raccourci* so narrow that he had to get ashore and push or pull the clumsy dory through the beds of mauve water hyacinths that were like blankets of pale orchids set in emerald green. And presently Agnes forgot her disappointment and became lost again in a kind of waking dream in which strange thoughts and colored fancies passed through her brain like shadows in a magic lantern show.

In New Orleans the news of the fate of the *San Cristobal* was brought up the river by a Philadelphia schooner. The Captain reported that a Spanish ship had been found drifting in the Gulf. Apparently she had dragged her anchor and at last broken the cable which held it. On board the ship there was no one but the

Captain dead in his cabin of what appeared to be cholera. The ship's papers showed that she was bound from Havana to New Orleans with a mixed cargo. The Philadelphia schooner, *Betsy Ann* by name and commanded by Captain Philander Pike, had towed the boat inshore and anchored her there. No member of the crew was willing to stay aboard her.

In a little while, the news of the ghost ship spread everywhere in the city, along the wharves and then through the French market and into the cafés, where with each repetition the tale grew in fantasy until it was reported that the ship was manned only by a crew of skeletons and that when she was first sighted, at night, she was ablaze with light. Around Congo Square it was even told among the negroes that the ship herself was only the ghost of an old Spanish slave ship which had gone down with everyone on board during the great hurricane of 1809.

About noon the news reached David Wicks, sitting in the port authority's office in place of Tom Bedloe who had not come in at all that day. All morning David had waited for him, uncertain in his timid, dreamy way of what decisions to make in the cases which had come up before him. Once or twice he had considered sending a black boy round to Tom's billet to inquire after him, but each time, after hesitation, he had decided that Tom had had a bad night at the Café Imperial and would turn up before it was time to lunch.

But in the end the hour of lunch had come without any sign or message from Tom and he went out into the hot streets, vaguely alarmed but unable to decide upon any course of action. In any case he could not afford to be late to lunch.

He was having noon-day dinner at the General's house and it was not an engagement to which he looked forward with pleasure. The bullying manner of the General always made him uncomfortable and the General's wife terrified him.

The dinner was not good. Even David who had small concern for food was aware of its indifference. It was a kind of New England boiled dinner prepared with contempt by a black Louisiana cook in the kitchen adjoining the horses belowstairs and it was sloppily served by a middle-aged soldier in uniform, thus saving the expense of an extra servant. Nor was there any conversation

[99]

worthy of the name, but only a series of tirades denouncing everything in the State of Louisiana, delivered by the General as if he were addressing an assembly hall filled with people. The only interruption came from the General's wife whose pouter-pigeon bosom rose and fell with pleasure at the General's denunciations. Now and then when he paused for breath Aunt Louisa managed to put in a word, urging him to fresh outbursts. Meanwhile, David sat there dreamily, trying to eat the bad food, half-listening to the long account of fresh outrages committed by the citizens of New Orleans against the innocent, well-meaning Union troops and the benevolent carpetbaggers, and wishing vaguely that heaven and nature had not allied him to Uncle James and Aunt Louisa.

And then just as the baked apple was brought in, an orderly appeared with two messages for the General. Opening them he read them both through, his face growing slowly more and more purple with indignation. When he had finished he turned to the orderly and said, "Tell Colonel Moss he is to send out a battalion at once and round up every one of them. Shut them up and keep them shut up."

The man saluted and went out and when he had gone the General slapped the papers on the table and said, "Damned foreigners!" and asked the soldier who served them to bring him a glass of baking soda dissolved in water.

"It's a damned shame! What chance has a man's digestion . . . always being disturbed even at meal times."

He tossed the messages across the table for his wife and David to read.

The first was simply a report of the finding of the *San Cristobal* with its Captain dead in his cabin. The second was more grave. A messenger had come up from down river to report that three sailors, Spanish by origin, and members of the crew of the *San Cristobal*, had been captured. A detachment of Union soldiers had come upon them on a marshy island near Pilotstown. They were starving and ill and half-devoured by mosquitoes. At first the detachment had believed them to be escaped Confederate prisoners, but when, at last, a man was found who could speak Spanish, they learned that they were deserting sailors who had left the *San Cristobal* because of the cholera aboard. Thirty-seven of them in all had left the ship and were now scattered among the islands in the Delta, all of them possibly carrying the horrible disease with them. It was bad enough already with yellow fever gaining daily in the city and the adjoining parishes; the presence of cholera would only increase the panic that was beginning to spread through New Orleans.

But at the end of the message there was a line or two the significance of which the General in his agitation had overlooked. It was his wife who caught their meaning. She put down the paper suddenly and going a shade paler, she said, "James, did you read the last of this?"

"Yes, of course I read it. I read all my dispatches thoroughly."

For a moment she hesitated and then turning toward David she said, "Would you mind, David, going into the parlor for your coffee. I'll send it in to you. There's something I must discuss privately with the General."

So, David, relieved at the prospect of peace in the drawing room went away and when he had gone, Aunt Louisa said, "James, you didn't read all of it! You didn't read about the two women."

"I read about the two women. Creoles probably . . . rebel strumpets! Trash!"

The General's wife picked up the dispatch. Her hand was shaking now. She read, "The escaped sailors spoke of two American ladies, accompanied by a giant negro, who had been passengers aboard the *San Cristobal*. They said the ladies were left on board. The ship was empty when discovered and we have been unable to find any trace of them. The fugitives described them as a middle-aged woman and a young girl."

The General regarded his wife and bluntly said, "Well!"

"Well nothing," said his wife. "It sounds to me as if it was Tam and Agnes."

At that the General showed faint signs of agitation. "It couldn't be," he said. "They were safe with Captain Hazlitt on the *Allegheny*. I know Hazlitt. He's not the sort of man to permit such a thing. Tam and Agnes aboard a dirty Spanish freight boat. It's impossible!"

His wife was silent for a moment. "I don't know," she said. "I hope you're right. I'd agree with you but for Tam with all her crazy ideas. . . . You've got to do something about it. Ethan would never forgive us if anything happened to Agnes. She's a silly young girl who knows nothing about the world . . . and Tam is no better."

The General gravely drank his baking soda pausing only to belch. Then he said, "It would be very unfortunate . . . very unfortunate indeed."

He had scarcely finished speaking when the answer came in the form of the Captain of the U.S. Gunboat *Tallahassee*. He was a tall thin man with a sallow face. When he had saluted, he said, "I am afraid I have bad news for you, sir."

His boat had come, he said, straight from Havana and he brought a message which concerned members of the General's family—by name, Miss Abigail and Miss Agnes Wicks. They were aboard the *San Cristobal*. He already knew the fate of the ship. He had a letter from Captain Hazlitt of the *Allegheny*, but Captain Hazlitt could not have known what had happened to the *San Cristobal*.

At this point, the General's wife, who was experiencing strangely mixed emotions, partly excitement over the story and partly a feeling of faintness over its implications, sent the orderly to fetch her a glass of port.

Silently, indignantly, as if all the inhabitants of the terrestrial globe were joined in one vast conspiracy to torment him and aggravate his dyspepsia, the General tore open the letter and read. When he had finished, he said, "You were right. It's that damned Tam."

"Where are they?" cried the General's wife. "What has become of them?" Her voice trembled with hysteria. She was, it was clear, on the verge of one of her "attacks." "Answer me," she cried, "don't sit there like a fool!"

At this, the General said in a loud voice, "How am I to know? How is Hazlitt to know in Havana? Good God! Woman! Show some sense!"

The General's wife gave a faint scream and said, "General Wicks! I won't be spoken to like that!" And the Commander of the *Tallahassee*, fearing a dramatic scene, made a respectful but uneasy exit, leaving word where he could be found, if needed.

When he had gone the General rose pompously and said, "All this, Louisa, was your idea—the idea of having Tam and Agnes come here, and the idea of surprising David and Tom Bedloe. I shouldn't like to face either Tom or David with the news. That is your job, Mrs. Wicks. You thought up this romantic nonsense. I am off to the St. Charles Hotel to do what I can to find out what has become of that fool Tam and poor little Agnes."

And before she could attack him or scream, or faint, he was gone.

For a moment she contemplated running after him, forcing him to come back and help her break the news to David, innocently drinking his coffee in the other room. But she remembered that after all it had been her idea to bring them here and to bring them secretly. The General had been against it from the beginning, believing that a solid business man like Ethan Wicks would never accept so wild a plan. There was no romance in the General —no one knew that better than his wife. Indeed the whole plan, like her tantrums and vapors, grew out of starved romanticism, out of being married to a man who regarded the marital act merely as a rather unpleasant necessity like physicking once a week.

All without knowing it she had planned a romantic meeting for Agnes and Tom Bedloe as a vicarious pleasure. In the long hours in which there was little to occupy her—for she had no female companionship save the hostile black cook and the crow-faced and even more hostile wife of the Quartermaster—she had remained for long periods engaged in reveries in which hazily she imagined herself to be Agnes Wicks and her lover to be Tom Bedloe. It was, when she thought of it, a very silly diversion, but because she enjoyed it she tried not to think how silly it was. For in spite of the fact that she came from Maine and was "smart" and a penurious housekeeper, the pathetic fact remained that God had made her flesh in the mold of a female, and females at a certain period of their lives when very often their attractions had already faded, were subject to an exaggerated romanticism. Although it had never occurred to her, simply because she refused to allow it to occur to her, the fact was that she herself was a little in love with Tom Bedloe, not only because he was good-looking and young, but because he was everything the General was not, and because he was a symbol of all she had missed in life, all that it was now too late ever to experience. In her less excited moments, she herself saw that the whole idea of Aunt Tam's and Agnes' visit was folly, but for the remainder of the time, it seemed to her not only perfectly logical but romantic and exciting.

The anger caused by the unchivalrous, the rebellious behavior of the General brought on hot flushes again, and before she went in to relate the news to David, she took two of the large pills advised by the Quartermaster General's wife as efficacious under such circumstances.

She was glad that it was David and not Tom Bedloe whom she was to face. David was a poet and a milksop, and Agnes was only his sister. It would be different with Tom. She shuddered, not without pleasure, at the thought of what he would say to her, at the thought of the curse-words he would use. She would tell David first and David, in the natural course of events, would tell Tom.

So, pulling herself together, she opened the heavy doors of the MacTavish drawing room which always awed her a little by its size and elegance, and went in to tell David.

He seemed to take the news calmly enough, in his dreamy way, as if he did not understand the full seriousness of it. He listened and when she had finished, he only sat still without speaking at all, as if turning the thing over in his mind. And now the calmness which she had hoped for at the beginning of the interview, only irritated her. There was no drama whatever in the scene. It was all flat. So after a moment she said, "I hope you appreciate what it means. They may be dead . . . both of them, of cholera . . . a loathsome disease. Or they may be held prisoners by the drunken crew. They may be suffering worse than death. Even if they have escaped, the prospect is a terrible one. All that swamp country is overrun by renegade negroes and escaped war prisoners and convicts. What chance have two gently bred women in a vast swamp filled with alligators and snakes in human form?"

Even this catalogue of horrors seemed not to move the boy. He sat staring at her with his large blue eyes, and she thought, contemptuously, "He ought to have been a girl! Agnes is the boy of the twins." The General's wife under other circumstances might have developed strong tastes in men.

Then he rose and said, "It is very serious. I think it was a very foolish idea in the beginning. I'll find Tom. He'll know what to do."

"The General," she said, "will of course do everything possible, even to sending out a whole regiment if necessary."

But he was already out of the room, leaving her with a baffled feeling that this callow, feminine young poet believed her as big a fool as did the blustering General. As he went out the door it dawned upon her that his silence was not the silence of indifference but of contempt.

He hadn't said anything to the General's wife because he could think of nothing to say. An odd thing had happened to him while he sat there listening to her. While she told her story, justifying herself always, there rose inside him an odd tumult of contempt and hatred, and when she began her wretched and sadistic catalogue of the things which might have happened to his sister Agnes and poor old Aunt Tam, there crystallized out of the tumult of his emotions a grain of pure distilled hatred for the dumpy, middle-aged frustrated woman, not hatred for her because of the misfortune she had brought into the midst of his family, but hatred for all the things she was and stood for, all the things which he hated in his own background and in New England. It was as if he understood for the first time all the things which crippled his own existence and stifled whatever talent he had, so that he always wrote restrained and sentimental verses about snow-storms and graveyards, instead of writing of the odd turbulent things he sometimes felt deep inside him. As he went out of the room he thought, "I will never see Aunt Louisa again, no matter what happens. She is a horrible, monstrous, woman."

He was young, not yet twenty-one, and for his years he was young, having lived always under the shadow of a powerful, protecting, dull man, Ethan Wicks. He had lived always in books and in fantasy, and so for a little time the horrible implications of his sister Agnes' possible fate had no reality for him. His own love for her, that special curious love of one twin for the other, had caused him pain so great that sometimes at night his pillow was damp with his own tears. No, nothing must happen to Agnes! Nothing could happen to Agnes! Things such as Aunt Louisa had just recounted did not happen to people like his own family, living respectably and quietly in Boston, secure in the knowledge that they had only to step outside the door to have a reassuring glimpse of the Common, or perhaps even of Mr. Emerson or some member of the Lowell family. There was something sensational and indecent about the whole thing, an indecency which had somehow to do with Aunt Louisa and possibly even with Tom Bedloe.

The element of Tom was always in the background, menacing and riotous and bewildering. In the beginning he had hated Tom because Agnes was always talking and thinking of him, and then presently he had become used to him, especially after Tom brought him to New Orleans and Agnes was no longer at hand to watch him with abnormally bright eyes and pink cheeks. He had got used to Tom but he never understood him. He had never even hinted at Tom's philanderings in his letters home, partly because it would only make trouble and unhappiness, and partly because he was not quite certain of how dangerous and significant the philanderings were. In his vague, bookish way he was both ignorant and innocent, more like Agnes herself than a soldier. He knew vaguely about the violence and untidiness of the lives of most of the common soldiers, but his own fastidiousness drove him away from any close knowledge of the details of their lives. What puzzled him was that Tom, who was such a nice fellow and a gentleman when he chose to be, appeared to lead much the same sort of goatish and disorderly existence, on a more expensive and elegant scale to be sure, but otherwise not very different.

Yet Tom was at the same time, secretly and curiously, also a hero to him, partly because to David, Byron was not only a great and romantic poet but a great hero, and Tom, with his wildness and lady-killing, was like Byron. It was very odd to feel inside you that you too were like Byron, and still be unable to do anything about it, always to be chained by doubts and fears and paralyzed at the merest contact with women, always driven back to books and dreaming instead of action. The reason, he divined, vaguely in the midst of his rage and hatred for the General's wife, had something to do with Aunt Louisa, with all her kind of people and her kind of life—a life that was mean and small and thin-blooded with no color or excitement. Sometimes he thought that if only he could overcome or destroy these subtle chains which held him prisoner, if just once he could accept the invitation to life which Tom had now and then held out to him, he might be a great poet writing passionately as Byron and Shelley wrote, instead of writing pretty small things about snowstorms and graveyards.

How to escape, he did not know.

What he did know was that in such a crisis as he now found himself, Tom was the person who would know what to do—not the General or the General's wife or anyone in all New Orleans, either Yankee or Rebel—but Tom, because Tom would act. Tom would go to the rescue of Agnes, as knights went in other days. He would find her. He would save her. It was Tom he must find.

So he hired an old fiacre drawn by a broken-down mule, as good a vehicle as was to be found in all the city, and set out for the port office. Tom was not there and he ordered the driver to go direct to the de Lèche house.

Outside the door he stood on the step, his head and his heart still on the borders of hysteria from the confusion of his emotions. He pulled the bell again and again, listening to the distant jangle at the far end of the closed garden and at last the door was opened by an old negro whom he had never seen before.

Quickly the old man told him that Monsieur Tom was not there. He had not been there since meal time the evening before. Nor were any of the family there. The old Baroness had gone into the country to stay with a cousin taking old Seraphine with her. The young Baroness had gone to the plantation Bel Manoir.

In Tom's room he found nothing which gave him any hint of what had happened. It was exactly as Tom had left it, as if he had walked out meaning to return in a little while. The papers on the desk were in the same disorder, the bed unslept in. For half an hour, he went through the papers trying to discover some clue to his whereabouts but there was none. There were two letters from Agnes written long before she left Boston, and a great many official documents which to David meant nothing. That was all.

He went to the doorway and stood for a time looking out over the gallery into the garden, considering what he should do. Only one thing, he knew, remained and that was to go to La Lionne's establishment. Tom might be there. The tumult in his heart had abated a little but the sense of rebellion remained. He was filled with an odd reckless fury, feeling a wild desire to live as Tom lived, wildly seizing every pleasure that came his way.

Until now he had never gone to the Café Imperial, even at Tom's half-mocking invitation to take him there and "break him in." There had always been dread in his heart. Now the dread suddenly was gone, lost in his fury at the General's wife and his fear of what had happened to Agnes. Poor little Agnes!

It was three in the afternoon with the muggy heat creeping in through doors and windows, when Big Ernestine came into La Lionne's room with her black coffee to draw back the red brocade curtains and let in a thin hot line of daylight.

La Lionne was in better spirits of late; the change had come over her since Mama Tolanne began working her spell. She had hope again. She resumed her efforts at elaborate make-up to conceal the ravages of twenty-two years of hard living. She had even given up thinking of selling the Café Imperial. She lived for the moment on the blind hope of a woman turned romantic at the approach of middle-age, a wild hope, based upon folly and desire and so all the more desperate.

This afternoon Big Ernestine had come in grinning. She said, "Mama Tolanne's spell has begun to work. There is a young man downstairs to see you. He is a friend of Major Tom."

At that La Lionne first asked for her mirror and then as Ernestine put the coffee on the table beside her, she said, "What kind of a young man?" And Big Ernestine described him. Very young, she said he was, with blond hair and blue eyes. She chuckled, "Un vierge, sans doute! He looks frightened of the place."

At once La Lionne knew who it was because Major Tom had told her about David, describing his shyness and his blond good looks and his fear of the rowdy life of the Café Imperial. At the same moment, a plot formed itself in the head of the French woman, not a very new plot certainly for a woman in her business but one which sometimes worked. She said to Ernestine, "Send him up to me in ten minutes and tell Clélie to get up and dress herself and come here as quickly as she can."

In the ten minutes, La Lionne rose from the bed and made up her face and dusted her hair with the imitation gold powder, put on a *peignoir* trimmed with lace and got back into the ebony and mother-of-pearl bed. She had done none of this in order to lure the boy for herself. She had no illusions. She knew that anyone as experienced as herself would only terrify him and that to a boy so young she would seem an old woman. She meant merely to make his call as attractive and charming as possible. The rest she would leave to Clélie who was younger even than the boy himself, younger at least in years.

He came in shyly and at her invitation he sat on a chair on the far side of the room. For a moment he looked about him, with a bewildered air and La Lionne watching him thought, "What a charming boy! He looks like an angel!" and gave a faint and sentimental sigh. Then she went into her role—that of a *femme du monde*, gracious, charming, simple and inordinately respectable. Only her voice betrayed her, the champagne-husky voice, which long ago, out of many brawls, had taken on a coarsened quality like the voices of street women.

He told her almost at once what he had come for—but he told her nothing of the whole story, that he was trying to find Tom because his sister, Tom's fiancée, was either lost or dead or held a prisoner. This was not the place to mention the name of one's sister. As he talked he seemed to relax a little as if he found the place less terrifying than he had expected and La Lionne herself not very different from what European ladies must be. In Boston, of course "ladies" were quite different, but even he understood that the world was larger than Boston. He found her accent fascinating and surely there was nothing sordid or rough about the voluptuously decorated room.

She told him that she herself had not seen Major Tom for more than a fortnight, and she was distressed that he had disappeared. At the same time she pulled the bell-rope beside the bed and almost immediately the door opened and Ernestine came in. She had not far to come for she had been standing all the while just outside the door, listening.

"Bring some iced champagne," said La Lionne, "unless (and she turned to David) you would prefer something made of gin or rum."

For a second, only a second, he hesitated. He had never in all his life drunk anything, but now he was rebellious. The hatred of the General's wife and the thought of Byron was still driving him into emotional recklessness. He heard himself saying, "Champagne, thank you."

While they waited, La Lionne made worldly conversation, about his life, how he liked New Orleans, what career he meant to take up after the war, but all the time, behind the wild hope that somehow through Mama Tolanne's charms and friendship with this boy, she might get Tom back, there hid a terror, perhaps that Tom was kidnaped and prisoner, or even dead. She thought of Les Défenseurs with their record of assassinations of carpetbaggers and Union soldiers. Her Tom was a good mark for them, involved as he was with the General and all the corruption over cotton and shipping. But she said nothing of this. It could come later on.

Then the door opened and Ernestine came in closely followed by the girl Clélie in a crimson ball gown, dressed for the evening's entertainment. She was a slender girl, not yet eighteen, with a skin of satin washed with pale gold and great black eyes fringed with long lashes. As she moved she had the quality of a lily about her. It was not for nothing that she was the favorite of La Lionne and that La Lionne meant to take her to Paris. The girl had pride and intelligence and wits. Some of the best blood of Louisiana flowed in her veins. And she had a trick of smiling, a wide, honest charming smile, at the same time casting down her eyes as if suddenly stricken with shyness. In Paris she could have what she wanted; she was too good for New Orleans, even in the old days when gentlemen still came to the Café Imperial, much too good for the cheap, disorganized city it had become, when one no longer saw a gentleman or a *connoisseur*.

La Lionne, from the bed, presented David Wicks to Mademoiselle Clélie Legrand. "She is a great friend of mine and of Major Tom. I thought you would like to meet her."

David bowed gravely, a little shy and a little timid, but much less shy than the girl herself appeared. Her downcast eyes and the faint smile gave him courage; they even made him feel bold.

Big Ernestine poured the champagne with a glass for La Lionne propped up in bed, and they all drank to the health of Major Tom and the hope of finding him very shortly. La Lionne took over the conversation boldly, telling David that she meant to take Clélie with her to Paris where Clélie would study to be a singer and actress; and for a time while they drank champagne, she talked of Paris, and for the first time there was a nostalgic fire and beauty in what she said.

For a little time she made the great and beautiful city come alive for the two young people who had never seen it. For them she made live all the life and light and color of the boulevards, the immense ordered spaces of the Place de la Concorde, the splendor of the Louvre and the Tuileries. She told them about the balls she had gone to as a young girl and the famous men she had known well—the composers, the painters, the Princes and Dukes, the singers and actresses.

"Ah," she sighed, slipping back into French, *"c'est une belle existence qu'on mène à Paris . . . une si belle existence. Comme je voudrais avoir la jeunesse et la beauté de Clélie."* And in her broken English, "Life is so beautiful when one is young. One ought never to deny it. Pleasure, love and beauty do not last for long."

She had barely finished the speech when there was a soft knock at the door and Big Ernestine came in to say that it was necessary to see Madame for a moment. La Lionne got out of the bed, drawing the *peignoir* modestly about her, slipped her feet into pink mules and went to the door. In the doorway she turned for a second and said, "The place is yours, *mes enfants.* I will not disturb you."

As she closed the door behind her the tears came into her eyes. They were no longer tears of self-pity. She had intoxicated herself with talk and homesickness. She wasn't thinking now of Major Tom or herself, but of the two young people—*si jeunes, si beaux, si simples,* with all life and love before them.

And inside the room she had achieved a miracle, leaving behind her a boy who was no longer timid and shy, because in her nostalgic description of Paris, there was a poetry which his own poet's nature recognized, a poetry which stimulated the faint halting desire he had experienced at the first glimpse of Clélie in the doorway. Yes, life was something to be enjoyed, not denied and tormented as the General's horrible wife had treated it, as all his world had treated it. It should be gay and friendly and beautiful and a little wild.

The champagne too was doing its work.

The girl looked at him, her great black eyes shining. *"Vous êtes beau,"* she said, and like a child speaking, *"Vous êtes gentil."*

With his schoolboy French accent he answered, *"Vous aussi, Mademoiselle . . . vous êtes très . . . très belle."*

"Merci." She poured him more champagne and as she gave him his glass their fingers touched for a moment.

"La Lionne est une brave femme," she said. *"Elle a toujours été très gentille pour moi."*

"Oui . . . elle est très généreuse."

Then she asked him if he had been before to the Café Imperial and he told her that he went out very little. Most of the time he stayed at home writing and thinking.

"Un poète?" said the girl. *"Un philosophe?"*

He smiled and told her that he only hoped one day to be a poet, a philosopher. For a little while longer they went on talking, politely, correctly, like two well brought up Boston young people on a sofa in a Beacon Street house, but presently the girl said,

"Vous ne connaissez pas l'amour?"

He blushed, and said in his bad French, *"Non. Vous savez que dans mon pays les choses sont différentes."*

"Quelle dommage." A dreamy look came into her eyes, *"L'amour est si beau."* Then she touched his sleeve gently, *"Je peux vous servir comme institutrice. Ça me fera du plaisir."* She spoke as if she were saying politely and innocently, "If you like, I can give you lessons in French."

He took her hand and kissed it, partly because that was what Lord Byron would have done and partly because she was so understanding and so charming.

"Je le veux . . . Clélie."

"Bon . . . David." She laughed and kissed him, not on the lips but on the cheek. *"Tu est gentil."*

It was true that Clélie had great talents, that she would go far in Paris. La Lionne was quite right, for Clélie adapted her style to the subject.

And so David stayed.

It was nearly six when he left the Café Imperial. He was no nearer to finding Tom and he still did not know what had become of Agnes and Aunt Tam. But it was an afternoon which he remembered for the rest of his brief life, gratefully, for it changed everything. From that afternoon of his life, he was free. He had been freed in the strangest fashion by three women—the dragon Aunt Louisa, La Lionne and the child Clélie. The stars moving in their heaven had brought them together at exactly the right moment in exactly the proper fashion.

He walked through the noisy crowd in the bar of the Café Imperial and out of the door, his chest thrust out a little, his head back, a little the way Tom Bedloe walked, as if he owned all the world with all the beauty and pleasure there was to be found in it.

The King himself had given the first de Lèche the rich acres of the doomed plantation of Bel Manoir. When the great house was built near the end of the eighteenth century and filled with silver and furniture and fine linen, the great river had been a mile from its great painted mahogany doors. Big French houses had to have avenues and so the first de Lèche had planted an allée of live oaks from the house to the landing stage on the bank of the river. Each spring when the flood waters swept down from the north carrying with them the rich earth of the wilderness, they had cut urther and further into the banks, moving closer each year to the great house itself. Each year in March the landing stage was swept away and each year when it was replaced, it was anchored nearer to he house. The descendants of the first de Lèche measured the advance of the mighty river by the number of oak trees it devoured each season from the long rows of the allée. Some years it devoured wo or three. In one great flood year it had devoured eleven. Each ear it carried away more acres of rich plantation land. Each ear it came nearer to the great house. Before the young Baroness reached the age of the old Baroness the river would devour the house itself with all its gardens and dependences. Where once Bel Manoir had stood there would be only the turgid waters of the Mississippi.

It was a true French-Spanish house, unlike the great Georgian houses built by the Americans who had come in after the Louisiana Purchase, built in a style which had grown out of the very soil, not a style imported from another world and another civilization, and so it seemed more than the other great houses in the neighborhood to belong there, set solidly on the rich earth in the midst of marshes and bayous, cypresses and live oaks all hung with silver gray moss.

The walls were of pink brick brought down from Natchez which time and dampness and heat had turned to a silvery rose color. A wide veranda ran all the way round the house at the second floor, suspended between the house itself and the thirty-two white columns which supported the great sloping roof of pinkish tiles. On the side facing the river there was a wide double stairway, in the shape of a horseshoe, with wrought iron balustrades of extraordinary lightness and beauty of design made by the mulatto blacksmiths in the great forge near the slave quarters. Because of the dampness, there were no living rooms on the first floor but only kitchens and vast storerooms which in the great days of the plantation had been filled with rich foods, enough to feed an army. On the second floor were a dining room, a ballroom and a great *salon* and a small library and above these were the bedrooms opening onto a great hall.

When the old Baroness had come to Bel Manoir as a bride straight from Spain, the house was new and the center of life for all the parish. In those days the plantation was like a town with people coming and going constantly in carriages and on horseback for visits that lasted weeks. Rarely was a single bedroom of the house without a cousin or a friend. The slave quarters—a whole village of cypress log cabins beneath the low-spreading live oaks— were filled with happy negroes who themselves entertained relatives and friends from all the countryside and New Orleans itself.

And then when the old Baroness was only twenty-seven, her husband died of the yellow fever in the great house and a curious thing happened to his widow. She had loved him in her cold and passionate Spanish fashion and after his death she came to hate Bel Manoir and the swamps and the bayous and the deathly gray moss, and spent less and less time there. For months at a time the big house was empty save for the house servants and Eugénie the octoroon housekeeper. The Baroness stayed in Paris or Madrid or Seville and sometimes she spent long visits at the family estates in Martinique. She had never really learned to speak English and she never felt comfortable with the Americans who had come in from other parts of the South to take up plantations in the neighborhood of Bel Manoir. They seemed to her strange, sometimes barbaric people, too simple and direct and healthy for her Spanish taste.

The house appeared to return the hostility of the Baroness for when her only child, a son, was twenty-five, he was thrown from a horse and killed at the very foot of the great curving stairway. After that she never again visited the plantation, but her grandson, child of the son killed on the doorstep, returned to Bel Manoir with his bride, the young Baroness, and died there of consumption before he had been married a year.

The old Baroness in her bitterness blamed the house and the young Baroness. The girl was a distant cousin and poor and her mother was an Irishwoman who had been an artist's model in Paris, and the grandson, known as the young Baron, had married her in spite of every intrigue and influence against it. The bitter, icy old Spanish woman knew in her heart that he had died of too much love and that the young Baroness had killed him without even bearing him a child. The old woman hated her granddaughter-in-law most of all because Bel Manoir and all the property in New Orleans and Martinique now belonged to the girl, not only as the widow of the kin but because she herself was a de Lèche. After the young Baroness the only heir was the old woman's nephew, the one-armed young man with the white face whom Tom Bedloe had met in the big house in New Orleans . . . a youth whom the old woman hated as much as she hated the young Baroness because, although he too was tubercular, he had survived her own son, and because he, like her son, was also the victim of the young Baroness, a miserable, bitter victim who in his decadent way found pleasure in his own misery.

And so Bel Manoir had become a place which none of them ever visited. The great house stood empty year after year and the garden ran wild, the camellia trees scraggly and unpruned, the azaleas overrunning the flower border like jungle plants. In the damp, hot climate, houses went to pieces very quickly if they were not tended with love and care, and rot and mildew quickly worked havoc with Bel Manoir. Tiles slipped from the roof and were not replaced. Spindles in the balustrade of the big veranda rotted and fell unnoticed to the ground. Dampness warped and shattered the beauty of the marquetry floor brought long ago from France, and the grass and weeds grew high and deep in the long alleé which led from the house down to the hungry menacing river.

The neighbors said the young Baroness cared nothing for the place save for the money it brought in. She never came near it but she hired an overseer from the North to manage the slaves and operate the place. He lived in a house of his own between the great house and the slave quarters—a leathery-faced, lantern-jawed Yankee from Pennsylvania, Elias Sharp by name, who kept great dogs in his house and slept with the doors and windows locked and barred. In the day time he rode on a big gray mule surrounded by dogs which at his order would have torn to pieces anyone who threatened him.

He was a hard man, living alone save for two mulatto house servants who were also his mistresses. The gentry of the neighboring plantations never saw him; even the storekeepers and overseers passed him by without any sign of recognition when they encountered him on the muddy roads; for Elias Sharp had the most evil of reputations. From the moment he came to the plantation, the old easy life of the Bel Manoir slaves was gone. They worked long hours. They were whipped even for so slight a thing as a rebellious look. And among the slaves of neighboring plantations there were stories of evil punishments, of mutilations and obscene tortures, conceived only in the brain of a madman and a sadist. In the slave quarters of the great houses of the parish, mothers frightened naughty black children by saying, "Eff'n you don't behave yo' self, Elias Sharp'll git you."

Among the slaves there was only one rebel—a great black negro called César. This César was a prodigious fellow, a goat in love, a great singer and the father of half the children in the quarter, and for him Elias Sharp had a special hatred because César was what the ill-favored, sour Sharp would himself have liked to be. And César was shrewd too like a goat, fomenting trouble and singing rebellious songs in the parish dialect which Elias Sharp could not understand. And although Sharp tried every plan of catching him in some rebellion, he never quite succeeded until he at last ordered César's wife, Emilienne, to leave the slave quarters and come to the overseer's house as cook. The same night, César waited outside the house until Elias Sharp went to the privy. There César trapped him and beat him until one of the mulatto girls, hearing Sharp's cries, released the dogs and César escaped into the bayou where the dogs refused to follow him. But that was what Sharp wanted. Now he could have César arrested and hanged. The sheriff of the Parish, no matter how much he detested the evil overseer, could not refuse to arrest a slave who had tried to kill a white man, his master.

But César was already gone, down the river to New Orleans and on to Cuba.

With their leader gone, the slaves at Bel Manoir grew discouraged and the cruelties of Elias Sharp redoubled. For the poor black people there remained only the consolation of song and out of their misery were born a hundred new songs, melancholy and beautiful, which sounded at night across the bayous from the fires of the slave quarters.

But no de Lèche came near the Bel Manoir after the young Baron died. The war broke out between the North and South and the Yankees captured New Orleans and the young Baroness returned from Martinique, but she never came near Bel Manoir. And then one evening about sunset there arrived at the plantation a man named Abraham Hunter.

He was a squat man with bowed legs, a squint and a bald head and he came from Connecticut where he had been bankrupt three times. With him came ten Yankee soldiers.

While the slaves gathered about the soldiers, Abraham Hunter knocked at the door of Elias Sharp's house. The overseer came out, surrounded by his dogs, and Abraham Hunter told the overseer that if he did not keep his dogs in order he would command the soldiers to shoot them on the spot.

Then he proceeded to make a long speech in which he told Elias Sharp that he had come to dispossess him. Reports of his cruelty had reached the military governor of New Orleans who had issued orders that the overseer Elias Sharp should be sent away. The plantation, with its stored cotton and cane, its mules and horses and the great decaying house were now the property of himself, Abraham Hunter. They had been bestowed upon him by the military governor. And at last the squat little man launched into a peroration of fearful hypocrisy. Turning to the slaves he told them that they were now free and their own masters. He would pay them for moving the cotton to the river pier for shipping to New Orleans. No more would they suffer the cruelty and persecution of their overseer. They were a noble people wronged in the past. From now on, liberated by the great people of the North, they were the equal of all whites. They would be able to vote and send negro men to the legislature.

"Raise up your heads!" cried Abraham Hunter, "you are now free men!"

Two or three of the slaves who understood English translated for the others. They listened, their big mouths hanging open in astonishment. Dazed, they kept silence for a time, while the Pennsylvania overseer and the Connecticut carpetbagger glared at each other. One of the dogs leapt at a soldier. There was the quick report of a carbine and the dog, shuddering a little, was dead. The sun dropped below the flat horizon and suddenly it was night, with only the faint glow of the oil light from the overseer's house lighting the black faces of the startled slaves.

Elias Sharp said nothing. Then suddenly he spat a stream of tobacco juice on the ground, turned and went into the house, closing and bolting the door behind him.

The closing of the door appeared to release the choked emotions of the negroes. They began suddenly to shout and sing, to dance and to bellow like cattle along the levee, and as the carpetbagger moved off to take possession of the great house, they followed behind him, still singing and shouting and rolling on the ground. They followed him all the way to the house and up the horseshoe stairway, streaming through the dark hallways while the old housekeeper with a lamp led her new master from room to room showing him the warped and mildewed splendors of Bel Manoir.

He ordered a fire to be built in the great bedroom where the old Baroness had come as a bride, and chose the finest sheets to be warmed, and wine to be brought from the cellar. And slyly he watched the crowd which followed him, noticing the young girls and especially the light-colored ones. At last he selected one called Anastasie, a timid, doe-like girl of fifteen, for his companion. It was all easy and safe for he was in the ring that was bent upon punishing the Secessionists. Together they could loot plantation after plantation. They could take what they liked. Thus was Connecticut liberating Louisiana.

Before Abraham Hunter bedded for the night, the light of the great bonfires from the slave quarters illuminated the whole of the great bedroom, and the sound of wild singing and the beating of tom-toms echoed through the big house. Down among the cabins a half-mile from the house, there were orgies in progress, born of sudden release from years of bitter cruelty and suppression.

When Elias Sharp, the overseer, went in the house and bolted the door after him, he discovered that it was empty. He went from room to room looking for the two mulatto girls, calling out their names and swearing. The dogs followed at his heels sniffing, their tails between their legs. In the bedroom he found the cupboard doors open and empty. In the kitchen there were no signs of any preparations for supper. Then he understood. They had simply gone away. Somehow they had learned of the coming of Abraham Hunter and known that the reign of Elias Sharp was finished.

The sight of the empty, untouched kitchen filled him with a vague alarm and something like fear. In his hardness and self-sufficiency he had never thought before of being lonely or alone. He had never thought of being afraid or of flight. Now, standing there, in the empty dimly lighted house, he was alone, and for the first time the idea of retribution occurred to him. That damned Yankee interloper would be of no help. All he wanted was to get possession of the cotton, sell it and clear out for fresh thieveries.

Through the window he saw the rising fires in the slave quarters and heard the sound of the tom-toms and the wild cries and the jungle singing. That damned Yankee had told them that they were free . . . free! The word echoed in his mind. Already they were like wild animals turned suddenly out of a cage. They might do anything. They might . . . he tried to turn his thoughts away from what they might do, but it was no good. Even when he tried to think of other things, the visions of what they might do, horrible visions, kept turning before his eyes.

And then suddenly a curious shivering sensation crept along his spine. It was like the hair rising on the back of a dog and he knew that he was being watched by eyes he could not see.

Quickly he put out the light so that the whole house was in darkness and still, so still and empty that he could hear the breathing of the great dogs even above the shouts and screams and drums from the slave quarters.

He thought, feeling suddenly cold, "I could make a break for it to the big house. They'd have to protect me."

But would they? By now the carpetbagger and his soldiers were probably all drunk or wandering about in the overgrown garden watching the fires and the dancing. All the carpetbagger wanted was to be rid of him. He remembered senselessly the long record of cruelties he had perpetrated, finding even now in his fear, a sinister satisfaction in them that was like looking at a naked young girl. He was a hard man who had never given or asked for mercy, and now he knew there was no use in asking any from the blacks he had whipped and tortured for so many years. And again, even in the darkness, the feeling of being watched returned and the hair along his spine rose like the hair on the backs of the growling dogs.

He thought, "I might get away into the swamp. I could find a *pirogue* there and make my way to New Orleans." And then the afterthought, "If I can get as far as from here to the edge of the bayou . . . if it was dark I could do it. I might have a chance." But it was not dark. The great fires from the slave quarters illuminated the whole landscape. Anyone could see you making a break for the swamp. And he was certain now that he was being watched.

[120]

Half to himself, he said, "I'll send out the dogs. That will draw the fire if they are watching the cabin."

He had no feeling for animals. He fed them with his own hand to keep them attached to him. The death of the dog outside the cabin had caused him no regret. He would not need them any longer. The only thing that mattered was escape. He must get away and he would be safe alone in the swamp. The dogs would only serve to betray him.

So cautiously he opened the door a little way and two of the remaining three dogs rushed out barking. That side of the house was on the far side from the fires in the slave quarters with a rectangle of black shadow. As soon as the dogs emerged into the band of firelight a dozen rifles were fired and they fell kicking, without a sound. A bullet struck the door sill beside him as he closed and bolted the door. So that was it. Either the Yankee soldiers had given the negroes their carbines or they were drunk in the big house and the negroes had taken them.

He moved a table against the door and waited, for what he did not quite know.

The shouting and singing outside had now changed to a kind of rhythmic wail, guided by the beat of tom-toms, a wail straight out of Africa, led, he knew, by Tombo, a great skinny black man only a few years removed from the jungles of Senegal. It was always Tombo who led them, even some of the mulattoes and octoroons with white blood and great grandparents born in slavery, back to the jungle. Tombo had been whipped and branded for it, but nothing had stopped him. When he was seized with an attack of nostalgic misery, the big bony negro would sit over his drum and begin to pound and wail, while one by one the others gathered round him from all points of the slave quarters, moaning and wailing in unison. Tombo had them again. Tombo could make them do as he chose. Now in the blackness of the room he saw Tombo's face, contorted, his eyes rolled back until only the whites were visible, spittle drooling from his lips, as he beat his drum and wailed and jerked his head until the bones of the neck cracked.

"Escape," he thought, "I must get away to the swamp."

Kneeling, he put his ear to the door and heard the sound of breathing on the opposite side of the panel. Quickly he took his revolver and fired through the door and then listened again. This time he heard no breathing but only the sound of "Bon Dieu! Sauvez moi!" and two low groans in quick succession.

"That'll put the fear of God in their black hearts," he thought, and then almost at once he knew he had made his case more hopeless. They had no fear in their hearts now. Nothing could put fear into them. That damned carpetbagger had told them they were free and could do as they pleased.

He was sweating now. He did not feel hot but the drops ran down his face and he could smell his own sweat. He began to curse, himself, the slaves, the carpetbagger, his own mother for having brought him into the world. And then above the smell of his own fear-sweat, his thin flaring nostrils caught the odor of smoke. He sniffed again to make certain he had made no mistake, and then he knew they were firing the house. Outside the glare was heightened, showing bright through the cracks in the shutters. Then he understood the sound of rustling and scratching; they had piled brush and dried reeds close against the house on all sides and set fire to it. He could hear the crackling of the flames and in a second, it seemed, they were licking at the bolted shutters.

Turning toward the kitchen he knocked over a chair in the darkness. The last dog began suddenly to howl and blindly he kicked at it. Stumbling he found the water pail at last but when he lifted it he found there was little water in it. The sluts hadn't even bothered to fill it before running away. Hysterically, he flung it against the smoking shutter, but the fire was all about him now, on every side of the house, licking at the shutters and even creeping through the cracks about the door.

Cursing, he took up his pistol, thinking, "I'll run for it and shoot as many bastards on the way as I can hit." There wasn't much time. The room was suddenly hot like the inside of an oven. Pulling away the scorched table and releasing the bolt, he swung back the door and leapt through the flames.

As he ran he headed for the cane brake, thinking that once there he could find his way to the swamp. Half way across the open space he heard rifle shots but the bullets did not hit him. The last of the dogs somersaulted and dying, tripped him, and as he scrambled to his feet a gun butt struck him forward again on his face.

They had shot at the dog. They had not meant to kill him; they wanted him alive.

Consciousness came back to him as the beating of the blood in his head took on the rhythm of the thumping tom-tom. It was pain which awakened him, a fierce bright stab of pain across the muscles of his abdomen, and as he wakened the smell of burning flesh was in his nostrils. Out of the haze which enveloped his consciousness he knew suddenly that the flesh was his own flesh.

He was surrounded by faces, some black, some gray, some yellow, peeking and peering at him in the wild firelight. They were all the faces he knew— the faces of the men and women, the boys and girls, he had starved and whipped and branded since he had come to Bel Manoir. There was a strong smell of rum in the warm damp air and above the tom-toms there rose the sound of wild singing. The faces were wild like the faces of beasts, so frightening that he closed his eyes again as the stabbing flash of pain accompanied by the smell of burning flesh smote him again.

They had stripped him naked to lay him on a table outside the door of the forge like a hog at butchering time. Inside the forge they kept the irons at a white heat over burning charcoal. They were branding the name "Bel Manoir" across his abdomen as if he were a steer. As consciousness came and went in waves he felt a fresh stab of pain and knew with a cold horror that they had gelded him. Then a hand scratched full across his face, the long nails tearing out the flesh and with it pieces of his coarse beard, and opening his eyes in agony, he saw the two mulatto girls he had kept as prisoners in his house. They were bending over him, tearing his flesh away in long strips.

He tried to call out, to make the carpetbagger and his soldiers hear him, but the sound died in his throat. Above the din of the drums and the singing they could not have heard him.

At last when they had finished the branding, they lifted him and turning him over on his face began to lash him with the same bullwhips he had used on the backs of the powerful black men who now wielded them. He bit through his lips. The pain flashed before his eyes in patches of light like the Northern Lights he had watched as a boy in Pennsylvania. He prayed to die, but he was tough, with that same toughness which had made him an animal through all his life. He cursed it now wishing he was weak as a woman.

The whips sang and fell in the wild light and between the flashes of pain he felt the warm wetness of his own blood in the small of his back and across his thighs. Then mercifully the sounds blurred and the firelight turned to blackness.

For a long time they went on beating the unconscious body and at last when they lifted up the head and it fell back again with a thump against the planks, they raised him, trussed like a pig, and with four negroes carrying the mutilated still living body the mob set out toward the cane brake. A great procession followed—old men and women, young girls and children, carrying burning faggots to light the way, screaming and yelling to the sound of the tom-toms.

Trampling the young green cane, they went toward the swamp by the very path which Elias Sharp had planned to use in his escape. After half a mile the procession came to the end of the field and entering the high reeds, broke a fresh path to where the black cypresses hung with gray moss caught the wild light of the torches. When they reached the edge of the water they laid the body of Elias Sharp, white and pink like a freshly butchered hog on the damp fertile mud and two of the negroes set to work driving two great stakes into the earth. As they worked there appeared here and there on the surface of the black water small bright pin points of light, always in pairs, sometimes in clusters of six or eight or ten. They were eyes and the eyes caught the light of the torches and turned it back.

Then the two big negroes fastened Elias Sharp by head and by feet to the heavy stakes. One of them bent over him, touched the chest and grinning, cried out triumphantly, "He libbin' yet!" Then the ringleaders, yelling and driving the screaming crowd before them, moved up the bank into the reeds once more. As the torches moved away the pin points of light closed in upon the spot where the blood from the overseer's beaten, tormented body dribbled across the mud into the black water. Then as the torch-light faded away among the reeds and the hanging moss, the alligators crawled out of the muddy bayou, following the trail of blood to where the body of the overseer lay tied to the stakes. There was a sound of grunting and tearing in the darkness. No one would ever find any trace of Elias Sharp.

In the big house lights shone from all the windows, for life, tempestuous, violent, had come back suddenly to its shuttered loneliness. Lamps that had not been lighted for twenty years were brought out, their wicks trimmed and lighted. In the second floor ballroom the half-burned candles in the great chandeliers were lighted again and to the music of banjos and violins and drums a kind of witches ball was in progress with field hands and mulatto girls and Union soldiers dancing, without pattern or reason in a wild orgy of rum and music. The negroes came and went from the ball to the slave quarters to watch the slow death of Elias Sharp, bringing back reports on the progress of his torture. Frail gilt chairs were turned over and shattered, panes of old glass cracked and tumbled on the marquetry floor polished by the dancing bare feet of the negroes and gouged by the hob-nailed boots of the soldiers.

At one end of the ballroom Abraham Hunter, the liberator, too fat and too flat-footed to enjoy dancing, sat enthroned in a great gilt chair surrounded by girls who came and went, now dancing wild steps with negro bucks for his amusement, now drinking rum by the side of the carpetbagger. The girl Alouette chosen as his consort, dressed now in an ancient ball gown of the old Baroness, fell into a drunken sleep with her head on his knee.

In the midst of all the wild singing and dancing, a negro would bellow suddenly, *"Libre! Nous sommes libres!"* Free! Freedom! The shouting set the crystal pendants on the chandelier to tinkling.

From his throne, his bald head shining in the light of the candles, Abraham Hunter raised his glass of rum to shout, "Free! That's right! You're all free now!"

Toward morning, after the alligators had dragged Elias Sharp from his stakes under the black water of the swamp and the embers of the overseer's cabin had turned to ashes, Tombo came from the slave quarters to the ballroom with his drum and there under the wild rhythm beat out by his bony black hands, the dancing ceased to be dancing and turned to a wild orgy, punctuated still by wild cries of *"Libre! Nous sommes libres!"* and *"Elias Sharp est mort!"*

The great house, with its wild garden doomed by the great river, was alive again, not with the life of the de Lèche family but with the primitive life of the jungle. Fallen on the polished floor, Abraham Hunter, the liberator, lay at last flat on his face snoring, dead drunk.

And along the muddy roads in the rising dawn hobbled a handful of old slaves who remembered the days of the old Baroness. They were fleeing to nearby plantations to the shelter of the cabins of good niggers. Among them was an old negro called Pierre who rode on a big black mule. He was headed for New Orleans. He traveled all the night, halted twice by picket lines, and arrived only the next night to burst into the drawing-room of the de Lèche house and throw himself down before the young Baroness while she and the old Baroness and M'sieur Amedé were receiving Major Tom Bedloe.

For a long time after they shut him into the cabin Tom Bedloe sat on the bunk, his head between his hands, trying to pull himself together so that he could think clearly and shrewdly. It was difficult, for in addition to the dull feeling in his head, there was a houn' dog howling outside the window and a faint distant sound of beating drums, like the drums he had heard once or twice in Congo Square.

At first he could not remember how long it had been since he left New Orleans, nor had he the slightest idea where he was. Three or four times he went over his skull carefully, feeling it gently with his fingertips to make certain it had not been broken by the terrific blow which came out of the darkness, out of nowhere, as he followed his black guide.

On thinking it over he was certain now that the negro had led him astray deliberately, that all the time he had been in the pay of the men who had caught him and shut him up here in this dark cabin with the howling houn' dog outside. He had been a fool, just picking up any negro who said he knew the way to Bel Manoir. Clearly they had planted this negro as a trap and he had swallowed the bait like any stupid catfish. He remembered a saying among the common soldiers, a saying as old as time—that there was something which had no conscience. Well, it hadn't any common sense either. It was that something that was always getting him into trouble, and he never seemed to learn anything from experience. But he didn't care very much; he was glad after all that he had that something. It made him better than most men. He grinned and the movement of the muscles in his face set the blood throbbing again in his bruised head.

It wasn't anything to grin about. They had him shut up here in this cabin. He didn't know what it was they wanted or why they had captured him, but it was clear that they wanted something or they would have killed him outright on any dark street corner in New Orleans, the way they had killed the carpetbagger in front of the French Opera House.

But who was it that wanted him?

He lay back on the straw of the bunk and then sat up again because the straw was stinking damp and because the blood, rushing to his head, made him dizzy once more. The houn' dog outside kept on howling.

He remembered suddenly Big Ernestine standing at the foot of the bed in La Lionne's big room with the red curtains and gold baldequins, "Ef'n you Yankees stay long enough you'll be done up proper . . . women and drink and the climate." Well, he felt pretty done up right now, but he knew that tomorrow he would be himself again. Tomorrow or even tonight he'd think up a way to escape. And in the meanwhile the General and David would have missed him and sent troops to search for him.

But almost at once he remembered that wherever this cabin was, it was a long way from New Orleans, farther perhaps than any troops short of a regiment dared to venture. After all, the Union Army only held New Orleans and a small circle of territory. The rest of the country was overrun with guerillas, escaped prisoners and remnants of the Confederate Army. He knew he was a long way from New Orleans, because with the negro leading him, he had traveled all one day and well into the night. He fell to thinking again of his guide, a thin-faced negro with features stamped by some high-bred French or Spanish ancestor. Down here in Louisiana the negroes weren't what he had expected. They weren't at all like the negroes in Mrs. Stowe's book. A lot of them didn't seem to want freedom; they wouldn't even leave their masters. Only the bad ones seemed to take advantage of their freedom, swaggering about under the General's protection, consorting with Northern carpetbaggers. It was all very puzzling, the way these Louisiana people themselves were puzzling.

He was aware presently that the sound of the drums had died away but the houn' dog kept on howling and presently a gray light showed him the openings which passed for windows in the cabin. As the light rose, he saw that the cabin consisted of one room about fifteen feet square made of cypress logs chinked with mud and Spanish moss. There was no glass in the windows. They were so small that a heavy man could not have forced his body through them. His own slim tough body could have made it but the windows were half closed by heavy cypress planks nailed across them. The floor was of beaten clay, sticky with dampness. Water stood in one corner of the room. "It must be," he thought, "in swampy land," like the wide stretches they had crossed yesterday in the afternoon.

In the gray rising light he saw that his blue uniform was covered with mud and he thought, "That's from rolling in the mud after they knocked me off the horse." Of what happened after that he could remember nothing.

He thrust a hand into his pocket and brought out a piece of pale blue paper. The sight of it gave him a feeling of reassurance—that he was not mad or dreaming. Opening it, he read the message, written in rather fine neat writing like the writing of a man of character and determination, not at all like the hand writing of any woman he had ever seen.

I am going away to the plantation where there is trouble. That is why you will not see me again. Good luck and a long life—Éliane de Lèche.

It was a brief enough message, easy to remember, but instead of throwing it away, he put it, folded carefully, back in his pocket.

No, all that part was true—about the message and the sudden necessity of following her. Now, sitting on the bunk filled with damp straw, with an aching head, the whole thing seemed ridiculous folly—to leave in the middle of the night to follow a woman he scarcely knew into the swamps and bayous of a strange and hostile country.

He was not a man given to reflections or analysis; action was his role. But now he considered why he had come on a journey which ended here in this moss-chinked cabin. This morning it seemed to him that the man, all eagerness and impatience, who set out on the journey was another person having no relation to the self who now sat in the damp cabin. That stranger had followed a woman because he had been under a compulsion; he could not have done otherwise. And he had gone because of a challenge which he had divined from the moment she turned away from the vase of camellias and smiled at him. He had to follow her, aware in some part of him that if he did not follow this adventure to the end, he would go to his grave, regretful, incomplete and baffled. Beside this adventure all the countless others he had known seemed cheap and easy and unexciting. It was all very odd and unlikely that it should be happening to him.

When he felt a little better he rose and made a circuit of the cabin. That he was a prisoner did not disturb him; on the contrary it was a challenge which filled him with a sudden sense of exhilaration. He was not well enough to escape yet but tomorrow the sense of dizziness and faintness would be gone and then he would show his captors, whoever they were, what it was they had caught.

The door was bolted on the outside and the planks across the windows were heavy and spiked firmly into the logs. Even his wiry strength would not be sufficient to loosen them. There was in the cabin nothing but the flimsy bunk without a piece of wood in it heavy enough or sound enough to use as a battering ram. In any case there must be guards about somewhere.

Through the crevices between the planks he studied the landscape outside, seeking some clue to his whereabouts. Close at hand on one side there was a cane-brake and beyond that clumps of cypresses hung with gray moss. They emerged now like ghosts out of the mists rising from the damp ground. On the opposite side he could see another cabin, damp and moss-grown, like the one in which he was imprisoned save that one side had been scorched by fire—fire which had destroyed a building that once had stood quite near it. The fire must have happened recently for the white ashes still lay undisturbed about the half-wrecked brick chimney. In the distance so veiled by the mist that it appeared like a mirage, he could make out the faded pink roof of a great house rising from among clusters of live oaks. Except for the howling of the houn' dog there was no sound or sight of life in the whole landscape.

About the time the sun had cleared away the last of the mist, he heard the sound of footsteps and then the creak of hinges as the heavy door swung open and a negro came in. He limped from a deformity of the foot and carried a tray on which there was a silver coffee pot and a silver-covered dish, a cup, saucer and spoon and a long cigar of the kind which came from Cuba. The man had a scar across one eye which showed blue against his black skin. He looked at Tom Bedloe with a single side-long glance and put the tray down on the bunk. Then he made a sign to him that he was to eat, thrusting the ends of his fingers into his mouth and grinning.

Tom Bedloe said, "Who are you?" but in reply the negro only grinned in idiotic fashion. In a louder voice Tom Bedloe said, "Where am I?" but again the only answer was a grin and a gesture indicating that he was to eat, and then Tom Bedloe understood that he was not an idiot but deaf and dumb.

The negro then made a series of complicated pantomimic gestures accompanied by incoherent sounds, neither of which conveyed anything, and as Tom lifted the silver cover of the dish, he limped out of the cabin closing and bolting the door behind him.

He was recovered enough now to be hungry and the smell of the food and the coffee excited him as all physical sensations had a way of doing. Beneath the silver lid there was fried fish adorned with a sprig of parsley and two hot buttered muffins.

"Elegant food," he thought grinning, "for a prisoner."

When he had finished the meal, he poured out the last of the coffee and lighted the cigar. It was then for the first time that he noticed the crest and monogram. The silver was soft and so old and worn that the design was scarcely any longer decipherable, but after studying it for some time, comparing the coffee pot and the covered dish he made a curious discovery—that the crest and monogram were the same as those on the bit of paper on which the young Baroness (Éliane was her name, he thought, a pretty name) had written the note. Taking the paper from his pocket, he compared them. The design on the silver emerged clear and unmistakable.

He gave a low whistle and then grinned, because suddenly he understood a great deal. He had been a bigger fool than he thought. This cabin must be at Bel Manoir and the silver must have come from the plantation house, and the whole thing had been a trap. She had left the note, believing, even knowing, that he would follow her to the plantation. On the way his assailants, whoever they were, could capture him easily. Very likely she had not gone to Bel Manoir at all but only with the old Baroness as far as the lake. It may have been that she had never even left the house in New Orleans.

The idea of the plot did not anger him. He understood now a little that sense of challenge he had experienced each time he encountered her. All the time she had had for him very likely little more than a feeling of mockery and contempt. She must have known a great deal, to have been very sure of herself to *know* that he would follow her. But he saw almost at once that she was, after all, like no other woman he had ever known. It was no simple thing, this difference, but very profound, coming out of a life, a background, a civilization that was strange to him.

And yet . . . there was one other element, which in his experience, he could not regret, even now in his humility at having been duped by the most ancient of games. That element was the expression in her eyes when she looked at him, the look of an experienced woman who found him desirable. That was a look which belonged to women of experience, no matter what their color, race or nationality. It was the look of a whore who enjoys her profession at sight of a stranger who attracts her. La Lionne had looked at him in the same fashion, but without mockery, for La Lionne was a direct and uncomplicated woman. The look was that of what the world called a "bad woman"—a woman who lived like a man.

His head felt clearer now and he lay back on the damp straw smoking the cigar, to consider the revelations. The deaf and dumb negro came and took away the tray but Tom Bedloe scarcely noticed him this time, especially since all communication with him seemed impossible.

When he was alone again, he was aware that his desire for the young Baroness had not abated; on the contrary she was an obsession, for his feeling was complicated now by a desire to revenge himself for having been made a fool. When he escaped, if they did not kill him first, he would follow her until there was no longer any question of which was the master. She had asked for the contest; she had challenged him from the moment he caught her in his room, going through his papers.

Nothing happened after that for a long time. Twice he got up and made a round of the windows peering through the crevices between the planks and as the mist cleared he discovered that not far away—perhaps five hundred yards—there was a cluster of cabins, some made of cypress logs, some of sawn wood, some partly brick nestling among a grove of immense live oaks. It was a whole village but deserted. No smoke rose from the chimneys and although he watched for a long time he discovered no sign of life save for an old cat and two chickens. Outside the houn' dog had long since ceased howling and he divined that the man who had been with the dog on guard had gone away too.

It was all very odd, being shut in this cabin in the midst of this dead deserted landscape. There was something evil about it and the sense of evil passed over his body quickly like a wave, causing the skin to rise with a thin prickling sensation.

"That is all nonsense and rot," he told himself quickly, "and now is the time to get away."

So he went to work, trying the planks over again only to discover no way of moving them. They were heavy cypress and nailed with great spikes. He thought of the roof but it was beyond his reach, even when he stood on the bunk, and was made of heavy cypress planks. As he examined it, he thought, "This has been used as a prison before now. It is not just an ordinary cabin." And for the first time it occurred to him what the stains on the wall might be —those dark brown stains discoloring the logs and the cracked plaster which closed the chinks between the logs. The walls were splattered here and there save in one spot where at the height of a man's shoulders the plaster had been drenched not once but perhaps many times. At the realization of what the stains were, the same prickling wave of alarm went through him. It was like the rising of the hair along the back of a dog entering an empty room where he *smelled* danger. He understood now why the houn' dog with the man on watch had howled so persistently. It was said that dogs howled in the presence of death.

"All this," he thought, "is not nice. All this is very unpleasant."

Then he tried the heavy door and even hurled himself against it. He was a powerful man but weight made no more impression against the strength of the solid door than the hurling against it of a pebble.

"Others have tried it before me," he thought, considering the stains on the wall. "Others stronger and heavier." Cypress was wood which never decayed.

The futile attack on the door left him dizzy and faint. He lay down again on the damp straw and almost at once lost consciousness.

He was wakened by someone shaking his shoulder. It was dark again now and as he wakened he saw a man in riding clothes standing over him and beside him the deaf and dumb negro holding a lantern. The man was young like himself and blond and well built. His clothes were well made and expensive.

As Tom Bedloe sat up he said, "I am sorry to disturb you but there is urgent business."

Tom looked at him for a moment, "Where am I? Why am I kept here? Who are you?"

The man answered him without smiling. It was a handsome face, what you would call a "clean" face with a square cut jaw, a firm chin and eyes that were blue even in the dim light of the lantern. It was not an evil face but one in which there was determination and an inflexibility that was almost as frightening as evil.

"I am not here to answer who I am or where you are. I am only here to tell you why you are here."

As he listened now and through the speech that followed, Tom Bedloe knew, without thinking it out, that this fellow defeated him. There would be no way of getting round him as he frequently got round people when he was in a bad spot—by grinning and using the good looks and charm God had given him. It had worked always with women and often with men. This time it would not work.

There was something familiar about the man—nothing more direct and complete than the memory of the striking face of a passerby on the street. It was as if he had seen him before in some other life.

The rather rich deep voice went on speaking, "You are here as a hostage. I have written to your friend, the General in Command of New Orleans, that if he does not cease his persecution and make certain concessions you and two or three others we have taken, will be shot."

"What are the concessions?"

"They are simple enough. He is to release the good citizens of New Orleans he has imprisoned in Fort St. Philip. Most of them are elderly men who are guilty of no more than of calling him a thief and a murderer, and in that they are only truthful. And he is to return to the rightful owners the gold he has taken from the Planters Bank and the property he has confiscated. He and his carpetbagger friends are to stop stealing and selling our cotton, our cane, our horses."

"And who are the others you have taken?" asked Tom.

"That, my friend, is none of your business. Your business is to write to the General to say that you are a prisoner and threatened with death. You are to ask him to grant the concessions and save your life." Tom did not answer him and he said, "You are young. You love women. It is worth doing."

"No, I won't do it and to hell with you."

He looked up again at the face and noted its inflexibility. It was not the face of a fanatic or a madman. It was a suffering face. An avenging angel, he thought, must have a clean, stern blond face like that.

"You have about twelve hours in which to make up your mind. If the General refuses we shall shoot you here in this room." He sighed, "Don't expect us to be soft. We have killed. We shall go on killing, in cold blood like this, or by assassination in the streets of New Orleans because we are forced to do it, because we cannot fight openly. We should prefer it that way but we no longer have any choice. A Yankee, the kind of Yankee there is in New Orleans at the moment, is less to us than a bad nigger ready to be hanged." Again he sighed, then passed the back of his hand against the high white forehead and added, "You had best think it over. We mean to do as we say. We have plenty of reason for vengeance." To the negro, he said, "Leave one of the lanterns and put the food on the bed." And again to Tom Bedloe, "I am sorry we cannot make you more comfortable but the circumstances are special. They keep my father's brother below water level at Fort St. George. He is an old man and ill."

Then he turned away and the negro with the lantern followed him, and as he turned, something in the clean profile, sharp like a cameo but vigorous, gave Tom Bedloe the clue. He saw the face now exactly as he had seen it on the night he came back from the General's party, with the soft light from the candles behind it, bending over to look at the wound which the young Baroness was dressing while Old Seraphine held the basin. This was the one called MacTavish. This was the one who owned the house the General had taken, to quarter his horses in.

He was hungry again and there was no way of knowing the hour, for his watch had stopped at two o'clock, very likely the hour he was knocked off the horse. There was on the platter cornbread and fried oysters and coffee. It was all well cooked and still hot, but this time the silver coffee pot and the covered dish were not there. In its place was some sort of cheap yellow crockery. At first he thought nothing of the change and then a curious thought occurred to him. Perhaps she had managed to send the silver the first time as a sign, a signal to let him know where he was and that she was somewhere near. For a little time the thought excited him, but the memory of young MacTavish's face blurred the pleasure from it.

There was no doubt of it. He was in a tight spot. He knew what lay behind that flinty look in the blue eyes of MacTavish—the murder of young Mumford, the insults to the wives and fiancées and sweethearts of New Orleans, the presence everywhere of the thieving carpetbaggers and the "bad niggers," the thievery, hypocrisy, the New England "smartness" of General Wicks and his wife.

There was plenty of reason for that look. There was plenty of reason for MacTavish to shoot him in cold blood without another thought.

He finished the meal to the last crumb and lighted the cigar. Then he put out the lantern. There was no need for light and the darkness relieved the feeling he had that he was being watched by someone through the crevices between the planks.

For a long time he sat with his head between his hands thinking of many curious unrelated things—the look of his room as a small boy in New Bedford, the story that he was always a bad boy because his grandmother had been a Frenchwoman, of his first experience with "love" and its ugliness, of women he had known, of the General's wife and her curious obsession for him as if he were her son, only more than that, and of the singular depravity of New Englanders which was born of the brain rather than the body and seemed to him green in color.

It did not occur to him that he would be shot. He did not doubt that at the end of twelve hours MacTavish and his gang—Les Defenseurs—would shoot him if he were still here. But between now and then many things could happen. He would not be here. He had no feeling of death. Death was something which could not happen to him. And presently he heard a footstep outside and the breathing of the houn' dog as he sniffed at the crack under the door.

He called out to the man outside the door but got no answer, and then it occurred to him that possibly the guardian, even if he were not the deaf and dumb negro, very likely spoke only French.

He lay down again, bored and restless. Now that the ache in his head was gone, he felt the old necessity for physical action which always drove him, and presently he sat up. At the same time he heard a faint and distant roar. As he listened, the faint roar began presently to disintegrate into bits of sound—shouts and screams and the barking of dogs. Outside the door the hound whimpered and began to howl again. Then he was aware of a faint quavering glow of rosy light on the spattered wall opposite. Standing on the bunk he looked out between the planks.

The night was clear now with an immense full red moon rising behind the moss hung cypresses. Far away on the edge of a distant cane brake there were lights moving above the damp earth like will-o'-the-wisps above a marsh. They moved backward and forward and presently he discovered that the lights were torches carried by a mob. Before them ran barking and howling a great troop of mongrel dogs.

Then from one of the slave's cabins a flame broke through the roof and leapt toward the sky; then another and another, and as the fire spread from cabin to cabin and the fierce heat increased, flames and sparks and fragments of burning cane thatch and bits of burning cypress wood were carried high into the air. As they rose the faint wind from the Gulf carried them toward the cabin where he peered between the planks. With each surge of the flames they came nearer and nearer falling on the damp ground where they burned out, some of them lodging in the dry moss of the trees which flamed up so that the live oaks were filled with small lights like trees decorated for a fête.

Suddenly he thought, "They'll set the roof of the cabin on fire and I'll be roasted alive." Turning to the door he shouted and kicked at it, calling out to the man who stood on guard outside. But no answer came from the other side of the heavy door. The man and the houn' dog had gone away. He threw himself again at the heavy door but it held, solid as the cypress logs of the cabin walls.

Again it was not death he feared but the manner of death—to die horribly without a fight. He had never prayed and he could not pray now but only curse as he fought the door. It was no use attacking the planks at the windows; they were too high up and there was no way of finding purchase for his strength.

Outside the sparks and bits of burning wood fell now like a shower of flaming rain. The whole of the slave quarters was aflame and the fire rose high in the air. The sound of the wild approaching flames drowned even the yells of the mob. The only sound that came through was the deep sinister steady rhythm of a great drum.

Still cursing, he stopped battering at the door to regain breath and strength, and as he stood there drenched in sweat, he heard suddenly above the roar of the fire and the drum a faint crackling sound above his head, and at the same time he experienced an extraordinary sense of evil—the evil of the past with which the very walls of the cabin were saturated, the evil of the hot damp swamps and the whole lush landscape, the evil of the hanging gray moss and that distant house with its roof rising in the waxing moonlight above the jungle of camellias and chinaberry trees. It was an evil place drenched and permeated with evil.

Wildly he thought, "The fire may burn a hole in the roof and I can climb out that way." And he began to tear apart the flimsy rotten bunk planning to make of it a ladder to climb the blood-stained walls. The sound of the drum beat into his brain now, even above the crackling sound overhead. And then suddenly from behind him he heard a voice saying, "Come with me! Come quickly!" and he saw her standing in the doorway, her figure lighted by the flames from the burning roof.

After that first day Aunt Tam and Agnes and black César no longer traveled by daylight. In the morning when the two women awakened they found a pot of coffee on a freshly built fire but César was gone, and for a moment Agnes felt a sudden panic lest he had deserted them, leaving them to die there forgotten and lost like Manon Lescaut in the desert of Louisiana. But Aunt Tam was more optimistic. "He's gone scouting for food," she said. "He'll be back. Let us make an exploring trip."

And so with her niece, both of them freed now of their fashion-able crinolines, she made a tour of the island where they had spent the night. It was not a long tour for the island was small and they were forever coming to the edge of solid earth where it gave way to reeds and mangroves and palmettos and tall black cypresses. But the activity made them feel better.

They had been wakened at dawn by the clamor of the aigrettes when an osprey swooped down over the live oaks, at the moment when the sun, rising over the swamps, painted the wheeling and plummeting birds a pale pink. The air was still cool but already touched with the rich smell of growing vegetation.

To Aunt Tam it was like wakening in paradise. In her elderly bosom, her heart beat with a joy she had never before experienced. Her dress was rumpled and stained with sea water and primeval mud. Her straight hair usually crimped into tight waves with a small cluster of curls on each side of the horse face, hung lank and stringy in the damp air. Dipping water from the bayou into the kettle out of which they had eaten their supper the night before, she managed a crude toilette, and all the while her heart kept singing and one wicked thought kept turning over in her mind. It was that no one would find or rescue them for a long time, that she could go on living in this wild and beautiful world. But of this she said nothing to Agnes.

Something was happening to the girl, but what it was she could not quite make out. Before they left Havana, she had always been simple and frank, like a child, but in the last few days she had changed. It was nothing Aunt Tam could put her finger on. If she had not known the girl so well she would perhaps have failed to notice the difference. Because it was very subtle, a kind of withdrawal of the spirit, betrayed by the look in the eyes and the strange remarks and observations which she occasionally made. As they walked over the island, with Aunt Tam discovering and pointing out the strange plants and birds, Agnes was curiously silent instead of running after her Aunt uttering small child-like cries of delight as she did when they went for a walk on the farm at Dedham.

When they had made a complete tour of the tiny island, Aunt Tam took out her journal and wrote a meticulous and uninspired description of what had happened to them and what they had seen since they drew away from the side of the rotting plague-stricken *San Cristobal*. She wrote for a long time, ten pages in all.

It was Agnes who saw black César returning across the lagoon. He was in a tiny boat that looked like a floating log, his great muscular body naked from the waist up. Delicately, skillfully, he handled the fragile craft. He belonged here in the beauty of this scene, like the aigrettes. As she watched him coming across the dark water, she felt a sudden pang, as if her spirit were growing. It was like the physical pangs she had as a small girl which her father had told her were "growing pains." It was as if the whole world opened up before her, a new world she had never before entered.

Then César grounded the frail craft and grinning, came ashore and told his story.

He had gone off just before sunrise on a scouting trip leaving the heavy dory behind, hidden among the reeds. Alone through the morning mist he had made his way now swimming, now wading, between the low islands, until he came to an abandoned settlement of Sabines—a special race of crawfishermen and shrimpers and hunters who were part Indian and part Negro. Most of the houses in the settlement had been burned, but among the ruins he had found the *pirogue* in which he returned now.

On his way back he had come through a *raccourci* scarcely wide enough for the *pirogue* to pass, into the wide bayou he had been searching for, and there in a hut he came upon two Sabine women who had run away into the swamp at sight of him. But in the hut he had discovered an old man, paralyzed and unable to flee and too old to be terrified by the prospect of death.

There in the hut he had learned from the old man what it was he wanted to know, and what he learned was worse than he had expected. All this part of the Delta was overrun by bands of thieves and cutthroats. Among them were "bad niggers," deserters, escaped prisoners, bad "Cajuns" and Sabines, convicts and even a few Indians. They lived off the settlements and the smaller plantations, pilfering and burning.

There was, as the old man told him painfully, no law of any kind now the Yankees had come. The old man had never seen the *Yanquis.* He had merely heard of them, robbers and bandits from up the river who infested the city of New Orleans. He had heard, he said, that all slaves were now free and that there was trouble everywhere and many of them had turned to murder and thievery, working with stray *Yanquis.* The river, he said, was more unsafe than the swamp. There were big *Yanqui* boats but also there were pirates and convicts.

Then César bargained with the old man for a sack full of corn and one of rice and one of dried shrimps and went away.

And now, said César, they could no longer travel by day. They would rest and sleep during the daytime and travel at night. He knew his way so long as they did not take too many *raccourcis*. It would be better that way because at night it would be cooler. In a day or two they would be in familiar country where they would eat well.

Then quite simply he went to work preparing lunch, leaving the two women alone on the crest of the island where the live oaks grew thickest.

Again Aunt Tam asked, "You aren't afraid?"

The girl thought for a moment. "No, I'm not afraid. Papa will be worried and David . . . and Tom."

She was not telling the truth, because she had never thought whether her father or David would be worried. It was only Tom of whom she thought, and even in this she had lied, because she could not be certain that he would be worried when he discovered what had happened to them. Sitting there miles from him, it seemed to her that she was beginning to know him for the first time.

Why this was so she could not explain to herself, much less to Aunt Tam, and so she did not talk of it at all. She was in the midst of an experience, half-mystical and half-physical, to which many elements contributed and so confused her. There was the beauty of the aigrettes and the terror and sickness of the hurricane, the curious animal beauty of the great black negro who had saved them, and that mysterious gesture made by the sailors, a gesture at once puzzling, exciting and terrifying. There was the smell of fertility from the damp earth and the beauty of the sun rising above the vast swamps to burn away the mists. All these had somehow made Tom real for the first time.

Until now he had been a kind of romantic figure cut out of paper, like the heroes in the few novels she had been allowed to read, and all the quality of the feeling between them had been romantic and literary. Sitting there on the island while Aunt Tam took out her journal and began to write down the things she had forgotten, the girl blushed, partly out of shame for the new and alarming thoughts which had come into her head of late.

She wanted to see him. She wanted by some miracle to fly through the sky and be at his side. She wanted . . . and she blushed more furiously . . . to touch him, his hands, his rough curly hair, his throat. She wanted to see his straight back and watch the slight swagger with which he walked, and hear again the curious deep soft voice that seemed to wrap itself round you, warming you. A slight shiver ran through her body, as if it too like her perception were growing.

Then looking with a quick sudden glance at Aunt Tam to remark whether she had noticed anything, she thought, "I should be ashamed."

One of the girls at the school—a bad girl—had told the rest of them what it was like to let a man make love to you. Afterward there had been some mystery and they had sent the girl away from the school and her parents had taken her to Europe and people said the family had left Boston forever because the girl was a "bad girl." "Maybe I am like that," she thought. But she was not ashamed. She was happy. She wanted suddenly to sing and dance and run through the dappled shadows beneath the live oaks, but that of course, she could not do. Aunt Tam would think her crazy.

All that day they hid among the trees and at dusk as the color faded out of the West and the rim of the moon showed through the cypresses on the opposite side of the lagoon, black César helped them aboard the dory and thrust it out from among the reeds.

Sometimes rowing, sometimes poling, the great negro drove the clumsy boat out of the lagoon into the bayou. Silently it slipped over the black water, so silently that they could hear the rustling and chortling of birds disturbed in the rushes, and after a little while the girl fell asleep, her head against the flat breast of the old maid.

For a long time Aunt Tam stayed awake watching the movement of the negro's body as he thrust the boat on its way. In the golden light of the rising moon there was rhythm and music in all his movements like the rhythm of the music Aunt Tam had always yearned for and been denied, the music of Mozart which she sang so badly, the beauty of fulfillment as a woman which with her had never gone much deeper than a chaste admiration for Mr. Emerson and Mr. Alcott, and jottings, romantic and florid, in the book she carried in her reticule.

Now the touch of the girl's head against her breast became poignant and unbearable, as if in some way the girl were a part of her, as if through the girl she might somehow touch, even distantly, all the things which for her had been forever beyond reach.

"Agnes must have passion in her life and excitement and glory and fire." And immediately she was ashamed, thinking, "You are an old fool! Abigail Jones! A romantic old fool!"

[142]

Then she fell to watching black César again as his shoulders rose and fell with the powerful thrusts of the pole. Presently he began to sing in a low voice so that the sound would not reach the banks, the nostalgic song he had sung on the river

Mo gagnain soutchien la Louisiane malle oir ca ya de moin . . .

The voice hung suspended in the stillness above the water. Aunt Tam dozed and fell asleep. In a little while, César climbed down and with elaborate care placed his ragged jacket across the knees of the two women, tucking it under their feet gently so as not to waken them. They were his charges. *Le bon dieu* had sent them to him, and he loved the old lady the way he loved his children at Bel Manoir and his mules and the pet raccoon. She was a good and simple woman.

All through the night he poled and rowed and at sunrise Aunt Tam stirred and wakened. They were in a wide expanse of water, clotted with water hyacinths, the whole surface pale blue and mauve as far as the eye could see.

From the moment David walked out of the room without a word to the General's wife, she began to plot—against no one in particular but against all that world of New Orleans and the South which in a few short months she had come to hate with all the bitterness of an unhappy woman. Somehow in her troubled mind everyone had turned against her, even the husband for whom she had felt no affection in twenty years.

As the boy turned from her she felt a sudden fierce hatred and contempt for him, for his gentleness, his ambition, even for his virginity which she divined by a fierce female instinct. How dared he be insolent to her, sitting there quietly as if she were a fool when everyone knew that she was the one who had made the General's career?

As the door closed belowstairs, tears of rage came into her eyes. She would punish them all. She would have more citizens arrested and thrown into the fortress prison. Aunt Tam was a fool and now Tom had disappeared and the General acted as if the whole disaster were her doing.

As she left the room she called over the long curving stairway, "Private Higgins! Private Higgins!" in a voice so loud and furious that it set the crystals of the great MacTavish chandelier above her head to tinkling.

The dreary soldier on duty came running up the stairs. She said, "Go and ask Mrs. Gilpin to come here."

She hated the Quartermaster's wife as much as Mrs. Theophilus Gilpin hated her, but in all New Orleans she was the only woman with whom she held any communication, and the only thing both hated more than each other was New Orleans and Louisiana and all Secessionists, not so much because they were rebels or slave-holders as because they had an easy life and great houses and ease and beauty. Mrs. Wicks and Mrs. Gilpin, whose own lives were singularly barren of all softness and beauty, looked upon all these things not only as symptoms but absolute evidence of lush immorality.

Mrs. Theophilus Gilpin arrived, puffing and blowing despite her wiry, crow-like figure, because she had hurried all the way knowing that the General's wife would not have sent for her except for some important and exciting reason; and she was in no good temper because on the way three different women, two of them obviously loose in character but one unmistakably a lady, had lifted their skirts and crossed to the opposite side of the street as they had seen her approaching. For this she could have had them all arrested under the General's latest decree and thrown into prison as prostitutes, but there was no soldier in sight and she had been forced to ignore the insults.

The orderly took her straight to the small drawing room where the General's wife sat to do her mending. Once inside she closed the door behind her and said, "Well!"

"Sit down, Melanctha," said the General's wife. "There is a long string of fresh outrages!"

Mrs. Gilpin sat down, flattered by the fact that the General's wife had addressed her by her Christian name, and unbuttoned her jacket and with an air of going to work said, "I have just been insulted three times on my way here."

Then for two hours their sterile, pinched spirits gossiped and plotted against the gaiety, the color, the life of the stricken city. Despite the oppression, despite the bitter decrees of the General, the city still showed too much spirit.

"They act as if they hadn't been licked!" said Melanctha Gilpin.

"They never *were* Americans!" ignored Aunt Louisa. "They were always foreigners and immoral. It's the French in them."

At last, after many diversions they arrived at the means of punishment and revenge. New Orleans must be purged of its wickedness. The woman from Maine and the woman from Indiana would make it a clean city where people would be moral because the law compelled them to be so. They would see that every bar and brothel and gaming house was closed.

"I'm sure the General will be of our opinion," said Aunt Louisa.

"I'm certain he will," said Melanctha Gilpin, "and the Quartermaster too."

"We shall begin with a place called the Café Imperial," said the General's wife. "It's a stink in the nostrils—a pit of Sodom and Gomorrah."

"I've heard of it," replied Mrs. Gilpin, her nostrils expanding with pleasure.

"The General himself is in no good mood."

About dusk, Mrs. Gilpin, buttoning up her jacket, and setting her bonnet at an angle which expressed both determination and an indestructible virtue, bade the General's wife adieu and set out for home, feeling washed free of sin and bathed in the blood of the Lord. When she had gone Aunt Louisa sat down to await the General and hear what progress had been made in the search for Aunt Tam and Agnes.

He came in late, rather purple in the face and perspiring from the unhealthy heat of the city he hated. Everything, it appeared, had gone wrong. Tom Bedloe had disappeared. David, in search of him, had vanished for the whole afternoon. He had summoned the Commander of the Fifteenth Regiment to send him out with a search party and found the Commander was in bed, delirious with malaria. Two enlisted men were reported dead of cholera. At St. Louis Hospital the nurses reported that yellow fever was spreading in the district about Congo Square.

"And what about Aunt Tam and Agnes?" asked his wife. "Have you done nothing about them?"

"Of course I've done something about them. Two battalions have been sent down the river to search the Delta Country."

"Melanctha Gilpin was insulted on the street again this afternoon."

For a moment, a ghost of humor showed in the General's puffy eyes. "It must have taken a pretty desperate man to pick on Melanctha Gilpin."

"Don't be vulgar, General. And it wasn't a man. It was three different women."

"Why didn't she have them arrested?"

"As usual," retorted his wife, "there was not an enlisted man in sight. Very likely they were all off whoring and gambling."

"Those are not words for a New England lady to use."

"It's the truth. When I think of the well brought up New England soldiers who are being debauched by this town, it makes my blood boil."

To this the General made no reply. He had considered again and again closing down the dives of New Orleans but each time he had met objection from his own officers. He wanted to eat his supper in peace. After a little time he did say, scornfully, "Well brought up New England boys, indeed! Mostly ruffians and hired substitutes!"

They had reached the pudding, still indignant with each other and with the world, when the dejected orderly who served them at table, handed him a message. He tore it open while his wife, tortured by curiosity, watched his face. When he had finished reading, he said, "Damn!" in a terrific voice.

"Well! What is it?" asked his wife. "Do you want me to faint from curiosity?"

"That's enough," he said, slapping the paper on the mahogany table. "I'll close every place in town down to the poorest coffee house."

"What's happened?" cried his wife. "For God's sake, don't act as if I were a fool!"

He pushed the paper across the table to her. Like a starving dog snatching a bone, she took it up and read.

The dispatch was brief. It merely stated that there had been a riot and shooting affray in a place called the Café Imperial. Two men, a Union officer and a merchant from Salem, Massachusetts,

[146]

had been killed and four other men wounded. The place had been wrecked.

But that was not all. It seemed that all the trials of the day had only mounted toward the climax which was to occur as they left the table. The depressed orderly delivered another message. It was written on blue paper and clearly not an Army dispatch. The General said, as he tore it open, "More threats, I suppose."

This time his wife was standing beside him instead of being at the opposite end of a great mahogany table, and this time she did not have to wait for the satisfaction of a curiosity which was a kind of disease, like kleptomania. Seizing one corner of the paper, she read with him line for line the disturbing message.

It was brief enough, considering its character. It stated simply that Major Thomas Bedloe, Captain Andrew Benson, and Captain Elias Burden were being held prisoners in undisclosed places of confinement and that their lives would be forfeit, ruthlessly and without compassion unless the General in Command of New Orleans saw fit to meet the demands of their captors. These demands were simple. The General must rescind the order reducing all New Orleans women to the status of prostitutes. The General must return to its rightful owners the gold seized from the Planters' Bank and other private banks. The General must exercise his power in stopping the theft and sale of cotton, sugar, horses, mules and other commodities belonging to citizens of Louisiana by carpet-baggers and northern merchants including relatives of the General and the General's wife. At the end, the document again warned that the General must act and within seventy-two hours, or the lives of his officers would be forfeited. It was signed simply *"Les Defenseurs."*

The General did not read the document to the end before he shouted to the orderly to seize and arrest the man who had delivered the paper. By the time he had finished reading it, the orderly returned to say that the bearer had vanished.

"What did he look like?" asked the General.

But the orderly was a dull fellow and not very observant. He did not know what he looked like except that he was a boy, not more, he thought, than fourteen or fifteen years old.

"Even their spawn is evil!" cried the General, and then to the orderly, "Get out, doughhead!"

His face was quite purple now, and for a moment he could not speak. He had had too much to bear in one day, and he knew that at any moment his wife would begin again to denounce him as a fool.

But she was strangely quiet. She looked at him for a long time waiting for him to recover and at last she said with astonishing calm, "What are you going to do about it?"

"I don't know yet. Give me time to think. Go and bring me some whisky!"

Like a dove she went away, not even protesting against the whisky which she allowed in the house only for medicinal purposes. The General thought, "Women are demented creatures," and felt suddenly empty and defeated and old and tired. He had expected a row. He would have welcomed an argument that would have permitted him to swear and call her a fool. It would have helped to restore his spirits and annihilate the growing weariness and sense of defeat and impotence. These damned Louisianans would not admit it when they were licked. He had tried everything. You trampled them down in one place and they rose in another. If they had behaved themselves in the beginning, if they had accepted their defeat and treated him with proper respect, they could have gone on selling their cotton and sugar like any sensible "smart" business men would have done. But they were full of high-falutin ideas about honor and glory and dignity. He interrupted his pacing up and down the room, thinking, "Well, if a man cares so much about honor and glory and dignity he'd better give up the idea of making money." If a man was "smart" in business, he forgot these things.

But the return of his wife made him realize that he had solved none of the problems which were tormenting him, and the sight of her coming in with a dove-like but sly and conniving expression, brought on one of those rare flashes of doubt, a terrifying, soul-shattering doubt, that he was too small a man for his job, that he and Louisa together had somehow made a desperate failure, not only of New Orleans but of their whole existence together. This woman carrying the whisky to him, was suddenly a monster to

[148]

whom he had been married for over thirty years without ever seeing her as she was. In that illuminating flash she appeared wrong in this beautiful room with the scent of the garden coming in at the open windows, she appeared ugly and hateful and mean. She did not belong here in New Orleans. He should never have permitted her to come. She had always been responsible for his worst actions, his worst decisions. She always managed to goad him into a fury and then taking advantage of his anger, to turn it in the direction she chose. As she handed him the whisky, he felt for her a wild surge of murderous hatred.

"What do you mean to do, General?" she asked.

He swallowed the whisky and was silent for a moment, reflecting that when she addressed him as "General" she was always the most dangerous.

"I don't know," he said, "I must go to headquarters and talk to the others."

"A fine lot they are," she said, bitterly. "If you had listened to them, we'd all have been run out of New Orleans long ago."

He began pacing up and down again and as he walked she watched him, her small, cold blue eyes bright with contempt. Presently in a terrifying voice, she said, "I've thought of the only thing to do. Put the Mayor and about ten other leading citizens in jail and announce in the *Daily Delta* that if any harm comes to Tom and the other two, you'll hang all of them right off the way you hanged that Mumford boy for tearing down the flag."

The mention of the Mumford boy made him wince as it always did. He would go on shuddering at the name of Mumford until he died.

"That way," she said bluntly, "you won't have to give up the gold or stop selling cotton. That's the only way."

She was beginning again to "work on" him, and she was quite calm and cold, and that frightened him.

But there was one thing he did not know and that was that for once it was not avarice which moved her. It was, of all impossible things, love. For in the moment she had gone out of the room the shock of the threatening message had made her see what until this moment she had not even considered—the fact that she, at forty-eight, was in love with Tom Bedloe who was twenty

[149]

years younger than herself. They must not harm Tom Bedloe no matter what happened, not even if it meant an end to the plundering of a rich and helpless city. In the excitement she experienced suddenly, even her avarice withered and died. The hot flushes returned, and she became hysterical. In the dining room she had leaned against the table thinking wildly, "I must pull myself together. I must keep my head now—more than ever before in my life."

So, she had taken one of Mrs. Gilpin's giant pills and pulled herself together, and suddenly she saw quite clearly what was to be done. Hostages, of course! Hostages always gave you an advantage! It did not matter if they shot the entire population of New Orleans. Tom must not be harmed. For Tom had become precious to her. He was wicked. He was everything that was disreputable. The idea that she could love him was ridiculous; that he should even think of her in such a fashion was preposterous. But it did not matter. He was everything she had never known, everything the General was not and never could be. He was son and lover rolled into one.

The wild freedom of that moment passed quickly and she was suddenly calm again and cold. But in that wicked moment she had experienced ecstasy for the only time in her life. For the only time in her life she was a woman. Then quickly it passed. She took up the whisky and with a firm step started toward the MacTavish drawing room, her heart black with hate against the General who had robbed her of everything . . . everything.

As she opened the drawing-room door a strange thought rushed through her tormented brain, "I should never have come here to this accursed city. I should never have left Bangor."

When Tom Bedloe turned and saw her standing in the doorway, his terror, the fire, the threats of death all vanished. His instinct, well-trained, said, "It's all right now. I've won!"

She did not give him time to speak. She only said, "Follow me. And run!"

Together they ran through the ashes of the burned overseer's house to the tangle of trees which surrounded the big house. The light from the burning cabins illuminated the whole stretch of

rough ground and he had a sudden momentary feeling of naked-
ness and panic and fear, of what he did not know. It was like the
fear of a small child running down a dark passage pursued by
someone, something, he cannot see.

As they reached the shelter of the trees, she stopped running
and standing very still, she said, "Be very quiet now." Then for a
moment she stood listening, straining to hear the small sounds
beneath the curtain of screaming and shouting and drum-beating
which came from the burning cabins. He could hear nothing at
all save a very faint rustling of leaves in the hot breeze from the
Gulf.

Then once more she said, "Follow me," and led him past the
garçonnière at one end of the big house into a small door set in
the pink brick wall. Opening it she went inside and in the darkness she said, "You had better take my hand. I know my way. If
you knocked over anything they might hear you."

He took her hand and the touch of it filled him with inde-
scribable excitement. It was soft and warm but firm and sur-
prisingly strong. She led him up a narrow dark stairway and then
into a large hallway illuminated faintly by the glare of the distant
fires. Then up a wide stairway and at last into a room with a
sloping roof and a single window facing the slave quarters.

Here she closed the door and as she attempted to free her hand,
he suddenly seized her and tried to kiss her. For a moment, in the
half-light from the fire, she resisted fiercely with a strength which
astonished him and then suddenly she yielded, pressing her body
fiercely against his with a kind of savagery. The whole of the great
house seemed to sway beneath him and the light of the burning
cabins suddenly to fill the whole room. The kiss she gave him was
the kiss of a passionate woman of experience, a kiss that would
have terrified a weaker man by its implications.

Then she freed herself and in the dim light he saw her press
the back of her hand against her mouth as if to destroy the meaning
of what had happened, and she said in a curious tight voice, "Well,
that has been done."

He did not know what she meant and to have asked would have
changed the whole mood of their relationship. He did not much
care for he had achieved what he meant to do; he had broken

down that curious puzzling wall that had made it all so difficult and impossible since the beginning. For it was not as if he had kissed her forcibly against her will, although it began that way. She had kissed him too, with more than willingness, with abandon, with a quick savage depravity. He was aware that for the moment at least he had dominated her utterly, completely.

Now she was free again. She said in her old manner, "I expect you to stay here. If you tried hard enough you could very likely escape. But I think it would do you little good. You'd be shot by the first man, black or white, who saw you. The others will think you have escaped. You are no longer their possession. You are mine."

"They must have seen us coming here."

"I don't think there is anyone in the house. MacTavish has gone to see if he can get help. The others are hiding in the cane brake watching the mob. The house is not easy to defend. It's too big and it's surrounded by trees. They mean to shoot them wholesale if they start across the open ground toward the house."

"I suppose none of them cared whether I was cooked alive."

"Only MacTavish and he is gone. The others are bitter."

There was a little silence and then quite boldly she said, "I have need of you."

"Was that why you left the message for me?"

But he did not trap her. She said, "I only left the message because it was good manners."

"You didn't think I would follow you?"

"I didn't think anything at all. Why should I think such a thing?"

He knew that again he could not press the point if he was to keep his advantage. They were still, despite the sudden embrace, too strange to each other. It was as if a part of them were already intimate, another part remote and distant and even hostile. The sense of the old challenge was there, exciting him, constricting his throat.

She said, "I will lock the door and keep the key . . . just to make certain you do not walk out . . . and to keep the others from coming in. I shall say that I have taken the key to keep the others from coming into my room."

"It is your room?"

"No. My own room was wrecked. They were all here. The same mob that is burning the cabins." Her voice hardened, the same voice he had heard singing across the courtyard. "They will not come here again . . . at least not without losing a good many of them. I am going away now. I shall be back."

She opened the door. "I am sorry there is no light. It is too dangerous."

He grinned, and said boldly, "What makes you think I shall not try to escape?"

He could not see whether or not she was smiling, but in her voice there was a suspicion of mirth. "If you go away," she said, "then you will not be the man I think you are and I should be a fool."

"I shouldn't want to make you a fool."

Apparently she received this remark with contempt as banal and naïf and cheap, for she said nothing more, but only went out closing the door behind her. Almost immediately he heard the key turning in the lock.

He sat down on the bed thinking, "She is right. I won't go away. I won't go away until this thing is finished."

He knew again, more surely than before, that he could not go until this thing between them was settled, because if it was not settled the sense of its incompleteness would haunt him for the rest of his life. The thought of death no longer troubled him because this thing was more profound, more urgent than any fear of death could possibly be. On death he was willing to gamble.

Outside the flames of the burning cabins had begun to die down a little, although the beating of the tom-toms and wild cries and shouts still continued. Then suddenly there was a burst of gun-fire—a dozen reports clustered together and then three or four isolated shots.

Three or four miles to the south, Hector MacTavish made his way on a mule along a muddy road, keeping always in the shadow of the trees. He did not like mules but in the whole countryside not a horse remained. All the good horses had been taken long ago for the Confederate cavalry and the old and poor ones which remained had been stolen and shipped down the river to New Orleans to be sold for what they would bring by the Northerners who had come in the wake of the Union Army.

As he rode the bony gray mule along the shadowed road, the thought of his own horses gave him a sick feeling at the pit of his stomach, for he was a man who owned horses not for show or for betting but because he loved them with a tenderness almost like that which he had bestowed on the two or three women who had been lucky enough to attract him. Each horse for him possessed its own character and personality.

There was Aldebaran, the black stallion. He was a warrior who when he moved brought up pictures of banners and armor and music. And Kitty, the little bay mare, who was skittish and melodramatic and made up stories like a precocious child. There was no dullness when you rode her, for she invented things to shy at An inert log became a dragon, the hanging Spanish moss overhead became garlands of snakes, a flying bit of paper became to Kitty something to turn her whole sleek body to shivering. And Regina, the black broodmare, who was so gentle and maternal, bringing up one foal after another with no trouble to anyone, always gentle, nuzzling at your neck for sugar. As he rode, he smiled at the memory of her, almost feeling the soft muzzle against his cheek.

They were gone now, forever, with all the others. Aldebaran, the black stallion, went with General Beauregard himself, and that at least was an honorable career, and little Kitty had gone with the Louisiana cavalry. But what had become of Regina and her soft muzzle he did not know, for she had been stolen by the Yankees, and what Yankee knew how to treat a horse decently? At the thought of her a lump came into his throat.

He hated these men who had come into New Orleans not because they had been ruthless but because they were both dishonest and dishonorable, and because in his heart his was the contempt of the man who lives on his own land for the men who kept shops, a contempt as old as time itself. It was bearable to be conquered by a decent and honorable foe but not by a contemptible one like that Yankee general who lived now with his wife in the great house of the MacTavishes.

He had other more personal reasons for hating that New England army which plundered New Orleans. There was his sister, Jeanie, who had spent a whole night in jail, treated and tried like a prostitute because she had refused to salute the Yankee flag, and his Uncle Henry, an old man enfeebled and ill, held in the forts as a hostage. It was odd, but the thought of poor old Regina and the memory of her soft nose against his cheek hurt him most. He would never know again that warm special feeling about his heart when she came across the paddock toward him, whinnying. He would never again have her look up at him, with a new-born foal by her side, as if to say, "Isn't he a beauty?"

Half-aloud and bitterly he said, "Damn them all!" And shook his head as if to make himself forget the bitterness.

It was gall too to ride like this, like a hunted animal, along the roads he knew as far back as he could remember. This was his own country and now he had to ride by night and hide by day to save his life.

And he was bitter too against certain of his own people, like Amedé and Éliane de Lèche. He was riding now in the shadow along this moonlit road partly because of their wickedness and because of that evil, degenerate Elias Sharp, their overseer. They had never cared for their land or their slaves as they should have done, loving them and cherishing them. They had only squeezed from their land all the money they could to spend in New Orleans and Paris. Because they were evil, their slaves, goaded by that loathsome Yankee who had come to steal their cotton, had turned on them and on Elias Sharp.

He knew the horrible end of Elias Sharp, every detail of the whipping and the torture, even to the death in the mud, dragged from the stakes by the alligators; but try as he would, he could feel no pity for the man. A dozen times he had ridden over to Bel Manoir to admonish or curse the overseer and advise him to mend his ways. Out of the whole parish he was the only one who had taken that trouble. And it had done no good to speak to the de Lèche family. The old Baroness had only told him coldly that even though Sharp was a Yankee, he was a good overseer; the revenues of the place had never been so good as during his regime. No, Elias Sharp had asked for the end the "bad niggers" gave him.

And the de Lèche family had suffered too, almost as if there were such a thing as a God and retribution. Every male in the direct line for three generations had died before he was twenty-five, so that Bel Manoir and all their riches were left in the care of women. And now to plague them there was the bad Éliane de Lèche, not an outsider but one of their own family, who had married her own cousin. Not only was her position faintly incestuous, she had caused nothing but trouble for them since she returned from Paris as a girl of fourteen. It was as if the curse of the whole family was somehow crystallized in her dominating character. She was like a man as the old Baroness was like a man. The men of the family who still existed were like women, spiteful and vengeful and weak and vacillating—Amedé, with his one arm and his tubercular pallor, the worst of them all.

He should never have tried to save them by bringing his own men to Bel Manoir to drive the carpetbagger out of the great house and protect it from the revolting slaves. He should not be riding now to find men, white or black, in the parish who would join them. The honest men who were not away fighting were all in hiding. The good niggers had all gone away in terror at the uprising. Only the bad niggers of the parish were left to join those in revolt at Bel Manoir.

He knew he would find no one. He had known it before he left. He had volunteered to go for help because this was his parish and he knew every lane and bayou and *raccourci* and because he had wanted to get away for a little time from the great house. Even this melancholy ride was better than the strange evil atmosphere of the half-ruined place. And more than anything, he had wanted to be free for a little while from the presence of the young Baroness.

But even here on the bony gray mule miles away he was not free of her. She was there beside him annoying him as she had done since he saw her for the first time among the still well-tended gardens of Bel Manoir, arrogant even then and vulgar as any octoroon's bastard offspring, but far more clever and ruthless. The little girl with the oval face and the ivory pallor had not been a child at all but a kind of monstrosity, full of precocious knowledge and wit and grossness. They said her mother was an Irish whore and one could believe it. What other sort of mother could have produced such a child? After the first month his sisters had been forbidden to go to Bel Manoir or to invite her to Rosevale. And now she was back again alone, with twenty men, fighting beside them to save Bel Manoir and her cotton and sugar cane.

The idea of making love to her had never occurred to Hector MacTavish; he could not support bold, dominating, arrogant women. In the very idea he found something unnatural and a little terrifying, yet there was something about her which fascinated him. Each time he saw her, the idea of her took possession of him. He would find himself thinking of her in unguarded moments as he was thinking of her now while he rode along the lonely moonlit road, resenting her boldness and shamelessness, her superior and contemptuous airs, as if she were more clever than any of them.

He thought, "To hell with her!" and kicked the gray mule on his bony ribs. At the same time he turned to look behind him and saw that the whole of the sky to the north was aglow, and he thought, "They have set fire to Bel Manoir. Well, let it burn!" and continued on his melancholy journey, falling after a while into a kind of dream thinking again of his horses and especially of old Regina and her soft muzzle. All night he rode and in all the lush and fertile country he saw no man, black or white.

The reflected light from the fires had almost died away when Tom Bedloe, still awake, lying on the great bed under the eaves, heard the key turning in the lock. He sat up, thinking, "Perhaps they have come to shoot me." But all the time he hoped that it was the young Baroness returning. Since she left the room he had thought of nothing else, seeing her clearly in his mind, allowing his imagination to lead him deeper and deeper into a kind of green morass of sensuality. She had been right; he would not go away. He could not go so long as she was at Bel Manoir.

The door opened and she came in, closing it behind her and turning the key. She was dressed all in black, her face as white as the collar at her throat. She was carrying a carbine and almost at once he heard her saying, "Are you still here?"

He rose from the bed, "Yes."

"I knew you would be." She placed the carbine against a chair.

"We killed a lot of the black devils. They won't bother us again tonight."

In her voice there was a quality of excitement, a curious unnatural excitement. As he came out of the shadows, she said, "Help me! Save me!" She seemed about to fall and he put out his arms to save her. As he caught her, she appeared to faint and then after a moment her body grew taut and she seized him, kissing his rough unshaven face and his throat wildly, crying out, "I killed them myself. They're lying out there in the moonlight. They're dead!" She laughed and said again, "They're dead! They're dead!"

For a moment the insane quality of her passion confused and embarrassed him.

All that which followed was full of fire and fury and evil, and when it was finished, she lay for a time very still, scarcely breathing, so that for a moment he was alarmed, thinking she was dead. But in a little while she opened her eyes and stood up and said abruptly, "Good night, I will bring your food in the morning."

He started to speak but said nothing for her voice was cold suddenly and full of self-possession as if he were no more to her than a prisoner. It was the cold dispassionate voice of the jail keeper.

"I advise you to keep away from the windows by daylight. They will not come up to this floor, but they may see you at the window."

Then quickly she picked up the carbine and went out the door, closing it and locking it again. For the first time it occurred to him that she walked and spoke more like a man than a woman.

It was nearly dawn before he fell asleep, for the experience left him bewildered and in a strange way, chastened. He had believed himself a man of many adventures and of experience, but never had he encountered anything like this passion which was like a white flame which seared but left no scar. And he was aware that he had never possessed her at all. It was as if he were the woman, as if he had been slowly and deliberately seduced, used, and immediately forgotten. And there was in it all a sinister and frightening element . . . the way she had cried out about death and the men she had helped to kill, as if in some way their death had roused in her a shameful and uncontrollable passion.

The burning sun was high above the half-wrecked house when

he was awakened by the opening of the door and saw her coming in with a tray and food. At sight of her he experienced a singular embarrassment, as if she were two women and he did not know which one of them had come in the door.

Looking at him she said, smiling, "Good morning. I hope you slept well."

"Very well. Thanks."

He was aware again of the old air of mockery which he found so confusing. There was nothing in her manner which gave even a hint of recognition of what had happened the night before. This woman carrying the tray was the one who had made him miserably uncomfortable that night in the *salon* of the house in New Orleans. Yet there was a difference; it was as if she assumed an understanding between them, as if somehow they were different from all other people on the earth, stronger, more certain of what they wanted. He had an odd feeling that they had known each other always, that they had been together thus, since the beginning of time.

She said, "Hector MacTavish has come back."

"What does that mean?"

"Nothing . . . only he reports that every plantation for miles around is deserted. And the niggers have all gone away into the swamp. The carpetbaggers have gone down the river. Two of the men we killed last night were Yankee soldiers. The rest have gone with the carpetbaggers."

"Does that mean that you are safe here now?"

"MacTavish doesn't know. They may come back."

She poured the coffee for him and as she did so he noticed that on the tray was the same ancient worn silver which had come to him on that first morning in the cabin prison. He said, "There is something I want to know."

"Yes, what is it?"

"Was it you who sent the silver coffee pot that first morning to let me know where I was?"

"Yes."

"Why?"

She did not answer him in words. A smile spread slowly over the curiously attractive but unbeautiful face.

[159]

The coffee was excellent, strong and very black. She said, "I made it myself . . . the way we make it in Martinique. The coffee in Louisiana is too often like dishwater."

He scarcely heard the speech for he was trying to discover exactly what she meant by the curious slow smile. He knew now that she was not in love with him, any more than he was in love with her. This was something more than love and something less, with the inevitable and impersonal quality of the attraction of iron for a magnet.

Like an excellent housewife she began putting the room in order. He watched her for a long time as he drank the coffee. She went about her task, picking up a chair overturned in the violence of the night before, drawing the curtains across the windows the better to conceal his presence. She behaved as if he were not there at all.

"Who is this Hector MacTavish?" he asked.

Without interrupting her housewifely tasks she said, "A neighbor. I've known him since he was a small boy. I once frightened him by being too impetuous. We were both about seventeen." She laughed, "He was a virgin. He has never liked me since."

"I didn't mean exactly that." He had the feeling that it was now his turn to mock her. He knew that she understood his mockery but she betrayed the understanding by no sign.

She said, "He is the leader of the lot. 'Silver Spoon' Wicks is living in his family house in New Orleans. MacTavish is what you would call an estimable southern gentleman." With the last sentence her voice was colored by an extraordinary contempt and bitterness, betraying two things—her own scorn of respectability and the likelihood that "estimable southern gentlemen" did not approve of her. "He has," she added, "what is called a Presbyterian conscience."

"So that's it!"

"Yes. That's it."

She had finished her tasks by now and stood waiting.

"Does no one know that I am here?"

"No. They all believe you have escaped. MacTavish gave them hell when he came back."

"You could do me a great favor."

"What?"

"Bring me a razor and soap and hot water." He rubbed his stubbly chin. "I must be pretty nasty looking like this."

"I like you that way. A beard makes a man seem more a man. But if it pleases you. . . ."

"It will please me."

"Very well."

Then she picked up the tray and went out, and when she had gone he went to the window to look out across the rough open space between the great house and the slave quarters. Where the slave cabins had been there were only piles of ashes and charred beams. The cabin where he had been imprisoned, with its evil memories of Elias Sharp the overseer, was only a heap of ashes. He grinned, thinking that if she had not come to save him he would now be nothing more than a heap of white carbonized bones, scattered among the ashes.

On the grass between the slave quarters and the house there were great dark splotches of blood. Someone had carried away the bodies; in the heat they would become unpleasant sights within a few hours. Beyond the quarters the flat lush landscape extended for miles until it became lost in a faint blue haze of heat. Suddenly he felt tired and relaxed, and again he experienced a quick flash of desire for the clearness of the New England air, the sight of pine trees and scrubby pastures and stone walls, gray and sharply outlined in the clarity of the atmosphere. All that was far away. He had a sudden sense of being lost, of having wandered a long way, of having been driven on and on by something beyond his power of control.

The sound of a knock at the door brought him sharply back to reality. He was about to speak when he thought quickly. "It cannot be her. She does not knock." And he made no sound. The knock was repeated once and again and then a man's voice which had a familiar timbre, said, "Open up or I'll fire through the door."

Stealthily he moved along the wall so that he might place himself beside the door out of range. The voice, now more familiar, said again, "Open up! Open up!" and then in quick succession two shots were fired. The bullets splintered the panels of the door and buried themselves in the bed opposite.

For a moment there was silence and then the voice said, "I will return."

Listening he heard the sound of retreating footsteps but, fearing trickery, he still remained pressed against the wall beside the door. He was still there when he heard the sound of the key turning and thought, "Well, there's nothing to be done now. They've got me this time."

But when the door opened, only the young Baroness came in. She was carrying a pitcher of hot water and shaving implements. She had an absurd settled air of domesticity, and smiled at the sight of him with his body pressed cautiously against the wall. She put down the shaving things and said, "It was my cousin Amedé who shot at you. He must have followed me up the stairs this morning."

Grinning, he said, "He didn't come anywhere near me."

"He won't do it again," she said.

"I hope not. I wouldn't have got off so easy if I'd happened to be on the bed."

"He was my first lover when I was seventeen. He lost his arm in a duel over me. He killed a man who called me a Créole whore."

She spoke perfectly calmly, almost flatly, so that he felt a desire, partly born of hysteria, to laugh.

"And what is going to happen now?"

"Nothing . . . until they hear from New Orleans."

"And then what?"

"Perhaps they will shoot you. Perhaps they will let you go. It depends on 'Silver Spoon's' reply."

"Yes?"

"Yes."

He laughed, "In any case, I'll be shaved and clean for the funeral."

He laughed because he knew now there was no danger of his being shot. He knew it from the tone of her voice and the look in her eyes and because in a swift moment of intuition, he saw that she was very like himself. She would not let them shoot him so long as she had reasons for wanting to keep him alive.

At a little before sundown, one of the band, a boy of eighteen named Callendon, brought back the answer from New Orleans. The General had not troubled to answer them directly. He had answered them in the columns of the *Delta*. The newspaper announced the arrest of eight leading citizens, most of them men over fifty who had stayed in New Orleans to safeguard as far as possible the interests of their fellow citizens. Each one of them had many relatives and many friends even among Les Défenseurs. A cousin of Hector MacTavish was among them.

Following the announcement of their arrest and imprisonment there was a statement from the General in Command of the City of New Orleans. It was brief, stating merely that the prisoners had been taken as hostages in reprisal for certain acts of a band of renegade outlaws known as "Les Défenseurs" who had seized three officers of the Union Army. If any of them came to harm, the General announced, the hostages would be summarily shot.

In the parlor at Bel Manoir the little band gathered while Hector MacTavish read the announcement. As he read the line of the square jaw grew hard and the color went out of his sunburned face. When he had finished, he put the copy of the *Delta* on the table beside him and said, quietly, "Well, it seems that we must find some other plan."

Young Chauvin Boisclair, a dark impetuous boy, cried out, "We'll take the forts and free the prisoners."

"With what?" asked Hector MacTavish. "How? With fifteen or twenty men?"

"There must be some way," said the Lafosse boy. "We could think up some way."

Then Amédé de Lèche spoke. There was a wild look in his black eyes. The quality of the white in his face had changed from waxen to chalk. With his one thin white hand he was twisting the buttons on his jacket. He said, "There's only one thing to do . . . shoot the prisoner anyway!"

MacTavish did not answer him, but the young Baroness said, "You tried that once, cousin. You had best not try it again."

MacTavish heard her but he said nothing. The clear blue eyes saw everything and sometimes a great deal which to other eyes was not visible. Then he said to young Boisclair, "Come with me. I want to make sure the canebrake is empty."

[163]

He saw that the young Baroness was watching him. The corners of her mouth trembled a little with the shadow of a smile. In the eyes was the light of mockery—a mockery of many things, of her cousin Amedé, of that scene long ago when her boldness had disgusted Hector MacTavish, a mockery of all the men in the room, as if she said, "I am stronger and more clever than any of you."

He gave no sign of recognizing the mockery. He simply turned away and taking the Boisclair boy with him, went out of the door. The broad shoulders drooped a little, but there was no other sign of weariness or discouragement.

When he had gone she took up the copy of the *Delta* from the table and went out. As she passed Amedé de Lèche she said, "Remember what I told you, cousin. You had best not try it again." There was something vicious in the color of her voice as she spoke the word cousin.

Then she left the room, taking with her the newspaper up the stairs to the room where Tom Bedloe was kept a prisoner. When she had closed and locked the door behind her, she showed him the message of "Silver Spoon" Wicks.

"We've been checkmated," she said. "You're free now. There's no point in keeping you. You'd only be a nuisance."

Quickly he read the blustering statement. Then he grinned and said, "I don't know whether I want to be free. I rather like being a prisoner."

She shrugged her shoulders. "The decision is entirely up to you. I shouldn't think it was very safe. Anyone might take a pot shot at you just for luck."

"What are you meaning to do?"

"I don't know. It depends on what MacTavish plans."

For a moment he considered this, knowing perfectly well that he meant to follow her wherever she went, not only because of the compulsion upon him but because there was still the necessity to subdue her, to establish his own position as the dominant one. It was a sense of incompleteness more than anything which tormented him. Then he said, "What's this MacTavish like?"

She looked at him quickly as if she hoped to find that he was jealous. Then she said, "He is quite a fellow. He's the kind of man other men look to . . . especially younger men."

He watched her with a curious look and asked, "What will he do?"

"I don't know."

"He's fighting a losing fight."

"Why do you say that?"

"His material is no good. It's full of rottenness."

Again she shrugged her shoulders. Then she gave him the key. "There," she said, "you can do as you choose. Only I would not go walking about and I should keep my door locked. I think my cousin is insane. Consumption produces very queer effects. I don't think that even MacTavish can control him."

"And what am I to eat?"

"I will bring you your meals until I go away."

She had told him what he wanted to know—that what happened the night before was not to be merely an isolated experience.

Then she went away and when she had gone he sat for a time thinking of her, puzzled and excited again. But after a time, he remembered the newspaper and taking it up, fell to reading it in an effort to discover what had happened in New Orleans since the night he left so unexpectedly to follow her to Bel Manoir.

There were the usual items regarding transfers and appointments and the arrival of ships. An account of the arrest and trial of two New Orleans ladies as "prostitutes" because one of them had displayed a small Confederate flag on the lapel of her jacket and the other had hummed "Dixie" as she passed a Union officer. Another Yankee officer had been wantonly attacked and beaten by rebel dastards. It was all Yankee news for it was the only newspaper General Wicks permitted in the stricken city and it was no more than an organ of the General himself and his satellites.

Slowly he turned the page and there he found an item of singular interest. It read simply, *"Following the disorders at the Café Imperial on Thursday night when the place was wrecked and two officers of the loyal army badly hurt, the Commander of the Army of Occupation has ordered the closing of all cafés, restaurants and establishments of dubious reputation until further notice. Madame Duchesne, also known as 'La Lionne' has disappeared and the military police have been unable to execute the warrant for her arrest.*

It is believed that she may have fled the city aboard a French vessel which sailed yesterday for Bordeaux."

He put down the paper and lighted one of the cheroots the young Baroness had brought him.

So La Lionne had disappeared! He experienced a swift feeling of regret, partly because he was fond of her and admired her character and independence, partly because there was always in the back of his consciousness the knowledge that when this other thing was finished, when it was complete, he could go back to her. She was that sort of woman. It occurred to him that he had scarcely thought of her since the night when, returning from the General's party, he had resisted the temptation to enter the Café Imperial and had gone on to his billet to discover the young Baroness dressing the arm of the wounded Défenseur. It occurred to him that everything had become immensely complicated, that in this sultry half-tropical country, the slightest thing might lead to changes and passions and incredible complications. Here everything—even daily life—had a kind of theatrical, melancholy, overwrought quality. It was not at all like New England, or even Virginia or New York. Here there was too much romance; it was laid on thick like the plaster from a mason's trowel. Everything was romance and love and duels and assassinations, carried on always in an atmosphere in which the odors of fertile mud and disease and the scent of jasmine were equally mixed. And he had again the sense of having been carried away like a swimmer caught in a rip-tide, beyond his depth.

What was happening to him had its fantastic side. What had begun by being merely another conquest had become melodramatic and mysterious and complicated in a wild setting in the swamps with fire and torture and death just outside the windows of a great ruined house. Beside this any other love affair he had ever had, even the one with La Lionne, was pallid and tame. It all seemed foolish and dangerous and yet the very folly and danger gave it a savor and a satisfaction which made every other experience he had ever known seem narrow and commonplace.

He knocked the ashes from his cigar and taking off his shirt in the rising heat he continued his reading, thinking, "Perhaps it is better that she has gone back to France. She might have become troublesome."

Out of boredom he read everything, even the notices of sales of household goods and legal announcements of petty lawsuits, and so his mind had become quite dull again when he turned to the final page and discovered the most astonishing piece of news that he could possibly have conjured up even in the wildest flights of his imagination.

It was given a great deal of importance, with the lead in large chunky black type.

STORY OF MYSTERIOUS SHIP CLEARED UP. IDENTITY OF TWO LOST LADIES ESTABLISHED—THEY ARE NIECE AND SISTER OF GENERAL WICKS

Casually he began to read and almost immediately the cheroot fell from his mouth and he swore aloud.

It couldn't possibly be true—what he was reading—that Aunt Tam and Agnes were in Louisiana. David hadn't known it, or Aunt Louisa. It couldn't be true. They were both safe in the house in Pinckney Street sitting before the fire in the long drawing-room, embroidering and gossiping with the other female relatives. Somebody must be crazy!

Then he read on about the "mystery ship" and the cholera and the flight into the bayous and swamps and finally the news that General Wicks had sent four battalions of soldiers to search the swamps and rescue them.

Twice he read the story through and still he could not believe what he was reading. He rose and began walking up and down the room, filled with a desire for action but not knowing what form it was to take. He would escape and go to New Orleans but almost at once the idea seemed absurd. Even if he succeeded in escaping he would have to make his way back to the city on foot, and he did not even know whether Agnes was alive. It was very probable that both she and Aunt Tam were dead of cholera or by violence somewhere in the muddy fertile reaches of the Delta. How could two gently bred women of the North survive in all this wildness and violence?

Into his mind came a sudden picture of Aunt Tam and poor

little Agnes, dying there in the wilderness. He saw Agnes very clearly, blonde and young and child-like, helpless and alone with Aunt Tam who was only a fool. The tears came into his eyes, genuine tears at the moment, born of genuine masculine pity for the girl's helplessness. He began to curse again saying over and over, "God damn the fools! God damn the damned fools!" He did not mean Agnes and poor old Aunt Tam but those who had permitted the journey and encouraged it. And he thought, "It was that old cow, Aunt Louisa. She sent for them because no woman in New Orleans would speak to her." That must be the only reason—that the General's wife had been lonely, that she had wanted for support the presence of stalwart and virtuous New England women like herself.

Then as he grew calmer, he sat down again and lighted another cheroot, with the newspaper propped before him. With the first excitement gone out of him, he saw that there was very little he could do beyond trying to return to New Orleans as quickly as possible. And if he returned there—what? Either he would find that Agnes and Aunt Tam were dead or that they had been rescued. If they were dead, they were dead, but if they were alive there would be complications. He wanted to marry Agnes; she was exactly suitable and he was, in spite of everything, sufficiently in love with her, but this other thing was not yet finished and Agnes, backed by Aunt Louisa and Aunt Tam, might not be the gentle lamb she had always been.

"That damned Aunt Louisa," he thought. "That damned, bumptious woman." She was always meddling, always directing. For the first time he saw clearly how much trouble she had caused; he saw that she and not the General had really been the ruler of New Orleans, imposing her nasty smallness upon the pattern of the stricken city. He had never thought of her one way or another until now when her muddling directly affected his existence. He had laughed at her, humored her, even now and then smacked her backside—a liberty she would have allowed no other person on earth, not even her husband—because the friendship of the General and herself was important to him. Through that he had led a free life, with no disciplinary annoyances; through good relations with the satrap from Massachusetts and his wife, he had achieved promotion and grown rich in a few months. If he had been in the General's house in New Orleans instead of being shut up here a prisoner in a ruined plantation house he would have told her off for her muddling. Damn the old cow!

As evening came, the heat abated a little and the grim ruins of the slave quarters took on a kind of beauty in the violet light. In the shadows of the room he forgot Agnes and Aunt Tam and the General's wife and fell to waiting. Only one thing was any longer of importance—that she return. By the time it was quite dark he was trembling as if from a chill and at last when he heard footsteps in the hallway outside he hurried to the door and flung it open.

She was standing there, the curious, provocative face lighted by the candle on the tray she carried. She was smiling at him and he noticed almost at once that the tray was set for two people with a bottle of wine and a bottle of ancient brandy.

He said, "I was afraid you weren't coming." And for a moment in the smile and the light in her eyes there was the gleam of that devastating intimacy which he had never encountered in his relations with any other woman. It was a kind of understanding which placed the two of them on some plane high above all other people in the world in a kind of sulphurous glory, the devastating bond between two purely sensual people who had no sense of sin and knew no shame.

As she put the tray on a small mahogany table, he closed the door and locked it quickly, shutting them in from all the world outside.

A little after ten o'clock Hector MacTavish set out upon his patrol, riding the big gray mule. Keeping always to the shadows, his nerves alert for any sound, he turned toward the road leading to his own plantation meaning to cross the bayou by the ferry at Pont-a-Mousson. There would be no one there to operate the boat but with luck he would find it on the Bel Manoir side and with his own great strength he could manage to propel it to the other side. The ferry would save him more than three miles of heavy roads.

As the mule jolted along, MacTavish thought of many things— of his own house, pilfered and deserted, of his horses, of what was to come. Although he was an immensely strong and active young man, he was, like most leaders, given to grave and sometimes despondent periods of reflection, and gravity had settled upon him now like a mantle of gray.

Many things induced the mood—the checkmating of their plan by "Silver Spoon" Wicks, the rumors that with the rising heat the fever was spreading again, this time bringing with it black cholera. But most of all it was the small scene which had happened so quickly between the young Baroness and Amedé when she said to him, "You tried that once, cousin. You had best not try it again."

MacTavish was a simple man for all his intelligence, and what he had seen in the eyes of the last two surviving members of the de Lèche family as they looked at each other, was something which frightened him and brought a faint chill of horror, partly because what he saw there he could not understand through his own thoughts or experience. He was not a prig and he loved women, but in that glance between the two cousins there were intimations of dark and complicated things which made him feel soiled and uncomfortable, emotions which he himself was incapable of feeling. And then the sudden awareness of what was happening between Éliane de Lèche and the Yankee prisoner in the room on the upper floor filled him with a sense of distaste in which there was more than a shade of anger. It seemed to him that not only was she unmoral but disloyal, an altogether reprehensible woman whose ways he could not fathom.

It was not that he was jealous of the Union officer, nor even envious, but that the woman herself raised doubts in his mind as to the virtues of decency, that she raised intimations of sensual mysteries and delights which he did not wish to explore but which tormented his imagination.

Half aloud he said, "Damn the woman!" The mule hearing his voice, supposed that he was being urged on his way and sank back into a slow ungainly walk.

Then for a time he put her out of his mind and fell to brooding over what lay ahead when this bitter war was finished, if it ever was finished. In his heart he could not see victory for either side. He believed in the Confederacy, he had fought for it, not for the preservation of slavery alone; the issue was much more complicated and profound than that. To him it was a war between the landowners of the South and the factory owners of the North, between one system and another, between two kinds of civilization. He had never believed that slavery was inevitable or good, and he did not believe that it was a system which could be thrown out over-night without violence and tragedy and confusion for slave and master alike. He did not believe that negroes were meant by God to be slaves—that was an argument of the tricky politician or the pious hypocrites; he did not believe it because he knew his own slaves and loved them as he loved his horses, which was with a high and noble love which he gave to few white men or women.

He believed in Secession because he did not see how the great landowner and the great rich industrialist elements could survive in partnership; their interests were too profoundly opposed. One or the other must go down in ruin and he knew that any economic battle in which the bankers took part must go against the landowner.

What discouraged him most was the character of his own people. As a rich planter and the youngest congressman from the South he knew them—in Alabama, in Georgia, in South Carolina; and sometimes in his heart he despaired of them for their decadence, their grace, their charm, their ineffectiveness. It seemed to him, riding the mule through the scented darkness, that the Louisianians were the worst of all with their quadroon mistresses, their laziness and extravagance, their overripe emphasis on romance and gallantry. It was not from such stock that one recruited the strong men and the able women who would be needed if they were to survive.

To his tough Scottish blood there seemed to be a curse upon the whole state of Louisiana, as if the dark blend of French and Spanish blood and the fertile beauty of the country carried in themselves the seeds of ruin and decadence. Since the beginning the history of the state had been one of violence and corruption. In its future and present he could discover only the same elements. It was as if Éliane de Lèche and her cousin stood in a strange fashion as symbols of the evil that corrupted everything it touched, the evils of decadence and cruelty, of greed and indifference which ate like gangrene at this very country where he was born and which he loved so much.

When he thought of the little band he had brought together to fight a vain guerilla war against the pilfering shopkeeping Yankees, his heart grew heavy. They were brave enough and dashing enough —young Chauvin Boisclair and his cousin Faucon and Javolle DeMouy and all the others, even poor dying Amedé de Lèche, but they had no character and they were spoiled and as badly educated and ignorant as his own slaves. They lived for drinking and women and horses. They were romantic and pretty, but for what lay ahead, the building up of all this ruined province, men of stronger faith and fiber were needed, men with even a dash of that toughness and materialism of the Yankee prisoner who was at this moment entertaining Éliane de Lèche. For the defiance, the toughness, the recklessness of that fellow he had a certain respect.

He had passed the burned *garconnière* of the Boisclair plantation and was descending the muddy lane which led down to the ferry when he heard faintly the sound of a man's voice singing softly. It came across the water of the bayou and as the song took form in the still night he recognized it as an old slave song he had heard all his life.

> *Malle couri dan deser*
> *Malle marche dan savane*
> *Malle marche su piquan doré*
> *Malle oui ca yu de moin*

Swinging down from the mule, he tied the beast to a tree and slithered down the bank to the edge of the water. Here, hidden among the tall reeds by the landing he waited, watching. The boat was an ordinary skiff with three persons in it. One, a big man, was poling it through the clotted water hyacinths. In the dim light of the rising moon he could make out the figures of two other persons but not their sex. The voice continued singing—a deep, rich voice full of homesickness. The memory of the song it was singing and the quality of the voice itself brought sudden tears into the eyes of Hector MacTavish. The man was singing a nostalgic song about "La Louisane" which had never been and perhaps would never be.

Then he became aware that the man in the skiff was bringing it in shore to the ferry landing. It came nearer and nearer and with the effort of thrusting the boat through the hyacinths, the boatman stopped singing. In silence, with one mighty thrust of his powerful shoulders, the man pushed the boat through the reeds into the soft mud at the ferry landing. Then Hector MacTavish saw that he was black and at the same time something familiar in the easy thrust of the great shoulders made him know that the man was big César from Bel Manoir who had run away after nearly killing Elias Sharp.

At the same moment the two figures seated in the rear of the skiff stood up and Hector MacTavish saw that they were women and white or very light colored octoroons.

Drawing his pistol he stepped out of the reeds and said, "Good evening, César!"

At the same time César quickly drew the long knife he carried in his belt and turned toward him, ready to attack.

MacTavish said quietly, in French, "You know me, César. What are you doing here?"

In the moonlight the big negro's teeth shone white in a wide grin as he put away the knife.

"Ah's comin' home," he said, "and ah'm fetchin' two white ladies. Mis' Jones and young Mis' Wicks. Ah fetched 'em all the way from Cuba."

MacTavish, having put away his pistol, bowed to the two women, noticing that one was old and ugly and one very young and very pretty with a skin which in the moonlight was white as milk. Standing there in the mud, he welcomed them to his own country, thinking glumly that it was an odd place and time to offer hospitality to strangers.

Then he explained who he was, while big César kept saying, "M'sieu MacTavish fine man." And "M'sieu MacTavish friend of all black people," and "There ain't no reason to be afraid of M'sieu MacTavish."

MacTavish said, "You had better come with me. The country is not safe now. There's no place safe to go but to Bel Manoir. I can't offer you a carriage. There isn't a horse within miles."

Then César asked in French if it was true that all negroes were now free and if it was safe for him to go back to Bel Manoir, and

MacTavish told him what had happened there and about the savage murder of Elias Sharp, and César, rolling his eyes, asked, "Ma wife and chillun? What is become of 'em?" And MacTavish said they had gone away, probably to New Orleans with the other good negroes.

Then the older of the two women made an astonishing statement. She said, rather primly and with importance, "We are on our way to New Orleans to visit General Wicks. It is very kind of you to look out for us."

For a moment MacTavish did not answer her. The statement seemed astonishing, even impossible. It was as if God had delivered fresh hostages into the hands of the Defenseurs. But his mind worked quickly and almost at once he saw the futility of any plan of using them. "Silver Spoon" still held the relatives and friends in the forts.

He said, "It is a pleasure to do what I can for you ladies—even though you are relatives of General Wicks. I will see that you arrive safely in New Orleans, Madame."

Then rather stiffly he said, "It's a good four miles to Bel Manoir. I cannot offer you a carriage but I have a very serviceable old mule. He will carry the two of you."

The older woman said, "That's very kind of you, but we do not mind walking. We have been through a great deal and feel rather hardened."

But he insisted. Bringing the old mule out of the bushes, he bade César lift up the two women. Aunt Tam got up in front with Agnes behind her, holding firmly to her waist. The strangeness of the situation and the awareness that they were on opposite sides in a bitter struggle, left them all silent. Only big César seemed unaware of the sense of strain. He kept on muttering in a strange mixture of English, Spanish and *patois* French that M'sieu MacTavish was a fine gentleman and that they had nothing to fear.

Then they set out, César leading the old mule with Hector MacTavish walking beside him, his pistol drawn in case they encountered anything troublesome. Now and then in the French of the Parish he asked César questions, edging out of the negro the whole story of the fantastic flight. Once he smiled, saying to César, "You are a remarkable fellow." And César said, "They are kind, good ladies. The old one is a very good lady. The young one is only a baby chick still with the down on her."

On the back of the mule Aunt Tam and Agnes rode in silence. Agnes was tired and felt sleepy but Aunt Tam remained alert, partly because she was not certain of her balance and partly because she kept straining her ears in an effort to understand what the two men were saying, but even when she heard a word or two it meant nothing to her for she could not understand anything of the *patois* in which they conversed.

She was having one of her elevated moments when her spirit soared. The adventure which she feared was nearing an end, had opened into a whole new chapter. At first she had been terrified at the spectacle of a stranger with drawn pistol emerging from the rushes. For a moment or two she had visions of violence and rape and ransom and perhaps even murder, but the fear went out of her when the stranger began to talk. He spoke like a gentleman and he had the manners of a gentleman, but it was not this which stifled her fears. She knew there were plenty of men with good manners who could be villains at heart. It was first of all the sound of his voice and then the sight of his face as he lifted his hat with the moonlight falling full upon him. The voice had a peculiar warm timbre; it was the voice of a wise and strong man, and the face was a remarkably pleasant face, strong and simple and handsome and young, a straightforward face which her instinct told her was the face of a man to be trusted. She had an odd feeling that she had known him before, and she liked the way he spoke to César who was her friend. Almost at once she had whispered to Agnes, "He's all right. There's no need to be afraid."

In an indignant whisper she had received the reply, "I'm not afraid."

And now here she was, a prisoner of the enemy, riding on a gray mule through wild abandoned country infested with escaped convicts and renegade soldiers and murderous escaped slaves. The adventure had not yet come to an end; she wasn't yet forced to sit evening after evening quietly talking with Louisa and the General about Cousin-this and Cousin-that and what was going to happen to old Uncle Edward's property.

[175]

The prospect of visiting Louisa had grown daily more distasteful. She had never cared much for Louisa, now that she thought about it—but until lately she had never known the reasons. Now, riding in the moonlight of deep Louisiana she understood; it was because Louisa had no largeness of spirit, no "expansion." Everything about her was controlled to the bursting point, like a too tightly laced fat woman. Louisa always took a small mean view of everything, mocking the spiritual flights of men like Mr. Emerson and Bronson Alcott. Now, far away from Boston and New England it seemed to Aunt Tam that there were only two kinds of people in that bleak northern country—either they were like Louisa and her own brother, materialistic, "smart" and small-minded, or *spiritual* men like Mr. Emerson and great reformers like William Lloyd Garrison and Margaret Fuller. Nobody in New England seemed simply to relax and be merry and enjoy themselves.

Thinking about Louisa and the General she wondered now whether she could tolerate a visit with them. So much had happened since she last saw them; she felt quite a different person *inside* as if she had been growing, expanding, warming. It must, she thought, primly, be the sort of feeling which a healthy pregnant woman experienced, the sort of *triumphantly* pregnant woman who could be so annoying, as if what had happened to her had never happened before to any other woman.

Suddenly her thoughts were interrupted by her awareness that the mule had stopped. Ahead of them in the moonlight on the muddy road, two men were advancing toward them. They themselves were in the shadow of a great live oak. Mr. MacTavish was standing with his pistol drawn. For a little while he stood silently, tense and still. Then suddenly he relaxed, dropped the pistol into the holster and called out, "Chauvin! Élie!"

The two men on the moonlit road stopped and Mr. MacTavish called out again, "C'est moi, 'Ector!" and went out into the middle of the road where the three stood talking for a time. Then the two men turned back and Mr. MacTavish came to where Aunt Tam and Agnes were waiting under the tree. Aunt Tam noticed how tall he was and how straight and how he walked as if he were accustomed always to be on the back of a horse.

He talked again with big César and then instead of going ahead along the road, big César turned the mule, and Mr. MacTavish with his pistol drawn again led them into the underbrush.

For nearly an hour they moved through scrub and swamp and presently they emerged into a cane brake and here Mr. MacTavish took the lead, advancing with his pistol drawn, fifty feet ahead of them. To Aunt Tam and Agnes, tired with the jolting of the old mule, the journey through the brake seemed interminable. The bruised cane gave off a sickening sugary smell in the hot damp air. It stood higher than the back of the mule.

At last they came to an open space of many acres beyond which a dark clump of enormous trees with the roof of a house rising above it showed black and gray in the silver light. On the edge of the brake Mr. MacTavish stopped and whistled, making a sound like the night birds Aunt Tam and Agnes had heard again and again on the long journey through the swamps. From the clump of trees on the opposite side the whistle was answered. As if to make certain there was no mistake, Mr. MacTavish repeated the call and again it was answered. Then he led them across the open space and through a gate in the pink brick wall into a big garden, black with shadows and overgrown with flowering shrubs.

In the great hallway on the second floor there was a light which illuminated faintly the stairway up which the little party followed Hector MacTavish. As they reached the hallway itself with its shattered mirrors and wrecked furniture, big César gave a cry and in French said, "God have mercy on us, M'sieu MacTavish. What have they done?"

MacTavish did not answer him. He had discovered at the far end of the hall the figure of Amedé de Lèche. The small wiry body was half hidden in the shadows of a great armchair. The single light, a hurricane lantern, stood on the rosewood table beside him. Near it was a bottle of brandy. Amedé was huddled in the chair, a glass in his hand, a pistol across his knee. He was very drunk and the brandy in the glass he held stained the gray trousers. At sight of him MacTavish divined what was happening. He had been drinking to drive his courage to the striking point where he had the will to climb the stairs and kill his cousin Éliane and the Yankee. He thought, "We came back none too soon."

Quickly he walked over to Amedé and took the pistol off his knees. "What are you doing?" he asked. "Why aren't you on guard duty?"

Amedé de Lèche lifted his head unsteadily, the face as white as paper in the dim light. His lips moved but no sound came out of them. MacTavish knew then there was no danger—the man was too drunk to move. Although no sound came from the lips, the black eyes, so black they seemed to have no pupils, were eloquent. There was in them a look of utter despair and misery. It was as if in the sodden body, the spirit somehow remained sober and clear. The face, so deadly white in the light of the hurricane lamp, was, MacTavish thought afterward, like the face of a man looking up from hell, the face of a man hopelessly damned. The look in the eyes was that of a man who wanted revenge, a man in torture of jealousy and hatred who was paralyzed by fear.

MacTavish thought quickly, "It's that damned harlot! He's afraid of her. He's afraid to kill her." And suddenly he wished that he had not arrived so soon. Wickedly he thought, "It would have been better if he had killed her and himself." The damned Yankee did not matter; he was white trash. No one would have missed him save perhaps a woman or two he left behind.

MacTavish took the glass from his hand and said, "You'd better let me take you to bed, Amedé."

But Amedé de Lèche did not answer him and suddenly he began to cough violently, the paroxysms shaking the thin body in waves of violence. MacTavish, filled with quick pity, leaned over and put his arm about the shoulders in an effort to stop the awful coughing, and then the hemorrhage came. The blood poured out of his mouth and over the torn Aubusson carpet. For two or three minutes the horror endured and then Amedé de Lèche collapsed and lost consciousness.

As MacTavish bent over him, he was aware of the presence at his side of the great gaunt woman he had found at the ferry landing. She said, "We must get him into bed and put heat at his feet. I'll help you."

MacTavish picked up the unconscious man. Against his own great strength the poor thin body of Amedé de Lèche had no more than the weight of a child. He said to the horse-faced woman be-

[178]

side him, "Come with me . . . and tell the girl to wait here. She ought not to see such things."

Then he led the way, cursing under his breath and thinking, "It's that damned harlot! She cost him his arm and his happiness and now she has killed him!" And as he crossed the great hall, carrying Amedé de Lèche, he kept seeing her, with her voluptuous figure and mocking black eyes in which there was too much evil, wisdom and provocation.

But the girl did not stay behind. When they went into the wrecked library next to the hall, she was there. When the older woman tried to send her away, she said, "No, I can be of help. I mean to stay." And looking at her, Hector MacTavish saw her clearly for the first time by the light of the hurricane lantern black César held above the body of the stricken man.

It was a child's face with scarcely a hint of maturity in it and yet there was firmness and character. The lips quivered a little and MacTavish thought, "She is afraid because she has never before seen death but she is brave and will not go away." Something in the face, perhaps its youngness and courage, brought an odd lump in his throat. She was beautiful too in the dim light, even in the soiled dress with her hair all awry.

They laid Amedé de Lèche on a sofa and César returned in a little while with stone jugs filled with hot water and a basin and some torn sheets of fine linen brought long ago from France as part of the old Baroness' bridal trousseau. Then Hector MacTavish and Aunt Tam sent Agnes out of the room and they undressed Amedé de Lèche and bathed the poor thin body and put the jugs of hot water across his heart and at his feet.

When MacTavish had felt the feeble pulse he said, "I must go now. I shall be back at daylight. You will be all right with César. He can find things to make you comfortable."

But Aunt Tam said they would watch at the side of the sick man and nothing could change her determination.

Very politely Mr. MacTavish said, "I would not go but for the sake of your safety. I am sorry we cannot make you more comfortable. It wasn't always like this at Bel Manoir." Then he smiled, a curious smile, easy and simple and friendly, as if he had known them both for a long while. "I hope you will not think this is Louisiana hospitality."

What he did not tell them before he left was the message given him by the two young men they had met on the road . . . that yellow fever had broken out in the camp of the revolting slaves and renegade soldiers in the swamp and that in terror they had begun to scatter again over the countryside. Three of them had been shot pilfering the ruins of the MacTavish plantation.

In the darkness he climbed the old mule and set out again down the highway lined with great oak trees which led to the edge of the menacing river. Then he turned south on the muddy lane which ran now along the top of the levee.

The news of the dispersal of the renegades disturbed him. Since the night they had been driven off, leaving eleven men and a woman dead on the open space between the house and the slave quarters, they had kept together on an island in the depths of the swamps. It was easy to watch them there; dispersed they might attack at any time in the night in small groups. But he had a feeling that they would not come again to trouble Bel Manoir. There were still plenty of defenseless plantation houses and stores for them to loot. They had, he knew, only chosen to attack Bel Manoir because of Elias Sharp and their hatred of the whole de Lèche family and because once, long ago, the splendor of the house with its plate and crystal chandeliers and French furniture had been famous. Certainly they would not come to attack the house in the rising dawn with no darkness to protect them.

And he was riding now to fetch the priest for Amedé de Lèche, because a priest was necessary for Amedé to get to heaven. As he rode through the rising dawn he reflected on these Catholic neighbors and friends of his, full of wonder for a thing he could not himself comprehend—that they should lead whoring wicked lives with sudden periods of repentance and devotion, that Amedé de Lèche should believe it necessary to have a priest at his side when he died in order to speed him into paradise. It was a strange belief, comforting perhaps but in his mind full of weakness and lacking in responsibility, convenient perhaps for men like Amedé and the other Créoles but not for himself. There had never been any formal religion in his life, for his grandfather, educated in France, had been a worshiper of Voltaire and Voltaire's love of humanity, and after him there was no church, either Protestant or Catholic, in the MacTavish family, a thing which had always been a scandal in the parish and which caused the MacTavishes for three generations always to marry outside of Louisiana.

And here he was, a MacTavish riding to fetch the priest, Father Desmoulins, who, despite everything, was his friend—a tall thin rosy-cheeked man with blue eyes and a clear and reasonable brain, who looked like an eighteenth century miniature of a French statesman-prince-of-the-church. Father Desmoulins forgave him things his neighbors would not because Father Desmoulins was in his way a great man who had spent most of his life among the Indians and the Negroes and the Sabines of the Delta, believing they were as much children of God as the men and women who lived in the great rich houses of New Orleans and the plantations. Father Desmoulins was one of the great things which had come down from the riotous corrupt past of the province.

The band at Bel Manoir had had no news of him since before the burning and looting began, but MacTavish knew that very likely he would find the old man at his little house at Beaupré.

He had too a second reason for the journey. He hoped to find a boat in which he might send the two women he had found by the ferry landing down the river to New Orleans. In a boat the journey would be much easier and simpler. He wanted to be rid of them, why he could not say except that deep within him the instinct to send them away was strong. There were times when the *Fey* quality of his Scottish blood was more acute than the quick intuition of the volatile Créoles. There was something wrong about the presence of the two New England women in the decaying doomed house of Bel Manoir. They did not belong there and no good could come of their presence.

He was tired. He had not felt the weariness until the moment he rode away from the great house down the avenue, and the weariness brought with it a loneliness of spirit which was rare with him and made him feel uneasy and discouraged. As he rode, the scene of Amedé de Lèche's collapse kept returning to him, taking on the proportions of symbolism. It was as if Amedé stood for other great families like his own who had gone the way of decadence and waste and futility, families which had come long ago out of the confused, dark beginnings of the province and had long since lost their vigor.

The MacTavishes were not like that. The MacTavishes, coming in after the Louisiana Purchase, were newcomers, vulgar and recent in origin, but vigorous. The thought occurred to him as it had occurred many times before, that there was a curse upon this country which he loved. It had produced again in cycle after cycle so much beauty and richness entangled always with corruption and decay, as if the very heat and fertility of the place carried with it a miasma of destruction. It was a country where there existed only the very rich and the very poor, where there had been much beauty and luxury and splendor, but always just beneath it much poverty and squalor. It was a country in which only the Negro ever seemed to be adaptable and comfortable. It was a negro's country, like the fantastic worlds you sometimes saw portrayed at the Opera.

And as he rode a curious thought came to him—that neither he nor any of his family had ever been at home here, because there was something in their blood which could never reconcile itself to the soft and easy life, to the heat, to the extravagant perfumes, to the rich, spiced foods.

In a moment of revelation he saw that all his life he had been contemptuous of men like Amedé de Lèche and Chauvin Boisclair and his neighbors, for their laziness and gaiety, for their duels and drinking and lush romanticism. At times all these things had in turn tempted him and he had yielded to the temptations, out-drinking, out-racing, out-loving all the others because the animal in him was more vigorous; but in none of it had he ever found more than a momentary sensual satisfaction, and afterward he had suffered disgust and disillusionment because the very core of their romantic debauchery was false, like the brown center of an apple which appeared bright and pretty on the surface. Their sensuality was not that of animal vigor like the brute sensuality of the Yankee prisoner nor the vigorous sensuality of an experienced woman like Éliane de Lèche whose harlot mother had somehow redeemed the taint of her de Lèche blood, but the wan sensuality of laziness and boredom—the same laziness and boredom from which their slaves and their plantations suffered. There was something soft and effeminate in it all which distressed him, not because of any finicky disapproval but because it was wasteful and sterile.

"The truth," he thought, smiling unconsciously in the rising gray light, "is that I am a Scotsman and by their standards a vulgar man."

At heart he was a reformer, a builder, a colonizer, a creator. He wanted always to change things, to alter them for the better. This life had always been too easy, too luxurious, lacking in hardships. It was like the hot nights when sometimes, unable to sleep, he had lain awake thinking of cold fogs and ice and snow to ease the sense of suffocation which tormented him.

Life for a young man should be a finer, sounder thing than mistresses and wine and rich food and slave servants. There should be in it, if it was to have any savor or satisfaction, struggle and the sense of building. A young man should love his wife and breed children, not alone for the delights of sensuality, but because he needed strong sons and daughters to work upon the structure begun by his own imagination and ambition.

The sense of building, of creation—the hunger for it was strong in his brain, his great chest, his loins, and now the whole structure which had come to him from his father—the plantation, the great house and the slave labor upon which it was all founded so precariously—was in ruins. It might be rebuilt—there would be a task! But, riding through the darkness, he doubted that it would even be worth rebuilding in this accursed beautiful country. What good was there in breeding strong sons to see them and their sons slowly corrupted by the very earth itself.

He found no boat nor did he see a living soul on all the long journey, save an old negress who looked at him in terror and vanished in the mists rising out of the swamp.

At last when he had ridden for nearly two hours, the blunt spire of the little church of St. Jean Baptiste appeared out of the rosy mist of dawn and as he came near to it, he saw that from the chimney of the house alongside at the edge of the bayou, smoke was rising. There was something homely in the sight of the smoke which touched him and filled his heart with warmth for the priest who, despite everything, had remained in his parish among what was left of his people.

At the little fence of unpainted cypress pickets he swung down from the mule, even his horse-accustomed legs stiff with so much riding of the stomp-gaited mule. At the little portico beneath the chinaberry tree he knocked on the green painted door and it was opened almost at once by Father Desmoulins himself, his face rosy and smiling despite the earliness of the hour. Behind him, pouring his *café-au-lait*, stood the old negress Célimène who was his only servant. At sight of MacTavish, her black face opened half its width in a toothless grin of welcome. In all the parish she loved MacTavish next to Père Desmoulins. She prayed to the Virgin every day of the year that he might be converted so that in the next world when she opened the door of her cottage there, he would be standing outside. For he had always been good to her people.

The old priest said, *"Bon jour, mon fils,"* and MacTavish said, *"Bon jour,* Père," and they shook hands, the handclasp lingering a little longer than that of men who know not the richness of their kind of friendship.

"You are in time for coffee," said the priest.

"I cannot stay," said MacTavish. "I've come to fetch you. Amedé de Lèche is dying."

"Dieu bénisse!" rumbled the old negress, crossing herself. *"Le pauvre mince gar'!"*

He quickly drank a bowl of *café-au-lait* and then the priest climbed up behind him on the tough gray mule and they set out for Bel Manoir. As the mist melted away beneath the rising sun, the heat, damp and enervating, began to settle down over the muddy river and the flat country below the levee.

Amedé de Lèche, the last male of his family, died a little after dawn on a torn sofa in the ruined house at Bel Manoir with two strange women from Boston watching, one an Episcopalian, one a Unitarian, at his side. He died quietly; one moment he was there and the next he had left the emaciated white body and it lay white and still and empty against the torn purple plush. That Father Desmoulins was not there beside him did not matter much to the peace of his mind for he slipped without consciousness into death.

It was Agnes who noticed that he was dead. It was the first time she had ever seen death, but some instinct, old as time, told her that the last faint sigh was the sign of death. She had been watching while Aunt Tam dozed, now and then wakening for a moment's bewilderment when she looked about her. Aunt Tam was asleep when the boy died.

For a long time Agnes sat watching the body, not seeing it, but beyond it into regions where her thoughts had never before entered. She wept not for the loss of this young man whom she had never known, but because he was young and therefore there was tragedy in his death, a kind of universal tragedy touched by a sense of waste. Death brushed close to her too because the dead youth seemed not much older than her brother David whom she loved. Her tears were in a strange mystical fashion for all the world, for the tragedy of this ruined strange house in which she sat and for the deaths which had happened here and in all her country North and South. In a moment or two before she roused Aunt Tam a tremendous thing happened to her. Whatever there remained in her of childishness after the hardships and perils and adventures of the last month, whatever remained of the child who had left Boston with Aunt Tam, died forever at the sight of the tired white young face of this stranger. She became aware of things—experiences and even adventures—which had never happened to her in this life. It was as if a kind of wisdom had come down to her from heaven, as if this sight of death were in some way the culmination of all that had begun with the obscene gesture made by the degraded crew of the *San Cristobal*.

Rousing herself from the trance which had seemed to paralyze her, she shook Aunt Tam gently and when the older woman had wakened, she said, "He is dead, Aunt Tam."

For a moment Aunt Tam was silent and then as if only half understanding where she was and what had happened, she said, "It's God's mercy! The poor little thing!" Why she said this she did not know. Quickly, as if embarrassed, she said, "I will stay with him. You go and find César or Mr. MacTavish."

But Agnes did not go at once. She rose and, going to a huge

[185]

gilt framed mirror that hung on the opposite side of the room, she stood for a moment regarding herself with a peculiar concentration as if she were looking at a stranger. Then quickly, as if embarrassed, she began to rearrange her hair and when she had finished she turned to Aunt Tam and after looking at her for a little time, she said, "What is to happen to us, Aunt Tam?"

"I wouldn't worry, child. God seems to take care of us. We shall get to New Orleans in God's good time."

"I don't mean that."

"What do you mean?"

"I don't know. Only everything seems so changed, as if something had happened to me or the world. It isn't the same any more."

Aunt Tam looked away from her and pretended to fiddle with the hurricane lamp. "Don't begin to talk in that high-falutin way, like Mr. Emerson. In any case it's not the time for it. Go and find César or Mr. MacTavish. He will have to be laid out and there doesn't seem to be any regular person to do it here."

So Agnes, still bewildered, went out and when she had gone, Aunt Tam went to the mirror in her turn and looked at herself. The reflection of the horse-face seemed strange to her, and as she looked into her own honest eyes, she understood a little what Agnes meant when she said, "What is to become of us?" for never again could they go back to that small, protected life of the house in Pinckney Street where everything seemed to be without blood or splendor or richness. It was queer that she understood only now that it had always been like that, all those years of her youth and even in Paris where somehow her family had managed to keep themselves forever immersed in the same atmosphere of remoteness and sterility. It was bitter to her that she had discovered these things now, so late in life.

As she stood half-enchanted by the strange look in the reflection of her eyes, she became aware in a dreamy way of the presence in the mirror of a strange figure. It was that of a woman—a young woman—dressed all in black. For a second it seemed to her that the face was that of the young man who lay dead here in the room with her, but almost at once she saw that it was a different face, very like that of the dead man, but stronger, more

[186]

vigorous, more determined. The woman was watching her. She did not know how long she had been looking at her own reflection nor how long the woman had been standing there. She felt a sudden embarrassment and annoyance as if she had been standing there naked. As she turned away from the mirror the woman said, "Is he dead?"

"Yes. He died only a little while ago."

"He is my cousin," said the woman.

She had a warm, rather deep and moving voice, but she spoke flatly without emotion.

"I am sorry," said Aunt Tam.

"You need not be sorry," said the woman. "There is nothing you could have done. There was never any hope for him . . . from the beginning. He was always a foolish boy. He believed in love."

To this extraordinary statement Aunt Tam was unable to find any answer. Before she could recover herself, the woman asked, "Who are you? How did you come to this God-forsaken place?"

To Aunt Tam it seemed odd and lacking in respect for the dead to continue such a conversation callously in the presence of a corpse. So she said, "My name is Abigail Jones. I come from Boston. Colonel MacTavish found me and my niece on the bayou last night." She did not know why she said "Colonel" save that the nice young man seemed to have an air of authority. Rather tartly, she asked, "May I ask who you are, Madame?"

The woman said, "I am the Baroness Éliane de Lèche. This is my house."

"I hope you will forgive our being here," said Aunt Tam. "I was brought here. It was not a matter of choice."

The stiffness, the awkwardness of the first encounter had changed now into something else. The quality was intensified, crystallized into something very near to hostility as if in some way the principles of good and of evil confronted each other. Aunt Tam was rather like an alarmed cat with its back arched, its hair bristling. She found this woman "disgusting" but what troubled her most was the feeling of hatred she experienced. She was a simple good-natured woman to whom hatred was a disturbing and uncomfortable emotion. For the first time in her life she understood what hatred was. The quality of mockery in the woman seemed to pervade her whole being, even to the black of her dress.

The young Baroness said, "I'm sorry that you arrived at such an unfortunate time with death and ruin in the house." And then when Aunt Tam said nothing in reply. "It was very good of you to sit up with my cousin."

"Any one would have done it." As Aunt Tam spoke, it struck her for the first time how odd it was that in such circumstances Mr. MacTavish had not roused the owner of the house, even more odd that this woman should not have appeared at all and when she did appear that she behaved in this strange inhuman fashion.

But at that moment Mr. MacTavish and black César appeared in the doorway. With them was a priest, a pleasant looking man whom Aunt Tam liked at once. She stood now by the side of the dead man, as if to shield him from the presence of the woman. She saw that MacTavish understood that death was in the room. But he seemed not to notice death. He was looking at the young Baroness. His blue eyes had turned to cold bits of marble and the square jaw had turned to iron. For a moment he and the woman stared at each other. Then MacTavish said, in a voice of ice, "What are you doing here?"

The woman smiled, "It is my house. Amedé was my cousin."

MacTavish started to speak and then appeared to choke. He swallowed, and finding words at last, said, "You are not to stay here! You are to go—do you understand?—back where you came from! And you are to stay there!"

"I shall do as I please, Hector MacTavish!"

He moved over to her and took her arm. "This is once when you will not do as you please. If you do not go I shall make you go by force. All this is obscene."

"Let go of my arm."

He moved away from her and said, "I beg your pardon . . . but I still mean what I said."

Then she smiled at him and went out the door. As she left big César turned and raising the first and little fingers of his great black hand, spat seven times between them in the direction of the door.

In French MacTavish said to him, "You are right, César. She is a witch."

Then to Aunt Tam he said, "You had better go, Ma'am. This is work for men. César and I can do it."

But Aunt Tam would not go away. Out of all that had happened while she stood listening, she could make out nothing whatever. It all seemed a hodge-podge of melodrama and mystery, but her instinct told her that it all had to do with the dead man on the purple plush love seat. Her instinct bade her pity him and pity him she did. He was like a poor and miserable orphan who had never known a woman's tenderness. Why she *knew* this, she could not say. It was perhaps only more of Mr. Emerson's nonsense.

Firmly she said, "No, I will stay and help. I am an old woman to whom modesty is of no concern. This is a woman's work."

MacTavish thinking how strange it was that so homely a face could suddenly seem beautiful, turned to César and said, "You go find planks and make a box. We are going to New Orleans tonight and must finish this business."

It seemed to him now, more than ever, that he must get the young girl out of this doomed and evil house.

Throughout the strange scene, the old priest had said nothing at all. He only stood by the doorway, his kindly blue eyes filled with compassion and understanding.

As if to clear her head, to find her way, Agnes, when she left the room, walked out into the open gallery at the top of the curving stairway. But the air brought no relief as New England air would have done; it was warm and damp and heavy with the odor of the flowering shrubs from the garden below. She was frightened, why or by what she did not know, but despite the fact that a hot sun had risen above the line of the opposite shore of the river, she felt that there was no sun but only a kind of misty darkness enveloping the whole landscape. Scarcely knowing what she was doing, she descended slowly the long stairway leaning on the wrought iron balustrade for support. When she reached the garden she set out slowly along a neglected pathway in which the weeds and grass grew between the moss-covered flags.

It was very different from the bright summer garden at Dedham with its banks of bright clean delphiniums and dahlias. The flowers here seemed heavy gross flowers like the thick-scented waxen petals of the magnolia blossoms which lay in a drift of creamy white across the path. She experienced a vague and curious desire to see crisp bright-colored flowers and blond people and she thought suddenly how odd it was that since she and Aunt Tam had left the army transport in Havana they had seen only negroes or swarthy people—all save Mr. MacTavish. She saw his face very clearly now with the honest eyes that were the color of clean blue water. There seemed to be a cleanness about his face for which she was hungry as she was hungry for the crisp air of New England.

Moving along the path she came at the end of the garden axis before three statues half-concealed in niches of a ragged unkempt hedge of magnolias. The statues were stained by fungus and partly overgrown by moss—the figure of Venus and Priapus and Dionysius. Half-dreaming she stood inspecting them, thinking at the same time that there was something strangely indecent about the nude figures, something which became associated vaguely with the puzzling gesture of the sailors on the *San Cristobal*. Once the sight of such marble figures would have shocked and frightened her but now they roused in her no more emotion than a casual interest in their physiological peculiarities, for they revealed to her things which her prudish education had left rather hazy.

She was thinking how wild and beautiful and romantic this garden was, all overgrown and flowering with a lushness that was almost stifling, when the sound of a footstep on the path caused her to turn and she saw coming toward her a woman not much older than herself, dressed all in black. She was smiling, a warm and friendly smile it was, full of welcome and friendliness. At sight of her, Agnes felt confused and blushed as if she were an unwelcome intruder.

But the woman, still smiling, said, "Good morning. I only discovered you were here. I am the Baroness Éliane de Lèche."

"My name is Agnes Wicks," said Agnes. "I came here with Mr. MacTavish."

"I've just heard the story from your Aunt. Have you had breakfast?"

"No," said Agnes, thinking it was very odd that the Baroness should behave in so cordial a way with a man lying dead in the house.

"I can't offer you much. It isn't as if we were living here. Come, we'll go along to the kitchen. Do you like the garden?"

"I think it is very beautiful."

"It was lovely once . . . a long time ago."

Back toward the house, the young Baroness led Agnes through another *allée* roofed with rotten lattices covered with the purple drooping garlands of wistaria. As they reached the house, she turned between the arms of the horseshoe-shaped stairway to a central opening where the great doors, standing open, hung sagging on their hinges. Inside, the walls of the wide passage were damp and moss grown. At the end they came to a huge kitchen with a fireplace large enough to roast a whole ox. Over a small fire built in one corner of it bent an old negro, lame and with a scarred face. At the sound of their footsteps he rose and bowed and gave the Baroness a curious vacant smile.

The Baroness said quickly, "His name is Aristide. He was born deaf and dumb." Then she made signs of drinking and the old man opened a cupboard and brought out bowls of heavy crockery and lifted from the fire a great tin pot of coffee.

"We have no milk. They have driven off all the cows."

"I don't mind," said Agnes politely, "I like it black."

"And there is only molasses to sweeten it, and only army biscuit to eat with it. You see we have been in a state of siege." The accent seemed strange to Agnes. It was precise yet beautiful. The woman spoke as if the words she uttered were fragile and delicate, each one a bit of crystal which might be shattered by too rough a touch. And now and then as light creates in crystal a gleam of color, there was a faint echo of a foreign accent. The English she spoke sounded nothing like the flat colorless English of Beacon Hill. Listening to her, it occurred to Agnes that English could be a lovely and musical tongue.

The woman fascinated her. There was a grace about the body that was animal, slow and flowing, like the easy grace of a cat. And she used her hands, which were beautiful, delicately, like a cat. Watching her made Agnes feel awkward and blunt and very young. And she had a worldliness that was new to Agnes and therefore dazzling. Sitting there at the crude table in the vast damp kitchen with cobwebs hanging in the corners, she managed to invest their frugal breakfast and the crude furniture and the very room with a kind of elegance. And she did not ask stupid questions nor allow any shy and aching pauses. It was as if she were aware that the girl opposite her was young and frightened. She enveloped her in friendliness and warmth, telling her about Bel Manoir and the burning of the cabins and the attack on the place.

Only once did she seem to change and that was when she told of fighting by the side of the men and of herself killing three men. Then for a moment the violet eyes seemed to change their color. Her hands clasped the edge of the table in her excitement until the veins which showed through the white skin stood out like cords drawn tense.

The Baroness said suddenly, "When I return to New Orleans you must call upon me."

"Is it nice there?" asked Agnes politely. "Is it a pretty town?"

The Baroness smiled again. "It is a strange town—not like any other I've ever seen. It's both pretty and ugly. It's prettiness is very pretty and its ugliness is vile."

"Do you think I'll care for it?"

"That I couldn't answer."

She pushed back her chair and stood up. "I should think you might need some sleep."

"It's all right," said Agnes. "I'm used to going without."

The woman did not answer this remark but only said, "Come with me. I'll make you as comfortable as possible."

The bedroom was enormous, with a high canopied bed set in the middle of the room and a small stepladder beside it to aid the sleeper to climb in. The mattress lay bare on the cording and the Baroness said, "I apologize. There is no bed linen. It was all stolen and taken to New Orleans."

"Who stole it?"

"The Yankee who came here to claim the cotton and free the slaves."

The Baroness smoothed the pillows and said, "I'll leave you now.

Sleep all you can. MacTavish will probably want to send you on your way tonight."

When the woman had gone Agnes took off her outer clothing, climbed the stepladder and lay down on the high bed, but she did not fall asleep at once. The heat, already pouring in at the great windows, was stifling and she could not sleep for studying the room. She had never seen a room like it. Despite its wrecked condition, there remained a kind of sultry splendor about the mouldy green painted walls, the great baldaquins of gold above the windows and torn curtains of crimson plush. Her own bedroom at home seemed tiny in comparison, and chaste and clean and cool. Here even the furniture seemed enormous, as if it were a room belonging to a giantess.

And she pondered for a long time about the strange woman who had been so kind to her. She was like the room, like the house, like the whole fantastic journey through swamps and bayous with Aunt Tam and black César. She had never seen anything like her, "She is one of those women I have read about," thought Agnes, "who have only to put on a frock and a bonnet to make it appear fashionable."

For what had impressed her most about the woman was the elegance which had a quality of unreality. The dress she wore was of some cotton stuff dyed black, with a simple white collar, a dress even soiled and torn, yet the woman had invested it with elegance. It came about, thought Agnes, trying drowsily to discover the secret, from the way she walked, moving smoothly and erectly, and from the carriage of the head on the long curve of her neck, and from the awareness she gave you of the perfection of the body which the shabby frock concealed, as if its beauty and splendor were something which nothing could hide. And she had an ease and a graciousness which Agnes had never before encountered, a way of making the wicked decaying house seem a sound and beautiful place.

She thought, "How wonderful it would be to be like that, to be so certain of oneself that one would never be shy or afraid." Women like this one must have some secret that none of the women she had ever known possessed.

It was very odd too and difficult to believe that this woman was,

[193]

like herself, an American, that she too must have had grandparents and great grandparents like Grandfather Wicks and Great Grandfather Jones. "But then," reflected Agnes, "it is no more strange than that this peculiar house and the peculiar country through which we have been traveling for so long are also in America. Maybe people should travel and mix more. Maybe there would not have been this dreadful war if Americans had known each other better."

"That's it," she thought, brushing away the buzzing flies which kept returning to annoy her. "That's it. When we get to New Orleans we shall go about and get to know people. Aunt Tam will like that. It will just suit her. Aunt Louisa must know *some* people there."

But even if Aunt Louisa knew nobody, there were always ways of meeting people. Even in Havana Aunt Tam had found a way.

And probably Tom and David would have friends there. Even if there was a war, people who lived in the same town would have to speak to each other. David might not be very good at knowing people because he was so shy, but surely Tom would know people —nobody could call *him* shy. And everybody always liked him.

Then in the heat she began thinking about Tom, in this new way she had come to think of him—as something warm and precious. They could perhaps be married at once, as soon as she arrived. Aunt Tam would approve of that; she would think it adventurous and romantic. It would make her father furious and all the aunts and cousins at home, but that did not matter. They seemed very remote now, like creatures in another world, sprinkling the carpets with pepper and formaldehyde in Pinckney Street to keep out the moths for the summer, and opening the windows and taking off the dust covers at the house at Dedham. Half-asleep now, she did not give a snap of her fingers for all of them, and in the illumination which came to her, lying there between wakefulness and sleep, she became aware of a dreadful thing—she did not love her father; she had never loved him. This bearded heavy mountain of authority and protection was a humbug. Even when she thought that she might never see him again, it did not trouble her.

"Perhaps I'm really like Aunt Tam," she thought. "They all

think Aunt Tam is queer and crazy because they're so mean and narrow and limited. They just don't understand her."

There was something magnificent and adventurous and indestructible about Aunt Tam, about the way she was friendly with everyone and never had any trouble with people. Even though she was plain and eccentric, everyone liked her at once. In a funny way, there was something in Aunt Tam that was like the Baroness —the way she swept aside all the things that troubled most people —the shyness, the suspicions, smallness and "tightness" of people like Aunt Louisa. Aunt Tam and the strange Baroness didn't seem to have these things which wrapped you round and tied you into an inert and stupid bundle. And Tom was like that in his way too— sweeping everything aside which usually separated people from each other. It was funny that three people as different as Aunt Tam and the Baroness and Tom should be alike, even in the smallest way.

The discovery excited her and dreamily she thought, "Maybe I am going to be like that too when I've really grown up into a person." And as she fell asleep she experienced the queer sensation of being a fledgling bird who was growing wings which one day would enable her to soar above the world of ordinary people.

It was Tom she dreamed of, dozing and waking now and then as the flies settled on her bare arms. It was Tom she wanted more than anything in the world. She wanted to be married to him, to have him here beside her. The dreams would have horrified "dear Papa" and the kinfolk in Pinckney Street. Once or twice during the long journey through the nocturnal swamps, there had been moments of dreadful doubts when she suspected that all those nice people in Boston sometimes had "wicked" thoughts too and hid them away, choosing always to live in a false and constricted world that began to seem to her to be the apotheosis of dullness. She began to understand about the "wicked" girl who had been expelled from Miss Dignum's boarding school.

But to Aunt Tam, coming into the room after Amedé de Lèche had been bathed and dressed and put into the crude coffin made by César out of boards from the kitchen table, Agnes, asleep on the huge bed seemed small and frail and innocent and childlike. For once Aunt Tam felt tired, so tired that she even put off writ-

[195]

ing in her journal the extraordinary experiences of the past few hours. It would need an hour's writing at least to put down all her impressions of the extraordinary things her sensibilities had recorded in this frightening house.

Without troubling to remove her outer clothes she climbed the little stepladder and lay down to sleep beside Agnes in this strange world which seemed to doze through the hot days and only come to life after the sun had gone down and night had come.

Mr. MacTavish had advised her to get some sleep because they would set out at nightfall on the last lap of their journey to New Orleans. She would do anything Mr. MacTavish asked her to do. She would trust herself and Agnes to his care. In the last two hours she had discovered a great deal about him. There was no nonsense about him, and he had been gentle and tender as a woman in all the sad business of preparing the dead boy for the grave. The kind, sad look in the blue eyes she would remember as long as she lived.

Belowstairs, MacTavish and Father Desmoulins laid Amedé de Lèche in his coffin and MacTavish drew the curtains across the window and went away leaving the priest to light the candles he had brought to place at the head and feet of the dead man and kneel to pray beside him.

The old man prayed but the sonorous Latin words were so familiar to him that after a little time his mind wandered away from them and occupied itself with other thoughts while his lips went on moving. But it did not matter for it was not his lips which prayed but his heart, while his mind wandered into more worldly paths. It was the form which would have brought peace to the heart of Amedé de Lèche and all the millions of others of the poor, fallible human race.

Father Desmoulins was old enough to be detached and aloof as if he himself were already dead. It was this which had saved him now when all the province he loved was torn and destroyed, when all those, black and white and brown, among whom he had worked for so long were ruined and embittered and dying. He had stayed behind in his parish house by the little church of St. Jean Baptiste at Beaupré because he knew that those who needed him would come there to find him, out of hiding in the swamps and forests, as Hector MacTavish, an infidel, had come. He had no fear of death or violence. He was ready to die if death came to him but he had no enemies. And they *had* come to him out of the swamps and forests, negroes and mulattos and white people, in the middle of the night or in the first light of the hot Louisiana dawn, to knock at his door for confession or the last sacraments. He would stay there until death at last removed him.

And so as his lips moved automatically, repeating the prayers for the soul of the poor sinful Amedé de Lèche destroyed by the passions of his body, the goodness in him understood much and achieved forgiveness with God. For it is certain that God understood and found a friend in Father Desmoulins. God saw them all in that ruined house through his priest and understood and forgave them—Chauvin Boisclair and great black César who was a splendid animal like one of MacTavish's lost stallions, and Hector MacTavish who was troubled because two nights ago he had killed three ignorant niggers driven half mad by rum and the monotonous beating of Tombo's drums. And poor deaf and dumb Aristide hidden away in the kitchen who was innocent as the birds in the garden were innocent, and the Yankee in the room on the third floor whom God had made beautiful and desirable to all women and endowed with a vitality which gave him no peace, and the two strange women from the North, out of another world, who were the most difficult of all for Father Desmoulins to understand, and even Éliane de Lèche, doomed like her poor cousin lying in the crude box before him.

She was, he thought, as his lips moved mechanically in the prayers for the dead, one of those whom the ancient prophets would have described as possessed of a devil, a Jezebel. For she was brilliant and gifted with life and intelligence and even beauty far beyond most women, yet they were gifts which she had always turned toward evil and destruction as long as he had known her, since she first came into the parish as a child. He had known everything about her and he had known everything—sometimes dark and evil and corrupt things—about all those in the Parish who came to him for confession. By now there remained little concerning the weakness and folly and evil of mankind to astonish him, but the demon which possessed Éliane de Lèche was something he had rarely encountered. He had known her wickedness since the beginning. He had known the whole story of her and poor dead Amedé. He knew even of her curious, intense love for Hector MacTavish and her attempted seduction of him. At confession, he had heard mirth in her voice as she confessed her sin. And he knew how the curious idealism of MacTavish had defeated her in the midst of a world in which morality of that kind was so often of small importance. Her very boldness and wickedness had defeated her, yet she had never admitted defeat. She had come back again from Paris and Martinique, all the way to Bel Manoir to be near MacTavish, to fight by his side using a gun like a man.

There were times, thought Father Desmoulins, when it was as if God placed one's own hell inside one at birth. It was like that with Éliane de Lèche, daughter of a harlot raised in the wickedness of Paris, for God had made her love the one man whom she could never reach. In her wicked heart He had made her love him because he was a good and honorable and serious man. God had given her many gifts but among them He had given her a blackness of heart which revolted Hector MacTavish who was a strong man. And her defeat, instead of chastening her wickedness, only drove her on and on to greater and greater depths of folly until one day in an evil and sordid end she would die without ever having lived, because Hector MacTavish had never loved her.

Oh, it was a dark and complex thing—this short span of existence, and hard and bitter for many of God's children. He was not like so many of the heretic preachers, hard and stupid and denouncing, abusing and condemning the weakness of their brothers. In the heart of Father Desmoulins there was the pity of God, and so as his lips moved in the prayer for the soul of Amedé de Lèche his heart prayed for the soul of the dead man's tormented cousin. Amedé de Lèche was at last at peace, but the hell of the passionate and defeated woman abovestairs went on and on. It would go on until at last, weary and lost, the grave would bring her the only peace she would ever know.

When MacTavish left the room where Amedé de Lèche lay dead, he went to the room which he shared with Chauvin Boisclair during the few hours of daylight when it was possible to snatch a few hours of sleep. Chauvin had not returned and the room was empty, drowsing in the heat with the insects singing in the bands of coppery sunlight.

He wanted most of all to shave and bathe for he had a curious vague desire to wash himself clean of this house, of the wild garden, of the death and corruption which seemed to infest the whole place. He had taken off his jacket and poured the tepid water from the cracked pitcher in the bowl when there came a knock at the door.

He continued rolling up the sleeves of his shirt as he called, "Come in," and the door opened to admit the young Baroness. She smiled, apparently untouched by his violence earlier in the morning.

"What is it you want?" he asked.

"I came to tell you that I am going back to New Orleans."

"I think it's better that way. There's no use staying on here. It's only a matter of time until the Yankees will march in and hold both banks of the river."

She seated herself on one of the carved rosewood chairs, "That is an odd way for a Secessionist to talk."

He took the tiny piece of soap and began to wash his hands as if the urgency had become uncontrollable. "There is no use in deceiving ourselves. We can't even hold this band together, let alone a good disciplined fighting army." Bitterness came into his voice, "We all ought to be dressed in shining armor riding white horses. It's every man for himself. Every man must be a knight, a hero, himself rescuing the whole of poor demoralized Louisiana. That's not good enough to fight an army made up of tough and disciplined shopkeepers. Chivalry is dead, Éliane. It is dead of futility and corruption in the province of Louisiana."

She had taken up a bit of the torn curtain and was unraveling it, looking away from him. Her long white fingers worked with the nervous speed of shuttles. When she spoke she said a strange thing, "Do you suppose I ever liked all of that romantic rubbish?"

"You always seem to flourish in the midst of it."

She looked up quickly and then back at the bit of torn curtain. with the quickness of a passing shadow, her face took on an expression of torment. She said, "What are you going to do with the Yankee?"

He glanced at her with astonishment, wondering if she believed he was deceived by the casual way in which she referred to him as "the Yankee."

"Do with him as you wish."

"He is not my prisoner," she answered without looking up. He allowed silence to speak for him, eloquently, and she said, "Oh, I know what you think, Hector MacTavish. It is not true. I am not in love with him . . . not that much." And she measured an infinitesimal bit of the tip of her little finger. "Not at all. He is a fool, a coxcomb. He fancies himself irresistible."

"Does it make it better that you are not in love with him?"

There was a curious sense of tormenting intimacy between them, curiously like the intimacy between lovers who need speak very little since their thoughts are already known to each other. It was a bitter intimacy, perverse and baffled, as if fate had meant them to be lovers but had put some curse upon them. She did not answer him and when he had finished washing his hands and drying them, he turned toward her and said abruptly, "What is it you want?"

"Nothing. I only came to tell you I am going away. Everything here has been ruined or stolen. What happens now can't matter very much."

He began walking up and down, impatient for her to be gone, but she had one more thing to tell him. She said, "I have discovered something."

"What?"

"That girl you brought here is the fiancée of the Yankee. She came to Louisiana to see him."

He stopped his pacing and looked at her sharply, but she was still absorbed in unraveling the bit of torn brocade. He could not see her eyes.

"How do you know that?"

"The Yankee told me. He read in the *Delta* about them being lost."

For a moment MacTavish thought over what she had said. Then he asked, "Does he know they are here?"

"No."

"Then you had better not tell him, under the circumstances."

"I hadn't meant to."

He looked at her sharply again. "You understand," he said, "you are not to tell him."

She did not answer him and he said, "I think the quicker he clears out of here the better. If anything happens to him . . . if anyone happens to take a pot shot at him, it might be bad for the others in New Orleans."

"I think when I go, he will leave too."

She looked up at him as if to see the effect of the remark, but there was no effect. He was looking out of the window, wishing that she would go away because the sight of her here in the bedroom with him was disturbing, and because he wanted to get some rest. It was odd that she should always put strange thoughts into his head, thoughts which excited him but made him at the same time alarmed and cautious. He was thinking, "No good ever comes of making love to a witch."

She had stopped unraveling the piece of brocade. Her hands were trembling so that she could no longer control them. She managed to ask, "What time are you burying Amedé?"

"After the sun goes down and it cools off. You had better not come."

"Why not?"

"It would be indecent."

She shrugged her fine shoulders and gave a laugh that was more like a cough. "You have an odd way of looking at things."

"Yes, I have. And now, Éliane, if you'll go away, I'll get some sleep. I haven't had much for the last three days."

She stood up. Her whole body was trembling now. She said, "How am I to get back to New Orleans?"

"You can go with the two women if you like. We shall be leaving as soon as the sun goes down. Father Desmoulins knows where there is a boat. César can bring it back. Does that suit you?"

"As well as anything does."

She did not go away and he could not make out what she was waiting for. After a little time, he said, "Why don't you go back to Paris, Éliane? Louisiana is no place for you." In his voice there was a sudden unexpected softness of which she seemed immediately aware. The trembling ceased and she looked at him directly for the first time. "There's nothing here for you any more than there is for me. Both of us belong in different worlds. Europe is your world . . . not this half-barbaric place."

"And you?" she asked.

"I'm going to the West."

The softness went out of her and in a hard voice she said, "I shan't leave New Orleans until I get back the gold which belongs to me and all the property they've stolen. Money means a great deal to me. Money is power and I can't live without power."

"What makes you think you'll ever get it back?"

"You will see."

She went away then, abruptly, leaving him alone, but he did not sleep for a long time, perhaps because he was too exhausted to sleep, perhaps because the visit had disturbed him too profoundly.

At sundown César came in to waken him. He wakened slowly out of a dead sleep, dazed at first at the sight of the wrecked bedroom in which he found himself. As he dressed César told him that the two Boston ladies were awake now and wished to go to the burial.

When the little party collected—Aunt Tam and Agnes, Father Desmoulins and MacTavish, César and deaf and dumb Aristide—they set out for the de Lèche burial ground, the four men carrying the rude wooden coffin in which lay Amedé de Lèche. It weighed very little for the boards were dry and old and the body inside was little heavier than that of a child. The journey was not long. Less than half a mile from the great house stood the low knoll of consecrated ground with its tiny chapel falling into decay with a leaking roof and moss-grown walls.

Long ago the first de Lèche had chosen the knoll for a burial ground because it lay above the level of all the swampy landscape and he had hoped that he and his children would have a resting place that was dry. But there was water everywhere, even when one dug deeper than three feet on the little knoll covered with live oaks, and so all the dead de Lèches had been buried in the end above ground in brick tombs faced with slabs of carved marble or limestone. The tombs had been placed here and there at random among the trunks of the great trees, and some of them through neglect had begun to fall apart in the dampness. They were of all sizes according to the age and sex of the corpses they contained. Always those of the men had been the more imposing and expensive as if the men of the family had in death sought to fix their importance in a family where for generation after generation the women had been the more powerful. From some of them the carved slabs of the tombs had fallen away exposing the faded pink brickwork of the inner tomb.

But for Amedé de Lèche the last of the family, there was no such tomb for a resting place but only a hole dug in the ground already half-filled with tepid yellow water. There had been no brick mason nor any workmen to solder a leaden coffin over the frail body.

Very gently the four men lowered the clumsy box, so gently that the yellow water swallowed it without so much as a ripple. Then they knelt together, black and white, Catholic and Protestant and Agnostic while Father Desmoulins repeated the service of the dead. And as his lips repeated the sonorous sounds, MacTavish thought, "Back to the earth he has gone, not to a tomb but to the earth, the fertile soaked soil which bred and corrupted him." He was glad that Éliane had not come to kneel there with them. These were good people, even old deaf and dumb Aristide. With her there it would have been very different. There would have been ugliness and uneasiness with her perverse presence in their midst.

When they rose from beside the grave it was nearly dark and the aigrettes, crying in the dusk, were settling themselves for the night in the cypresses of the nearby swamps.

As they moved across the uneven ground on their way home MacTavish walked beside Agnes, so near to her that at moments in the darkness their hands brushed for a moment, and twice he took her hand to cross small ditches where the water drained away toward the bayou. The touch of his hand gave her a small *frisson* of pleasure, why she could not quite make out except that he seemed very strong and simple. In her mind the pleasure seemed to spring from the look of the square jaw and chin and the kind blue eyes. She was aware that she did not feel at all as people should feel returning from a burial. There was a kind of singing in her heart and a curious sense of freedom.

While they were gone at the burial ground, Eliane de Lèche was in Tom Bedloe's room. She had come there to tell him that she was going away, that she had found a way back to the city. He listened to her sitting sleepily on the edge of the bed, satiated and for the first time a little bored.

She said, "And so I am saying good-by. You are free now to go where you like. They are leaving here. You will have the house to yourself." In her voice there was a fine edge of arrogance and mockery. She was like a man dismissing a mistress of whom he had had enough. But it was less what she said than the peculiar quality of her voice and the look in her eyes, which suddenly annoyed him.

He said, "Oh, no. You don't do that."

"And why not?"

"Because what we have begun isn't finished yet."

She did not answer him directly. She said quite coldly, "I am sailing for Martinique and then to France. I've finished with this accursed country."

"What if I went with you?" He had not the faintest idea of any such madness. With her assumption of domination, the sense of satiation faded away, its place taken by the old challenge.

"You wouldn't be such a fool."

There was about their conversation a curious quality, almost inhuman. It was the conversation of two sensualists disillusioned and without warmth.

He said, "You will not soon find another man like me."

She laughed, "There are plenty of men better than you."

He laughed and said, "This is a silly conversation considering . . ."

"Considering what?"

"How we felt about one another." He did not wait for her to answer. "You can't deny that. There are certain things in which a woman cannot deceive a man."

But again she escaped his domination, "Women sometimes have great curiosity . . . which may be satisfied very quickly."

"I shall see you in New Orleans."

"Perhaps . . . I shall leave by the first boat bound for Havana or Martinique."

"Why are you going?"

"Because what I have come for has failed and there is no longer any use in staying in a hateful city."

"What was it you came for?"

"To protect the property that was mine. It has been stolen by you damned Yankees. I wanted to recover it but there seems to be no way."

He was thoughtful for a moment. Then he regarded her slyly, "I might be of use."

"How?"

He came a little nearer to her. "Will you trust me? Will you let me try?"

The hardness, the sense of antagonism seemed to melt away.

"If you like. I see no reason why you should."

"Because I am more sentimental, more romantic than you. I would like to do you a service."

"I have no wish to be paid."

"I didn't mean it in that way."

"I apologize for being ungracious."

He took her hand. "Why are you like that? Why is there no warmth in you?"

She looked at him in astonishment, "No warmth in *me*!"

"No warmth."

She sighed, "But I *have* warmth."

Quietly he put his arm about her. He tried to kiss her but she drew away from him. "No," she said, "not now . . . in New Orleans, perhaps. Not now. I don't want to begin all over again. I can't! Not here again! Oh, God save me!"

The desperation in her voice, the real anguish of her cry stopped him. Freeing her he stepped away a little, looking at her almost with distaste. She recovered her self-possession quickly and said in a flat voice, "I must go now. They want to be off as soon as it's dark. How are you going to reach New Orleans?"

"I could go with you."

"That's no good. Any of them but MacTavish might take a shot at you just for luck. You can't trust them. MacTavish is a man but the others you can't trust."

"Do you really care very much how I get to New Orleans?" It would have been a silly speech, almost the speech of a coquettish woman but for the bitterness in the voice and the intensity of the look in the eyes. It was the first time he had ever been bitter. Bitterness was not a part of his exuberant nature.

"Of course I care," she said. "You have only to go to the river and follow it until you come to the city. And travel by night. It is not difficult if you use your head and keep moving. If you want to eat, stop at Father Desmoulins'. It's the first village inside the levee. It's called Beaupré. I'll tell him to expect you. Don't leave here for a couple of hours after they're all gone. They're going away for good. I'll never see this accursed place again. I wish I had never seen it. I wish they had never brought me here from Paris. Wait till they're well out of the way and then follow the avenue to the river and turn left and keep straight on until you reach the city."

"In New Orleans then."

"In New Orleans. . . ."

Then she went away. It was quite dark now and the waning moon had not yet appeared. As he stood in the doorway her figure in the black dress faded into the darkness before she reached the top of the great stairway. The feeling of boredom and satiation was gone now. He was awake and a healthy animal once more, hungry and filled with a faint sense of excitement at the prospect of returning to New Orleans and his luxurious quarters. From belowstairs in the darkness he heard a faint sound of voices and for a moment it seemed to him that one voice, flat and a little strident and unmistakable which might have been the voice of a woman or of an effeminate man, sounded a little like Agnes' Aunt Tam. He went as far as the well of the stairway to hear more clearly, but by the time he reached it, the sound of the voices had ceased and he returned to the room, thinking that his imagination had played him tricks. It was beyond the imagination—the idea of Aunt Tam turning up in a place like ruined Bel Manoir. It would be as if the poles had come together.

But the sound of the voices brought back the thought of Agnes. What was he to do with her in New Orleans? What had become of her? Perhaps she was dead. He hoped not. The wild experience of the past few hours had for a time extinguished the very thought of her. But now she seemed desirable again, if only for the reason that she was so different from this woman who had just now melted away into darkness. One day he would marry her and make her a good husband, but that time had not yet come. This other thing had yet to be finished.

When the moon came up its light fell upon an odd bedraggled procession moving in the shadow of the levee. At the head, following MacTavish, came the old mule carrying two women led by César, Miss Abigail Jones and the Baroness Eliane de Lèche. On foot behind came Miss Agnes Wicks, Father Desmoulins in his black soutane, black, small, gnarled Aristide and finally young Chauvin Boisclair carrying a carbine. Now and then a word was spoken in a low voice but most of the time the party moved in silence, squashing through the puddles of dark mud where the water from the river had seeped through the levee. Every half-hour the procession halted while one of the women dismounted to ex change places with the one following on foot. Because of her age they had urged Aunt Tam to keep her seat the whole of the journey but this she had refused first on the ground that she was quite as strong as the others and secondly because she considered a place on the back of the gray mule a doubtful privilege.

"I shouldn't," she said, "be able to walk for twenty-four hours afterward if one of you didn't spell me."

They talked little partly because of the danger from the escaped slaves and renegades dispersed by the fever, and partly from sadness. MacTavish was sad because he was leaving the parish where he was born and which he loved, perhaps never to return. Aunt Tam was sad because the adventure was nearly finished and because she was leaving two new friends of whose rare quality and goodness her sound heart was convinced. It seemed to her cruel and idiotic that you should find friends like Mr. MacTavish and Father Desmoulins only to lose them again, perhaps forever because there was a war and people fighting and hating and killing each other. As she sat perched on the bony back of the gray mule, she thought that some day she would write an essay on the subject.

The world, she thought, planning the essay, ought to be delivered over to an aristocracy of good people like MacTavish and Mr. Alcott and Father Desmoulins. In them there was neither greed nor guile, nor the wishing of ill to anyone. If the world could be ruled by such men, there would be no wars, no fighting and no trouble. She had a mind for a moment to include Mr. Lincoln but people said so many different things about him that one couldn't be certain. She would have to see him herself to form a judgment. Her heart she could trust far more than gossip or the cheap viciousness of the newspapers. It was, she knew, the greedy people, the dishonest people who made the troubles and the wars . . . people, she thought ruefully, like her brother Ethan sitting smugly at home in Pinckney Street always putting his business ahead of everything—decency, morality or kindliness. No, you could see what people were by their faces. The goodness shone out of them as it shown out of the faces of men like MacTavish and Father Desmoulins and even poor black César. Mr. MacTavish's goodness had an aggressive quality; he would fight for it. And the priest's goodness was gentle and understanding. And César was like a great, faithful beautiful dog.

She was still composing her essay when Mr. MacTavish halted the mule and said that it was Miss Agnes' turn to ride. So Aunt Tam got down to trudge along in the mud beside Father Desmoulins, and MacTavish, cupping his strong hands, bade Miss Agnes step on them while he lifted her up.

Once she was aboard the mule sitting in front of the Baroness who put her arms about her waist to steady her, he said, "I reckon you'll be glad to arrive in New Orleans and have a good soft bed again."

"Yes, Mr. MacTavish, I will be."

"You're a mighty brave girl and a strong one."

"Thank you, sir."

Then he took his place again at the head of the procession and as they moved off Agnes settled herself and turned to ask politely if the Baroness was comfortable. She got no answer and when she turned she saw in the moonlight that the woman's face was wet with tears. Embarrassed, she did not repeat her question, thinking,

"The poor creature is crying at the thought of her ruined house, of going away and leaving it to all those wicked people."

The sadness of Father Desmoulins was for all the Parish and all the world, for the killing and destruction, for all the crosscurrents of passion and feeling he felt about him in the little party of lost refugees. He was tired and, being old and wise, rather enjoyed his sadness and the prospect of reaching his own bed and the attentions given him by his old servant. All the others, save for the nice horse-faced old virgin from Boston, were young and while the young, unworn and unarmored by wisdom, suffered more bitterly from tragedy and disappointment, they had in its place the strength to support and endure these things. It was out of the fires of their resistance that their characters were born. The weak grew weaker and the strong calmer and more enduring.

Behind him young Chauvin Boisclair swung along, happy in his carelessness and the optimism of youth. He did not know where he would lay his head tomorrow but it did not matter to him so long as Hector MacTavish was there to decide for him. It might be that they would set out for Virginia to join the Confederate Army there or that they would stay on here leading the guerrilla life of the Defenseurs. Once or twice his full red lips pursed as he began to whistle, only to be reproved into silence by a word from MacTavish.

In the whole party only he and the young girl on the mule were really happy, he because he was young and being alive on a fine moonlit night like this was a wonderful thing. His desire to whistle was born of the impulse which made the mocking bird sing in the chinaberry tree. And Agnes was happy because she believed that in a little while she would be seeing her Tom. Somehow in the long journey he had come to life. He was no longer a kind of romantic figure out of the only sort of novel she was permitted to read. The Tom she was traveling to meet was of flesh and blood. Bumping along on the mule with the arms of the Baroness encircling her waist, she trembled suddenly at the thought that by tomorrow she might be held thus in Tom's arms.

It was nearly ten o'clock before, coming round a bend of the levee road, they came suddenly upon the tiny hamlet of Beaupré and the squat spire of Father Desmoulins' church.

The old black woman was awake waiting for the return of the priest but she had not expected the others and there was a great scurrying about to make coffee and heat up cakes for them. While she worked, aided clumsily by Aunt Tam, MacTavish said to Agnes that he wished to speak to her alone. They had only to step through the doorway. Once outside, he said, "There is something I wanted to tell you. It's about your fiancé. He won't be in New Orleans when you return. Perhaps he will return in a day or two."

Even as he spoke he could not think why he had troubled to tell her this except that he felt sorry for her because she seemed to him so childlike and trustful. He knew that he was being silly and sentimental and was meddling in things which did not concern him, but he could not help himself. His instinct told him that she had need of protection, not so much against violence, as against Éliane and the Yankee. Slowly he had come to the conclusion that these two were a pair—suited to each other. Neither of them should be permitted to hurt others. The Yankee, he believed, was very like some of his more worthless neighbors except that there was no decadence about the Yankee. It was his vigor which made him dangerous.

Quietly he told Agnes the story of Tom Bedloe's capture and imprisonment as a hostage, only he was careful to lie a little, dressing up the story to make it seem that he was being held prisoner in some remote part of the delta.

"He is free now and I know that he is safe. He has only to make his way to New Orleans. He is not stupid. He ought to arrive there safely in a day or two. I did not mean to cause you worry but I thought you should know, because when you arrive in the city he won't be there and no one but you will have any idea where he is."

"It is very good of you," she said. "I understand." Then it occurred to her how strange it was that he should know about her and Tom and she asked, "How did you know he was my fiancé?"

He had thought of this so he said quickly, "I heard it from your Aunt." It was a lie but they would be leaving in a little while and it might never be discovered.

Then he said, "There's one thing more I should like to ask of you. It may sound silly but I must ask it. It would be a great favor to me."

"What? If it is anything I can do I shall be glad to do it. You have been very good to my Aunt and me."

In the shadow of the little portico he blushed, "I should like to have something of yours to remember you by."

She laughed, "But I haven't anything to give you. I haven't anything left but what I'm wearing."

He was silent for an awkward moment. Then he said, "Don't trouble. I understand. I thank you just the same. I think we had better go inside now."

He was aware suddenly of Éliane standing just inside the doorway and again he was overcome by the feeling that this girl should be protected from her. But Agnes laid her hand gently on his arm and said, "Wait! I could give you a button from my frock, if you had something to cut it off with."

He knew now that Éliane was watching and listening, so he said quickly, "No, I have no knife. It's not important. We shall meet again no doubt."

He turned toward the door leaving her no choice but to go with him. She wanted to stop him but there seemed no way. She wanted to explain to him that she had not meant to hurt his feelings.

But there was no time. The old black woman was serving coffee and Chauvin Boisclair was saying that they should be on their way if they were to get to New Orleans under cover of darkness.

And then Aristide discovered the fire. He had been in the woodshed to fetch more wood and he returned in a high state of agitation, gesticulating and making incoherent noises. Seizing MacTavish by the arm he pulled him to the doorway and pointed toward the west.

In that direction the whole sky was aglow, throwing the branches of the live oaks along the levee into black relief. It was MacTavish who understood.

He said, forgetting the ladies, "The damned bastards have done it! It's Bel Manoir that's burning!"

No murmur followed the announcement but only a silence as all of them came out of the house to stand watching the light in

[211]

the western sky. It was the young Baroness who broke the silence. In a low voice she said, "The Yankee. What's happening to him?"

MacTavish said, "He's got away. He's no fool!" He was not answering the young Baroness. His words were meant for the girl, Agnes, in case she had overheard and discovered his lie.

The light of daybreak lay across the oily waters of the river when the boat bumped against the granite wharf near the French market. There were many other boats there already—small barges and skiffs and bumboats manned by Negroes and Indians and Sabines who had come out of the swamps and bayous bringing their vegetables and fruits and fish and shrimp to the market. They were shouting and quarreling among themselves and so not much notice was taken of the bedraggled party which César brought ashore. Only at the end of the quai did anyone notice them. A Yankee sentry stopped them but he was drunk and the young Baroness wheedled their way past him. In the French market they waited while César went to find a conveyance. He knew the city. He knew the MacTavish house which General Wicks had taken over.

Miraculously he returned in a little while with two bedraggled *barouches*. The Baroness and Aristide set out in one of them. Aunt Tam, Agnes and César went in the other. As they turned into the narrow streets of the old quarter, they saw for the first time the barrels of pitch placed here and there on the banquettes. They had been burning all the night and from some of them fire and smoke still emerged.

It was César who said, "It's de fever. It's bad in New Orleans. They're burnin' to clear up de night air."

Things had not been going well for General Wicks and his wife. It was as if their own characters were, in the Greek fashion, bringing about their ruin. The pompous little man with the pouter pigeon figure and a squint, a lack of all scruples, who had always been accustomed to shouting and bullying his way toward achievement, found himself baffled and defeated at every turn in this strange half-tropical city. It had a velvety softness about it, a drowsiness that was as deceptive as that of a sated, sleeping tiger which with one lazy blow of its paw can maul and lacerate. He did not understand the ways of the people. They had no respect for him and gave him ludicrous and libellous names such as "Squint Eye," "Pot Belly," and "Silver Spoon" and "Molasses Eater." The epithets were repeated to him by his own officers, sanctimoniously but with a secret satisfaction, since few of them liked him any better than the citizens of New Orleans liked him. And they came to him in a series of abusive and anonymous letters which his wife Louisa always read avidly with a curious satisfaction, partly masochistic and partly because, discovering in them names she herself had frequently longed to call the General, a secret part of her soul was satisfied.

She had followed him everywhere, through every campaign he had conducted. She had seen all his failures, one after another, and she knew even now that there was no victory for him in the occupation of the city. The work had been done by the fleet of Farragut. After the forts had been forced and the city deserted, nothing remained but for the General to make a pompous landing from one of Farragut's ships to occupy the city.

And now his failure to placate or bring any sort of order without brutality and violence had done a dreadful thing to her. For the first time, perhaps because of the peculiar and irritating qualities of the New Orleans people, perhaps because of the climate and the remarkably upsetting changes in her own physiology, the disillusionment she had been thrusting beneath the surface of her consciousness for half a lifetime, began to seethe and boil and force its way to the surface. In awful moments of clarity, in the solitude of her exile's existence, she found herself composing speeches which one day she meant to fling at her husband. She would imagine the whole scene. Sometimes in the vividness of her fancy, she would throw herself about in her chair or begin to walk up and down the room in agitation, saying aloud, "General, you are a fake and a humbug! You have bought or bullied your way everywhere! You have been a demagogue in politics and a blunderer in the long military adventure! You are a swindler and a martinet! I have known it all along but I have never dared to say it even to myself!"

And now she *was* saying it to herself.

In calmer moments her disillusionment was even more unbearable. She knew the General as no one else knew him. She had seen his paunchy body in redflannel underwear and so she knew what lay beneath all the gold lace with which he covered his pompous front when he paraded in public. She had observed in her own violent fashion, that there was an odd likeness in men between their bodies and their characters, and the sight of the General, bleary-eyed and gray-faced, his thick round calves protruding from beneath his nightshirt became intolerable to her and there were nights when she left the vast bed she shared with him for a room of her own, saying that she suffered from *migraines* and could only sleep in solitude.

Everything he attempted seemed to her, always to end in disaster. He had been a failure in the army. He was a humbug in politics. He had sought to bring order to the occupied city and had produced only rioting and chaos and rebellion. He had succeeded only in making money and in being "smart" and for this success she was coming slowly to have little esteem. Making money, she knew from observation and experience required no great talent nor very great brains. When she went over the list of rich men she knew back in New England, her respect for this achievement fell even lower.

She even blamed him for the tragic disappearance of Aunt Tam and Agnes and the failure to find them, and for the disappearance of Tom Bedloe, the one person who had made the lonely, barren life in New Orleans supportable. It was the loss of Tom which she resented more than any of the countless disappointments. The sight of him always cheered her. His low jokes made her laugh. His healthy vulgarity was the only outlet of a vulgar spirit which respectability had always kept tightly corseted.

Being a respectable middle-aged American wife with a certain background, it rarely occurred to her that many of the General's blunders and mistakes had come about from her own brow-beating and bad advice. There were, at times, doubts in her mind, but these she managed quickly to stifle by a cloud of excuses, largely religious in origin.

Things seemed to grow worse rather than better with each day. The insolence of the people, the anonymous letters, the defiance, increased. The General had ordered the town to be cleaned up and quarantines established, making the citizens of New Orleans pay for the expenses, but the yellow fever and cholera crept in just the same out of the swampy parishes all about the city. And worst of all there were distant rumblings of discontent with the General coming all the way from Washington. The General had already received three "insolent" letters from the Secretary of War, advising him to soften his tactics and try methods more human and wise and conciliatory. There were even whisperings among his own officers that his removal was only a matter of time.

In all this Aunt Louisa fancied she discerned the hand of Mr. Lincoln, an upstart from the wilderness of Illinois, his own blood drawn from the Rebel South. Mr. Lincoln, she thought, was a fool. He would not support the New England business men who favored slavery nor would he back men like the General who wanted to crush and exterminate all rebels. Mr. Lincoln had none of the qualities of what she and the General referred to as "New England gentlemen" and "people of substance." She could not bring herself to contemplate the humiliation of the General's removal for incompetency. The satisfaction of their enemies here in this foreign city would be something she could not contemplate.

And so, although until now she had been more ferocious than the General himself, she began to see advantages in a policy of conciliation. They had won over a handful of Confederates to co-operation, although in every case the question of money-making was involved. With a little compromising they might win over others and stifle the dissatisfaction in Washington, for a little while in any case, long enough for the General and his family and the officers to finish their deals in cotton and sugar and dispose of the property they had acquired by dubious methods.

It was not only the internal troubles which made the General's wife irritable. There seemed to be no end to the petty annoyances which disrupted each day. There was the incident of the letters.

It had begun the day after the General issued his orders closing all cafés and ballrooms in New Orleans. She had found the first letter in her work basket when she opened it to set about mending some of the General's undergarments. It lay on top of the materials—a blue envelope, large and square and foreign looking, an envelope in which a great deal of expensive paper had been

[215]

wasted. The scent of patchouli came from the envelope, violating the chasteness of work basket which was the property of a respectable New England woman. It was addressed in a flowing emotional hand—"*Madame la Generale.*" Although Aunt Louisa knew no French and considered it a depraved language adapted principally to intrigue and unmorality, she divined that it was meant for herself.

Aware with a rush of blood to her head that this was perhaps another abusive letter, she lifted it out as if it were a bit of *ordure*, but a curiosity which amounted almost to a mania, would not permit her to leave it unread. With shaking hands (for rage was already taking possession of her) she tore it open and read what was written in the same large handwriting which covered most of the envelope.

She read: *Madame la Generale, You are a hypocrite and a harlot. You are an evil witch. It is shameful that you should love a man young like Tom Bedloe—a fat old woman like you. He hates you and laughs at you. Madame, we have put a curse on you. You will suffer pains in head and belly where we are sticking pins. You and your husband may close and steal my establishment. You may try to arrest me. You may steal everything in New Orleans but in the end you will not gain nothing. You had better leave the city before you die.*

It was signed simply *La Lionne.*

Shaking with rage and indignation she read the letter through twice and then started tearing it up, but when she had torn it twice across, she checked herself, thinking shrewdly that it was foolish to destroy what might be a clue to discovering the whereabouts of the writer. In this brief second she stood there holding the torn letter in her hand, the woman who wrote became a symbol of the evil city itself, a monument upon which to fix her hatred. La Lionne! The proprietress of a brothel! A scarlet woman! A procuress! Daring to write this to the wife of the General in command of the city. She knew about Tom and the Café Imperial and the knowledge made the latter all the more bitter. So this woman, this vile woman had discussed her with Tom, and they had laughed at her!

The dreary man climbed the stairs wearily to face a woman who was purple with rage, whose voice shook when she spoke.

"Who have you let into the house?"

The poor man who was not very bright, answered, "No one, Mrs. General. No one but the General himself."

"You lie to me! Someone brought a letter here."

"I didn't see anybody, Mrs. General. Honest, I didn't." His blank face turned gray with fear. "I ain't seen anybody in the front hall but the General himself."

It was clear even to the General's wife that the man was too stupid to plot or lie. Otherwise she would have had him sent away, back to the labor detachment. He was probably drunk or asleep when the letter was delivered, or it had been left there by someone inside the house.

With the letter still in her hand she swept down two flights of stairs to the basement. Here in the dark kitchen the cook and the young mulatto who came in by the day to clean had to face her rage.

"It was in my work basket," she kept screaming. "How could anyone put it into my work basket without anybody seeing it?"

But neither of them knew anything. She sent away the mulatto girl saying she was lucky not to be arrested. She discharged the cook and then, aware that it was difficult to find any sort of cook who would work for the General, she changed the order and went upstairs again.

When the General returned in the evening she said, "You must find her and arrest her. It's outrageous. Have we no dignity in our position which cannot be violated."

"It appears not," said the General, and after a moment, "We have been trying to find the woman. We have had a warrant out for her arrest for forty-eight hours."

"Well, you'd better find her. This can't go on."

But the General did not show much interest. He looked sallow and tired and consumed a great amount of baking soda to make him belch comfortably. He had had a bad day filled with more trouble than usual and ending with the arrival of one of those irritating letters from Secretary Seward advising him all the way from Washington how to govern a rebellious city filled with stink ing Secessionists. His own government was now making an uproar about the gold belonging to the Planter's Bank which he had seized illegally from the Belgian Consulate. The French Consulate and the English Consulate had complained of him as well, charging him with being highhanded and dishonest.

And now to have to face his wife in so violent a mood seemed too much even for a man of his small sensibilities to endure. There were times when he wished that she would threaten him with returning to Boston so that he might send her, but her threats never went that far. She had never left the General for a day in any one of his disastrous campaigns and she did not mean to leave him at this late date when all the world seemed to have turned against him.

Silently the General reflected that all luck seemed to have abandoned him.

It was a miserable night they spent in the vast MacTavish house, irritated, hating each other, unable to sleep. The General worried and afraid, his bully's heart weakening in the face of trouble, the General's wife angry, snorting from time to time into her pillow. The heat was terrible—damp and heavy with not the ghost of a breeze from the hot Gulf.

In the middle of the night she fell victim to a terrible *migraine* and felt shooting pains in her abdomen and nothing could keep her from thinking of the passage in the letter about the pins they were sticking into her. But worse than the pain or the thought of the pins was one awful passage engraved upon her consciousness like Calais on the heart of Bloody Mary.

It is shameful that you should love a man young like Tom Bed-loe . . . a fat old woman like you. He hates you and laughs at you.

In the darkness she could see the sentences as if they were written in letters of fire in the big sprawling handwriting.

It was not true that she loved Tom Bedloe. Was that what people were saying in New Orleans? Had he gone about saying things? She would make him pay if he had. She would have him stripped of his job and his rank. She would have him arrested for stealing from the Port Office. She would show him! In love with him! A whippersnapper like that! A coxcomb! A lady-killer! A libertine

[218]

But all the time in the back of her mind was the delicious consciousness of that curious moment of ecstasy she had experienced in the dining room when she had gone to fetch the whisky for the General.

The annoyance did not come to an end with the incident of the work basket. Two days later the new orderly brought her another blue square envelope addressed in the same sprawling handwriting. At sight of it she flew into another rage (which brought on a violent *migraine*) and she upbraided the orderly for accepting it.

Who had brought the note? Why hadn't he arrested the bearer on sight? Didn't he know his duty? What kind of a lunkhead was he? Turning her back upon him she went out, slamming the door, to face the awful temptation of the letter. Alone, she paced the room, struggling with the desire to read it. Her common sense told her to burn it at once, but her curiosity, the curiosity which at times reduced her to the level of a monster, would not permit her. In the end to stifle the torment she tore it open.

This time it was brief. It read:

Madame: How are your pains? Worse and Worse. They will get worser. We are sticking fiery pins into your belly and head. You will never see Tom Bedloe again. You had better get gone off New Orleans and leave honest people alone. La Lionne.

That night when the General returned, he found her in bed. He had a lonely supper, but for the first time in days a peaceful one. He even found no need of baking soda to make him belch properly. It was long after midnight when fearfully he joined her in the great bed.

When the tirade had worn itself out, she asked, "Where is Tom Bedloe?"

The General didn't know. No one knew.

"It is shameful," she said, "that a whole Union Army hasn't been able to rescue him."

A third letter she found on her bed in the middle of the afternoon.

This time she determined to discharge the cook but when she descended to the kitchen she found that the cook already had her few belongings tied up in an old sheet and was leaving. At first the woman would tell her nothing. It was only when she stood in the doorway and refused to let her pass that she said the house had a doom on it. A *poupon* had been found in the doorway. It was directed against someone in the house. The someone was certain to die. There was no saving that someone.

Nothing could make the woman stay.

After that it seemed to be easier. The letters appeared mysteriously on the doorstep, in the kitchen, even in the storeroom where the horses were stabled. And each day the General's wife had new attacks of pain in the head and abdomen. The General issued special orders for the apprehension of La Lionne, and privately, although it caused him pain very nearly as great as that suffered by his wife, he offered special rewards out of his pocket not only for the capture of the Lioness but for the discovery and rescue of Tom Bedloe. In the confusion and agitation, Aunt Tam and Agnes were very nearly forgotten.

La Lionne was safe enough. She was hidden way in the house of Clélie's mother in a crooked street not far from Congo Square. It was a pleasant house, small but with a nice walled garden which gave it privacy, the gift of Clélie's white father to her quadroon mother when he married and broke off their liaison. He had been a generous lover and left Clélie's mother ten thousand dollars in French bonds as well as the house, and so in that dim half-world of pale golden women and girls, the woman known by the name of Josélie Drélincourt was a person of importance who had married a free negro named Legrand with a fruit and vegetable business. They had placed Clélie with La Lionne when she reached the age of sixteen because they were ambitious for her and wished her to have opportunities and training which her mother had never known.

La Lionne had been good to her, teaching her to speak French properly, not the garbled French of her mother's people but the pure French of Paris. La Lionne had taught her grand manners and supervised her taste in clothes and saw to it that the girl met only the most distinguished young men. The plan had always been that when La Lionne sold the Café Imperial, Clélie was to go with her to Paris to a brilliant life beside which even the world centering about the Quadroon Balls was nothing.

And it had gone well, as planned, until the fall of the city. From then on the Café Imperial had become a different place, vulgar and cheap and disorderly, and to protect Clélie, La Lionne had kept her apart from the other girls, giving her special protection. Because Clélie herself was young and accomplished and prettier than the other girls, the task of protecting her had grown more and more difficult until that afternoon when a shy Bostonian had come to the Café seeking news of his missing friend. From that moment until the disastrous evening which ended with the closing of the establishment, the problem of Clélie was solved. She had a protector who was a gentleman. The sudden inspiration of La Lionne was successful beyond her wildest hopes.

So, on the night of the rioting when the Café was demolished and two men were killed amid the smashed mirrors of the barroom, La Lionne and Clélie, accompanied and protected by Big Ernestine, made their escape by the back door into Bourbon Street and, hurrying along the muddy banquettes, went directly to the house of Josélie Drélincourt. There she remained, hidden, in a bedroom on the second floor.

The Lioness who hid away in the little room of Josélie Drélincourt's house was a different woman from the Lioness whom Josélie knew when she first took her daughter Clélie into the gilt and red plush bedroom above the Café Imperial. She still kept the proudness of her carriage—that fierce erectness which was at the same time supple and provocative—as she walked after nightfall up and down, up and down, like a lioness, in Josélie's small garden. But the glow was gone. All the fierce vitality which gave her a kind of incandescent glow and made her seem a woman far younger than her years, was no longer there. The loud, rather coarse but immensely human laugh was no longer heard.

In the beginning Josélie, who was a woman of no illusions and vast experience, had believed that the change in her came through disappointment and anger at the destruction of her fortune. The Café Imperial had been a rich property—none knew better than Josélie how to appraise property—and now it was worth nothing, the interior wrecked and ruined, the clientele which had made it so distinguished a rendezvous, dispersed, ruined or dead. What might have been sold for seventy-five thousand in gold dollars, no longer had any value at all. And such a disaster was, thought Josélie, enough to ruin the health and change the disposition of any woman, even if there had not been added to it the fact that La Lionne, once so rich and even so powerful in the affairs of the city, was now being hunted like a criminal.

It was only after days of watching her and of gossiping with Clélie and Big Ernestine that Josélie began to discover the truth. La Lionne fasted and stayed in bed all day weeping, she went stealthily to early Mass, she muttered to herself, she went with Big Ernestine to visit Mama Tolanne after nightfall, not because her business had been ruined, but because of a man.

It took a long time for Josélie to feel the discovery credible. She was, after all, herself a woman of experience but she had never felt any such violence of emotion for any man as that displayed by La Lionne. There were, she knew, girls who sometimes became the slaves of their *maquereaux*, but La Lionne was not a stupid girl. She was a clever woman, good at business, with strength of character, who had fought her way through life like a man. She was no young girl to swoon and become the victim of the first good-looking fellow who came along.

So for days, while Josélie cooked and marketed and kept her husband's account books and received and helped entertain her daughter's young Yankee admirer, she brooded over the strange behavior of her guest, and as she brooded, a complex sense of envy came to be born. La Lionne must have experienced something which it was too late for her now ever to experience. She determined that when La Lionne had calmed down a bit, she would question her intimately to discover the secret of the man's fascination. It would be a good talk between experienced women. She looked forward to it.

There were other things which troubled Josélie since the ruin of the Café Imperial. It was true that the house was filled with comings and goings and that there were always extra mouths at every meal, but this she would not have minded because she liked people and excitement. What disturbed her most was the presence and personality of Clélie's young admirer. He was like no young

[222]

man she had ever seen. That he had reached the age of twenty and was still a virgin when he discovered Clélie seemed to her unbelievable and faintly scandalous. In New Orleans a Créole boy in a similar situation would have been regarded as peculiar as if he were deformed or half-witted. Very likely, if there could be such a boy, his family would be forced to send him out of the community as something shameful.

Over her housework she reflected upon what the world must be like out of which he had come. A dull world, she thought, a peculiar and unhealthy world which kept its young men in such unnatural suppression and ignorance. No good could come of it, except monsters like the ogre who ruled New Orleans. The more she reflected upon the situation the more shocked she became. It was like not teaching a child to read and write and prepare it for earning its living.

But she found too a kind of vicarious pleasure in the idyllic and childlike quality of the romance between David Wicks and her daughter Clélie. This quality was something which she herself, in all her experience, had never known. They were, she thought, like a pair of mourning doves, slim and young and pretty. She found them charming to watch, on the love seat in the *salon*, or as they walked up and down the little garden together their arms about each other's waists, or at the gate of the garden, when at last he chose to leave.

In less sentimental moments Josélie was, it is true, troubled by somewhat maternal doubts concerning the future of her only child. She had thought it all out. It was unlikely or impossible that the young Yankee would remain in New Orleans and undertake the support of Clélie and her security for the future, and from what she had heard it did not seem possible that he would take her back to Boston and set up an establishment for her there. What was most troublesome of all was the awful discovery that Clélie was in love, and in love in a strange and unnatural fashion—romantically and sentimentally. Being in love and in that peculiar fashion, had made her stubborn and irritable and superior. With the boys she was gentle as a dove, but with her mother she displayed stubbornness and even contempt.

When Josélie attempted to explain her situation to her in realis-

[223]

tic terms, the girl only said that her mother could not understand things like this because she had never been in love. When her mother tried to explain that women in her peculiar position could not live forever upon swooning and mooning but had their futures to think of, the girl simply slammed the door and left her.

"What about Paris?" her mother asked her. "What about the stage and the career La Lionne has promised you?" The girl only said, scornfully, "Paris! Career! Look at La Lionne herself, growing thin and haggard and old all because of love. Why doesn't she go back to Paris? There's nothing here to hold her any longer but that Yankee, and more than likely he's dead. She's had lots of experience and she's no better than I am. Where is *her* common sense?"

To this of course Josélie had no answer or rather only a poor one—that La Lionne's love sprang from sensuality and therefore was more bitter and savage than the sentimental love between her daughter and the boyish Yankee. She attempted to explain, almost in physiological terms, which Clélie resented and would not hear because it seemed to spoil her own dream.

And so Love, for which Josélie had always lived and still lived, began to become a bore and a nuisance in her own settled respectable home. Her husband Joe was no help. He was simple and uncomplicated and direct and satisfactory as a lover, but he was, Josélie told herself, black and savage and did not understand romance as she had always known it until she married and settled down. She began to wish that La Lionne would take herself back to Paris and the young Yankee would return to Boston where men apparently remained virgins until they married.

As for David, he allowed his golden hair to grow even longer until now it fell below his ears. His life, once so orderly, spent between the Port Office and writing poetry about graveyards and snowstorms in his hotel bedroom, became disorderly and Bohemian. The strange household of Josélie with its amorality, its laughter, its comings and goings of Josélie's octoroon friends, with La Lionne hiding in her bedroom moaning and groaning with baffled love, and Clélie always waiting for him with her innocently experienced caresses, became a kind of paradise. It was not only that he had discovered a life violently opposed to anything in Pinckney Street and Dedham, it was also that he felt that he was now leading the life of a poet. He drank and sang and made love to Clélie and hated Boston and succeeded in tangling the accounts of the Port Office far beyond the point of confusion in which Tom Bedloe had deliberately and carefully left them.

He knew all the time of the presence of La Lionne in the house. He knew of the rewards offered for her apprehension. He knew presently even of the voodoo tricks being played on Aunt Louisa by Big Ernestine and La Lionne during their secret nightly visits to Mama Tolanne. He even came to know through Clélie of the letters which found their way into the house of the General's wife.

He would not in any case have betrayed La Lionne. He was too grateful to her for the extraordinary change she had made in his life, for the freedom she had given him. But there were reasons even more profound for protecting her. She was revenging him upon Aunt Louisa, and so upon all the things for which Aunt Louisa stood, the things which might have deformed his whole life—all the meanness, the tightness, the aridness which, he believed, were death to a poet.

And all the while this was what mattered most to him—that he should be a great Byronic poet, singing of love and death in the heroic manner. All the abandon, the good nature, the sensuality of Josélie's household was only a part of the experience he must have, the trimmings and background of the heroic role he was to play, the stage trappings before which he was to strut.

There were even times in this new existence when the fate of Aunt Tam and his sister Agnes faded into insignificance. The curious feeling of an intense affection for his twin sister, born of his long dependence upon her as the stronger of the two, disappeared. Agnes and Aunt Tam would turn up some day, as Aunt Tam, the indestructible, had always had a way of doing. Life would go on, only he would be different.

He began to grow chesty and lose some of the boyishness and to swagger and to drink and swear. Sometimes, it was true, it required a certain effort, but it became easier each time he indulged himself, just as, once the first shy, halting step had been taken with Clélie, love had become a simple and natural function. He had never been popular with his fellow officers who had always thought him a milksop protected by old "Silver Spoon" and Tom Bedloe. Now they thought him a dude and a popinjay.

And then one night returning from Josélie's and feeling bold and wild he opened the portfolio where he carefully preserved his poems about snowstorms and graveyards, tore them up and threw them out of the window. And almost at once he began a great epic poem which he called, "Don Juan and Oriana." Clélie of course was Oriana, a simple, lovely child dwelling in a forest of magnolia and chinaberry trees among the savage Indians.

He wrote far into the morning, verse after verse, describing the trees and flowers and jungles of the background and the beauty of Oriana who had been carried off as a child among the savages and by her sweetness and beauty had come to rule over them. Oriana was regarded as a goddess whose virginity was a sacred thing.

It was already daylight when he wrote "Canto 11" on a blank sheet of paper, making it ready to receive the story of Don Juan arriving from the North. Then he undressed and tired but happy and at peace, fell asleep.

At a little after nine he was awakened by a pounding on the door and opened it to admit Aunt Louisa's orderly who told him that Aunt Tam and Agnes had been found and were even at this moment having breakfast at the General's house. The strange part of the story was that they had been rescued not by the troops sent out by General Wicks, but by a band of rebel guerrillas who delivered them to the General.

The breakfast was the first happy experience for weeks in the life of the General's wife.

The General always kept Spartan hours, not because he liked them but because it eased a little his conscience of being a mere politician turned soldier, and so they were both seated at the table having a huge and indigestible breakfast of ham, eggs, pancakes, hot breads and coffee when the orderly came running up the stairs to say that Miss Abigail Jones and Miss Agnes Wicks were in the hall below.

There she and the General found them, rather bedraggled, hatless and in torn clothing, talking to a huge and very black negro.

Aunt Tam was telling the negro to go and find his wife and children and return when he had seen them. Aunt Louisa saw her give him a gold piece as she ran down the stairs crying, "Tammy! Agnes!"

In the anxious days after their disappearance she had lived many times through the scene of the reunion. She had pictured Aunt Tam and Agnes, faint from weakness and hunger, bursting into tears at sight of her, perhaps even fainting away on the spot. But nothing like that happened. They both seemed, despite their gypsy appearance, to be well and strong and in good spirits. They returned the overwrought kisses and embraces of Aunt Louisa firmly but without hysteria, and when she cried, "You poor dear things, you must be weak and ill!" Aunt Tam only answered her in a matter-of-fact way, saying, "No, we are both very well and very hungry."

Then the General's wife noticed that although Aunt Tam appeared to have lost very nearly everything else, she still had her reticule with the journal in it.

They went upstairs to breakfast and while Aunt Tam and Agnes ate like two river roustabouts, the talk flew. The General's wife, almost hysterical with curiosity, wanted to know everything at once—why they had left the safety of the transport, why they had left the deserted ship and plunged into the delta swamps, why they had not come straight up the river to the safety of the Union Army. The questions poured out of her, one question after another, giving the General no time to speak or Aunt Tam or Agnes to answer her questions properly. She took the tone of a practiced, sensible woman dealing with a pair of half-wits—something which at the moment irritated neither Aunt Tam nor Agnes who were far more interested in the ham and hot cakes.

"You must have suffered terribly, you poor dears!"

But Aunt Tam only answered, "Not very much. We didn't eat very well and we had a little trouble with mosquitoes."

"And losing all your clothes . . . the lovely new clothes you bought for the visit."

"They aren't lost," said Agnes, with what seemed to the General's wife a kind of tartness. "They're hidden in the swamp."

"César is going back to fetch them," said Aunt Tam.

"Who is César?" asked the General.

Aunt Tam explained and Louisa made a clucking sound of alarm while the General, rather like a fat duck, shook his head to emphasize his words, "I shouldn't trust a nigger like that," he said. "You can't trust any of them nowadays . . . you can't trust anybody in this God-forsaken place."

Now Aunt Tam had always believed the General to be a pompous fool but never more profoundly than in this moment. She was aware that he had always thought her a fool too, but she saw there was no use arguing with people like him. Their skulls, in her opinion, were filled with a mixture of sawdust tinctured with self-importance. While she listened to Louisa's cackling and watched the General's face grow redder and redder as he stuffed himself with food, she felt a sudden sense of extraordinary superiority tempered by pity. In the past, throughout all her life, they had, like all the rest of the family, patronized her, speaking of her as "poor Abigail" or "poor Tam" as if she were slightly half-witted. She *knew* now that this wasn't true. She *knew* that the rest of them were poor-spirited and material and narrow and limited people who would go to their grave without ever knowing the glories that could come of merely being alive. She meant to save Agnes from them, although she could not at the moment anticipate how it was to be done.

Abruptly she replied to the General, "I would trust César anywhere with anything," in so firm and decisive a voice that the General only grunted with an air of saying "You will see!"

The reference to the trunk troubled Agnes only through vanity. She had brought all the frocks, now molding in the damp of the swamps, to make herself pretty for Tom, and now they might be all lost or ruined. It was luck, after all, she thought, that Tom was not here in New Orleans to see her bedraggled and untidy, looking her worst.

In the midst of these thoughts, she asked, "And David . . . how is David?"

At the mention of the name an extraordinary change came over Aunt Louisa's pudgy countenance. All the lines, relaxed and happy only a moment before, reappeared. The eyelids drooped, the lips were pursed. She appeared about to burst into tears. She sighed so deeply, so ferociously that the high-corseted bosom seemed about to pop the row of tiny buttons on the front of her dress.

"I don't really know, my dear. I haven't seen him for a long time. He hasn't been near the house. But from what I hear, David has changed. He has altered so much that it's possible you won't know him."

"Changed?" asked Aunt Tam. "How?"

Aunt Louisa's expression altered again, this time from deep sorrow bordering on tears, to suavity and superiority and to an expression which implied, "There are things I know which I couldn't repeat." It was exactly the expression of a little girl in a corner saying, "I've got a secret! I've got a secret!"

Aloud she said, "Well, I don't know how to explain it. He's become wild. He's got . . ."

Here the General interrupted her. "Louisa!" he said fiercely, "I think your explanation has gone far enough." To Aunt Tam and Agnes he said, "He's wild. He drinks."

But it was Agnes who forced the issue, with a suddenness and boldness that was like the explosion of a bomb.

"If you mean that he's running around with women, I'm glad."

The General said, "Agnes!" And Aunt Louisa said, "I don't think you understand what you're saying, my child."

"Yes, I think she does," put in Aunt Tam. She made the remark viciously, almost with hostility.

"There's one thing you must understand, Aunt Louisa," continued Agnes, "I am not a child. And I do understand what I'm talking about."

"It's not very lady-like at your age, Agnes."

Aunt Tam interrupted, "Lady-like!" she said with a snort, "Pish. Tosh!"

"Abigail!"

"What I want to know, Aunt Louisa," persisted Agnes, "is when are we going to see him?"

"I've sent him a message," said the General's wife. "I hope he will care enough to take some notice of it. He's taken no notice of the others I've sent him. I haven't seen him since . . ." The face drooped and grew immeasurably sad again, "I'm afraid I have other bad news for you. It's about Tom."

[229]

But Agnes only replied brightly, "I know all about Tom."

"How," asked Aunt Louisa in a tone of irritation, "could you know anything about Tom?"

"Because Mr. MacTavish told me. Tom's free. He'll be back in New Orleans in a day or two."

"What MacTavish?" thundered the General.

"Colonel *Hector* MacTavish—the same one I told you about, who sent us here," said Aunt Tam, again conferring rank upon her friend, this time partly from a vague desire to irritate the General who was annoying her by his grunts of disapproval and superiority. "He was very kind to us."

"Fiddlesticks!" said the General. "You sound like a rebel talking."

His wife interrupted him impatiently, "What did he tell you about Tom? Is he all right? Is he safe?"

"He's all right. He's got away. Mr. MacTavish knew all about it."

The face of the General's wife had now undergone another startling change. In her eagerness it had become quite red. She said, "It's a relief to hear that. We were afraid for a long time that something had happened to him . . . that he might have been . . ."

The General was chuckling, "I never really worried about Tom," he said. "He'll always take care of himself. There's a fellow who could get himself out of any scrape. You're going to have your hands full, Agnes, when you marry him."

He took the napkin from under his chin, stood up and pulled his coat down tight over his pot-belly. "You girls will have to forgive me, but I must go to headquarters. We've plenty of trouble down there, but I'm fixing them. Leave it to me and we'll have order and decency in this town, or someone will have to pay for it."

Aunt Tam wanted suddenly to say "Pish! Tosh!" again but she held her tongue.

The General said, "I'll see you tonight," and went off. The three women, each one of them in her way aware of something strained and peculiar in the atmosphere, did not speak until the sound of the General's thumping descent of the stairs had died away.

Then Aunt Tam said, "This is a very nice house, Louisa. You've done very well for yourself."

"It's not a convenient house," said Aunt Louisa. "It's too big and everything is inconvenient. It's like all these southern houses . . . all for show and no matter how much dirt gathers in the corners. I like a smaller house that you can keep neat and clean."

"I understand," said Agnes, "that it is Mr. MacTavish's house."

"Mr. MacTavish's house, my eyes," said Aunt Louisa. "Everything in the city of New Orleans belongs to the Union Army. You'd think from the way these people carry on that we hadn't beaten them." She sighed, "Oh, you've no idea what the General and I have been through. Only a man of his character and strength could have stood it."

Aunt Tam was aware that they were about to be treated to one of Louisa's long tirades on the subject of her martyrdom, and she was right. There was nothing to stop her now, not even the fact that she had not yet heard in detail the more horrific part of the adventures of Aunt Tam and Agnes, the terrifying voyage on the *Cristobal* and the hurricane. She went into detail concerning the unruliness of the Louisianans, their persecution of the General and herself, and all their own self-sacrificing attempts to bring order out of chaos and morality out of immorality. Upon this subject she dwelt for quite a long time, finally ending with the story of the abusive letters in blue envelopes which kept turning up mysteriously, and the story of La Lionne who could not be found, omitting however to mention Tom's familiarity with the Café Imperial.

She might have gone on for the rest of the morning but for the fact that she was interrupted by the sound of footsteps coming up the stairs, three treads at a time. From the impetuousness of the arrival the three women at once thought, "It must be Tom," but almost at once and to their astonishment David appeared in the doorway.

At sight of him Agnes knew at once how much he had altered. It was natural that the fair-haired, delicate boy of Pinckney Street and Cambridge should have changed, but this was more than change. This was a new David. It was not only that he was heavier

[231]

and looked healthier but he swaggered into the room almost as Tom would have done.

Aunt Tam thought, "He went away a fledgling and he has turned into a man."

The David who left them in Boston to join the Army of the Potomac would have come into the room blushing and shy, waiting for Agnes to give him his cue, as he had always done since he was a little boy. This young buck came in with assurance, crossed directly to Agnes and lifting his sister out of her chair and on to her feet, hugged and kissed her.

"I knew you'd turn up," he said. "I wasn't even very worried." Then he hugged her again and turning to Aunt Tam hugged her until she lost her breath and giggled, "Davy! Davy!"

The General's wife, who had not left her chair, said, "Well, David," to which he only replied, "Hello, Aunt Louisa." And seating himself he turned to Agnes saying, "Now tell me all about it. What happened to you? How did you ever come to be on a dirty dago boat?" But before she had a chance to speak he leaned over and taking her by both shoulders, looked at her and said, "But you're different. You look different. You aren't a little girl any longer."

"You aren't exactly the same either, Davy."

"I'm writing poetry now . . . lots of it . . . real poetry. I'll write a poem about you and Aunt Tam and your strange adventures." He laughed, "What'll they think of all this back in Pinckney Street? Can you see Pa's face when he hears about us. This is a great city, Agnes. You'll love it. It's not like anything you've ever seen before."

"I guessed that," said Agnes.

"Well, well!" he said, looking her over carefully once more. "You're looking very handsome. You always were a pretty little girl but you look handsome now. You're a great beauty. You've got a face . . . a real beautiful face."

The General's wife interrupted them, "Perhaps we had better go into the parlor."

"Wherever you like," said Aunt Tam, brushing the crumbs off her knees. She was aware more than ever of the atmosphere of dissension and strain and was glad that the General had gone off to headquarters. David had certainly changed. If running after women had cured his namby-pamby manner, she was, like Agnes, glad he was running after women. He certainly no longer seemed like the girl of the family. She chuckled inwardly. He had certainly escaped with a vengeance the thwarted dreariness of Pinckney Street. She couldn't help chuckling inwardly at the prospect of her brother's reunion with his son. Ethan would be shocked as he had been shocked by Tom Bedloe's easy-going ways. But she wished David wouldn't wear his wavy blond hair so long, like a woman who liked to brag that she could sit on her hair. It *was* beautiful hair but that was no excuse for making yourself look like a naughty archangel in the uniform of a Yankee officer.

On the way through the great hall, Agnes said, "This is a wonderful house." To which Aunt Louisa replied sharply, "It is too big. Everything is too big. It's vulgar."

"I don't think it's vulgar at all. It's beautiful."

To Agnes it seemed that here in these great high-ceilinged rooms there was space, space in which to breathe and expand. And all the time, all through the morning she was defending Mr. MacTavish. Once or twice she had nearly lost her temper and insulted Aunt Louisa. Every time the General's wife abused the people of New Orleans, it seemed to her that she was slandering Mr. MacTavish personally. The people of Louisiana couldn't be as bad as Aunt Louisa said. Ever since the night before when Mr. MacTavish asked her for a souvenir, she had been troubled. She had, she felt, hurt his feelings in all innocence and she had never been able to explain to him that she *really* had nothing to give him. She had been rude to him without meaning to be, after all his kindness to them. There had been no time to explain. She wished now she had torn off one of the buttons with her own fingers and given it to him. He was so nice and so gentle and yet so strong.

The trouble remained with her all the way down the river in the boat, all the way in the barouche from the river to Aunt Louisa's house. It had returned, rankling, to spoil her pleasure in the breakfast and in seeing David again. She kept seeing the curious look of pain and anger in his face, dimly lighted by the lamp in the doorway of Father Desmoulin's little house. "Maybe," she thought, "it will haunt me always. I must see him again some time, some place, to explain."

But they were in the parlor now, a big room in pale gray and gold with a vast chandelier of crystal. Aunt Tam was standing by a round table covered by a purple plush cloth with a wide gold fringe. She was looking intently at something on the table. Then she turned and said, "Louisa, this looks like one of those blue envelopes."

The General's wife stiffened and her face again turned an alarming shade of red. She snatched it off the table and said, "Excuse me. I must go downstairs."

She went out, closing the door violently behind her, and when she had gone the others looked at each other for a moment without speaking. David was grinning.

"Why are you laughing?" asked Aunt Tam.

"I'm laughing at Aunt Louisa."

"You shouldn't," said Aunt Tam. "There's something the matter with the poor woman."

"There always has been," said David.

Agnes said, "I think she's horrible. I never knew how horrible they could both be. We can't stay here, Aunt Tam. We can't!"

"There's nothing else we can do," said Aunt Tam. "We came here to visit her."

David was grinning again, "You see what she's like. You see why I haven't come near here lately."

"She wasn't always like that," said Aunt Tam. "Something has happened to her."

"In her heart she was always like that," said David. Then quite suddenly he said, "When the war's over I'm not going back to Boston."

Agnes looked at him suddenly and then meekly said, "But what about Pa? He meant you to take over his business."

"I don't want his business. I'm never going back to Boston again if I can help it."

It was Aunt Tam who, a little shocked, spoke now.

"What do you mean, David? Not many boys have such opportunities as your father offers you."

"I'll do something . . . anything, but I'm not going to lead the

[234]

life Pa has led . . . back and forth between his factory and Pinckney Street. It's like being in jail." To Agnes he said, "And what
are you going to do?"

"I'm going to marry Tom."

"If you marry Tom, you'll not be going back to Boston."

Then Agnes said, "I think that's why I'm marrying him. I think
that's the reason I've always been in love with him. He's exciting.
With Tom you'd never know what was happening next."

"That can become very tiresome after a time," said Aunt Tam.
For a moment she had experienced alarm at the change in the
two children. Perhaps they were going too far. She remembered
what a Frenchman had said to her in Paris once, "Some of the
worst people I know in Paris are Americans from your New England. There seem to be no depths they are unwilling to plumb."
That was it. The pendulum sometimes swung too far the other way,
bringing ruin.

"I want to get out of here," repeated Agnes stubbornly. "It was
awful at breakfast. I'd rather still be eating what César dug up
for us. I am going to call on the Baroness as soon as I can buy
some decent clothes."

"What Baroness?" asked David.

"Her name is de Lèche. She came with us to New Orleans."

David did not answer at once. He did not know what were
Tom's relations with the Baroness de Lèche, but he had suspicions.
He found himself saying suddenly, "You mustn't go there."

"Why not? She was very kind to us."

"She's a rebel. The General wouldn't allow it." It was a weak,
implausible answer but the only one he could summon.

"I'm not an army private. The General cannot tell me where
I can go and where I can't."

Now David saw suddenly that he had taken the worse course. If
he did not tell her that Tom was quartered in the de Lèche house,
she would be suspicious at once. He had a sudden sense of being
very young and naïf and helpless and not quite the man of the
world he fancied himself to be. So he said, "Tom knows her. He's
billeted in her house. The family is very proud it seems. They've
had nothing to do with Tom." And again he felt himself getting
beyond his depth.

The opposition only seemed to strengthen Agnes' determination to call upon the young Baroness—opposition and the memory of breakfast which still impressed her. She said, "I didn't come all the way here to live in Boston. I want to know what this place is like."

To that argument Aunt Tam could find no answer. Her common sense told her that if she was to permit the General and Louisa to direct her existence they would eat New England boiled dinners and darn and mend and gossip and there would be nothing whatever to write in the journal. And David, with his secret, his miraculous release, could not well oppose his sister's impatience with much conviction. It was as if all of them were confused and at cross-purposes. Now that the first excitement of meeting had waned a little, a kind of exhaustion settled over them.

Agnes said, "I've got to have some clothes. I can't go out looking like this."

"Louisa must have a dressmaker," said Aunt Tam, "and I suppose the shops are still open."

"They're open," said David, "but there's not much in them."

Then Aunt Louisa reappeared, less red in the face, but still with an air of smoldering indignation. She was, thought Aunt Tam, like a volcano which from time to time erupted, giving off flame and clouds of smoke. She always had been like that.

"Well," she said, "have you got everything settled? Because your visit may be a short one. The General may be recalled to Washington soon. It seems that they need him there."

Aunt Tam didn't say anything but she did look at Agnes and saw that the girl's face wore a deeply sultry expression. In her own mind a plan had been forming . . . a wild, fantastic plan like the one of boarding the *Cristobal* at Havana. She distrusted herself, knowing that once she conceived a romantic plan, there was no stopping her. It was as if she became for a time quite a different person, a stranger whom she could not recognize in more sober moments. Drunkenness, she thought, must be a little like these wild flights of fantasy which sometimes seized her.

Now she held her tongue. Certainly with Louisa ready to explode, it was not the moment to propose anything radical. They were all sitting about the room, rather stiffly, their senses dulled, by the rising heat that crept in through the windows and beneath the door, when the orderly appeared saying that there was a negro with a telescope at the door. It was, he said, to be delivered to Miss Agnes Wicks. There was a letter too, sent by hand.

The General's wife said, "Don't let him bring the trunk inside. There might be a bomb in it."

Agnes took the letter and opened it. It was brief and written in a small, rather neat orthography, more like that of a man than of a woman. It read:

Dear Friend: Knowing you had no clothes at all I have sent my boy, Erastus, with a small trunk and four frocks which you may find of use until you can have some made. What you can buy in the shops is not worth much. I have a good couturière who will come to the house. She is Madame Célemene Dagereau. You can find her through the concierge of the Hotel St. Charles. I don't fancy that the clothes of the General's wife would be much good to you. You and I are somewhat the same size. I am looking forward to receiving you here. I fancy a de Lèche would not be very welcome at the General's house. Good luck to you and your Aunt. She is a splendid woman.

> *Sincerely,*
> *Éliane de Lèche.*

Agnes looked up from the letter and said, "You needn't be afraid. They are clothes for me, sent by the Baroness de Lèche."

"Who?" asked Cousin Louisa, as if she could not believe what she was hearing.

"Madame de Lèche," repeated Agnes.

"What an impertinence. You cannot accept them." To the orderly she said, "Tell the nigger boy to take them away."

Then a queer thing happened to Aunt Tam. Before Agnes could speak, she said to the bewildered orderly, "Wait!" And to the General's wife, she said, "Louisa, you had best get one thing clear. You are not ordering Agnes and me around. We are quite able to take care of ourselves. I found that out on the way from Havana. Either those dresses come into the house or Agnes and I go out the door."

The color rushed again to the face of Aunt Louisa. "Have you lost your mind, Abigail?" she said. "Do you know who this woman is?"

"I know her very well," said Aunt Tam (which was not altogether true even though she had ridden for miles on a mule her waist encircled by the arms of Madame de Lèche). "She has been very kind to us and there is no reason to be rude and discourteous."

"But the woman has a bad reputation. She is a rebel. She's mixed up with all the men who are making trouble for the General."

Aunt Tam stood her ground, "Louisa, is the trunk to be brought in?"

For a second it appeared that the volcano was on the verge of eruption. Louisa's face grew purple. She swallowed and then said to the orderly, "Very well, tell the boy to take the trunk up to the green bedroom."

When the orderly had gone away, she said to Aunt Tam, "You have put me in a shameful position, as if I could not dress my own kinfolk and had to ask favors of a rebel."

Aunt Tam, quieter now, said, "I'm sorry, Louisa, but I think you're being ridiculous. I do not see how either Agnes or myself could appear in public in your clothing. And there's no use slapping kindness in the face, there's little enough of it in the world."

Coldly the General's wife said, "I'll go and see about the rooms. Will you want to share a room or have separate ones? It is a big house."

Agnes answered her, "We want to share a room, Aunt Louisa." She had a vague feeling that if once she allowed herself to be separated from Aunt Tam, Aunt Louisa would force her back, back into the world out of which she had only but now escaped.

"You'll probably want to talk a little longer to David," said Aunt Louisa. "I'll go and see about the room."

When she had gone, David said, "You see what she's like. I think she's going crazy. That's why I didn't come here any more."

"I think she ought to go back to Boston," said Aunt Tam. "She seems very nervous . . . almost deranged. She ought never to have come here."

David was grinning, "Maybe none of us should have come here."

"I'm going after her," said Aunt Tam. "I'm going to apologize for losing my temper."

When she had gone from the room, David kissed Agnes again and for a moment he seemed like the old David, rather gentle and quiet.

He said, "Agnes, are you really in love with Tom?"

"Yes, I am. I wasn't sure before, but I am now."

"Are you determined to marry him?"

"That's why I came here. I didn't tell anybody that was the reason. If I had, Pa wouldn't have let me come."

David didn't answer her and she said, "Why do you ask me that? Why do you look so serious?"

He looked out of the window. "I don't think you'll be happy with Tom."

"Why?"

"He's not for somebody like you. He's for somebody like the de Lèche woman."

"Do you mean because he's been wild?"

"Yes." He frowned like a little boy. "But I don't think you know what 'being wild' means, Agnes."

Quickly she answered, "Oh, yes I do. I didn't, but I know now. I don't mind his being wild. I don't want to marry a milksop, David." She blushed suddenly, furiously, for the memory of the obscene gesture was in her mind. "I think I'd like a wicked man for a husband . . . wicked and experienced."

For a moment David did not know whether in his new role, to laugh or in his old one, to cry. He was only certain of one thing, that this was an extraordinary conversation which a little while ago would have been impossible.

He said, "I don't think you know what you are talking about."

"I do if you mean that Tom runs after women. That's not altogether his fault because he's like that and it makes women run after him. I've seen them even back in Boston—some of the most respectable and prudish ones. Even I have run after him, that's the real reason I came here. I was running after him. I'm not what you think I am, David. I never was, only I had to pretend to be something else because everybody always said I was and made me be somebody else. I wasn't like that. Sometimes lately I think I'm

[239]

bad. I know I must be what they call a 'bad girl' in Boston, like Sophia who was sent away from school. I know why now. It was because she was having a baby. I sometimes almost wish I'd been sent away like her. Anyway I'm not going back."

The wind completely taken out of his sails, he couldn't find any answer. In some vague fashion he failed to understand, she had outdone him again as she had always outdone him at croquet or hop-scotch or argument or anything else. She had forced him back again into the position of inferiority and timidity. And there was something indecent in such a speech.

She said in a firm voice, "I think I must be bad and I'm very glad of it."

He was aware now of a vague injury to his dignity and sense of importance. Byron and Don Juan had been affronted and rendered innocent by the boldness of Agnes' speech. In order to restore his self-respect, in order to make himself believe the role which he had been playing, to re-establish his sense of dominance, it was necessary to strike a bold decisive blow.

Almost without knowing what he was saying, he blurted, "I have a mistress. Her name is Clélie."

Now it was Agnes' turn to be overwhelmed. "Running after women" was a vague term she had overheard older women sometimes using. It was vague and general and mysterious and dashing, but to be confronted in cold blood with fact garnished by detail was quite another thing. She had not been until that moment even quite certain of the exact implications of the word "mistress." But she was certain now. David's manner, the spirited swagger, which accompanied the declaration made it perfectly clear. And she was shocked.

She said simply, "Oh, David!" and the very tone of her voice and the bright color of her face told him that his dominance had been re-established. Byron and Don Juan were vindicated.

"Don't tell Aunt Tam," she said.

"I hadn't meant to. I hadn't meant to tell you. It isn't exactly the kind of thing a fellow tells his sister."

She smiled and the blush faded away. "I'm glad you did, David." Then she covered her face with her hands, "I don't know what's come over me lately. Sometimes I'm scared."

"Don't worry. Sometimes I'm scared too."

"Do you feel like I do . . . that sometimes you're just carried away by a wave of something you don't understand?"

"Yes," said David. "That's the way I felt at first but it's beginning to go away."

"Do you think it will go away with me?"

"I don't know. Maybe girls are different."

She still kept her face covered. "Oh, David, I don't want to be like the women back home. I don't want to be like Aunt Louisa or even poor Aunt Tam. If Aunt Tam had gotten away when she was young it might have been different. I want to be like Madame de Lèche."

The statement alarmed him. He said, "I don't know what she's like. I never saw her."

"I want to be a great lady. I don't want to be just a stupid, common housewife."

And then Aunt Tam put an end to the conversation by returning suddenly. She said, "We have a very nice room, Agnes. It was Mr. MacTavish's sister's room." The speech brought no response and she was aware at once that she had interrupted a serious conversation not meant for her ears.

Agnes was thinking suddenly of Mr. MacTavish and the button, and wishing that he was here with them. Then she could explain about the button. But she also wished he was here because she felt lost and bewildered, like a bather unable to swim who has ventured beyond his depth. Mr. MacTavish was wise and sensible and experienced. Suddenly she felt a wild impulse to burst into tears. She managed to restrain herself, although she had to bite her lip hard in order to accomplish it.

In the bedroom on the top floor, waiting for nightfall, Tom had fallen asleep after the young Baroness left him. Like all violent and sensual people, he slept easily, dozing and waking as effortlessly as a dog lying in the sun. When he wakened he lay for a long time stretching and turning lazily. There was no reason for haste and he enjoyed this moment just between sleep and consciousness.

Indolently he thought, "It is quite dark. She has gone by now. I shall have to find her again in New Orleans."

[241]

Not being given to reflection, it did not occur to him that she was becoming an obsession, that his mind and body were occupied with her not only while she was with him but when she was absent as well. No other woman he had ever known had ever affected him thus. Yet, with the instinct of an animal, he knew that he was not in love with her. Even by his rabbit-like standards, love implied tenderness and respect and something like awe, and in his feeling for the young Baroness there were none of these things. He had for her, in spite of his healthy self-indulgence, no particular respect or awe. There was only a sense of *malaise* which at moments became a torment, and a sense of conflict.

Lying there, half awake, it seemed to him that his feeling for her was like the feeling a man might have if he could, like Narcissus, be in love with himself. It was her egotism, her savagery, the brazen sensuality which held him and, most of all, a vague feeling that there still remained depth after depth which he had not yet explored, which he had not been permitted to explore. He thought, "She is a wicked bitch!" But in the darkness he smiled in enjoyment of her wickedness, or at the memory of her experienced caresses.

Then he thought, "To hell with her! I've got to get out of here." And sitting up on the edge of the bed, he pulled on his boots. Then he stood up and put on the jacket of his uniform, wishing vaguely that he had some other clothing that would be less conspicuous until he reached New Orleans and the safety of the occupied zone around the capital city. At about the same time he smelled the smoke which had begun to filter up the well of the stairway and under the door of his room.

The smell was a smell of danger and at once he was alert. Opening the door he stepped into the hallway and heard the sound of voices. Going over to the stair railing he listened and from below-stairs he could hear what they were saying without understanding it, for the voices spoke in the *patois* of the country. And then leaning further over the well, he saw the heads of many negroes and of one or two white men. Two of the negroes carried torches. He heard one of the white men say, "We'll clean out the God damned place and burn it!" And by the accent he knew that the man was from the North, probably a deserter. They were bent on

[242]

plundering the last scrap left at Bel Manoir before setting fire to it.

Quickly he thought again, "I must get out of here."

He was aware that the lawless gang pouring through the rooms below would have small respect for his uniform of officer in the Union Army. The deserters might try to kill him just to get him out of the way. Then he remembered the dark narrow stairway up which the young Baroness had brought him on the way from the burning cabin to the room. Going to the end of the great hall he opened a door and there leading downward was the narrow stairway.

On the black descent he met no one. In the kitchen he made his way toward the dim moonlight which shone through the doorway leading into the garden. The garden, with its thick tangle of bushes was the obvious way of escape. Waiting in the doorway until the noise and shouting overhead seemed to increase in violence, he ran quickly through the curve of the great horseshoe-shaped stairway into the shelter of the camellias and the wistaria-covered arbor.

Then, hiding in the shrubbery, he watched the mob inside tearing down what remained of the curtains, smashing the windows and the mirrors by the light of the torches. While he watched a flame crept out of one of the windows and swept up the wall of the house, then another and another and he thought, "I must run now. They will be coming out."

But the sight of the burning house held a fascination and instead of going away he retreated down the path into the hedged enclosure where Agnes had found herself earlier in the day. Here from the shadow of a ragged camellia he watched the fire climb from window to window of the doomed house. It was like an animal, leaping now here now there, devouring whatever it touched.

The mob had fled now out into the cleared space between the great house and the burned slave quarters. Some still carried burning faggots although by now the flames from the burning building illuminated the whole countryside. Above the savage crackling of the flames he heard now and then the wild drunken shouting. One of the negroes had a drum—perhaps the same drum he had

[243]

heard from the windows of the sinister cabin where he had been imprisoned. He kept beating it wildly in a rhythm which seemed in a strange fashion to synchronize with the clamor made by the roaring flames.

They had spread now, the whole length of the façade and downward into the big ballroom. With a crash a part of the roof fell and through the opening the flames rushed upward carrying high into the air showers of sparks and bits of burning wood which fell among the mob and about the drummer. Through an opening in the shrubbery he could see the drummer now, black and half-naked, standing over his great drum, swaying with the rhythm which the fire seemed to define for him.

And watching the fire, he felt no sadness, no bitterness such as a man like MacTavish with his affection for animals and trees and houses and tradition would have felt, but only a simple kind of primitive ecstasy in the wild spectacle of destruction. He should have run away but he could not go until he had seen the whole great pile, with all its decaying beauty and its implications utterly foreign to him, crash into a shapeless heap of crackling, naked beams. There was a direct evil splendor in the spectacle like the evil splendor of that first night he had spent with the young Baroness in the room where the flames now devoured the bed, the chairs, every object to which he had become attached in a curious fashion through their association with her and what had happened in the room.

While he watched, he came perhaps near to seeing himself for the first time. In the ecstatic satisfaction which the contemplation of the spectacle brought his spirit, a satisfaction curiously like that which she of all women he had ever known had been able to bring to his body, he divined clearly many things, among them a kind of doom which hung over himself and her. Whether they met the doom together or whether he never saw her again and they met it separately, divided, there was nevertheless, no escape from it. It was as if a curse and an overwhelming gift had been placed upon them at birth, as if both of them were propelled, willingly and with perverse delight, toward destruction by a force stronger than either of them, as if they possessed a kind of special and vicious splendor which, fascinating others, men and women alike, by the very aura of sensuality, at the same time set them apart from those who had never felt and could not understand that dark, throbbing splendor. And as if in punishment for what they knew and for the incandescent evil of their knowledge, there lay before them a terrible and violent end.

The rhythm of the drum was in his veins now, beating in his very blood. The fire reared in a great column of flame a hundred feet above the flat soaked earth. He stood, watching it, forgetful of the danger of discovery, his feet apart, his body braced forward, his back arched above the buttocks like that of an amorous stallion.

Then suddenly with a wild sound of crashing timber the whole great house collapsed in an inferno of flame and flying sparks. The fire, in a last spasm of destruction leapt high above the scorched live oaks, and then subsided, slowly in rhythmic waves of diminishing violence. For a moment the sound of the drum was annihilated by the crash and when it was heard again it was no longer in his veins. He stood relaxed, silent and curiously sad.

Then after a little time, he became aware slowly of a sensation of being watched by someone or something which he could not see. He felt it at the back of his neck, an odd tickling sensation which gradually spread through his whole body as he slipped deeper into the shadow of the camellia thicket. Turning, crouched protectively like an animal, he looked behind him and there in the moonlight among the shadows cast by the flames of the burning ruin, he discovered three figures. A prickly sensation ran over the surface of his body and the hair of his head stood up like the hair on the back of a suspicious dog. It was a fear, a sense of alarm, he had never before experienced. It was not like the fear he had felt in battle or even at the moment when he had believed he was about to be burned alive in the cabin-prison. Such fear only stimulated him into physical action, into fighting. This was different. This fear, lacking a definite object against which action might launch itself, paralyzed him. It was a fear of these figures which, although they seemed to be half-naked white men, were, his strong animal instinct told him, neither human nor tangible. The fear was of something in the *place*, in the atmosphere, in nature itself.

It all happened quickly—the first terror, its passing into a sensation of cold, the calculated control in which his heart seemed no longer to beat, and the final action motivated by his own physical courage which commanded him to discover and annihilate the reason for fear. Stepping out of the shadows he moved toward the figures and when he had crossed the small circular open space and reached the pool of water which reflected the glow of the sky, he stopped suddenly and burst into laughter. It was laughter colored by an hysterical quality, but laughter none the less, at himself, at the grotesqueness of the whole scene.

The three figures watching him were of stone, of white marble, patchily covered by lichen, rendered phosphorescent by the play of moonlight shadow and the reflected flames of the burning house. Moving nearer he discovered that the central figure was that of a woman of beautiful proportions, in form very like the young Baroness herself. On either side of her was a male figure, each of them grotesque, one of them obscene.

The central figure, he divined, must be Venus but the other two had only for him the significance of grotesque. One of them was so comically remarkable that he laughed again. In the wildness of his youth mythology had scarcely touched his consciousness. Venus was apparent. Dionysius and Priapus were beyond him; but the juxtaposition of the beautiful female figure placed between them he understood with an instinct uncomplicated by legend or mythology. In the moonlight he was able to discover the aged and corrupt face of the monstrous Priapus figure. It, too, seemed to be laughing—a frozen, savage, ironical laugh—laughing back at him.

Suddenly he thrust his body forward and with all his strength pushed the evil figure. It was firmly fastened to its heavy granite base. Again and again he pushed, straining and sweating, until at length the rusted bolt which held it in place broke from its socket and the statue fell forward. Falling, it turned and rolled on its back, lying face upward, the face still grinning obscenely in the moonlight. Then swiftly he kicked the face with his heavy boots. The cynical joke of that first de Lèche who had placed the Venus between two lecherous grotesques had stabbed home at last by the light of the burning house into the consciousness of a man he had never even seen, who was not born when the Frenchman died.

The violence of his attack on the statue suddenly exhausted him and, standing there in the moonlight bathed in sweat, with the sound of the tom-tom in his ears, he felt a fool, the butt of some evil joke perpetrated by something or someone he had never known save through the awareness of his nerves.

The statue lay there, prostrate but still grinning, intact and triumphant.

Then he was aware that the sound of the drumming had ceased and there was only the crackling sound of the fire, greatly diminished as it burned itself out.

All around him nothing remained but desolation. Bel Manoir was finished. Nothing ever again could recreate it as it had been. For the first time, a feeling of desolation filled his consciousness. He hated the place, with its beauty and cruelty, with its disease and splendor. He hated her. He wanted to be free of it, quickly, never to see it again. He was filled with quick rage and hatred and disgust, against whom or what he did not know.

Fleeing from the shadow of one great live oak to another, he made his way down the long allée toward the menacing river which ate its way toward the ruined plantation, its muddy waters nibbling at the thick levee, swallowing up the minute cascades of damp earth that slipped away in the moonlight as the river swept on its way to the hot Gulf.

It was nearly dawn when Célimène, the old servant of Father Desmoulins, opened the door to find the Yankee officer outside. At sight of him in the yellow glow from the lamp she carried the old woman screamed; not only did the uniform frighten her but the face of the man and the look in his eyes. She did not like Yankees; the only ones with whom she had ever had experience were the renegades and deserters and thieves who had come into the country since the fall of New Orleans. Father Desmoulins, by gentleness, by reasonableness had been able to manage them. And he possessed, beyond his own priest's clothing and a few books and tables and chairs, nothing to steal. Yet they had been threatening and unpleasant and the memories of them now made this visitor a menace.

Father Desmoulins, already at his prayers, heard her scream and came to the door just as she was closing it.

He recognized the Yankee at once as the one Eliane de Lèche had told him would appear, and in his gentle worldliness he thought, "He is the sort she would choose. He is much more for her than Hector MacTavish."

"I am Major Thomas Bedloe," said the Yankee.

"I was expecting you," said the priest. "Come in and we'll have breakfast."

He was aware of the edge of hostility in the voice of the visitor and wondered whether it was hostility for his church, for himself, or for the fact that he was a Créole and a Southerner. He bade the old servant bring the breakfast and showed his visitor where he might wash, and in a little while they sat down together in a small room with a big window overlooking the one street of the deserted and looted village.

Conversation between them was not easy. Father Desmoulins spoke English well but it was difficult for him, and the visitor came out of a world of which he knew very little, no more than he had read in books or had repeated to him by planters who had made astonished visitors to New England. And in the blue eyes of the younger man he detected sullenness and dissatisfaction. Watching him, he thought, "Perhaps it was not hostility I felt in him, but only unhappiness and doubt." And then in a sudden flash of intuition the old man saw how similar the mood of the young man was to that of Éliane herself at those moments when, not mocking, she seemed impatient and furious and baffled.

They talked of the uprisings and the anarchy which had spread everywhere in the parish, of Bel Manoir and its utter annihilation.

"We saw the fire from here last night," said the priest, "lighting all the sky. We knew it was Bel Manoir."

The destruction saddened the old man, yet it was, he knew, inevitable. It was not like the wanton destruction of a plantation which was the property of a God-fearing family who were good citizens. The de Lèche family had been worldly and vain and greedy since the very beginning. He did not look upon the destruction as a result of the vengeance of God, but as the only logical end of a long record of evil arising from the heartlessness and wickedness of a family. Nothing, he believed, could have prevented the destruction and death of that family. It was as inevitable as the rising of the sun.

He was aware of the same sort of ruthlessness and vanity in the dark good-looking face of the young man opposite him. There was in his countenance the same pride and recklessness he had seen in the faces of one de Lèche after another. Lucifer, he thought, leading the rebellious angels must have had the same look in the eyes and the carriage of the head. He did not attempt to discount the power or the attraction of the Lucifers; that was what made them dangerous and destructive to others. He had no doubts that Lucifer himself was handsome, attractive and reckless. Only through wisdom and experience were you able to protect yourself from them. The odd thing was that, like Lucifer, his counterparts on this earth with all the vitality, the beauty, the animal attraction with which God had endowed them, were doomed to disaster. It was as if their own gifts, their own violence destroyed them. Sometimes, he thought, they were aware of intimations of doom; it was that which turned their willful brilliant spirits dark and malicious and evil.

The priest aloud said, "Celemène can prepare you more eggs if you like. There is not much else to be had but we have our own hens. They have not yet stolen them." And as he spoke his heart was saying, "God have mercy upon these dark angels."

Across the table from him Tom Bedloe watched the priest, listening with only half his mind to the banal and formal speeches of the old man. He was tired and he was sullen and the memory of what had happened in the garden of Bel Manoir during the burning of the house kept troubling him. It would not be shaken off. It remained there inside him like an obscure dull pain which would not be stopped either by will or by medicine. It was always there in the back of his mind, returning at the very moment when he believed it annihilated, when he felt for a moment his old healthy animal self. It had troubled him during the long solitary hours when he had walked along the river alone in the moonlight.

The experience in the garden was to him like a moment of insanity, as if for a little time his own brain had betrayed him, altering his whole body and spirit, so that he had become, at the moment he found himself kicking the prostrate statue, a kind of maniac whose actions his proper self could neither fathom nor control. That the days and nights of dissipation had weakened and depressed him, he accepted coldly as a physical fact; he was only troubled because the knowledge opened in his unphilosophical mind a small crevasse through which appeared the darkness of terrifying doubt. It would be like this to grow old . . . only it would go on and on—this sensation of lifelessness, of dullness, this strange sensation of wandering in emptiness. The sensation had no significance for him; it was only a feeling of profound *malaise*, like that of an animal that is ill. That it was the first intimation of the agony which becomes the horror of aging and impotent sensualists, did not occur to him. In his sullenness he only knew that he felt badly.

The presence of the man opposite him troubled him as a speech of reproval might trouble him. He was uncomfortable because he had never before spoken so much as a word to a Catholic priest. In his mind, priests were connivers and hypocrites, and it troubled him now that this man appeared to be neither. It troubled him even more that he seemed to resemble someone he had known or seen at some time, and it troubled him even more when he discovered that the old priest was very like Mr. Emerson, not only in physical appearance (although the priest was much older) but because his voice and his wise gentle manner were like Mr. Emerson's. Long ago he had dismissed Mr. Emerson and those other friends of Aunt Tam's whom he saw sometimes in the house at Dedham, as clever and somewhat tiresome creatures who were above or at least apart from himself and all that interested him in life. In his heart there always lurked the uneasy contempt of the man of action for the intellectual and the reformer, and now here was Mr. Emerson again, dressed as a priest seated opposite him in this tiny house in a Louisiana parish. His presence was like a reproach, from which there is no escape. The priest implied Mr. Emerson and the reproach implied Agnes, and Agnes had never appeared so cool, so clean, so shining as in this moment when he felt tired, soiled and bewildered. Yet his body, strong and assertive from years of indulgence, kept crying out, "You will go back to her. You will go back to her. You will see her tomorrow again," and the anguished cry of the body was not for Agnes. And the image was not that of Agnes, who seemed presently only something vague and white and shining and vaporous, but of the young Baroness whom he saw with agonizing yet voluptuous clarity, like a pain from which one derives an obscure pleasure.

He scarcely heard what the priest was saying and he remembered none of it. He was aware presently of the priest saying, "Celemène has prepared a bed for you. It wouldn't be safe to attempt going further by daylight. You had better rest here until nightfall."

In the priest's own small tidy bedroom Hector MacTavish was already asleep when Tom Bedloe came to the door. After the others had disappeared down the river with black César, he had gone out into the darkness to walk the levee. Overhead were only the stars and the rising moon and beside him the great river laden with the mud of all those northern states—Ohio and Indiana and Minnesota and Iowa and Kentucky—out of which his own country, this damp fertile Louisiana, in the passage of aeons of time had been created.

He was troubled about many things—the welfare of his mother and sisters whose whereabouts he did not even know, the destruction of his own plantation, and the gradual breaking up of the small effective band of which he was, by virtue of being what he was, the leader. They had begun to drift away and disappear, whither he did not know, although, understanding each one of them intimately, he was able to divine that some of them had gone northward and eastward to join the Confederate Armies, some of them east to Mobile and Atlanta and some of them back to New Orleans to hide away in that dim and languorous half-world of which Josélie and her daughter Clélie were a part.

And the memory of his horses was always there, like a dim pain that would not be destroyed; and now there was added another dim pain which grew out of the incident in the doorway with the Yankee girl when he had asked her for something to remember her by. The request had come out of him almost without his knowing it, a silly sentimental request more worthy of the professional romanticism of Chauvin Boisclair than of himself. But although he flushed now in the darkness at the memory of it, he was aware that it had come from something deep inside him which had reacted to the freshness and purity and the clear blue eyes of the girl, something which had to do with her courage and sympathy and intelligence as well. From the moment when she had stepped ashore at the ferry landing and he had seen her face in the bright moonlight, she had made no effort to seduce him with her femininity. She had about her a frankness, an honesty, a spirit that was like that of a boy. There had been none of the archness, the coquetry, the effort at seduction which the girls he had always known—even his Scottish Protestant sisters—would have practiced almost at once. There was nothing silly about her. She was rather like the clear cool air of early morning on the bayous before the burning sun had come up over the horizon. And he had admired the way she behaved in all the unhappy business of Amédé's death, trudging across the muddy fields to the graveyard to dissipate the bitter loneliness of the burial. And he had divined in her a stubbornness and strength, like the stubbornness and strength of the remarkable horse-faced aunt who helped to prepare Amédé for the grave—qualities which those first women who came to this country must have had before they turned luxurious and decadent and frivolous.

It did not occur to him that he had fallen in love, or that the presence in the same house of Éliane de Lèche with her sensuality and shamelessness, had made the girl seem to him a paragon of all the virtues. He was not in love. The feeling which led him to ask for a trivial souvenir was something at once more and less than love. His heart had led him to ask for a handkerchief, a button, an earring, anything, which in moments of despair and darkness, would bring back to him the illusion of her peculiar freshness and charm.

And then Éliane had spoiled the whole thing by appearing in the doorway vibrant with suspicion and jealousy and malice before the innocent, simple moment between them was completed. Because he was afraid of Éliane less for himself than for the girl, he had quickly and rudely led the girl back into the house. And after that there had been no opportunity for them to be alone again, even for a second, and she had gone away thinking him, no doubt, both a clumsy boor and a fool. His vanity suffered too. Chauvin

Boisclair with his full red lips and empty head and swan-like sensuality would have done better.

He thought, "I am no good at such things. It is not my line. I had better leave that sort of thing to the professional lady-killers." For Chauvin or the others the speech would have been a piece of gallantry, as glib as the tirades of a medicine man.

What troubled him was the knowledge that the whole thing had happened simply and sincerely, but must have had the effect of a cheap speech out of a romantic play. That was how he left her thinking of him, falsely, as just another professionally romantic Southerner. It was idiotic, he knew, to be disturbed over so silly a trifle, yet the knowledge of the idiocy did nothing to relieve the dull, aching sense of incompleteness. "Somehow," he thought, "I must see her again if only to explain that I am not the damned fool I seemed to be."

Then, as he walked above the muddy river, his thoughts wandered back again to troubles more profound—mostly concerning what the future was to bring. In his heart he knew that the cause of the Confederacy was lost; it had been lost since the beginning, but that troubled him less than the knowledge of his own weakness of spirit, that he could not believe in the cause, as those around him, his friends, even his sisters, believed recklessly, carelessly and gallantly, without weighing all those elements which went into the contest—the eternal weakness of the landed proprietor confronted by bankers, the feebleness and instability of a system founded upon a slavery which he himself had accepted but never approved.

Walking along the levee in the moonlight he tried desperately to believe in the cause itself and its eventual triumph, but belief would not come; the whole structure was too decayed and unsound. He fought now, he organized a band, he would go on fighting not for secession which his heart told him was a calamity, but *against* the cutthroats, the blackguards, the thieves who swarmed into Louisiana with the Union Army and in its wake. These he would have fought anywhere, at any time, ruthlessly, even with cruelty, because in his heart he despised them as he despised the whole de Lèche connection because they preyed upon and spoiled a world so lovely as this half-drowned, wild Louisiana.

He had turned now, feeling tired and lost and was walking back toward St. André de Beaupré when he saw a figure coming toward him. He knew by the walk, by the carefree swing, that it was young Chauvin Boisclair, coming to discover what had happened to him. The boy was like a faithful dog, a bodyguard serving him out of some almost mystical devotion. It was odd that such a child of nature should be so faithful. A person would have said that pleasure-loving Chauvin would have been the first of the band to drift away, yet here he was, almost the last of the band to remain. He felt a sudden pang of envy for the boy; it must, he thought, be wonderful to be so carefree, never worrying even about where you were to sleep or whom you were to sleep with. For Chauvin the world was a lovely place in which there was only pleasure.

All that morning until the sun rose high and the heat steamed up from the swamps, Father Desmoulins worked in his little garden. It was small and neat, each bed outlined with small hedges of boxwood with a chinaberry tree in one corner to shade the more delicate seedlings. In it he grew many strange and exotic plants sent him from Martinique and the Guianas, Mexico and Cuba and the depths of the vast Brazilian forests. There were herbs too from which he brewed simple remedies for the people of his parish and rows of seedlings and cuttings, all neatly labeled, which were a part of his experiments in pollenization. He knew each plant and its exact state of well-being. When they were ill, he suffered as if their illness were his own. When they thrived, when a cross-pollenization proved successful, his whole spirit flowered like the plant itself. In this garden, surrounded by a low wall which was high enough to keep out the half-wild pigs but low enough to permit him to talk to his neighbors and the passersby on the muddy street, he was happy, as if the low inadequate wall shut out all the stupidities, the vanities, the evil of the great world beyond.

This morning as he worked he was troubled by thinking of the three young men sleeping in his house. In his fancy they were a little like three sons he had never had. He liked their youth and their vigor and their difference. He would have been proud of them as sons—three strapping young fellows none of them perfect and all of them fallible and human. Chauvin Boisclair he had christened, and Hector MacTavish he had known since childhood —the one person in the whole parish whose mind was worthy of his own, who could talk of the philosophies, or politics or botany. Poor Hector was always troubled by doubts. The third young man —the Yankee—he had known only since this morning but he loved him too, with a love troubled by pity. Chauvin Boisclair did not trouble him. He was simple and as near to nature as one of the plants the old man cultivated. Life for Chauvin would always be pleasant and easy, like that of the amorous tom-cat that rubbed against the skirts of old maids.

But the old man really loved Hector MacTavish. He was the stuff from which heroes were made, not stupid heroes acting out of animal courage or stupidity in a single reckless act, but heroes who made for the progress of the human race. In his tormented fashion Hector was a good man.

As Father Desmoulins hoed and pruned, his fancy grew a little unruly and he fell to speculating upon whether if he had his life to live over he would not have chosen a different course. There were moments when even the serene peace which lighted up his pink face and created about him an aura of goodness, was troubled by worldly and at times even fleshly doubts. There were moments when he regretted not having been, like Saint Augustin, a wild libertine who repented. He had never really had anything serious to repent, since the day he went down the long allée of his father's *manoir* near Bourges to become a priest.

Now, under the hot sun, he allowed his imagination to play a game. He imagined that God had come to him as the Devil had come to Faust and said, "Father Desmoulins, you may be young again and enter the body of one of the three young men now asleep in your cottage. It is for you to choose which one of them you will be." And Father Desmoulins, wickedly, fancied himself as answering God by saying, "I would choose to be the Yankee."

Almost at once the old man was aware of his wickedness, but it did not change his desire to know what it would be like to be a turbulent fallen archangel.

In the city, the heat and the presence of the Union Army and the fever and the cholera seemed to destroy what little there remained of order and decency. There were riotings and assassinations. Along the waterfront and around Congo Square a dozen secret gambling dens and brothels came into being for every one suppressed by the order of the General. It was no longer safe for an honest citizen to appear in the streets after dark and unsafe for an honest woman to go unescorted in daylight. Now that the river was open all the way from Pennsylvania to the Gulf, each day brought new thieves and swindlers and cheap politicians to plunder the rapidly waning riches of the romantic city.

It was to this turbulent place that Tom Bedloe returned, landing below the Government wharfs and making his way on foot through the district about Congo Square back to the house he had left to follow the young Baroness. Walking along streets lined by barrels of blazing pitch, it seemed to him that years had passed since he quit the city on the adventure which had proved so fantastic. It was an adventure still incomplete, for neither warfare nor violence nor all that had happened in the room nor the burning of Bel Manoir had ended it. There was only one end as there had been since the beginning, and until that end was achieved there would be no peace for him. He was no nearer to it now than he had been on the night he set out for Bel Manoir. He knew her no better than he had known her in the old house built about the courtyard filled with wistaria and bamboo and camellia trees. It was no longer a woman whom he pursued but an obsession.

And so he hurried along the streets, losing his way once or twice in haste and dark turnings. It was as if she were always there, just a little way before him, now visible, now dissolved in the misty heat which hung over the city. Twice on the way he encountered the dead wagon making its rounds to collect the corpses of the poor who had died during the day of the fever. They carried out the bodies wrapped in sheets to lay them side by side on the great mule-drawn cart.

Away from the center of the city there were fewer barrels of blazing pitch and by the time he reached the narrow blind alley which led to the side door of the de Lèche house, the streets were black in the shadows cast by the hot dying moon. The sweat ran from his body and he trembled so that he fumbled in taking the key from his pocket and it fell, striking the stone of the banquette with a hollow ringing sound which echoed back and forth between the houses of the *impasse.*

It was only when he picked up the key and was fitting it in the lock that he discovered the black ribbon on the door. It hung there in a great bow-knot of satiny stuff, repulsive to the touch like the cold back of a snake. For a moment he was puzzled and then suddenly he understood. There was death in the house.

With the key half-turned in the lock he stood quite still, trying to absorb the shock of the discovery and recover himself. There were only two people in the house who could have died—Éliane and the old Baroness. They would not put crêpe on the door for a dead slave. He felt a sudden sickness at the pit of his stomach, and a curious devastating sense of dryness and desolation. His knees trembled and his thighs went suddenly limp. It was as if his body no longer belonged to him but had become something detached, apart, ill.

Quickly he thought, "She cannot be the one! It must be the old woman!"

Controlling himself, he turned the key in the lock and stepped into the gallery. Beyond lay the courtyard with its flowery shrubs in pots and the singing fountain filigreed with shadows. But the house itself was dark. It was not until he stepped into the courtyard that he discovered a light in one room on the second floor, gleaming dully through the closed shutters.

For a long time he stood watching the window, as if paralyzed and incapable of action. In all his life he had never known suffering, and now he was aware of an agony which seemed to penetrate into every part of his body, not an agony of mind, but of the body itself, as if all its functions had been suddenly arrested. It was difficult even to breathe. It was like the agony of a confined drunkard for the alcohol denied to him.

Yet his mind remained still and clear, almost cold, without grief or anxiety. It functioned apart, betrayed by the intensity of his body's desire. It was indecent to break in upon the solitude of the house, but it was impossible to go on in ignorance. In order to live it was necessary to know whether she was dead or alive.

Quietly, his body still moving as if it no longer belonged to his mind, he went along the gallery to the stairs, past the parrot chortling in the darkness, up the stairs and along the gallery to the soft yellow light that spilled through the shutters. There was suddenly no longer either excitement or apprehension in his mind or body, but only a dull sense of compulsion resented fiercely by some remote part of him. He thought, "To hell with her! I will never see her again!" But his body carried him forward along the moonlit gallery.

Outside the shutters he halted staring at the light, his arms hanging at his side, aware of the indecency of what he was doing. Then, before he could move the shutters opened quietly and she stood there in the doorway, her body dark against the light of the candles behind her. Inside the room the old Baroness lay upon an enormous canopied bed. By the light of the candles at her head and feet, the cold sharp profile of the old woman was like a cameo cut against the black background of the soutane of the priest who stood praying with his back toward the door before a small altar adorned by a Spanish Virgin dressed in lace and bedecked with small diamonds and emeralds like the marvelous doll of a rich spoiled child.

The young Baroness said, "I heard your footsteps. The old woman is dead." Then as if she divined out of long experience what it was he wanted, she said, "You cannot come in. I must sit by her through the night."

She leaned suddenly against the doorway like one of the women from the *cabanes* near Congo Square, her arms folded across her breasts, her head thrown back a little. In the tilt of the head and the slight sagging of the hips beneath the white *peignoir*, there was a vulgarity, a coarseness, a taunt of power, as ancient as time itself. Her whole body invited what her words perversely denied.

A wild, inexplicable anger seized him. He wanted madly to strike her in the face, to kick her, to call her every filthy name he knew. It swept over him like a gigantic wave submerging a weary swimmer. Then it was gone and he heard himself saying in a voice that sounded strange to him, "How did she die?"

"She died of rage over the death of Amédé. She said I had killed him. She cursed me. And then she fell down dead. She was an evil old woman . . . my grandmother . . . full of cold, cruel evil like all Spanish. She hated me but I won in the end. They all hated me because I was the child of a whore. But I won in the end. I outlived them all and now everything is mine!"

Against the droning sound of the voice of the priest praying before the gaudy Virgin, her voice was tense and fine and triumphant like the sound made by a taut thin wire when plucked. He was aware of a sickening feeling of indecency, yet the unashamed frankness of her hatred gave her a primitive force like that of an animal. For a second he came very near to divining what it was that created the fierceness of his desire; it was something direct, primitive, and overwhelming.

"You had better go now. I will see you tomorrow."

Without giving him any choice, she straightened her body and reaching out, closed one of the shuttered doors. Then she said, "If you are to help me with my affairs you had better act at once. I hear the General and his wife are to be sent away. Good night."

Then she closed the other door, shutting herself away from him, in with the priest and the dead woman, leaving him alone in the shadows feeling baffled and lost, with the memory of the priest, the glittering Madonna, the old dead woman and the young Baroness. Again he had the feeling of struggling beyond his depth with something too complex, too decadent for his experience or understanding.

He was exhausted now, more tired than he had ever been in all his life, as if the structure of all that had happened since he came by chance to live in this beautiful house had collapsed about him. It was a deep physical exhaustion like that of a man who has walked for days, without sleeping, through a desert. The muscles of his arms and legs ached. Yet it was not the weariness which brought sleep, least of all in the hot, scented darkness.

As he crossed the gallery to his own quarters, the sudden thought came to him that he should leave this place, this house and never return to it, never to see her again, but he knew at once that this was impossible, that he had to go through the whole thing to the end; it was something over which he no longer had any control.

Then he noticed that someone had lighted a lamp in his own rooms and when he came to the open door he saw that Old Seraphine was inside drawing the curtains. She turned toward him and said in her curious, thick accented English, "Bon soir, mon Major. I heard you come in."

He thanked her and then noticed that she was staring at him. He returned the stare angrily and the old woman said to him in a conciliatory way, "You look tired, mon Major. You look sick."

"I'm all right, Seraphine."

"Should I bring you hot water for a bath?"

"Not tonight." He wanted her to go away. He wanted to be free of the staring inquiring wise black eyes.

But she remained fussing with the curtains and taking a long time to turn the cover of the big bed. He stood watching her as if that would make her hasten with the task. When she had finished she gave the bed a pat and said suddenly, "I know where La Lionne is."

"Yes." His voice betrayed no anxiety or interest.

"She is hiding in the house of Clélie's mother, Josélie."

"That's all finished," he said.

She took a blue envelope out of the folds of her skirt and said, "She gave me this to give you when you came back."

"Thank you . . . and good night."

But still she did not go. "The young Lieutenant was here. He left a letter for you on your desk."

"Good night."

In the doorway she stopped again. His nerves cried out with the desire for her to go and leave him in peace. She said, grinning, "He is Clélie's lover."

"He is what?"

She repeated what she had said, and he answered, "Yes! Yes!" and almost pushing her through the doorway, closed the shutters behind her.

The news startled him because it seemed so fantastic and implausible. For a moment he forgot the blue envelope in his hand. Then he thought, "The old witch has made it all up. David with a mistress!" There was something almost unnatural in the idea and then he thought shrewdly, "It's La Lionne's doing," and tore open the envelope.

The letter consisted of many pages all covered with La Lionne's emotionalized writing. After the first sentence he knew what the rest of it would be—an appeal to him, an hysterical account of her loneliness and suffering, a demand that he return to her. He read only a little way and tossed the letter on the table. He had had letters like this before from other women, always pitched in the same key and written in the same vein of martyrdom. He felt nothing for her now. It was all over and finished. Whatever pleasure he had had with her was an old story, stale and dead.

He picked up the other letter. It was brief:

Dear Tom: I came to find you and went away again. Agnes and Aunt Tam are safe and are at Aunt Louisa's. I am at the office during the day. Agnes knows that you are expected back. Good luck. David.

He found himself smiling over the letter because it was so unlike David. It was cocky and nonchalant instead of being detached and slightly pompous. Certainly something had happened to David. Perhaps Seraphine was right. Once he would have sat in the room for hours waiting, and now he had obviously written this note in haste and hurried off. The smile broadened a little and half aloud, he said, "Good luck, David." Clélie was very pretty and gentle as a doe.

Then he picked up the letter of La Lionne again, looked at it for a second, laid it on top of the other and carefully tore the two neatly into small bits and threw them into the basket beside the desk. Before he tried to sleep he went to the shutters and opening them, stood for a moment looking across the courtyard at the lighted windows on the opposite side of the house where the young Baroness was sitting with the priest, the glittering Virgin and the dead woman. He had seen the old Baroness but once in life but he would remember her always, with the narrow bony temples, the black eyes, the arched nose and the cruel mouth. He could see again the chain to which were attached the black enameled boxes studded with diamonds that rattled together like bones. He could hear the hard voice, brittle with hate, saying to the young Baroness, "Honteux! . . ."

As he closed the shutters he frowned, thinking that tomorrow he would have to go back into that other life of Agnes and Aunt Tam and the General and his wife, of the Port Office—that flavorless humdrum life which suddenly seemed dreary and intolerable. Tomorrow he would have to tolerate Aunt Louisa again. Worse than that he would have to flatter her almost as if her fat squat body were feminine and desirable. Only through her could he work upon the General to release the gold in the Planter's Bank which belonged to the young Baroness.

Long after he had gone to bed and lay awake, listening with his nerves to the creaking sound of the ancient house and thinking of the young Baroness as she stood in the candlelight leaning against the edge of the door in the white *peignoir*, he heard from the street outside the crash of iron against cobblestones as the wagon going about to collect the dead, passed in the moonlight. He heard the voice of the driver calling out, *"Char de morts! Char de morts! Apportez vos morts!"*

Agnes saw him as she was hurrying down the stairs to speak to black César. He was talking to the orderly in the hallway and the sudden, unexpected sight of him caused her heart to miss a beat or two, not so much because of delight, as from the understanding that here he was at last, face to face with her before she had a chance to prepare herself for the meeting. In an odd way she did not want to see him, suddenly like this, without any preparation, without the opportunity of building up the part she was to play. Because during the months which had passed since she last saw him in the drawing room in Pinckney Street she had been living in a fanciful world of her own imagination, and in that world he had become a new kind of person, endowed with qualities which he did not, in reality, possess. He had become almost a lover she had dreamed of, or invented, and in her heart she was troubled by the instinctive knowledge of the shock which lay before her. For a second she experienced a wild feeling that she did not want to see him at all.

Then he saw her and smiled and came to meet her at the foot of the great stairway, and she was aware suddenly not of delight at seeing him but of a faint sense of disappointment because he was not as radiant and wonderful as he had seemed during those long still nights while black César poled and paddled them through the bayous.

His blue uniform was bright and clean and new, yet she had an impression of shabbiness which was utterly inexplicable. It seemed to her that there was something faded about him, like a once bright picture that has been exposed too long to brilliant sunlight. He put his arms about her and kissed her, but she was aware only of disappointment, because during the hours of day-dreaming, she had imagined this as a moment when she would grow faint with ecstasy. And now she did not grow faint. What she expected to happen did not happen and she thought quickly, "In time it will be as I expected it to be. It's just the shock of seeing him suddenly like this."

He held her at arms length and said, "Well, here you are all safe and sound. You were a bad girl to run off like that in Havana." And she was aware that his voice was different, not only from the voice she had created for him in her romantic imagining, but from the swaggering, rather too loud confident voice she remembered in the drawing room in Pinckney Street. It, too, seemed to have faded. It seemed almost commonplace, like the voice of any young man.

She said, rather primly, "Come upstairs. Aunt Tam will want to see you." Then looking at him anxiously, "You're all right? You're not ill or anything?"

"No, I'm not ill."

He followed her up the stairs into the small sitting room with the table covered with purple plush and there in the full hot light of the window she looked at him again, sharply and quickly, and saw that it was not her fancy which endowed him with the curious quality of dimness. He seemed thinner, as if the bones of the temples had somehow contracted, and his eyes were not the same. It was as if they were dimmed. And there were tired lines almost of bitterness about the sensuous mouth. She felt suddenly that she must go out of the room and find time to adjust herself to something she did not yet understand, and so she said, "I'll go and tell Aunt Tam."

"Couldn't you wait? Couldn't we be alone for a minute?" For a moment something of the thing she had remembered, or imagined, came into his voice, a spark of that fire which she had expected to consume her, that fire which somehow was associated

[263]

with what had happened on the *San Cristobal* and with the nostalgic songs of black César. But it was not enough. She had to get out of the room. If she did not escape at once something dreadful would happen.

"We'll have time enough presently," she said and left him.

When she had gone he looked about the room, seeing nothing because he too was a little bewildered. At sight of her he had not felt the sudden stir of excitement in his veins which always before had caused him to stand very straight, balancing himself on spread legs, and changed the very quality of his voice. She was prettier than he remembered her—or more beautiful. Certainly she was desirable. She would make a perfect wife, but perhaps a perfect wife was not what he wanted or needed. For a fleeting moment the thought of following the young Baroness returned to his mind. Perhaps that was where he belonged, in that other dark world, streaked with color and mystery and cruelty and excitement. He tried to discipline his thoughts, to think reasonably as he had once been able to do even in the most emotional circumstances; but nothing happened. Inside his brain was only confusion and indecision and a very clear picture of the young Baroness leaning against the lintel of the door in the white *peignoir*. He began to swear and he was still swearing when the door opened and Aunt Tam, tall, thin and horse-faced and the General's wife, dumpy, high-bosomed and short, came in with Agnes behind them. He thought, "Now, I'm in it for it," and braced himself for the encounter.

He loved women but he hated them in troops, and now the two older women fell upon him with motherly cries, in a burst of intimacy which excelled the bounds of any relationship which had ever existed between him and them. He had a sense of being claimed, kidnaped and imprisoned against his will. The face of the General's wife grew flushed with pleasure. Both women uttered little meaningless birdlike cries of excitement while Agnes stood by, watching. And then the torrent of talk began.

They wanted to know what had happened to him and how he escaped. They questioned him about his health and what precautions he was taking to escape the awful fever. Under the deluge of middle-aged female sentimentality he grew sullen, and thrust out his lower lip like a small boy. It was then that Agnes found him for the first time something like the Tom she had hoped to find.

But the excitement reached a peak of hysteria when he said he had been held captive in a house called Bel Manoir. In that excitement even Agnes herself participated.

When it was all over and the two older women had retired to leave the lovers alone, Agnes sat primly, looking at him across the table with the purple plush cover. Then she said, "Well?"

"I never knew you were there. I swear it. I was a prisoner."

"The young Baroness knew it. It's odd that she never told you."

"Maybe she didn't know we knew each other."

"I told her about coming to New Orleans to see you. I even told her your name. She never even told me you were living in her house in New Orleans."

He shrugged his shoulders, feeling resentful, for Agnes suddenly seemed to him now only a younger version of the two women who had just left the room. Women! Women! Women! He wanted very little from them and they were always hounding him. He was aware, too, of a resentment and a confused suspicion in relation to the young Baroness. He had a confused feeling of having been betrayed by all of them. Perhaps that was all you could expect of women in groups—that they should cling together.

"Tom," she said abruptly, "you needn't marry me . . . if you don't want to."

"I want to marry you. You're the only woman I ever thought of marrying. . . . And that's the truth."

"If you like the young Baroness better than me, marry her. I don't mind." She wanted to cry suddenly, not so much because her heart was broken as at the picture of herself, young, deceived and martyred.

"That's got nothing to do with it. I wouldn't dream of marrying her. And certainly she wouldn't dream of marrying me."

Innocently she said, "I don't understand."

"I hope you don't."

[265]

"You can go away any time you like, Tom. I'm not a prude, but I don't think I can see you while you're living with her."

He looked suddenly at her, puzzled. Something had certainly happened to her since he last saw her. This was no child talking to him.

"You don't know what you're talking about."

"Oh yes, I do."

"Well, you shouldn't know."

"And why not?" she cried with sudden passion. "Am I to sit around like an idiot? Women aren't what they used to be. I don't mind being betrayed nearly so much as being treated as if I were a fool."

"You've been talking too much with Aunt Tam. Those ideas are all right for an old horse like her. They're not for a pretty young girl."

"It's you who are talking like a fool!"

He began to feel angry because she was unmanageable. She was not behaving at all like a gentle, innocent young girl who would make an ideal wife.

He said brusquely, "You're not to call on the Baroness. You're not to see her. You certainly act foolish."

"I'm wearing one of her frocks at this moment."

"You're . . . what?"

She looked suddenly triumphant as if she had somehow outwitted and defeated him, as if she and the young Baroness were joined in a conspiracy against him. She repeated, "I'm wearing one of her frocks at this moment."

He tried to recover himself and said weakly, "You look very well in it."

"At this moment I don't care how I look." She crossed her feet and sat up a little more stiffly, "Tom, I'm not a child. I know about you. I thought I loved you. I think I still do. I certainly don't want to marry you now." She bit her lip as if to prevent herself from crying, "I wouldn't marry you now. . . . I don't think I'll ever marry anybody."

Now for the first time since he saw her, the old feeling returned, perhaps because the speech was like that of a child talking grown-up language. For an instant he was aware of standing at a division in a path, of being forced to make a decision. The paths led in quite different directions—one toward the bejeweled Madonna, the priest, the hatred, the voluptuousness, the excitement, the viciousness, everything that was in the strange world out of which the young Baroness seemed to emerge, standing in the doorway, her arms folded across her breasts, defiantly, like a whore in the doorway of a *cabane*. The other led toward women like Aunt Tam, and Aunt Louisa, knitting in the drawing room in Pinckney Street, and dull heavy men like Agnes' father, and thrift and meagerness and New England boiled dinners.

In that moment of insight, he chose neither path. He decided to sit by the road and wait until someone or something, unknown, nameless, shapeless, came along to make the decision for him. It was the course of a superstitious gambler. He wanted Agnes when he had finished with the other one, when he had possessed and subdued her, when the thing between them was finished. So, as gamblers will sometimes do, he lied with calculation. He said, "How could there be anything between me and the Baroness . . . anything more than a flirtation? She comes out of a world I know nothing about."

He stood up and began walking up and down. She watched him, admiring, in spite of her anger and resentment, his curious animal beauty—the broad shoulders, the narrow waist, the face that was not beautiful but more than that with its high cheekbones and sensuous mouth and surprising blue eyes and hard jaw. And she thought, "He's not like any other man I've ever seen, but don't let that deceive you, you little fool! If ever you are to marry him, if ever you are to find him possible, you must subdue him first. It is you who must rule." But all the time she was aware of a dim, fierce desire to let him take her, here and now, in this room, to do with her as he chose, now and forever. A distant small voice kept saying, "Perhaps that is better than all the rest—the security, the peace, the order, the domesticity to which all my life has been directed." But the other voice kept saying, "Don't be a fool! You can have him on your own terms—terms of decency and respectability." But the answer came back, "Would you want him tame and dull? Without his peculiar magnificence what would he be

. . . only a dull fellow." And she thought, "I will wait and see. I cannot decide now."

And then she was aware that he was speaking as he walked up and down, echoing her decision. He was saying, "I'm going away now and I'm coming back when you're calmer. This is no time to decide. We're both excited. There are a lot of things to decide. This isn't any place for you. You ought to go back to Boston."

She interrupted him, "Boston . . . I'm never going back to Boston! I've had enough of Boston!"

He halted suddenly, looking at her with an expression of bewilderment in his blue eyes, as if he was astonished by the collapse of his own cocksure calculations.

"You must be crazy!" he said.

"I may be, but I'm not going back to Boston, ever."

"And if your family says there's no money?"

"It doesn't matter. Aunt Tam has money. She'll share it with me. She doesn't care anything about money except for traveling."

"Well, I'll be damned!"

She stood up and said, "I think you're right. I think you'd better go now until both of us have calmly made up our minds what we're to do. Only don't think I'm a silly schoolgirl you can do with as you please. I'm not. I never was. I always knew what I was doing. But I never knew that I knew until just lately. I'm going now. Come back tomorrow when we're both not angry."

He came toward her. "Will you declare a truce and kiss me?" He grinned at her in a fashion that made her heart leap. It was a grin which seemed to dominate and take possession of her. She wanted to kiss him, wildly, passionately, as she had imagined it on those dark nights in the bayous. Now she knew was the moment. But she turned from it. She heard herself saying, "No, I won't kiss you. Sometimes you're as coquettish and unscrupulous as a woman."

The speech had a chilling effect. "I'm what?"

"You act like a trollop."

Then she turned and went out the door, and when she had gone he said again, "Well, I'll be damned!" and began to laugh. He sat down laughing helplessly, and when the laughter had passed he was aware of a kind of challenge which touched his

[268]

vanity, for in his heart it was difficult for him to believe that any woman could ever think of him with contempt.

He found the General's wife was alone in the small sitting room. She was darning and at sight of him she put down her work and said, "Come in, Tom. We can have a good talk."

In what she said there was no special significance but in the tone of her voice and the manner in which she settled back into the chair, there was an air of possession and intimacy which annoyed him. It was as if she had said, "Now that we're free of those two tiresome foolish women we can settle down and enjoy ourselves." For a moment he experienced a desire to flee and then, remembering what he had come for, he went over and patted her broad back with an air of affection.

"Well, Aunt Louisa, it looks like you had your hands full with Agnes and Aunt Tam."

She reached up and touched his hand, "I can't imagine what's come over them. Tam was always a little queer but now her head is filled with all kinds of crazy ideas. As if the General and I hadn't enough troubles already. Sit down here beside me. The house hasn't been the same since you went away." He sat down and she went right on, "You never told me why you did go away."

Glibly he said, "I was on my way to the end of the lake to do some business and I was kidnaped. I didn't go away, I was kidnaped."

She gave him a look of doubt and then uttered an obscene chuckle, shaking her finger at him as she spoke, "I can guess what kind of business."

He laughed because he knew she wanted him to laugh and said, "You know everything, don't you, Aunt Louisa?"

The excitement, mounting inside her, began to show in spots of red on her plump cheeks. "Was she pretty?"

"Yes, very pretty."

"Tell me all about it. You never told me about any of your girls." She leaned forward, resting her plump elbows on the upholstered arms of the chair, "Go along now, you naughty boy. Tell me."

"There isn't much to tell. It wasn't very satisfactory."

[269]

"Why?"

He laughed, "That would be telling a lot of things. Maybe some you wouldn't understand."

"Come now. I understand more than you think. After all, I've been married for more than thirty years."

The words echoed in his head, "Married for thirty years" to the General! He wanted to laugh at the naïveté of the statement—as if that had taught her anything. That was it! She knew nothing at all. She was trying desperately, with excitement, to find out what she did not know, what she turned over and over again in her imagination. He saw her now as she really was—a vulgar, full-blooded woman whose whole life had been cramped and stifled by restraint and prudery and hypocrisy. That was why she liked it when he smacked her backside in a friendly way. He understood it all now, and as he understood it, he thought, "That's it! I'll tell her. I'll give her a good time and then she'll get the General to do what I want for the young Baroness. That's how I can bribe her."

So he laughed and said, "All right. I'll tell you. But you asked for it. Don't be shocked and don't complain at what you get."

She was leaning toward him, the pupils of her eyes contracted as if she were nearsighted and peering into space at something which would not quite come into focus. She gave the impression of straining desperately toward some object just beyond her reach. He could hear the quickened pace of her breathing and was at once revolted and vengeful.

He did not hurry. Leaning back in his chair he told her of having fallen in love with a voice, with a woman he had never seen, taking great care to lead her away from the suspicion that the woman was the young Baroness. She lived, he said, in a house on the opposite side of the street. He invented a story of having spoken to her on the street, but from that point onward he recounted the story much as it occurred save that the consummation was placed in a great house on the edge of Lake Pontchartrain instead of at ill-fated Bel Manoir. And as he talked, the fire and obsession of his own passion crept into the tale. His eyes sparkled and the color came into his face as he went from step to step in the tale of the pursuit; and opposite him the dumpy, middle-aged woman grew more and more excited, until her face was quite purple and the veins stood out on the backs of her pudgy short-fingered hands. He noticed them, really for the first time, and thought how odd it was that this reputable New England woman should have the hands of a whore.

In telling the story he found a double satisfaction—that of spiteful pleasure in exciting the woman to the verge of apoplexy and the sensual, decadent pleasure of remembering all the dark details of the love-making. He found the memory of it, recounted to such an audience, almost as exciting as the experience itself.

Now and then, straining toward him and breathing with difficulty she would say in a whisper as if not to interrupt him, "So, it was like that! Like that! Go on! Go on!" Goaded by the effect he was achieving and by the pleasure he himself found in the story, he told her things he would not have told another man, astonished that they did not revolt or upset her. He became aware as he talked of the great heat that came in through the windows, and thought with some remote part of his mind, "Creatures in hell would look like Aunt Louisa at this moment." Tormented, baffled, unsatisfied. She should never have come to a country like this Louisiana. It was no place for a New Englander.

But he came presently to the end and said, "That's all!"

In a faint voice she said, "So, it was like that?"

"Yes, it was like that."

She leaned back in the upholstered chair, relaxing and closing her eyes. For a moment he thought that perhaps she had had a stroke of apoplexy and was dying, but almost at once he saw that she was breathing easily, like a child asleep. He sat watching her, thinking, "I must have done a good job to have knocked out the old girl."

Then she opened her eyes and staring before her, away from him, she said in a low voice, "So it is like that! Nobody ever told me. The old fool! The awkward old fool." She looked at him in a curious penetrating fashion and almost with dignity she said, "Thank you, Tom."

Now, he thought, is the time, and aloud he said, "There is a great favor you could do for me, Aunt Louisa."

For a second the shadow of suspicion crossed her small bright

[271]

eyes. "What?" she asked. "I'll do anything I can, Tom." But she answered him absently, as if her mind, her senses, her vision were still absorbed by the thing he had told her.

"It's not really for me. It's for the Baroness de Lèche . . . where I am quartered."

Quickly she asked, "She's not the woman, is she?"

Shrewdly, without change of expression, he said, "Of course not. It's only that she saved my life and I feel under obligation to her."

Then he told her again, this time in detail, of being locked in the burning cabin and how the young Baroness, risking her life, had crossed the moonlit open space and unbolted the door. He made the story sound romantic and when he had finished, he went on to explain how the Baroness had come from Martinique to save her property. First the cousin Amedé died and then the grandmother and now she was the last of her family, alone, young and bewildered. The General could help her by releasing the property and the gold belonging to her which he had seized on behalf of the Government. He had but to sign an order and it would be returned to her. He, himself, he pointed out again, owed her a great debt.

When he had finished she looked at him shrewdly and asked, "You are sure she is not the one?"

"No. She is not the one."

She shook her head, "I'll try," she said. "But the General is overwhelmed with troubles and he's very stubborn. I'll promise to try but I can't promise to succeed." Then as if she dismissed the subject as closed, she said, "And Agnes? Does she know about your gallivantings?"

"She knows."

"What is she going to do?"

"I don't know. I don't think she does."

Aunt Louisa chuckled. "She's no suckling dove. I always thought she was, but she isn't." She took up her darning again. "I think she might turn into almost anything." She drew in her breath. "I think she might even turn out to be bad. . . . I'd think twice before marrying her, even if she'll have you. You might live to regret it. She wouldn't be the first bad one in the Wicks family.

Her father had an aunt . . ." She started rocking again, making a clucking sound as he rose to leave.

The night which followed was for the General one of the worst in a long and varied experience. There was little sleep for him because the wife, lying beside him, would not permit him to sleep until she had won from him what she demanded. He fought against her request to release the gold belonging to the Baroness de Lèche, why, he himself did not quite know except that he was tired and worried and when he was like that he turned stubborn. Until long after midnight she harangued him. When he attempted to sleep, she poked his solid back. She argued and even tried blackmail, saying that if he did not do the favor for Tom, there were plenty of incriminating circumstances she could, in revenge, reveal. And at last when sleep seemed to the General a more precious thing than all the gold in the Planters' Bank—sleep and peace—he said, "Very well, I'll do it. But you must never speak of it to anyone."

Even after he had given the promise, he did not at once fall asleep, for he turned heavily after a little time, and asked, "Why do you want me to do this so much, Louisa, for a woman I've never even seen and you do not even know?"

"Because it will please Tom. She saved his life."

But that, she knew dimly, was not altogether the truth. It was all confused in her muddled brain—the hatred of the dull, heavy man at her side who had denied her all romance, all passion, all beauty, and her fondness for Tom. But most of all she had a vague sense of being herself the woman Tom had described to her. And in her woman's heart she had divined, despite all his denials, that the woman was the Baroness de Lèche. She was tired and growing old and disappointed and unhappy, and the whole experience was for her like a brilliant flash of light in the darkness she felt closing about her.

They did not bury the old Baroness at Bel Manoir between the lichen-grown tombs of her husband and her son. They found a place for her in the vaults of the old St. Louis Cemetery, a fate which would have shocked her arrogance and pride. At Bel Manoir nothing remained now save the graveyard on the knoll under the live oaks.

And in the house in New Orleans, the young Baroness began making preparations for her departure. Negroes came carrying cypress planks on their backs and the courtyard echoed with hammering that went on all through the day. On the night of the funeral the young Baroness did not return. In his room across the courtyard, Tom Bedloe waited, smoking cigar after cigar, going into the long open gallery now and then to pace up and down in the damp heat, until when the waiting at last became unendurable, he went downstairs and across the courtyard to the slave quarters to find Old Seraphine.

But she too was absent. The only person in all the great house was the white-haired old negro he had seen in the drawing room on that night long ago before he had gone to Bel Manoir. The old man sat dozing in a corner of the vast kitchen beneath row upon row of brightly burnished copper kettles. The old man he discovered knew nothing. They had gone away—the young Baroness and Seraphine—in the carriage after the funeral. The old man did not know where. He did not know when they would return. He knew nothing at all.

So he left the old man to fall asleep again and went into the garden to walk up and down among the flowers and potted shrubs, trying to plan what he meant to do, for he was aware of an intolerable confusion inside his head. It was clear to him that she meant to leave for Martinique despite anything he could do, and the sound of the hammering indicated that she was taking with her everything which could be moved. Perhaps she was going away forever, never to return. She hated Louisiana. She had, it seemed to him, no friend in all the city or the state. Once during the night she had told him that the country suffocated her, that she could not breathe for the narrowness and provinciality of the people, that she hated the very smell of the place, that curious mixture compounded of the smell of fertile mud and the fragrance of flowers.

He had planned to go to her tonight. All through the day, trying to bring some order to the confusion of dirty papers in the Port Office, he had accomplished nothing because his mind was here all the time in this house. He kept seeing her, now in the white dress, now all in black with the touch of white at the throat, now as he'd seen her for the first time in the yellow ball gown going through the papers on his desk. He knew now why she had been there. The knowledge grew out of experience, out of his very knowledge of her. She had been there spying on him, searching his papers in the hope that she might find some scrap, some fragment which she might use against him to recover the gold in the Planters' Bank. She was courageous and unscrupulous. And then suddenly it occurred to him that even then she might have been working with that band called Les Defenseurs. He had seen them here in the house on that night he had come back and crossed to the other gallery in the hope of seeing her again.

Again and again he stopped, fancying he heard some small sound from the house which indicated her return, but each time the sounds he fancied that he heard turned out to be only his imagination, save once when the wagon collecting the dead passed in the street outside. With each turn round the garden path, the agony grew more intense until at last he became aware that his whole body was trembling and that he no longer had any control over it. Then for the first time, a little after the death-wagon had passed, there came to him, perhaps for the only time in all his life, a moment of utter objectivity. He was standing somewhere in the gallery above looking down, seeing his own body pacing up and down the gravel paths of the big courtyard. He saw himself quite clearly and thought, "That man is a fool! No woman on earth is worth that much suffering . . . certainly not this she-dog . . . this . . ." His mind was flooded suddenly with obscenity, with all the evil words he had ever known.

Then the moment passed and the trembling ceased and he felt somehow purified and almost calm.

"To hell with her!" he thought. "To hell with her!"

He left the garden, opened the door and went out. He did not know where he was going but presently he found himself in the district between Congo Square and the river. He was hatless. A negro boy was plucking at his sleeve, saying, "Yaller girl, M'sieu. Nice yaller gal, M'sieu?"

"All right," he said. "Where?"

But it was no good. He only got very drunk on cheap rhum and came back to his room a little before dawn, more wretched than he had been on leaving the garden.

It was long after noon when he awakened, dimly conscious again of the sound of hammering in a distant part of the house, and that the heat was suffocating and his naked body was bathed in sweat. Lying there on the border between sleep and consciousness he was aware that someone was moving about in the next room. He could hear the faint sound of footsteps and the occasional tinkle of glass against metal. In a kind of fog, he thought, "That would be Seraphine putting the room in order." Half-awake, with his eyes closed he could see her fat figure, the bright-colored *tignon* covering her head, the neat apron over the full skirt. She belonged there among the soft colors of the room, among the scent of flowers that rose from the courtyard in the noonday heat. And dreamily it occurred to him that this was where he belonged, where he had always belonged, not in the white, neat world of New Bedford where he was born, with its clean white houses and bright green grass in summer, its clean white snow in winter. This was where he belonged; here he would stay, always, forever. He was like a wanderer returning home to a country where he had never been.

Then slowly the whole of the night before returned to him—the waiting and anxiety, the dreadful beat of baffled, thwarted, desire in his veins, and the blind, half-realized excursion into that dark, sordid, half-savage, sensual world beyond Congo Square. What happened after he left the house was not clear to him; it returned now like the memories of a man ill with fever, emerging in isolated fragments out of the fog of delirium—the memory of a low, hot, smoke-filled room with naked yellow girls dancing, of a ring of faces white and black, watching—the faces of roustabouts and negroes and evil, vulture-faced Yankees, the memory of drink after drink of rhum, of the music of banjos and drums, of a faro game. And none of these things had softened the misery not only of his desire, but of his doubts, for in that moment of sultry, half-conscious, clairvoyance it seemed to him that in some unfathomed way, she had become remote, that she had escaped him entirely, that he had never possessed her for a moment, but only her body, a shell without any significance beyond the borders of the sensual.

Waking, he called to Seraphine, believing he could discover from her where she was now and what she meant to do. The old fat woman appeared in the doorway, asking if he wanted his coffee.

He did not answer her but asked, "Where is the Baroness?"

"She is on the other side of the house, goin' through all the old trunks."

"Where were you and the Baroness last night?"

"We went to a meetin'."

"Meeting?"

"Yes, M'sieu, a meetin' on the other side of the lake."

"What kind of a meeting?"

"A magic meetin'."

So that was it. "What kind of people were there?"

"Black people. Mama Tolanne was there."

"Who's Mama Tolanne?"

"Mama Tolanne is a . . ." She hesitated for a moment and then used the French word, *"Sorcière."*

He had a sudden feeling of seeing beyond the walls of the room, beyond all the tormenting mystery which had kept her shut off from him even in moments of the deepest physical intimacy. Sitting up in the bed, he said, "Come here, Seraphine."

She looked at him for a moment, suspicious and hesitating. Then she came one step nearer the bed. He was aware that he was near to something which was of the greatest importance to him, some knowledge which would either free him or give him the power over her which would make life possible once more, a life of healthy, robust, satisfaction in which the morning brought pleasure and not misery upon waking. He was near to something which would destroy the whole evil spell which held him paralyzed and miserable.

Quickly he seized the wrist of the old black woman. A look of terror came into her face. He said, "Don't yell, or I'll kill you! I may kill you anyway!"

He was aware that he was acting in a ridiculous fashion. He felt an uncontrollable desire to laugh at himself, at the sudden terror of the old black woman, yet behind the stifled laughter there was a sense of terrible urgency, as if he were a dying man who could only be saved by the secret the old woman kept.

"Tell me. Why did she go there?"

The old woman did not answer him, but only rolled her eyes about, showing the yellowish whites. Again he said, "Tell me . . . tell me, or I'll take my sword and cut you into bits, you black devil! into tiny bits like chopped meat!" He twisted the old woman's wrist, harder than he meant to twist it. The stifled desire to laugh gave his face a maniacal expression.

The old woman said, "Ah'll tell you effin' you'll let me go, Major."

"I'll let you go after you've told me. Tell me! Why did she go there."

The old woman answered him in an almost inaudible voice, "Ah'll spoil the voodoo effin' I tell you."

Again he twisted her wrist, "I'll get my sword."

"She went to voodoo her man . . . to make him love her."

"What man?" he asked. "What man?"

"A man she's wasted her whole life a'lovin'."

"What man?"

The old woman sighed deeply, "M'sieu MacTavish," she said.

He felt sick and lay back, releasing Seraphine's wrist. "Mac-Tavish," he repeated. That was the man who had come to the cabin, the man who was leader of the Defenseurs, the man on whose head there was a price. He began to understand everything. The fragments began to fit together. That was why she had gone to Bel Manoir—to be with him. That was why she had lured him to follow . . . to do MacTavish a service or to use himself to make MacTavish jealous. That was why she had saved him from the cabin to lead him to that room on the third floor of the half-ruined plantation house.

The old woman had not gone away. He heard her saying, "You won't tell her, will you, mon Major? Effin' you told her, she'd tie me up and beat me like she beat Thomasine and old Michel. She near to killed Thomasine. Thomasine ain't been right in her head ever since. It ain't only she beat her. She did other things . . . awful things. You won't tell her, will you, Major?"

Dully he answered her, "I won't tell her."

The old woman seemed to relax. Like an old gossip, as if suddenly she was released to tell the whole story, she said, "It's always been like that. She's a one-man woman. She's always been like that after him and he won't have none of her. Doan tell her, mon Major! She might beat me to death for spoilin' the voodoo!"

He wasn't looking at her now. He was thinking, and through his thoughts he heard the sound of the bell at the street door ringing. It went on ringing and ringing, but the old negress only stood there staring at him, as if he were dying or mad. At last he said, "Go and open that door, Seraphine."

She went away then and in a little time returned bringing a letter. It was from the General's office and the sight of it brought back suddenly the extraordinary scene in the sittingroom with the General's wife.

The old black woman waited, still staring at him as he tore open the envelope. He knew what was inside. It was simple enough—simply the information that if Mrs. Éliane de Lèche would call at the General's offices, room 219, she would receive the gold held in her name among the deposits of the Planters' Bank to the amount of thirty-eight thousand seven hundred and eighty-four dollars in specie.

The General's wife had done her work well.

He thought, "And that too. She wanted the money too and I was the only one who could get it for her. That was why she led me on in the beginning. When she couldn't find any way to blackmail me she used her own body." He saw it all now and understood many things, most of all the source of his *malaise* and dissatisfaction. He had never possessed her at all but only her body, which like the whore she was, she looked upon as no more than an instrument which might be used by her to gain what she most desired, not love or even sensual satisfaction but the money in the Planters' Bank.

He gave the note to Seraphine, "Take that to Madame de Lèche."

She took the letter but still remained standing there, a curious expression of awe on her face.

"What is it you want, Seraphine?"

She swallowed twice and then asked, "You ain't in love with her, *mon Major?*"

"No . . . no . . . I don't think so. Now go and take her that letter."

The old woman started to speak and then checked herself and without another word went away, but after she went away, he kept seeing her eyes and the look of horror in them, a horror which must have had to do with the torture inflicted upon the girl Thomasine. He felt something of the same horror, only there was shame mingled with it. He thought, "Now I know how a prostitute must feel." It was thus she had treated him—as a procurer might use a prostitute—to satisfy his desires and earn money for him.

But he thought almost at once. "Perhaps it isn't true. Perhaps it is only something that black old witch had spitefully invented."

He had heard stories of that sort, of the strange power of slaves to corrupt and distort the lives of their masters. He remembered vaguely a story of a black woman who had imprisoned her mistress and her mistress' children and beaten and starved them. They had hanged the black woman in the square by the river. He tried to remember the black woman's name, searching his memory anxiously as if the knowledge would somehow make him feel less an idiot and a fool, but the name would not come to him.

Presently he dressed and set out for the Port Office to find David. David had connections now with that dim half-world which knew everything. From Clélie or her mother, from one of the octoroons who frequented Clélie's house he might discover the truth.

But David was not there. He had gone away a little before noon saying that he felt dizzy and had a fever.

Aunt Tam always slept like a horse and so for two nights she did not hear Agnes crying herself to sleep. The older woman had no suspicion of the girl's unhappiness, since Agnes told her nothing of what had happened in the drawing room between herself and Tom. Once or twice during the day Agnes had thought of telling Aunt Tam everything but in the end she said nothing, thinking, "What could Aunt Tam know of what I feel? How could she understand?" Aunt Tam who had never been loved by any man nor thought of any man in the way she had thought of Tom during those long dark nights when they had drifted over the black waters with the curious, wet, heavy fragrance of the water hyacinths always in the air. Aunt Tam could know nothing of things like that. She would be sympathetic but foolish, and it was not sympathy

Agnes wanted. Sympathy would only have made her weep; she wanted someone to tell her what to do.

For she did not know; she was unable even to understand her own complicated feelings—that she hated Tom and at the same time loved him, that her vanity and faith were hurt, that she flushed at the thought of the Baroness and the deception at Bel Manoir of which she had been made a victim. There were moments when that hurt most of all—that she had been made a dupe, that perhaps when Tom and that woman were together, they laughed at her innocence. The hurt to her pride was perhaps the worst of all—she had fancied herself wise and grown-up and she had appeared naïve and silly.

No, going to Aunt Tam was out of the question, and going to Aunt Louisa was as bad. What could Aunt Louisa, with her respectability, married to a yokel like the General, understand of the tempestuous, dark emotion she felt for Tom when he was not there. Aunt Louisa would only mock at her and tell her she was a wicked girl, a child, who did not know what love was.

She had never seen her mother and until now, as she lay beside Aunt Tam in the damp heat, she had never thought that a mother might be useful as someone to go to at times like this. Sometimes she had wondered what her mother was like, and now, thinking of her father, bearded, sober, devoted to routine and respectability, she wondered whether her mother, if she had been alive, would have been any greater help than Aunt Louisa. Her father, it seemed to her, could never have inspired any woman to a great love. He was not like Tom.

On the second night when she had cried until she thought she could have no more tears left, it came to her suddenly what she could do. It was a wild plan but it pleased her perhaps because it helped to cure the pain of her hurt pride.

She would show them both that she was not a child and that they had not made a fool of her. Alone in the darkness she worked out a plan in detail. Tomorrow, now that she had a frock to wear, she would pack up the clothes the Baroness sent her and return them and tell the Baroness that she had released Tom from his engagement and that the Baroness might have him. Then she would put him out of her heart, out of her mind, forever. Very likely she would never marry, but that would not matter. Aunt Tam seemed happy enough.

She began imagining the interview with the Baroness, making up what she would say to her, with dignity and coldness. She was still making up cold, proud speeches when drowsiness overcame her and she slipped off into unconsciousness.

But in the morning everything seemed different. Some of her courage was gone and in its place there was a small voice which kept saying "Why should you give him up when you love him? He is a rogue but you will never meet another man like him." To which another voice replied. "But he is no good. He is hopeless. He is a liar and a Don Juan."

All day through the heat she wandered about the house and garden tormented by indecision, avoiding Aunt Tam and Aunt Louisa. During the meager lunch, the two women tormented her. Aunt Tam with the kindliest motives, Aunt Louisa with the envious motives of a woman who had never known what love was like and now would never know because it was too late.

Aunt Tam told her that she looked peaked and needed a tonic, that she was afraid she had been living on her nerves and that only now were the hardships of the hurricane and the wanderings in the Delta beginning to show their effect.

Aunt Louisa asked sly questions about Tom and why he had not come back after that first visit. "It's a very queer way for a fiancé to behave. I know that Tom is wild and strange but I would have thought he'd want to see all he could of you after you'd been separated for so long. . . . After you've come all the way to New Orleans, after all you've been through."

Bravely she had answered, "I told him not to come. He's so busy with everything at the office. He works till late at night. When he's caught up with his work, he's coming to see me. It'll only be a day or two."

She bit her lip to keep from crying and tried to eat but could not swallow the food. So Aunt Louisa asked, "What is it, dear? Doesn't it suit you? Would you like something else? Has something happened to your appetite?"

It was like that all through the lunch, with Aunt Louisa waiting, watching, for every small chance to question her, to pry beneath the surface of her misery. Bravely she managed to sit out the lunch and to make a dignified escape to her room where she cried some more and at length fell asleep again like a child.

When she wakened the heat had abated a little and she thought, "In a little while it will be cool enough to drive through the streets," and, hurrying, she dressed and carefully packed the frocks the Baroness had sent her and then went downstairs to send César to fetch a *barouche*.

The great negro had found his family. They were living near Congo Square with a cousin of Madame César, enjoying the sights and excitement and splendor of city life and César had returned now to sit all day in the kitchen of the General's house waiting to serve the two ladies he had adopted long ago in San Cristobal de la Habana.

When she told him what it was she wanted, he said, in his queer language, "But it ain't safe, Mademoiselle, for any lady to drive through the streets. It ain't safe with the Yankee soldiers and all them men down from the North. Ah ken go with you, but a black man ain't no protection."

She insisted and in the end, shaking his head, he went away to fetch a carriage, promising he would tell no one of his errand. In a little while she saw him returning from the direction of the city. The carriage was shabby and the upholstery torn and ragged. It was drawn by a single bony mule and driven by a thin old negro who looked rather like a stork on the driver's seat.

She was dressed, waiting for him wearing a bonnet and a thick veil and carrying a parasol as black César told her to do, and at sight of the dilapidated carriage she took up the heavy valise containing the Baroness's frocks and hurried out of her room toward the stairs. She had kept the excursion a secret, knowing that Aunt Louisa and even Aunt Tam would oppose her doing anything so mad. But she should have known Aunt Louisa too well to believe that it was possible to escape without her knowing it.

As she reached the head of the stairway, she heard the voice of the General's wife, "Where on earth are you going, dear, disguised as a street woman?"

At the sound of the voice she wanted to cry. She said determinedly to herself, "Now I'm in for it. I'm not a child any more.

I'm grown up." And turning to face the woman she said, "I'm going to call on the Baroness and return her clothes."

"You can't do that. You can send the clothes. You needn't go with them. It's quite impossible." She placed herself between the girl and the top of the stairs, a formidable, squat figure. "You're in my care. I'm responsible for what happens to you."

For a moment Agnes was silent, wavering in her determination. Then she felt a sudden wave of contempt for this woman, for her mean life, and that gave her determination. She said, "Aunt Louisa, I'm going. Nothing can stop me. This valise is very heavy. Will you please get out of my way?"

A crafty look came into the eyes of the older woman, "There are other reasons why I can't permit you to go . . . reasons you wouldn't understand."

"Oh, yes I would. If it's about Tom, I know all about that. That's why I'm going to see her."

"You must be crazy. Ladies don't do things like that."

Agnes laughed, aware suddenly that she had the advantage. She had taken the wind out of Aunt Louisa's sails. "Who ever said I was a lady? That's the last thing I want to be—a narrow-minded, half-witted Boston lady!"

"You ought to be ashamed of yourself . . . talking like that and going to call on a loose woman."

Still Aunt Louisa did not move and again Agnes asked, "Will you please get out of my way?"

"Your father will punish you when he hears of this."

"Will you let me pass?"

"No."

Agnes acted quickly. Swinging the valise, she managed to strike the General's wife full in the stomach, knocking her aside. Without stopping to see whether she was hurt, the girl hurried down the stairs. As she went out the door past the startled orderly, she heard the wild screams from the floor above. She had to get away quickly before the screams awakened Aunt Tam.

Once in the barouche, she said, "Go! Go quickly!"

The old negro struck the bony mule across the rump and with a jolt which threw the hat over the back of her head, they started off, César muttering that he didn't like any of it.

The first portion of the journey through the Garden part of the city was decorous enough. With the veil drawn over her face and the parasol carried low to hide her, she might have been any lady out for an evening drive, if any New Orleans lady dared to drive out in the cool of the evening. It was only when they approached Canal Street that the first intimations of trouble came. From the sidewalk, two soldiers in the uniforms of the Union Army gave out loud whoops of delight at the sight of the ramshackle carriage drawn by a bony mule, with two negroes on the box and a slight woman heavily veiled in the back. Startled, she did not believe at first that the cries were directed at her. It was only when the two soldiers turned to follow the barouche and called out, "Hello there, Mrs. Secesh!" that she felt terrified and sick.

From his seat above her, big César said, "Doan you take no notice, Miss Agnes. There ain't nothin' ah can do. It'd only make it worse." But he leaned forward and whacked the mule. The animal went into a jolting mule's trot with the barouche rocking from side to side over the cobblestones, leaping in and out of the mud-holes. Agnes pulled the parasol lower over her face as if she could shut out the yells and catcalls.

On the *banquette* the two soldiers ran alongside yelling, "Lift up that parasol! Let's see your pretty face, Missis!" Attracted by the yells, men on the street ahead of them turned to watch the careening barouche drawn by a bony old mule coming toward them. Worst of all, they were suddenly in the center of the city with men everywhere—mostly Union soldiers but among them the coarse, hard-faced, rodent-faced men who had come in the wake of the army, criminals or near criminals, who watched the scene grinning with amusement or calling out jeers and shady remarks.

Beneath the parasol, Agnes' cheeks grew hot with anger and shame. She had never dreamed that it could be like this. It was worse than the mistily understood insults aboard the ship. In comparison to these lewd and mocking cries the ancient gesture of obscenity made by the sailors seemed primitive and wholesome. She felt like an animal with the pack in full cry. She might have stood up and cried out, "I am a niece of General Wicks. I will report you all." But she was aware that this would only make her the more ridiculous and in her heart something made it impossible for her to do this. She knew they thought her a New Orleans woman and her pride and fury made her accept their belief. If this was what honest women in New Orleans suffered, she would suffer it too. "The General," she thought, "ought to be jailed for what he has done, turning these depraved men loose like wild animals." Never again would she speak to him. Never again would she set foot in his house. "His house!" she thought indignantly. "The house he stole from Mr. MacTavish." When she got back to Boston she'd tell them about their gallant Massachusetts regiments. Riffraff! Ruffians! Trash! That's what they were!

Now, all along the length of Royal Street men, soldiers and carpetbaggers lined the narrow banquettes cheering the progress of the broken down barouche. At Toulouse Street the old negro, pulling in the mule to turn the corner, lost his worn top hat. As the barouche turned, Agnes became aware that a man had jumped into the carriage and was sitting opposite her. Through the veil she saw his face, red, broad, leering at her and grinning at the men on the sidewalk. He shouted, "Look at the girl I got me!"

A sudden wave of fury seized her and releasing the catch on the parasol she lowered it with incredible swiftness, and using it as a club she began beating him over the head. His hat fell into the street and at the same time he raised his arms to protect his face. César, leaning back from his place on the driver's seat, gave the ruffian a push which sent him sprawling into the street. Then he whacked the mule again into a final clumsy gallop and Agnes, standing up in the swaying barouche, heard herself screaming, "Long live Secession! Hurrah for the Confederacy!"

Dimly, through the veil, as she was thrown back on the seat she saw the faces along the banquette change from looks of derision to anger. The mule was really galloping now. Two or three soldiers ran after her and one man attempted to stop the mule and was knocked into the street. Then suddenly the faces grew fewer, the barouche turned on two wheels into another street which appeared to be almost empty. In the distance there were two negresses in *tignons* walking in the shadows of the setting sun. The old negro pulled in the mule to a walk and after a little way, turned the animal into a blind alley.

[286]

Through her sobs, Agnes heard big César saying, "Here we is, Miss Agnes. You didn't ought to have come."

With a great effort she managed to say, "I can't go in now, César. I want to wait a little before you ring the bell." While the negro waited she stopped sobbing and thought, "I'm come all this way. I can't come again. I must go in! I must! I should be a weak fool to go away now."

From the box César kept murmuring, "Doan you mind, little Miss Agnes. . . . Doan you mind."

"Get down and ring the bell, César," she said, "I'm all right now."

She did not get down until the door was opened by Old Seraphine who volunteered to go and see if her mistress could receive Miss Wicks. This gave Agnes a little more time to recover her composure. César took down the valise containing the frocks and in a little while Seraphine came back and said the Baroness would be glad to receive her.

Sitting there in the barouche, she had been hoping the woman wouldn't see her. Then she would have an excuse. She could have gone away even now, leaving the frocks, but all that was New England in her forced her to go through with what she had set out to do. Still trembling, she got down and followed Seraphine through the heavy door into the courtyard.

The sight of the interior made her forget for a moment her anxiety. It was the first time she had ever seen the inside of a French house. The MacTavish house where the General lived wasn't a French house; it was the new kind of house built by the planters who came in after the Louisiana Purchase. There were houses like it all over the South, and even big houses in New England that weren't very much different. This was a new world, a foreign world. This was Spain and Southern France and Italy, like the houses Aunt Tam had told her about—with its wide galleries all around the walls, with a fountain in the center and flowering trees and vines everywhere. It smelled cool and damp with a thin drift of flower scent. There was a foreign beauty about it very different from the clean bright perennial borders at Dedham. The courtyard enchanted her. She would have lingered, but the old negress did not wait.

[287]

She led Agnes up wide shallow stairs to the second floor and along a gallery with a wrought iron balustrade entangled with wistaria, and presently she opened a high shuttered door and told Agnes to sit down. The Baroness, she said, would be there directly.

The room was as enchanting as the cool courtyard. It was a big rectangular room in a kind of green twilight that came through the high shuttered doors. At first, coming in from the waning sunlight she was blinded and could distinguish only the more massive pieces of furniture, the piano and a great *commode* and the huge marble fireplace with the gilt-framed mirror above it. Then as her eyes accustomed themselves to the dimness, she perceived the peculiar quality of the room—its richness, its baroque elegance, the shimmer of crystal here and there on the walls and in the great chandelier in the center of the room. To her it seemed a suffocating kind of beauty, utterly foreign, very different from the massive Georgian elegance of the MacTavish house.

She was still lost in half-grudging admiration for the beauty of the room when she heard the sound of a creaking door behind her and turned. The young Baroness was coming toward her. She was dressed all in black with a shawl of Spanish lace thrown over her head. It hung low, shading the brilliant eyes.

As Agnes rose, her heart all soft and terrified, the Baroness said, "It was very good of you to come."

"I brought back the frocks. It was very good of you to send them."

It was all very formal now and confusing. The easy intimacy of the flight from Bel Manoir was gone. It was almost as if this woman in black were a stranger whom she had never seen before, as if they had not ridden together along the moonlit river for miles on the back of the old mule. For a little while they made "conversation," stilted and awkward talk about the heat and the fever and the fall of Natchez. Then suddenly the Baroness rose and going to the row of tall windows along one side of the house, threw open the shutters one after another.

"It was very stupid of Seraphine not to open the shutters at this time of day."

The sound of hammering came from another part of the house and as she returned from the windows the Baroness said, "You must forgive the noise, I am going away. They are at work packing things. You came just in time. Tomorrow they begin in this room."

Agnes' heart gave a leap. If she was going away, perhaps that would settle everything. Then she wouldn't need to speak. But almost at once she thought, "Perhaps he is going with her. Perhaps that is why I have not seen him." With the shutters open she could see the part of the house that lay on the opposite side of the garden. "Perhaps," she thought, "that is where his rooms are." She tried quickly, behind the talk, to imagine what they would be like with his clothes thrown about, his table littered with papers. She knew it would be like that. He was impatient and violent. The Baroness sat down in a chair near to her now instead of far across the room. It seemed to make a difference in the friendliness. As she looked at her, it struck her that the Baroness had put on the lace shawl because she had been weeping; the lace just covered her eyes and threw them into a shadow. It struck her as odd that a woman like this could weep or even be unhappy.

Then almost without knowing it she heard herself saying, "I came for another reason . . . about Major Bedloe."

"Yes," said the Baroness quietly.

"I know about Bel Manoir. I know all about everything." She paused for a moment and was aware that the body of the other woman was poised, tense, on the edge of her chair. Then with an immense effort she continued, "I only wanted to say that you may have him. I shouldn't want to claim him from anyone."

The young Baroness did not answer her at once. She smiled and then began to laugh. It was a curious laugh, subdued yet somehow hysterical in quality, as if she could not command her nerves. The laugh made Agnes suddenly angry. "It's wicked to laugh," she said.

The Baroness managed to speak, "I hadn't meant it to be unkind. I don't know what made me laugh. I only laughed perhaps because it seemed funny that you should think I wanted him. I don't want him. You may have him."

The speech bewildered the girl, because it struck at the very roots of everything upon which she had based her determination to come here to this house. If people behaved as Tom and this woman had behaved, then they were in love. Love was love. It was very simple. And now this woman was laughing at it.

She could think of nothing to say and she felt intolerably young and foolish. She had come here believing she was behaving like a grown woman, and now again she merely seemed silly. Love was love. It was very simple, not a thing to be mocked.

And the tone of the woman was neither feline nor hostile. She seemed actually friendly. "I don't want him," she repeated. "I never wanted him. He was useful to me . . . in a good many ways." She laughed again. "You mustn't think he's the only man of his kind."

Agnes swallowed twice before she spoke. Then she said, weakly, "It's very good of you. I didn't understand." She rose from her chair. "I'll go now."

The Baroness had risen and was holding out her hand. Agnes took it scarcely knowing what she felt. The whole foreign room and garden suddenly took on a nightmarish quality from which she had to escape quickly before she began to cry again. And somewhere in the back of her consciousness she was aware suddenly that she did not want him back. In the turmoil of her emotions she could not explain the queer feeling. But it was like not wanting back an old frock someone had tossed in your direction, like not wanting to keep the frocks she had returned.

The sun had gone down and the old house and garden were filled with the blue shadows of twilight, but there was still enough light for her to see when the young Baroness came near to her, that she had been right. The Baroness had been weeping. Her eyes were swollen and red. And again she was astonished.

The young Baroness pulled the bell rope and Seraphine appeared to conduct her to the door leading to the street. The sound of the hammering in the house was no longer heard and in the lower gallery, bordering the courtyard, it was quite dark. As she descended the stairs the parrot began to screech.

Then as they neared the door, a tall man stepped out of the shadows and gave the old negress an order in French and went away. It was MacTavish. Agnes recognized the deep, kind voice.

It was true that the young Baroness had been weeping. She had wept from the moment Hector MacTavish turned his back on her and left the room until a little time before Old Seraphine came into her bedroom and said there was a "mighty pretty young woman called Miss Wicks" come to call on her.

He had appeared in the house a little after *déjeuner* and sent word by Seraphine that he would like to speak to her mistress, and she had gone to the *salon* to find him standing there looking at a portrait of the old Baroness painted in Paris when she was a handsome woman in her thirties. So absorbed was he that he did not hear her come in and it was not until she was quite near to him and spoke that he noticed her.

She said, "The old Baroness was a beautiful woman." He turned then and said, "I did not hear you come in." And then, "She was very beautiful but there was nothing lovable about her even in that picture when she was young. My mother always said that where her heart should have been there was only a lump of ice."

She sat down and said, "What have you come here for, in broad daylight?"

"I came to get the papers which belonged to the band. You are going away. They must be destroyed." He sighed, "Anyway, it's all finished." And then, as if excusing himself, "I doubt that anyone could have held them together. Louisianians are like that. They're all right perhaps separately, but together they're not dependable."

He did not sit down but moved about as he talked, uneasily, trying not to look at her, as if he was afraid of something. She asked, "What are you going to do?"

"I don't know. Whatever happens I shall have to begin all over again. I was in debt before the war. Prices were bad for too many years in succession. And now with everything looted and burned . . ." His voice trailed off in a discouraged fashion.

"I could help you."

He ignored the remark and said, "We had better go about our business, Éliane."

The color came into her face and she rose from her chair. "Everything is in the old woman's safe," she said.

He followed her into the bedroom with the altar beneath the bejeweled Virgin and stood waiting while she drew back a piece of brilliant Spanish embroidery that hung on the wall. From a pocket in her skirt she took out a cluster of keys. She selected one and thrust it into the lock of the heavy safe hidden in the wall.

When she had opened the door she brought out a packet of papers tied together with a bit of string and handed them to him.

"Is that all of them?"

He unfastened the string and looked quickly through them. "That is all. May I burn them in the fireplace? I won't be at peace till they're burned."

"Of course."

She was watching him with a look of curious intensity. The black eyes seemed to devour him as he bent down, pulled the papers apart and made a little pile of them. The full red lips trembled as she leaned against the great carved mahogany bed. Then he struck a sulphur match and the two of them stood watching while the fire consumed the list of names, the secrets of the little band of men who had terrorized the Union troops and the Northern ruffians for so long. When nothing remained but a heap of burned ashes, he turned and picked up his hat.

She said suddenly, "I said I could help you, Hector."

"I heard you."

"Do you know what I mean?" Fierce color came suddenly to her face, as if the humiliation to which her body forced her was unendurable.

"I know you must be a very rich woman, Éliane. You did not have all your eggs in one basket. I know there is still Martinique and France . . . but I could not borrow from you. It's not possible."

"I did not mean to lend you money."

His impulse was to say, "You would be the first de Lèche who ever gave anything." But that was something one could not say. Instead he said, "I could not accept a gift."

He wanted to go away quickly but it was quite impossible for she stood between him and the doorway, squarely, as if she meant that whatever there was between them must be settled now, once and for all, here in the old woman's room. He was conscious of the glitter of the jewels on the Virgin as the fading light filtering through the tall shutters struck them into life, and suddenly he thought, "I do not belong in this evil country. I have always been a stranger here."

She was saying, "Do you hate me, Hector?"

"No . . . certainly not." But he knew there were times when he did hate her.

"I did not mean to lend you the money."

She seemed to choke and then, actually clasping her hands, she said, very quickly as if she must get the humiliation over, "I would marry you, Hector. I would be different, I love you. I have loved you always since the first time I saw you come riding up the allée at Bel Manoir. I would change. I would be your slave. I would do whatever you told me to do. I have always been a free woman. I have always lived like a man. That is why I can talk like this now. I never believed in woman's modesty. Why should a woman be modest and humble?" She began to weep but spoke no less quickly, "I have been wicked sometimes, but before God what ever I have done that was evil was because I loved you and because you would never show me even the faintest affection. I am no fool. I know what love and what desire may be. Do you think I could humble myself like this in the dirt if I didn't love you? You must know what that means to a woman like me? I will do whatever you wish. I will . . ."

She sat suddenly on the edge of the bed and buried her face in her hands, her shoulders shaking. That no sound came from her made the scene all the more unendurable.

He did not go to her. He still remained by the fireplace. After a moment he said, "It was never meant to be, Éliane. It is too late now. Only misery could come of such a thing. I'm going now." He waited for a moment but she had thrown herself face down on the bed where the old woman had died and showed no sign of speaking. Then he said, "Good-by and good luck," and went out the door. He was trembling as if the humiliation was as great for him as for her. To trample one's pride into the mud was a horrible thing. The spectacle made him feel sick.

So he had gone down the stairs to bid farewell to Seraphine and the old man in the kitchen. He talked to them, scarcely knowing what he was saying, and presently the bell had rung and Old Seraphine went to answer it. He was forced then to wait, since he did not know who might be at the door. She went away and returned and when she opened the door a second time he saw through the iron grille work that the girl from Boston had come in with her.

The sight of the girl did an extraordinary thing to him. The depression, the shock arising from what had happened abovestairs, left him almost at once. As he watched her crossing the lower gallery and climbing the stairs, he experienced an extraordinary sense of rightness, as if she had been sent by God at that moment as a kind of sign.

He thought, "I will wait and speak to her. Then I can explain what happened at Father Desmoulins."

But while he waited he was troubled by her very presence in this house. He was afraid for her, not that the young Baroness would in any way corrupt her young integrity, but because of the malice of the older woman. The girl, he reflected, should not be in this doomed place; she should be clear and free of its very aura.

So he waited and when she reappeared with Seraphine he opened the door of the kitchen and quickly crossed the gallery. It was almost dark; if he had not known that she was in the house he might not have recognized her in the shadows.

At the sound of his voice, she said, "Oh, it's Mr. MacTavish."

"Yes. I wanted to speak to you."

"You shouldn't be here in New Orleans with a reward out for your capture."

He smiled slowly, "I come and go as I like. They aren't very clever."

"It frightens me to think of you here."

"You needn't worry. I'm going away for good very shortly."

There was a small awkward silence in which the air was pregnant with unuttered thoughts and emotions. Then he said, "I wanted to speak to you about what happened outside the priest's door. I was afraid you thought me rude and a fool. I turned away and led you into the house because someone was listening to us. Someone who should not have heard what passed between us."

"I know," she said. At the same time she opened the reticule and took out a small lace-bordered handkerchief. She gave it to him, saying, "This time I have something to give you. I was afraid you thought me mean or ungracious . . . but I really had nothing to give you."

"Thank you, Miss Agnes. I'm sincerely glad to have it." Then he laughed. "I expect you think us silly and romantic here in the South."

"No. I think it's very nice." She sighed and said, "I must go now. They'll think something has happened to me and the General might send out a search party. That would make me seem very silly. I don't like to be treated like an idiot child."

He said quickly, "You didn't come here alone, did you?"

"No. There was a coachman and César."

"You had no orderly with you?"

"No."

The alarm was evident in his voice, "But you shouldn't have done a thing like that. Anything might have happened to you. You came in a carriage?"

She laughed, "I don't know what you'd call it. It's a rattle-trap thing César found." Then she was grave again, "They did follow us jeering and hooting. One man got into the carriage."

"I will drive back with you."

"Oh no, you couldn't do that. Someone might recognize you. It isn't safe."

He laughed again, "I've walked the length of Royal Street after dark without anyone noticing me."

"I couldn't allow it, Mr. MacTavish. I'm not as unprotected as that. If there was any real trouble I'd just say I'm the General's niece."

"There are too many men in New Orleans who wouldn't care whether you were the General's niece. There are too many who would like to do harm because you *are* the General's niece." He laid one hand gently on her arm. "You must listen to me. New Orleans grows worse and worse every day—and now they know old Silver Spoon is going to be recalled, they don't any longer respect his authority. I am going with you, Miss Agnes. You need not worry about me. I'm armed and I can put up a good fight."

She wanted to send him away and yet she wanted him to remain but she knew from his voice and manner that she had no choice in the matter. That he should risk possible capture and certain death to protect her brought a lump into her throat. But it was

[295]

his gentleness and the sound of his voice which moved her most. It was a voice that seemed to surround, protect and caress her.

She said primly, "You have no right to put the responsibility for your life on me, Mr. MacTavish. I assure you, I appreciate your kindness but I should be much happier alone . . . no matter what happens to me." But almost at once she was ashamed of the formality of her voice and speech. It seemed awkward and ungracious.

Very quietly he answered, "I am going to drive with you. Anything can happen in this city now. Come, it's dark enough now to be quite safe."

MacTavish was the guide. Now and then he leaned forward to give the old coachman directions, now to take this turning, now that one. The course led away from the center of the town where most of the soldiers and carpetbaggers concentrated their activities. It led through shabby streets thronged with negroes and half-castes and occasional poor-white families who had swarmed out of the ramshackle sheds and ruined houses into the muddy streets when the sun disappeared and the air grew a little cooler. The streets at intervals were lighted by great bonfires of wood, much of it torn from the sides of the ruined houses. Here in the poor part of the city no barrels of burning pitch were provided to "purify" the air and burn out the miasma of the dread fever, and so the inhabitants had made their own fires out of the very wood of the houses which gave them dubious shelter. Now and then a great fire built in the very center of the filthy street forced the barouche to turn and make a detour.

Sitting side by side in the carriage Agnes and MacTavish spoke very little. Agnes was happy without quite knowing why—because of the excitement and the curious wild beauty of the firelit journey. The faces and the bright ragged clothes of the women and children were like something out of another world, as unreal as an opera. The older people on the banquettes and the muddy streets stared as the ramshackle carriage passed and now and then a child cried out a shrill greeting.

Beside her MacTavish sat with the top hat pulled well over his eyes, absorbed in thoughts of a melancholy cast. The shame of the scene with the young Baroness still hung over him like a vague cloud and the sight of so much wretchedness and poverty depressed him as it always did. In Louisiana there seemed only to be a few very rich people and hordes of starving and half-starved whites and freed men. And now there would be very few rich people left save for those who had evilly made profit out of the misfortunes of others.

He wanted to talk to the girl at his side, to explain many things about his country which he knew must puzzle her, but the words would not come. He felt shy as a school boy, and it seemed silly to talk seriously to a girl from whom he would part in a little while and very likely never see again.

He realized presently that she was laughing and, puzzled, he turned toward her.

She said, "I was laughing at myself and how funny I must have looked beating that man over the head with my parasol. He looked so surprised." She laughed again and said, "But the funniest thing was that I was so mad I stood up in the carriage and shouted 'Hurrah for Secession! Long live the Confederacy!'"

He recognized the fine edge of nerves in her laughter. It wasn't simple, whole-hearted laughter. There was something tragic about it. He was aware that something must have happened during the visit to the young Baroness.

He said, "I'm afraid neither of us are very good partisans. Maybe it's because we see all around things."

She looked at him shyly, "Maybe that's it," she said, "but I guess there aren't many like us."

"A person can be too reasonable," he said. "It makes for weakness and bewilderment and indecision." Then after a moment he said almost as if talking to himself, "It's funny. I've been ruined like hundreds of others in Louisiana but I don't seem to care."

"Sometimes I wish I could get away from everything I've been, everything I've been taught and go into a new country where I could be myself—the way I feel I am inside." She smiled, "I guess that sounds silly. It's something I can't explain quite properly, the way I'd like to."

They were crossing Canal Street now at the far end away from the center of the city and he was aware that now if ever, he must be alert. But there were very few people about and none of them seemed to take any notice of the old barouche. When he did not answer her at once, she said, "You won't think me a fool, will you? It's only because I've never had a chance to know anything that's important. I feel lately like a chicken coming out of an egg."

He chuckled and said, "I don't think you're a fool. On the contrary I admire you very much." And again she had the feeling that the warm voice was enveloping, protecting, caressing her.

In the garden part of the city it was quiet and dark and the air was heavy with the odor of blooming flowers. Now and then a figure passed them, hurrying along against the wrought iron fences. As if the stillness and the beauty of the night had moved him irresistibly, big César on the box began to sing, and as if the sound of the deep voice eased the sense of shyness between them Agnes and MacTavish leaned back against the dirty worn lace which covered the torn upholstery. It was as if César by some aboriginal clairvoyance had been inspired to sing. Agnes could understand nothing of the *patois* but MacTavish knew every word of the song. He had heard it since he was a small child, an old Bretonne song about a shepherd and shepherdess which had become corrupted and changed by generations of slave singing into something lush and African. César sang softly in a low rumbling voice as a mocking bird moved by the soft languor of the night might sing.

Agnes, her mind lazily remembering all the excitement of the afternoon made a sudden strange discovery. She did not love Tom; she had never loved him. Tom belonged to someone like the Baroness not to herself. She heard again the Baroness' mocking, bitter laughter. "You can have him. There are plenty of other men as good."

And then through the sound of César's deep-throated singing she heard Aunt Tam's wild cry of "Agnes! Agnes!" And for a moment she was not certain whether this too was only a part of the curious dream-like drowsiness which had enveloped her. But she was aware that the barouche had stopped and César was no longer singing and Aunt Tam's face was close to hers. There was something frightening in the wild agitation of the older woman, as if it presaged all the calamity that was to follow. She had never seen Aunt Tam like this before.

She was saying, "David has the fever! We must go to him at once!"

David! The fever! The words and the curious panic in Aunt Tam's voice terrified her, and for one moment she experienced again the feeling she had had as a little girl for her twin brother, not that strange new feeling she had had when she saw him in Aunt Louisa's drawing room, but the old feeling of wanting to protect him and shield him from everything unpleasant which might hurt him.

Then Aunt Tam noticed MacTavish and the sight of him calmed her a little. She said, "He isn't at the hotel. He's at a house somewhere in the old part of the city. Here it is!" She held up a scrap of paper with an address written on it.

MacTavish struck a sulphur match, looked at the address and said quietly, "I know where it is. It's in a queer part of town. What is he doing there?"

Agnes answered him, "I think he has a friend there. It doesn't matter where it is."

"César knows," said MacTavish and repeated the address to the black man.

"We'll go straight there," said Agnes. MacTavish stepped down and helped Aunt Tam into his place beside Agnes. He took the small seat opposite them and for a long time as the barouche jolted along, they sat in silence, as if the horrible news had struck them all dumb. In Agnes' brain the same thoughts went round and round, "The fever! Nobody ever gets well from the fever! Poor David!" And leaning forward she called out to César, "Tell him to go faster."

But after a little time she heard Aunt Tam saying, "After you left, all kinds of things happened. You shouldn't have hit Louisa in the stomach."

"It doesn't matter now where I hit her."

"She went to bed and called the General's doctor and said that the pain was more than she could bear. She called you names and called the Baroness even worse names. I can't see why she should hate the Baroness so much. She said she was going to have her thrown into jail and all her money and property taken from her. She said awful things about her and Tom . . . and then the General came home with the news that Washington had sent him his walking papers and she screamed and fainted and came to and screamed and fainted all over again. And when the news came about David she paid no attention whatever."

Agnes scarcely heard her. The tears had begun to roll quietly down her cheeks. She tried to stop them, aware that MacTavish, opposite her, was watching her in the darkness. People died quietly of the fever, almost before anything could be done. "David! David!" she thought, "You mustn't die! You mustn't die!" And for the first time she felt sorrow for her father alone in Boston and wondered how much he was able to feel either sorrow or joy. So long as she had known him he had never shown any emotion. She saw him now as a bearded man of granite in a top hat with a shawl over his shoulders, punctual, unromantic, interested only in his business and factory. It was only now that she realized how little she loved him, that she would not care much if she never saw him again. It was really because of him that David was here dying of the fever in New Orleans. David, whom they were always trying to force into the dull mold of a New England business man, had gone away with Tom, who jeered at all that respectable world, to escape from it and from his father. She saw now that there was something monstrous and inhuman about their father, about the whole world in which she had spent her life until she escaped with Aunt Tam.

Leaning forward again, she bade César to hurry the old mule. The animal had grown tired and balky and could not be driven in his jolting trot.

Then she was aware of the light from a burning barrel of pitch on the banquette and saw the face of MacTavish clearly. She said, "You shouldn't be here. We're quite all right now. Someone will see you. Please leave us. We'll be quite safe."

But again he refused to leave. "This is the worst part of town. No one will recognize me. They wouldn't believe I'd dare to come here."

For a little while, distracted, she continued trying to persuade him, but it was no use.

He only said, "We'll be there in a little while."

Agnes thought again, "Poor David! You mustn't die! Oh God, dear God, don't let him die!" She had the wild feeling of being in a nightmare. It was all like the hurricane again, in which everything became confused and wild and unreal. She thought, "None of this is really happening to me. I have only dreamed it." She felt Aunt Tam's hand grasping hers, pressing it. Quietly and suddenly she had a moment of curious understanding—that Aunt Tam was only herself inside a plain rather battered body. She could always count on Aunt Tam as she counted upon herself, more than she counted upon herself. Whatever happened she must never lose Aunt Tam.

There was panic now in Josélie's house, and the good-natured, golden-skinned friends no longer came and went, scarcely knocking on the door or troubling to close it. Fever in the city had not terrified them for fever was always there in its season, sometimes striking here and there at random, killing only a handful of people during the long hot summer, sometimes sweeping over the whole city like a plague of the middle-ages, carrying off whole families in a few hours. When it was like that people left the city. Everyone who could escape, rich and poor alike, disappeared into the swamps or lost themselves among remote plantations and villages. The fever had been there for generations. Where it came from, no one knew. Some said it was brought in by slaves from the Gold Coast of Africa, others that it had come from Martinique and Cuba, and still others that trading vessels brought it from Rio and the Guianas. There was no way of knowing how it spread or why it was virulent in one season and light in the next. It was this mystery which gave it a peculiar horror, worse even than the horror of cholera and smallpox. Like black cholera it ran its course quickly; people sometimes fell down in the street to die of it. It was always there, a part of life itself among the Delta people.

And now it had struck at good-natured Josélie's house, and her daughter Clélie's *cavalier* lay dying, and the neighbors gathered in the garden and in the street outside, waiting for news. They were, most of them, women like Josélie herself, freed-women, light in color with small houses and a little money hidden away, and they had the interest of women in the fate of the young Yankee officer. They stood outside in the hot evening in little groups talking and relating their own experiences with the fever and speculating upon his chances of recovery, for sometimes, about one time out of five, a victim got well. They were, on the whole, good-natured women, who wished Clélie well. Now that they were middle-aged or old and settled, their romantic interest fastened itself upon girls like Clélie with all life still before them. In a way, through Clélie and girls like her, they could live again in the gay pleasant world of the Quadroon balls.

They had come too because they heard that the sister of Clélie's *cavalier* was coming to the house. This was something which had never happened in their world in all their experience—that a sister of a *cavalier* should enter the house of the object of his affections, and there was great dissension among them as to whether this was a proper thing to do. Some thought "yes" when her brother was dying; others thought that even death did not make *"bien élevé"* such an indiscreet action. And they had gathered too because none of them had ever seen a Boston woman. Talking about her they thought she must be cold and stiff and foreign and very different from Créole ladies.

And among other things they talked of La Lionne and the remarkable change which had come over her—that she looked tired and old and hard and that her loud coarse laugh was no longer heard. They knew that the man who had bewitched her was back in New Orleans and they knew that he had not seen her nor sent any answer to her letters. They knew that Mama Tolanne's voodoo had not brought him back and those who disliked Mama Tolanne scoffed at her as an old fraud who took people's good money but was able to do nothing for them. Some thought that La Lionne might die of love and others that she might kill herself, but all of them thought her a fool to be caught by a man younger than herself who would only grow tired of her.

And they knew too through the grapevine of rumor which had its roots in the bosom of Old Seraphine that La Lionne's young man was infatuated with the young Baroness. Some said that that would be sufficient punishment for him, and others crossed themselves and spat through their fingers at the very mention of her name.

Like birds, these golden-skinned women, no longer young, chattered and gossiped about love because love had been the beginning and end of their existence. Love had created for them a whole society, a whole world, endowed with something very near to respectability. Inside the garden and on the street outside the murmur of their voices rose and fell.

And there were other rumors about the Ogre's return to Washington and the lawlessness and violence which was creeping through the city like a winter fog. There were stories of assaults and robberies and murders which grew with each retelling, stories of the utter ruin of this great family and that one in which some of the women had protectors. Over them all hung a gray fog of uncertainty and insecurity, as if they felt about them, while they waited there in the garden for Clélie's fair-haired young lover to die, the dissolution of a whole world in which they had had a secure and protected place. They were accustomed to the violence of duels, but this violence of which they were suddenly aware was different, touched by brutality and terrifying lawlessness. That there was no grace or romance in it alarmed them. The sound of their soft, corrupted French filled all the garden as they talked about what was to happen in their dying world.

The arrival of the barouche brought a fresh diversion. Boldly but with a kind of deference they crowded about the gate to stare at the Boston girl. But they saw little of her for her face was covered by a black veil, and so they fastened their attention upon the horse-faced woman who accompanied her, a woman the like of which none of them had ever seen before. But the real sensation was the discovery as he turned toward them of M'sieu MacTavish. A rustle of whispering and indrawn breath went through the crowd. M'sieu MacTavish coming openly to Josélie's house when there was a reward for him dead or alive posted all over New Orleans! Any man could get one thousand dollars merely by shooting him down!

And the first murmur of astonishment was followed by a murmur of admiration. These women whose lives were based upon love, knew a man when they saw one, and their admiration for the figure and face of MacTavish was unbounded. And among them there were women who knew tales of his prowess and they became the centers of small groups listening to accounts of what they had heard or experienced.

He knew nearly all of them—as Boisclair's Eugénie or Dupont's Célimène, or Duplessis' Frédigonde or . . . Now he lifted his hat as he passed through them on his way into the house and said politely, "Bon soir, Mesdames." As he passed, giggles and small cries of admiration rose from among the women, as they chorused back, "Bon soir, M'sieu MacTavish! Bonne chance!"

Then as he went into the house, another figure came out of the door—that of a tall woman dressed all in black. She wore a veil over her face and walked very straight, making her way through the gossiping women like a tall ship through a cluster of market boats. She did not speak to them. She did not appear to be aware of their presence. The sight of her caused a pool of silence to spread through the little crowd of excited women. One of them said, "It is La Lionne on her way to Mama Tolanne's."

When she had gone, the murmuring and whispering and giggling died away as if they no longer had any heart for gossip and jesting. And in a little while they began to drift away to their own houses. It was as if a plague had fallen upon them. What they saw was to them a worse spectacle than death. They had witnessed the spectacle of a woman touched by death because of love —a strong and beautiful woman turned old and lost and alone and miserable. As she passed through them, Boisclair's Eugènie whispered, "The smell of death is on her."

The walls of the rooms inside Josélie's house were white-washed like a house in Martinique or Cuba and the heavy mahogany furniture was upholstered in bright materials—yellow and green and red and blue—clear, pure colors, that gave the inside of the house the effect of music, as if it were singing. When you looked at someone across the room by the light of the oil lamps it was like looking at a painting—against the white walls with all the bright colors about. That was the way it affected Agnes when she entered the little salon. She saw Josélie standing there in a dress of bright green taffeta, against the white wall and she thought, "What a pretty woman . . . like a painting!" Even through her terror she was aware of the beauty and the cheerfulness, like a note of bright music in the darkness. She thought, far in the back of her mind, "Some day, some place, I should like to have a house like this."

And then MacTavish was saying, "This is Madame Josélie Legrand."

He knew Josélie very well and that made it all easier. His presence seemed to change the quality of everything. There was no strain. Josélie said, "You ought not to be here M'sieu 'Ector . . . with all those gossiping women outside."

She spoke English with a strong accent and Agnes was aware that she was speaking it because she had good manners and wanted to make her visitors feel at home.

David, she said, was upstairs. Her daughter Clélie was with him. The doctor had gone away. He meant to return in a little while. There was nothing he could do. There was nothing anyone could do for the fever. It had to run its course. Her husband Joe had gone to a voodoo doctor. She, Josélie, didn't believe in voodoo but Joe did and in any case there was no harm in trying everything.

Then she led them up a small stairway with a pretty wrought iron rail. Aunt Tam followed her immediately and then Agnes and then MacTavish. Halfway up the stairs, MacTavish touched the hand of Agnes. As she turned, he said in a low voice, "Josélie is a cousin of the young Baroness. They had the same grandfather." Then they went on up the stairs. She did not know why he had told her this, except perhaps to make the whole scene easier and more natural. She saw at once that there was a likeness between the Baroness and the octoroon in the bright green dress, something about the eyes and the way Josélie Legrand held her head. For a moment before Josélie opened the door she had again a swift sensation such as she had known in the swamps, of growing, ripening, expanding.

Then she went through the door and saw David lying in an enormous teakwood bed inlaid with mother-of-pearl and beside him Josélie's daughter Clélie who was, she thought quickly, as the girl turned toward the door, like a white camellia.

The girl had been weeping but even the tears had not marred

her beauty. She wore a dress of purple printed stuff cut rather low so that nothing obscured the beauty of the throat and the poise of the head that gave her in turn a curious proud likeness to the young Baroness. Only this girl was younger and more beautiful, with none of the hardness which sometimes altered the beauty of the older woman and made it seem common.

The impression came quickly to Agnes and at the same time she thought, "Oh, I'm glad! I'm glad for David!"

It was as if there was a curious rightness and beauty not only about the girl but about the house with its whitewashed walls and bright colors and about the girl's mother with her soft, ripe beauty. This was a happy place and these were happy people, with a kind of animal happiness that was very close to the thing which had come to Agnes herself during the long journey through the swamps. David had found here what he had been searching for, blindly, what at home they had striven to keep from him and from herself.

It was very strange that at this moment, with David dying, she could feel a surge of happiness for him and for herself. Perhaps it was because he had known in the few short years of his young life what most people of his world never know. She knew suddenly what it was that made her fancy she loved Tom—because, without her understanding it, he had offered her a way out. He was all the things which she and David had never found in the stifled narrow world of Pinckney Street.

The boy lay unconscious now, his face scarlet with the fever, his soft fair poet's hair damp against the pillow of the great bed. As she crossed the room, the girl beside the bed leaned forward and with a handkerchief wiped away the dark trickle which ran from the corner of his mouth. MacTavish standing discreetly against the white wall, knew at sight of the black hemorrhage that there was no hope.

The girl rose and said softly, "Sit here, Mademoiselle." But Agnes said, "No, stay where you are, thank you. I'll sit on the bed."

She took David's hand, thinking how small it seemed and how delicate and sensitive—a poet's hand, the hand of a man born to suffering and death. The touch of it was like fire and she too knew then there was nothing to be done, since with such a fever it was impossible for anyone to live.

She said, "David!" softly and then repeated the name, "David! It's Agnes come to see you."

After a moment the eyelids flickered a little and then opened, but the eyes saw nothing. The pupils were contracted and sightless, "David!" she repeated, "It's Agnes." Although the eyes saw nothing, the sound of her voice reached some part of his brain for the lips moved and a faint gasping sound came from them, "Aggie . . ." the lips said, "Aggie . . ." and then "Clélie," and then there was only silence again and the sound of breathing growing weaker and weaker. A dark trickle appeared again at the corner of the mouth and the girl bent forward to wipe it away. And then suddenly the breathing stopped, and from the street came through the hot, still, scented air the sound of wheels creaking and jolting over the cobblestones and a long haunting cry, "*Char de morts! Char de morts! Apportez vos morts.*"

La Lionne was not bound for Mama Tolanne's sinister doll's house beyond Congo Square. At the corner of the Street, she turned in the opposite direction toward the old part of the city. She walked rapidly, with determination. She was bound for the de Lèche house to kill Tom Bedloe.

Her mind was clear now as it had always been until that night when he walked through the swinging doors of the Café Imperial. For it was finished now. It had been finished since the moment the morning before, near dawn at the hour when the weak and the old die, when it had come to her what she must do. As the misery was no longer tolerable, it had ceased suddenly. In the gray light she thought, "It is all finished. I am an old woman There is nothing for me to do but go back to France and die."

But there was something yet to be done. It was very clear to her suddenly, so clear that she was astonished that the idea had not come to her before now. It had not come to her, she knew then, because her body and spirit had been so miserable and confused. Now she knew that there was still vengeance to be exacted. There was still the misery, the haggard eyes, the deep lines in her painted face to be paid for.

Now that the passion had burnt itself out in frustration, she was once more what she had always been—a wise, hard, woman who in life kept her accounts as accurately and as shrewdly as she kept them in the Café Imperial. In life as in business, things had to be paid for. She had paid for her folly; she was an old woman. But Tom Bedloe had paid for nothing. He had taken what he liked when he chose and gone away without paying anything.

As she walked, rapidly, because she was driven by the passion to settle the account and have it finished, she saw him very clearly for what he was.

She had no illusions now. Even a fleeting memory of his prowess, of his grin, of his laughter could not soften her now. She had seen others like him in her long experience, men who by some animal power made wretched abject slaves of women. Until he had come into her life she had never believed in the power of such men over a shrewd woman like herself. She had warned her own girls against them; she had driven such men from her own establishment. She had looked upon them as fouler than rats feeding from a cesspool. But none of that had made any difference. None of that knowledge or experience had spared her the long hours of suffering when she had not slept because she was ravaged by desire, nor the humiliation of her pride and dignity and integrity caused by the pleading letters and the visits to Mama Tolanne. None of her knowledge had saved her from the humiliation of appearing a shameful and beaten old woman before Josélie and all her chattering friends.

No, there was a long and bitter account to be settled, not only for herself but for other women, all those who had gone before as well as those who were still to come, if she did not make the final entry and close the book.

She knew what would happen afterward. There would be a great sensation and the newspapers and the gossiping women at Josélie's would call it a *crime passionel* although there was no passion concerned in it now but only a cold, bitter sense of justice. And afterward she might be caught or she might escape to France. She did not deceive herself. She might be hanged for what she meant to do. But that was a gamble, and belonged to the future, and she was concerned now with a fierce concentration solely

[308]

upon the immediate. No one, she thought, grimly, would be able to say that the crime was unpremeditated. No one could honestly say it was a crime of passion. She had thought it all out carefully, even to the help from Old Seraphine. Afterward it would not be too difficult to escape, with the disorder in the city and the fever and the quarrels between the police and the soldiers. There would be plenty of people, plenty of women who would help her because they would look upon the murderess of a Union officer as a heroine. She would be like Charlotte Corday. And she would slip aboard one of the French ships loading stolen cotton and be hidden away by the sailors and be safe. She knew men, especially men like those who manned ships. They would help her because all her life she had understood them and had helped them and been their friend.

For nearly half an hour she hurried through the streets now silent and empty, now filled with crowds gathered about the blazing barrels of pitch. Now and then a voice cried out as she passed, but mostly the people were silent as if they were aware by some instinct of the errand of the black-clad woman, with the same instinct which had made Father Desmoulins read the doom in the face of the young man sitting opposite him at breakfast in his little house at St. Jean de Beaupré. As she hurried she ceased presently to be any longer simply La Lionne, ruined proprietress of the Café Imperial. She became a kind of symbol—woman seeking vengeance upon all men like Tom Bedloe.

And at last she came to the section where the rich Créoles lived and came presently to the blind alley and to the door which opened into the courtyard of the de Lèche house. In the darkness she pushed the door gently. It swung open easily on the carefully oiled hinges. It was not locked. Old Seraphine had kept her word and left it ajar. Inside the door, she kicked off her slippers and with her stockinged foot placed them side by side where she would be certain to find them when she came down again after the thing had been done.

And now it was all over and Josélie had drawn the sheet across David's face and for the first time the reality was clear to Agnes. She understood now what it was that had always troubled her. It had happened as it was meant to happen. She saw it now . . .

that David had only been loaned to life, that he had not been meant for this world because there was in him no toughness, no shell to protect him. All his dreaminess, his gentleness, his sensitivity were a part of the whole thing. That was why she had never in all her life, no matter how much she loved him, been able somehow to touch him, save perhaps for that single moment in the small drawing-room of the MacTavish house. It seemed now that she had always known it would end like this. It was an end which seemed right, an end which he himself might have chosen as an end to some romantic poem—dying in Josélie's house, far away from the narrow streets of Boston, with Clélie at his side. It was the way David always saw life, not in terms of reality, but veiled and lifted to a romantic plane beyond all the possibilities of reality. It was odd that she should be the sensible one—the "boy" of the twins.

She did not weep. Strangely she felt no desire to weep. She had only a sense of hazy uncertainty as if all that had happened since she struck Aunt Louisa with the valise had been a dream. She did not even know how she came presently to be in another room with Aunt Tam and MacTavish. Josélie and Clélie had vanished and she heard MacTavish saying, in his deep, clear voice. "Could I speak to Miss Agnes alone for a moment, Miss Wicks?"

Aunt Tam went out silently and when she had gone, he looked at her gravely and said, "I am sorry . . . so sorry." By instinct, without quite knowing what she was doing she held out her hand toward him. He moved a little nearer and took it in his big hand.

"I would like to do something . . . but there is nothing I can do. What Josélie says is true. I must go now. A hundred people must know by now that I am in this house. And I shall be no good to you hanging from the end of a rope. I must go away so that I can go on being of use to you."

"You can't believe I thought you a coward?"

"No, I didn't think that. I only wanted to be certain that you understood, because that means a great deal to me."

Now, suddenly, she wanted to cry, but the desire had nothing to do with David lying dead on the huge bed in the other room. Then through the flimsy wall of the room she heard the sound

[310]

of Clélie's soft sobbing, and she began to cry and knew that she was weeping not for David but because of MacTavish.

"You mustn't mind," she said. "It's because I'm tired and frightened."

He pressed her hand gently and said, "Where are you going now?"

"I don't know."

"There isn't much time and I don't know where to find you. You're not going back to Boston?"

"No."

"Even if the General goes?"

Almost passionately she said, "No. Certainly not with them."

Then Josélie came into the room. She, too, had been crying but she appeared excited now. To MacTavish she said, "You must go now, quickly! The soldiers are on their way. Someone has told them!"

He seemed to take no notice of Josélie's warning, "Where can I find you?" he asked.

"I don't know. You must go now . . . quickly."

"You can send word to Father Desmoulins where you are. . . . César can take the message."

"Go . . . please go."

He stood for a moment looking at her as if he meant to say something. In the silence the sound of marching feet was heard and then a cry of "Halt."

"Please go! Please go!" she said again.

He bent down and kissed her hand. Then he said, "I'll send someone to help you."

Josélie pulled at him, "Come . . . you can go out by the garden door . . . but quick."

Then he went away and she heard the nasal voice of a Massachusetts soldier belowstairs demanding entrance to the house.

It was quite dark when Tom Bedloe returned to his rooms. He had not come straight back from the Port Office. For nearly two hours he had walked through distant parts of the city in streets that were strange to him where he was certain he would encounter no one whom he knew. For nearly two hours he struggled with himself in a battle more violent than that between Jacob and the Angel, and when he returned at last he had made up his mind. He knew now what he meant to do. He meant to follow the young Baroness to Martinique, to France wherever she might choose to go. He had money. He could take more from the Port Office. In the confusion and disorder which had begun to settle over the unhappy city, no one would notice his absence until the ship was well out to sea.

It meant that he could never return to America but that knowledge troubled him very little. He had no family left and friends he could replace wherever he found himself. People always came to him wanting to be friends.

It meant that he would die and be reborn in another kind of world with the young Baroness the only flimsy bond between what had been and what was to come. He knew that if he did not follow her, if the thing was never completed, he would never again know any peace. Once or twice he thought of Agnes and consoled himself thinking, "Only her pride will be hurt. She will be lucky to escape me, for I could only have made her miserable."

With Agnes went too all the hopes he had had of settling down, of leading a decent life, of having sons of his own. All that, he knew, was finished. The road he chose would be a very different one with loneliness and perhaps ruin at the end, but it was, he knew now, a road which he could not escape. He had been born to it. It was a road that led to a life of magnificence and squalor, of ecstasy and despair, of adventure and excitement. He was not good with words. He did not think it out clearly. It was something he felt, emotionally and profoundly. There was no other road for him.

Back in his own rooms, he rang the bell for Old Seraphine to bring him water for a bath. He meant to dress carefully and cross the gallery and go to her. They were alone now in the great house, save for Seraphine and the old man in the kitchen.

The old black woman returned in a little while with the old man from the kitchen carrying two pails of water. They both stared at him in an odd fashion, as if he had changed in some way. Even when he bade them brusquely to go and leave him, Old Seraphine remained for a moment in the doorway, still staring.

When they were gone, he poured the cold water over him again and again, enjoying the sensual pleasure of the cold against his hot skin. His brain seemed clear now and free of confusion, and he gave himself up again to the feeling of exaltation at being alive and male and young. And while he bathed he heard again the music he had heard long ago before he had ever seen her. She was playing the piano and singing again in her clear perfect voice in the room on the opposite side of the courtyard. As he dried himself he paused now and then to listen, wondering that the voice of such a woman should be so pure and cold and perfect. It was as if the voice belonged to another woman, different from the one he had known in the ruined house at Bel Manoir.

He took the singing as an invitation, as a sign that she meant him to come to her, and he began to dress quickly but carefully, choosing the finest of the shirts which he had bought at the auction of a seized Confederate property . . . a shirt of transparent lawn, ruffled from the throat to the waist, a dandy's shirt which covered but did not conceal the body beneath it. He dressed with the care of a bridegroom going to be married.

He saw La Lionne then as he stood before the mirror brushing his thick, close-cropped black hair with the silver-backed brushes she had given him. For a second he had a strange feeling that what he saw was only something he had imagined. She was dressed all in black and the veil was thrown back so that he saw her face. It was the face which alarmed him, not only the look in the eyes but the haggard lines which showed through the thick rouge. It was La Lionne, but an old, tired, battered woman . . . not the Lionne he had known so well in the room with the red plush and gilt above the Café Imperial.

She said nothing. She only stood there in the doorway watching him. On the opposite side of the courtyard, the voice of the young Baroness still rose limpid and clear and perfect in the roulades of the aria from "Il Ré Pastore."

As he turned from the mirror and looked at her, he knew why she had come. He saw it in the hard green eyes. He thought, "I must act quickly and outwit her."

He said, almost with bravado, "Come in, Félice, and sit down." (Sitting she would be less dangerous. He wondered what weapon she carried—a knife or a pistol. A knife would be the likelier weapon. If he could keep her at a distance he could perhaps talk her into reason and induce her to go.)

She said in her strangely accented English, "I wrote you but you nevair answered me."

"I was away. I was a prisoner. You heard about that?" He spoke with an exaggerated casualness as if somehow it would restore his old power over her.

"Yes, I heard about that."

The sound of her voice was like the look in the hard eyes. He had a sudden sense of being cornered. As long as she stood in the doorway he could not leave the room. He thought, "I must rush at her and throw her to the floor." But he did not act, perhaps because the action appeared to him ridiculous and because a sudden excitement welled up in his blood.

"It is all over, Félice," he said. "It was all over a long time ago."

Above the sound of her hoarse voice he could still hear the other clear voice on the far side of the hot still courtyard.

"Yes," she repeated, with a sigh, "it's all over. I am going back to France away from this sacré place."

Then for the first time she moved. She stepped forward and he felt again the impulse to throw himself at her, but again he seemed to be paralyzed and could not act. Then, very quietly, she raised her arm. The long cape fell away and he saw that she held a revolver. He saw it very clearly—that it was one of the new Army models, a Colt, and he wondered where she had come by it.

"You're not going to do that, Félice," he said. "You're not going to be foolish." And he knew that he did not want to die . . . not now with the young Baroness inviting him by the sound of her voice on the far side of the garden.

He started toward her but she did not wait for him. He saw the flash of the pistol and fell, backward, as if he had been hit a violent blow on the chest. At the same time he heard the voice on the other side of the courtyard—pure, clear, passionless.

He said, "Oh, Félice! . . . Félice!" and then a black fog closed over the room, the face of La Lionne and the sound of the voice on the far side of the courtyard.

For a moment she stood looking down at the body. It lay on its side a faint trickle of blood discoloring the fine lawn of the ruffled shirt, and for a second she felt a sudden pang. He was young. He was strong. He was beautiful. He had been her lover. There were things about him which she would always remember even as an old woman. But the pang passed quickly, and as if to stifle it, she fired twice more into the back of the man who was already dead.

Then quickly, with the old walk which was like that of a lioness, she turned and went out of the room and down the stairway to the spot by the door where she had left her slippers. Quickly she thrust her feet into them and went out the door closing it behind her. As the darkness of the blind alley swallowed her up, she heard the sound of light footsteps hurrying along the gallery above her head and then a single scream.

For a long time the young Baroness stood looking down at the body. It was the sound of Old Seraphine's frightened whimpering which roused her. She looked at the old woman and said, "Who did it? Who did you let into the house you black devil!"

The old woman fell on her knees and covering her head with her arms, she began to rock back and forth moaning and making unintelligible sounds. Again her mistress cried, in French, "Who did it? You know, you evil witch!" But still the old woman only moaned.

Then the young Baroness took up the sword which lay on the chair by the dressing table. Taking it in both hands she began beating the old negress over the head. "You'll tell me or I'll flay you alive."

The moaning grew louder with each stroke of the blade and presently throwing herself flat on her face, she cried out, "*La Lionne! Fais pas ça*. La Lionne! I didn't know she meant to kill him! La Lionne! *Oh, le saligaud! Oh! la bête!*"

The young Baroness stopped beating her and threw down the sword. "Get up!" she said, "and send the old man for the police!" As the old woman scrambled painfully to her feet, there was the sound of a faint sigh in the room, and the young Baroness as if speaking to herself said, "*Je n'avais pas fini! Je n'avais pas fini!*"

A little after dawn Josélie came to the room where Aunt Tam and Agnes had spent what was left of the night. She said that

[315]

there was a gentleman belowstairs to see them. He was the Uncle of Chauvin Boisclair, she said, and M'sieu MacTavish had sent him.

They found him in Josélie's little salon, a small, delicately built old gentleman, dressed very carefully in rather faded elegant clothing. He was gentle and kind and kept punctuating his speeches with slight old-fashioned bows of deference. He talked very rapidly and with a faint and musical accent.

He had come, he said, to help them with all the painful arrangements. Mr. MacTavish had said they were alone in a strange city and would not know what had to be done. It would be a great honor for him to help in any way possible. He would stay with them, to serve them in any way he could until they no longer needed him. He had brought a note from Mr. MacTavish addressed to the young lady.

He gave it to Agnes and as she opened it to read, he asked Aunt Tam to come into the hall with him. There he said very gravely, "I have bad news for you," and told her that Tom Bedloe was dead.

For a moment the gaunt woman could not grasp the significance of what he was saying, and when at last she understood and accepted the news, she experienced a curious sense of relief, which made her feel ashamed. Tom was dead. It did not seem possible that anyone so alive could be dead. But the kindly old gentleman said so. He had been murdered in the most vulgar and shocking way by a woman who was the proprietor of a notorious establishment.

"Thank God," she thought first of all, "she was not married to him."

Then gravely she excused herself from the presence of old Mr. Boisclair and went down the stairway with the wrought iron grill work into the little garden where so many times La Lionne had paced up and down in the lonely scented darkness.

There were many things the elderly spinster had to consider before she could face her niece. It was not easy, she knew, thinking at the same time how curious it was that she had found herself, respectable, stiff and rather impregnable to all heartache, involved without her will in so much passion and tragedy. She thought how fortunate it was that they were not in Boston where Agnes could be pawed over by the women who would have come in, whispering in corners, speaking their oily condolences, secretly triumphant because in the end the girl had been robbed of a man of whom they openly disapproved but secretly admired. "Poor Agnes!" they would say, "how humiliating for her!" secretly satisfied in their hearts because death had destroyed this romance between a pretty young girl and a lover who was handsome and reckless and "fast." Aunt Tam, in her innocent wisdom, knew many things, among them the peculiar quality of envy which infected the hearts of women married to respectable solid dull men for a young girl who had attracted a reckless man like Tom Bedloe.

But Tom Bedloe was dead, and now the problem was when and where and how to tell Agnes. As she walked up and down the dewy garden, one thing became clear to her—that they could never return to the General's house and face him and Louisa, certainly not the Louisa she had seen screaming and moaning in baffled misery on the great canopied bed in Mr. MacTavish's house. It was better that they did not see Louisa at all. They could for the time being, take a room in David's hotel. Certainly she could not permit Agnes to be tortured by Louisa.

At last, her heart filled with sorrow for all young men like David and Tom, who died too young to have acquired wisdom, she wearily climbed the little stairway and pushed open the door of the room where Agnes and old Mr. Boisclair were sitting on Josélie's bright-colored chairs.

Agnes had been crying and Mr. Boisclair sat opposite her watching her with the eye of an old gentleman bewildered by the sorrow of a pretty young girl—an eye filled with kindliness and sympathy. But the odd thing was that despite Agnes' tears, there was a curious aura of happiness about the girl. It hung about her like a faint perfume. She looked up as Aunt Tam came through the door and said, "We're going to stay with Father Desmoulins, Aunt Tam. Mr. MacTavish has arranged it. I couldn't go back to Boston or to Aunt Louisa's house."

On the way to David's hotel no one molested them although there were rough men everywhere in the streets and there was a curious air of restlessness and violence in the crowds gathered here and there about the announcements plastered on the walls of shops and houses announcing a change in the command of the stricken city. It may have been the air of dignity and respectability about old Mr. Boisclair or the dragon appearance of Aunt Tam which protected them. Throughout the journey Aunt Tam worried over how she was to break the news to Agnes. It would be easier than she feared. She knew that the moment she saw Agnes' face on coming into the bright room at Josélie's. She knew then what she suspected on the night before when Mr. MacTavish had lingered with the soldiers of the Massachusetts regiment at the door. She was aware that the girl no longer loved Tom. Aunt Tam knew many things which did not come out of her pitifully meager experiences with romance, and now, thinking it over, she doubted that Agnes had ever been in love with Tom Bedloe. She had never looked at him as she had looked after MacTavish when he left her to escape into the garden on the night before.

At the hotel, Mr. Boisclair said he would wait in the bar while they went up to David's room.

They found the room neat and in order as he always kept it, but among his papers they found none of his old-fashioned poems about graveyards and snowstorms. They found only the manuscript of a long poem of which two cantos were complete. It was called, "Don Juan and Oriana."

While Agnes sat looking through it, Aunt Tam thought, "Now the time has come. If I do not tell her someone else will or she will see it in the *Delta*." And very gently she said, "My dear, I have bad news about Tom."

And then an odd thing happened. Agnes, glancing up at her with a curious look of pain in her clear blue eyes said swiftly, "I know. Something has happened to him. He is dead."

"Who told you that?"

"No one," said Agnes.

"How did you know?"

"I don't know how I knew." And then after a little silence, "I think I knew it when he left me that day at Aunt Louisa's."

She could not have explained to Aunt Tam if she had tried and it seemed to her now that she had always known that she would never be Tom Bedloe's wife because he was doomed. Once on the moonlit bayou it had come to her, almost as if a voice had spoken, and again in the garden of the de Lèche house as it melted into the darkness of twilight, just before Mr. MacTavish had spoken to her and again as she rose from beside David's bed when she knew that her brother was dead and would never speak to her again. The sense of his destruction had been very strong then but she put it out of her mind, telling herself that such things were nonsense.

Now she said quietly, "How did it happen?" and Aunt Tam told her, trying to disguise the sordidness and vulgarity of his death, but Agnes was not deceived, although she said nothing at all, except after a little while, "Poor Tom! Poor Tom!"

She herself knew then that she did not love him. Now she felt sorry for him as she would feel sorry for a naughty child. She was very tired. It was as if all her senses and perceptions were numbed. She never loved Aunt Tam so much as in that moment. The older woman made no effort to sympathize with her or to comfort her. She only said, "I am going out now with Mr. Boisclair. You had better try to get some sleep while I'm gone," and kissed her gently.

Then Aunt Tam left to find Mr. Boisclair and see to the business of the burial. She had a double task now, for she made up her mind that she would not leave Tom's burial to the disorganized Army authorities. She would see that he had a dignified and a proper funeral, for now she discovered that she, too, like all the others who had ever known him, had loved him. It seemed to her as it had seemed to Father Desmoulins that he had the brightness and beauty of a fallen archangel.

Autumn came slowly, almost imperceptibly to the Parish of St. Jean de Beaupré. The old priest busied himself about his garden during the hours when parishioners did not talk with him of their troubles in the confessional or in his tiny library. They were beginning to come back now, a few of the grand people to live among the ruins of the great plantation houses, the black and yellow people no longer either quite free or slave, the wretchedly poor white people who lived in the villages along the river.

In all the parish there was no such thing as money and there was very little to eat. The grand people learned to eat sowbelly from the half-wild pigs which roamed the swamps, and catfish out of the rivers and bayous, and even wild rabbit. Some of them lived again in simple cabins as their forefathers had done long ago when the whole state was a wilderness. And from all parts of the parish people of every station in life came to Father Desmoulins with their troubles. He acted as judge in disputes, as engineer and architect and schoolmaster and priest, and gradually the whole life of the community came to center about the small parish house which he shared with Old Célimene and the two strange Yankee women. Without him the whole story would have been a different one. Father Desmoulins had immense, unfathomable reserves of patience and understanding and wisdom.

Because he loved his fellowmen there was about him a quality of agelessness. He was as young as the children who crawled about the dooryards on all fours and as old as black Mammy Tita who said she was many years over a hundred.

In the beginning he found it odd and a little uncomfortable to have two strange women living in his house, but presently he grew used to their presence and even looked forward to conversation with them when he returned in the evening; and as the weeks passed he began to discover even at his age fresh evidence of the goodness of the human spirit. It was not as if the two women were of his race and kind and faith, speaking the same language; they were Anglo-Saxon and believed in a curious passionless and unnatural creed known as Unitarianism. They were everything which to him seemed curious and sterile.

He studied them, with that part of him which remained forever the scholar and the skeptic, as he studied the plants with which he labored in his small garden, and presently he made a remarkable discovery—that these two women appeared to be growing and flourishing like well-tended plants before his very eyes. The older one, whom God had chosen to make so ugly, was like a halfwithered plant that sprang into fresh and vigorous life with a little care and watering. She was like a friend sent from heaven to help him in the confusion and despair of the ruined parish. She was up at daybreak and worked all day even through the noon heat, going from house to house with a small bullet-headed black boy as guide, distributing food, helping in houses and cabins where there was illness, even acting on occasions as midwife. She appeared to have an inexhaustible store of energy and a body as tough as a swamp cypress, and after it grew dark, she sat for hours writing in the thick bound journal she kept in her bedroom.

Sometimes in her absence the old priest struggled with a fierce desire to open the journal and read what she wrote in it with such passionate and concentrated intensity. He believed that in its pages he would discover clues to many things which puzzled him— why these two women seemed so happy in this hard, spare life which was the best he could offer them, why they were never homesick for their own country, why each day seemed to be filled for them with new wonders and new satisfactions, why there was in both of them a toughness, a resourcefulness, a frontier quality which the women of Louisiana no longer seemed to possess.

It was the younger one, Miss Agnes, whom Father Desmoulins put in charge of the little school he set up in his own salon. In it were the very young children of the village and the neighboring plantations, brought together because the old man was unwilling even in the confusion and hardships of the moment that they should grow up ignorant as were their fathers and mothers.

Miss Agnes taught them their alphabets and she taught them to speak English. Learning English was an idea of Father Desmoulins and at first it was badly received, but he stuck to his purpose because, like Hector MacTavish, he divined that the old Créole world was doomed. Before the children sitting on their benches in front of Miss Agnes were middle-aged, the French language, he knew, would no longer be heard in Louisiana save among a few elegant people and in the remote lost parts of the Delta. In a little while, as time went, this soft Créole world which the old man loved, despite its violence and its decadence and evil, would have vanished. That other world, harsh and vigorous and practical and commonplace, pressing down from the North would have engulfed it, imposing upon it the pattern of life of the Anglo-Saxon shopkeeper.

But by that time he would be dead and buried in the little parish cemetery, above ground where the muddy water rising in the fertile earth could not reach him.

He watched the first signs of that transformation as Miss Agnes sat at her table with the children in rows on benches before her. Sometimes when he had a moment free from his heavy tasks, he came in and talked to the children in their own *patois* inventing childish jokes which made them laugh and explaining to them what the girl, in her faltering flat-accented French had not been able to convey. Her methods were simple. On the blackboard she would draw a picture of a cat and make them repeat after her the words "*Chatte*" and "cat," or it might be a dog or a chair or a table. They learned quickly and she was a good teacher, patient and even kind, but with a surprising sense of authority which gave her power over even the most mischievous of the children.

She was, the old man thought, an admirable young woman, pretty as she was intelligent and endowed with a firm character, and from day to day it seemed to him that she grew and ripened like a peach on one of his own trees. He was aware that her destiny was not that of schoolmistress. She was meant by God and nature to be a wife and the mother of many children. She would make a good wife; she would, the old man thought wistfully, be a wonderful woman for the man who won and kept her love.

He knew that man and the knowledge warmed his heart. He knew that while the girl stayed here in his house, teaching school, she was only waiting for a destiny as clearly marked, however different it may have been, as that of the young Yankee who had died by passion and violence in New Orleans. There were moments when Father Desmoulins, despite all his training, wavered perilously near to a belief in predestination, not by the will of God but by the character of man. It seemed to him that the life of every man and woman was determined by something inside himself. The combination of the inner being with the circumstance encountered outside constituted Fate and Fate, the old man knew, was a very old word, infinitely older even than his church.

It was Fate which had brought these two strange women out of their cold and narrow world into this other soft and sensuous and faintly decadent wilderness, and so changed the whole course of their lives. It was Fate which had turned Hector MacTavish away from the young Baroness from the very beginning; Fate too which destroyed the young Yankee by violence as certainly as the seasons followed one another. It was Fate that Louisiana should be defeated and plundered and in time changed beyond all recognition. All these things were written. There was about them something as inevitable as the rulers of higher mathematics. The sum of A plus B equals C. It was as simple as that. He knew because, in a curious fashion, he had never had any life of his own; he had always lived through and for his fellowmen.

And so he knew that Hector MacTavish would come back to claim his schoolmistress and he felt no surprise one afternoon a little before Christmas when he came home to find Hector in the little salon surrounded by Miss Wicks and Miss Agnes and Old Célimene, telling them of the wonders of the new country he had found in the West.

Agnes too had always known that he would return. She knew it from the moment he left Josélie's little house to escape from the soldiers who pounded on the door, from the moment when he took her hand and she knew that she had never loved Tom at all save in the romantic imagination of a schoolgirl brought up in a world of strange distorted values. There were moments when she trembled with fright at the thought of what might have happened to her if she and Aunt Tam had not run away from Havana on the *San Cristobal*.

Over the cropped heads of the children she saw him come in, his tall strong body filling the whole of the small doorway. Without looking at her he clapped his hands and cried in a loud voice in the *patois* of the parish, "School is dismissed! Today will be a holiday!"

Snatching their hats and their ragged jackets, the children ran away quickly. He stood watching them with a grin and when the last one had scuttled through the doorway, he crossed the room and took her in his arms and kissed her, without so much as saying "Good morning" or asking her leave. Then he held her at arm's length and looked at her smiling and said, "I've found the place. It's a wide green valley between high mountains and not a settler in the place. It's all ours for the taking . . . a whole bright new world."

Even though her happiness blinded and confused her, she was aware of a difference in him. The old sadness was no longer there and in its place there was a kind of radiance. She could only think, "This is how I knew it would be." This was what she had dreamed of during those long moonlit nights on the bayous. The odd thing was that she seemed to know him so well, as if she had loved him always, as far back as she could remember, even before she stepped ashore in the moonlight to find him waiting at the ferry landing. Looking up at him she said, "You're very dark . . . like an Indian."

"It's a wonderful country. Even the sunlight there is different."

"May I take Aunt Tam with us? I couldn't leave her . . . not now."

"Of course. I'm taking my mother and sisters. There'll be a lot of us."

She laughed and he went on, "And big César wants to go and all his family and Chauvin Boisclair."

"We'll be a whole village."

"Yes, we'll be a whole village . . . a growing village." He laughed again and kissed her again and it was only then that it struck her they had never talked of marriage and that he had never proposed to her in a proper fashion. It was as if they had known the story all so well that there was no need.

In New Orleans they did not hang La Lionne for they never found any trace of her. Like a lioness she went to earth somewhere in the swamps or among the shabby half-ruined houses of that world of harlots and freed men and roustabouts near Congo Square. In the confusion and lawlessness of the times the search was distracted and half-hearted, and there were hundreds of people in the city and in the swamps outside who would gladly have hidden the assassin of a Yankee officer, especially one who was a favorite of "Silver Spoon" Wicks. In the city some said, despite the evidence of the young Baroness and Old Seraphine, that La Lionne had not done the shooting, that the officer was only another victim of that band known as Les Defenseurs. But the band seemed to have vanished and its leader to have disappeared into thin air. For a long time afterward every one of the countless murders and assassinations was blamed upon the band, but the truth was that the band had ceased to exist on the day Hector MacTavish had burned the papers in the fireplace of the room where the old Baroness died.

About six weeks after the murder a French packet boat called the *Ville de Dunkerke*, laden with cotton and sugar stolen from the plantations and warehouses by the Yankees, sailed for Boulogne by way of Martinique. Aboard it traveled the Baroness de Lèche with three negro servants, an old woman called Seraphine, a very old man and a young black girl with dimmed wits and a perpetual look of terror called Thomasine. With the Baroness went twenty-eight trunks and countless cases of cypress wood filled with silver and pictures and carpets and mirrors, and five small heavy kegs containing thirty-eight thousand dollars in gold specie, mysteriously released from the gold stolen by the Yankees from the Planters' Bank.

On the same ship, hidden away in the depths of the hold there was another woman whose presence was known only to the sailors who smuggled her aboard and hid her. Until the ship reached Martinique she remained in her hiding place among the bales of cotton. At Martinique she went ashore after nightfall and came aboard the ship the next day to book a cabin not far from that of the Baroness de Lèche, as Madame Félice Mancheron, a resident of St. Pierre. She had a ravaged, bitter face which once must have been beautiful, and she appeared to have plenty of money.

On the evening of the day the ship left Fort de France, the woman, taking advantage of the calm weather and the balmy air came on deck to walk restlessly up and down. On her way she passed the Baroness de Lèche walking the deck on the arm of the Captain, and for a second the eyes of the two women met. Then both of them looked away quickly and never again throughout the voyage was there any sign of recognition between them.

When they had passed the Captain said to the Baroness, *"Quelle femme extraordinaire! Elle a le pas et l'air d'une vieille lionne!"*

"Oui," replied the Baroness, *"on l'appelle La Lionne à New Orléans."*

The Captain stopped. *"C'est elle, alors?"*

"Oui, c'est elle."

But it was too late now. The ship was on her way to France and the Captain was a Frenchman. To him a *crime passionnel* was no crime. Besides with a Parisian so distinguished, so fascinating, so alluring as the Baroness de Lèche on his arm, he had no interest or curiosity concerning ancient scandals.